CLNW

D0505027

We hope you enjoy this b
renew it by the due date.

You can renew it at www.r................................ or
by using our free library app.

Otherwise you can phone 0344 800 8020 -
please have your library card and PIN ready.

You can sign up for email reminders too.

Abby Davies grew up in Bedfordshire. She taught English for thirteen years and now lives in Wiltshire with her husband and daughter. *The Cult* is her second novel.

@Abby13Richards

Also by Abby Davies

Mother Loves Me

THE
CULT

ABBY DAVIES

HarperCollins*Publishers*

HarperCollins*Publishers*
1 London Bridge Street
London SE1 9GF

www.harpercollins.co.uk

HarperCollins*Publishers*
1st Floor, Watermarque Building, Ringsend Road
Dublin 4, Ireland

First published by HarperCollins*Publishers* 2021
1

Copyright © Abby Davies 2021

Abby Davies asserts the moral right to
be identified as the author of this work

A catalogue record for this book is available from the British Library

ISBN: 978-0-00-838954-3 (PB b-format)

This novel is entirely a work of fiction.
The names, characters and incidents portrayed in it are
the work of the author's imagination. Any resemblance to
actual persons, living or dead, events or localities is
entirely coincidental.

Set in Sabon LT Std 10.5/13.5 pt
by Palimpsest Book Production Limited, Falkirk, Stirlingshire

Printed and Bound in the UK using 100% Renewable Electricity
at CPI Group (UK) Ltd

All rights reserved. No part of this publication may be
reproduced, stored in a retrieval system, or transmitted,
in any form or by any means, electronic, mechanical,
photocopying, recording or otherwise, without the prior
permission of the publishers.

MIX
Paper from
responsible sources
FSC™ C007454

This book is produced from independently certified FSC™ paper
to ensure responsible forest management.

For more information visit: www.harpercollins.co.uk/green

For Tommy and Heidi

PART ONE

Chapter 1

LOVE

Age 6

September 1987

Shouts erupted from the barn killing the quiet. As if frightened, the sun retreated and a shadowy greyness swooped down smothering the farm like fog. Even the chickens, for all their greed, turned tail and fled.

Love placed her bucket of seeds on the ground and joined her sister and mother at the barn.

Peace hugged herself. She looked ugly in a green dress and sludge-brown boots. Mother slipped an arm around Peace and pulled her in close. Love watched them out of the corner of her eye and listened to the hot voice pound the air. It was Father. Angry. Again.

A frown twisted her mother's face. 'Love – stay here.'

Love ignored her and slipped inside the barn.

Father's cheeks were tomato-red. Trembling with rage, he jabbed a finger at her uncle. 'You're delusional.'

Uncle Saviour smiled down patiently at Father. He was a lot taller. Wider too. Like a bull towering over a calf.

As always, her uncle was calm and kind. 'If you don't like it here, David, leave. No one is stopping you. Besides, I think

3

you're probably right. You're a proud man. You need to earn your own keep. I only ask that you allow Charity to decide for herself. Let her stay if she wishes to.'

Father barked a laugh. 'Call her that name again and I'll—'

Uncle Saviour spread his hands and smiled. He took a step towards her father, closing the space between them. 'You'll do what? Hit me? Well, all right. If that's what you need to get this toxic rage out of your system, go ahead. Hit me. All I want is for everyone to live here in peace and harmony, but if punching out your anger helps, please do it.'

Love stared, keen to see what her father would do.

Father shook his head and kicked at the straw. He turned as if about to leave then lunged at Uncle Saviour and smashed his knuckles into his face. Her uncle staggered backwards and fell on the ground. Mother screamed and darted forwards, pushing Love to the side. Father climbed on top of Uncle Saviour, grabbed his neck with one hand and punched him again. This time blood burst out of her uncle's nose. He rolled onto his side and scarlet liquid dripped onto the dirty ground. Mother screamed again as Father shoved his face into the blood on the barn floor. Father whispered something in Uncle Saviour's ear, then stood up, dusted himself off, and strode towards the door, but Mother grabbed his shirt.

Love watched, heart racing.

Her father whirled around. Tears stained his cheeks. He was pale and dirty and his body shook as he grabbed Peace and Mother into a hug then pulled away. Love looked up at him, begging with her eyes, but he didn't even glance her way.

Love blinked. Once, twice.

'If you love us, you'll stay,' Mother said.

Father ignored her and strode out of the barn.

Love drifted into the cow field and knelt on the dewy grass. Scabs crusted her knees. Grit pressed into the scabs and stuck on the flesh between the cracks, but she didn't feel any pain. The air was cutting, the sun half-masked by clouds that resembled dead sheep. Dressed in only a cotton dress, goose bumps pimpled her skin, but she didn't feel the cold.

With trembling fingers, she stroked the petals of a poppy. The flower was red, like blood. There had been a lot of blood. The barn floor had been wet with it and the smell had crawled up her nose, down her throat and into her tummy like an invisible red mist.

Her stomach grumbled. Twisting the lid off a jam jar, she scooped out the final inch of black-blue jelly and slurped jam off her fingers, then froze as a buzzing sound caught at her ears.

Love stared at the poppy flower. Questions buzzed around her mind like the two bees whizzing around the flower's hairy tongue.

The buzzing grew louder, more intense, more urgent. She shuffled closer and leaned towards the poppy, edging in so she could see the fuzzy coat of each creature's body and the sting sticking out at the back. She was not scared of bees. Other children were. Her mother and sister were, but not her. Bees lived very short lives. They died when they stung you. They were stupid.

Love frowned, dug into her sock and pulled out the needle she had stored there earlier, the one she'd borrowed from her mother's sewing kit.

She frowned harder and rubbed a sore spot on her chest. Mother had told Peace that Father and Uncle Saviour had never got along, but that moving to the farm had made things worse between them.

They had been living here for three years and another family had come to live with them last month. Three families lived on her uncle's farm now.

Mother said Uncle Saviour was brilliant; that he saved people. That was why she had started calling him that name. Now everyone called him Uncle Saviour. Love couldn't remember what his old name was. At Christmas, Uncle Saviour decided all of them deserved new, better names. Names that meant something good and pure. She loved her new name. Her old name had been Zoe, which didn't mean anything. Love was a good name because it meant something important. Peace's old name had been Clare. Mother's had been Joyce and Father's David. Father did not want any of them to have new names and he hated his new one. Unlike everyone else, including the new family, Father moaned a lot and said unkind things about Uncle Saviour. She didn't know what the word delusional meant, but she was sure it wasn't nice.

Her sore spot went away. Love nodded to herself.

It was a good thing Father had left. He never smiled and his words came out too fast and jumbly. Uncle Saviour always smiled and his words were calm and clear. No one listened to Father, but everyone listened to Uncle Saviour. Father gave them nothing. Uncle Saviour gave them everything, including a roof over their heads. Father hardly ever hugged her. He cuddled Mother and Peace, but not her. Uncle Saviour hugged her all the time. He whispered nice things into her ear when no one else was listening; Father never did that. It was as though she was invisible to him. Once she'd heard him say that if she'd never been born, they would have been happy. He'd called her an accident. Said having another baby had been a big mistake. And when he'd said that, Mother hadn't argued.

The sore spot wanted to come back, but she pushed it away.

She picked up the jam jar and moved it closer to the poppy. As if sensing something was wrong, the bees grew frantic, buzzing louder and louder, so loud her head began to pound like an angry fist.

Looking at the needle, Love thought about what Mother would say. After a second, she shrugged. A smile tugged at her lips. She didn't care what her mother would say, only what Uncle Saviour would say, and he said blood was life. Besides, she was curious and no one would have to know if she didn't want them to.

Love glanced up and glared at a group of encroaching cows. They stared back at her with their slow, thick eyes. She wasn't scared of them either. She wasn't scared of anything.

Excitement wiggled inside her heart like a worm that had been cut in half.

The sun burst away from the dark cloud and sent a razor-sharp ray of light onto the poppy's blood-red petals. The bees seemed to relax a little, like they thought she wasn't going to do it. Like she was just a little girl who was too scared to do bad things. But she was seven soon and she'd seen something other girls hadn't seen and she hadn't looked away or cried or screamed or done any of those things. She had been calm, just like Uncle Saviour.

She inched the jar closer to the smallest bee. It was on the flower's hairy tongue now, too busy collecting pollen to notice the glass cage at its back.

Love placed the needle on her lap then picked up the jam jar lid. Keeping the jar close to the bee, she raised the lid in her other hand, edging it closer to the flower's bloody petals. With the jar in her left hand on the left side of the flower and the lid in her right hand on the right side, she stared at the bee, almost willing it to notice and fly away, to not be so stupid. But it didn't notice and it didn't fly away. If anything, it grew more focused on its work, a mindless worker bee going about its job for its clever, strong queen.

Her head pounded harder, her heart faster. She pinched her tongue between her teeth, held her breath and SNAP! She snapped the lid and jar together, trapping the little bee inside. Its friend immediately went berserk; buzzing and whizzing around in random directions, but Love only had eyes for her prize.

Inside the jar, the bee went crazy, buzzing so loudly she almost couldn't bear it. It bashed its body into the glass over and over again as if it were trying to kill itself. Love watched, fascinated as it landed in a fingernail-sized lump of jam near the top end of the jar and got stuck, its spidery legs wedged in the gloopy jelly like wellington boots in mud. Its buzzing intensified and so did its friend's. Love peered closer, her eyelashes brushing the glass. The bee was one hundred per cent stuck, but it wasn't giving up. She liked that.

She twisted off the lid and placed it on the grass beside her knees, then picked up the needle, pinching it between her thumb and reading finger. Angling the mouth of the jar towards her face, she held the cage up and moved the needle towards the trapped bee, which struggled with all its might and failed to free itself from its sticky trap. Still, its buzzing went on, louder and louder and louder, and Love's head banged and Father's face replaced the bee and she poised the needle-tip a millimetre above the bee's fuzzy back. Her mind was full of curiosity, laced with a need she didn't understand. Frowning in concentration, she pushed the needle into the bee, surprised to find it so easy, so soft. The needle went right through and the bee went still and its buzzing stopped. For a happy moment, she enjoyed the answer to her question. She did not feel excited, just glad that she had found out what would happen. The bee had died and it had bled, but its blood was not red like human blood. It was the colour of tree sap.

She felt a sharp pain on her arm and glanced at the bigger bee, which dropped off her skin onto the dewy grass, dead.

The sting was still in her arm. With a stab of anger, she plucked it out. After a few seconds, the pain died and her anger was replaced by curiosity.

Smiling slightly, Love brought the tiny silver blade up to her face and stared at it in wonder.

Chapter 2

HANNAH

Now

Hannah Woods heard the landing floor creak. Clutching her sheet, she stared at the bedroom door. Her heart fizzed like sherbet, then slowed as she told herself it was just her little brother sleepwalking again. There was no other reason for the weird creaking sound. No reason to be afraid.

With a humph, she tapped on her lamp, threw back her bedsheet, pulled on her heart pyjamas and slipped her toes into her still-sweaty unicorn slippers. She couldn't sleep anyway. Her thoughts were whizzing around like a bluebottle that wouldn't stop bashing into the window.

Outside her room moonlight turned the landing a tooth-yellow colour that made her think of ghosts and witches, not that she believed in that stuff any more. At ten years old, she was too grown up to believe in fairy tales.

Greg wasn't on the landing. Hannah peeped inside his bedroom. His bed was empty, sheet flipped onto the floor as if he'd been in a rush to leave.

She tiptoed up to her parents' room, smiling at Daddy's pig snores, and wondered whether she should wake them up so that they could sort out Greg. But they argued more when they didn't get enough sleep and she didn't want them to argue tomorrow. They were always arguing. Sometimes she worried they might get a divorce like Jack's parents, and the thought made her feel like she was drowning in soup.

Rubbing her tummy, she crept past their bedroom and stood at the top of the stairs.

It was darker down there. Scarier. A spiky stab of fear came but she thought about Greg and what he might do if she didn't get him back to bed. Who knew what crazy things went through people's heads when they walked in their sleep? And Greg was a bit crazy anyway. He was only seven and small for his age. He could try to climb the big bookcase in the lounge and pull it on top of himself and be crushed to death like the wicked witch in the *Wizard of Oz*. That would be horrible. Even though he was annoying, she loved him a lot.

Clenching her jaw, she rushed down the stairs and almost slipped.

Hannah grabbed the banister to stop herself falling and froze at a scuffling sound coming from the kitchen.

In the gloom she could see the kitchen door was open about halfway. Down there, shadows lurked like dementors, ready and waiting to suck out her happiness. Her heart raced, but she forced herself to focus on the 'bigger picture', as Daddy always said. Greg could be hurt. She couldn't let the darkness win. She had to be brave, like Hermione Granger. Hermione, with her big hair and super-clever ideas.

Sucking in a breath, she dashed down the rest of the stairs and peeked inside the room. Her little brother was kneeling on one of the kitchen stools at the cabinet next to the sink in his frog onesie. He even had his skate shoes on.

He jumped and looked around at her. Behind him the moon glowed through the blinds, making him look there but not there, stuck on the world like fake scenery in a bad film.

'Greg – what are you doing?' she hissed.

'You won't tell, will you?'

'Are you sleepwalking again?'

'No.'

'I don't believe you. You wouldn't be up otherwise.'

'I don't care,' he said with a pout, flipping his fringe out of his eyes.

She noticed his ladybird school bag lying open on the counter.

'What's that for?' Panic fluttered in her chest. 'Are you running away?'

'No, stupid.'

'Don't call me stupid, Greg. It's not kind.'

He looked away. 'Sorry. It's just, you're spoiling everything. No one's meant to know.'

'Know what?'

'Our secret.'

'Whose secret?'

'I can't tell you that.'

'Why?'

'Cos she made me promise.'

'Who made you promise?'

He opened his mouth to answer then shook his head. 'Nope. You can't trick me.'

She hid her frustration and lowered her voice, 'OK, if you're not going to tell me that, at least tell me what the secret is.'

He pretended to consider her demand for a second, then said, 'OK! *Promise* you won't tell?'

'Promise. Cross my heart and hope to die, stick a needle in my eye.'

He giggled and put his hand over his mouth. 'I'm going to see a fairy tonight!'

Hannah rolled her eyes. 'Fairies aren't real.'

He frowned. 'Yes they are.'

'No, they're not. Come on, go back to bed now and I won't tell Mummy and Daddy anything.'

He zipped up his bag. 'No way. I promised. I have to go.'

'Where?'

'It's a secret.'

'But you can't go out in the middle of the night on your own.'

'Why not?'

'Well, *duh*. It's dangerous. You could fall over and break your ankle and no one'll find you for weeks and you'll starve to death,' she hesitated then added, 'and insects will crawl up your nose into your brain and lay eggs, then the eggs will hatch and your brain will explode.'

His eyes widened at the thought, but he shook his head. 'I won't fall over. I'll be really careful. And I'll only be gone for a bit. It's not far.'

Hannah chewed her hair and tried to think of another reason he couldn't go. 'You could get taken by a stranger and locked in a dungeon. Stuff like that happens in real life you know.'

'No, it doesn't. You're just trying to scare me,' he said, carefully lowering his bag to the floor.

She shrugged. 'Whatever. Don't believe me if you don't want to, but you can't go. If you go, I'll run straight upstairs and tell Mummy and Daddy and they'll be so mad you won't be allowed to play on your Xbox for a whole week.'

His jaw dropped. 'You wouldn't! You're not a dobber-inner. And anyway, if you do, I'll tell them you kissed Jack.'

She gasped. 'How do you know that?'

He grinned. 'I saw you.'

Her heart pounded. She would definitely be in trouble for kissing Jack. Mummy and Daddy didn't approve of things like that. They didn't want her to grow up too fast. Whatever that meant. Also, Mummy didn't like Jack's mummy. They'd argued in the playground at pick-up and when Mrs Pickering had walked away, Mummy had held up her middle finger.

'All right. But I'm coming with you,' she said, crossing her arms to show him she meant business.

'I don't want you to.'

'Tough. I'm coming.'

'No.'

'Yes.'

'No, no, no.'

'Yes, yes, yes.' Hannah reached out and grabbed his bag, but he gripped hard and they fought over it.

'Stop, Hannah, stop! You'll wake them up.'

'I'll stop,' she ripped the bag out of his hands and held it high up above her head, 'when you let me come with you.'

He stared up at the bag then glared at her, flipped his fringe. She could see his little mind working things out. After a few seconds he nodded.

'Good,' she said, feeling guilty but relieved.

Greg held out his hand and she passed him the bag.

'What's in there anyway?'

He tapped his nose.

Her little brother grinned and heaved his backpack over his shoulder. Glad he was in a good mood again, Hannah smiled, but her belly twitched. What they were doing was naughty but no one would be awake at this time of night and as long as they got to wherever it was Greg thought the fairy lived and came back home really quickly, Mummy and Daddy would never realise they'd left the house.

Greg stood on tiptoe and grabbed the key off the hook beside the front door. Hannah glanced down at her unicorn slippers. They'd only be gone for a few minutes and it was dry outside. The weather lady said the heatwave was supposed to last for weeks.

She looked back at the gloomy stairs. Mummy and Daddy argued so much they'd stopped showing any interest in her. Even when she'd shown Mummy the Headteacher's commendation for her poison apple sketch, Mummy hadn't seemed interested. Greg still got looked after because he was the baby, but she had to look after herself most of the time. It wasn't fair. And Daddy was always too busy upcycling old bits of furniture to pay her any attention.

Her guilt was replaced by a delicious shiver of excitement. What she and Greg were doing was bad, but Mummy and Daddy would never know.

Greg unlocked the front door. Hannah took one last look back at the stairs, then followed him out into the muggy night.

Chapter 3

LILY

Now

Lily Woods heard the front door slam and sat up in bed, heart skittering like a baby bird. She rested a hand on her breast and glanced at the alarm clock, surprised it was only 2 a.m. John lay beside her snoring with the sheet tangled down by his ankles. He hadn't stirred, which was hardly surprising. A nuclear explosion wouldn't wake him up.

She looked at his peaceful expression and frowned. Last night they'd argued again and she'd started it. She felt bad for doing so but justified all the same. He wasn't himself at all. He hadn't been normal for a while.

Lily nibbled the torn skin around her thumbnail. The dull aching pain came again, spreading across her chest like a disease. They used to be so happy. Used to tease each other and cuddle on the sofa and talk about their days, but now all they seemed to do was get at each other about little things and argue. And the kids must sense it. Hannah especially. She only hoped the children hadn't heard them last night. They'd lowered their voices, but anger travelled.

Shaking her head, she got out of bed and slipped on her

silk dressing gown. The night was unbearably warm. Stifling. Lily was beginning to think she'd imagined the door slamming. John always locked up at night so there was no way it could slam, unless someone had broken in.

She stopped in the bedroom doorway and looked back at her husband, wondering if she should wake him. If she did, he'd probably moan at her and they'd argue again. Besides, she wasn't a person who got their partner to do that sort of thing for them. Built like an elf she might be, but weak she wasn't.

Jaw set, Lily slipped her feet into her slippers, grabbed her tennis racket from under the bed, and left the room.

The landing was cooler than the bedroom, which was a relief. She listened and heard nothing except for John's Darth Vader breathing. As always, her husband and kids were fast asleep while she was wide awake pulsing with thoughts and worries that were impossible to tame.

Greg's bedroom door was wide open. Pulling it to, Lily headed down the stairs slowly, pausing every two steps to listen. No strange noises crept through the air and she became convinced she'd dreamed the banging sound. She reached the bottom of the stairs, flicked on the light and looked to the right. The kitchen door was wide open. Lily crossed the hallway and entered the room. A quick scan revealed no intruders, no broken glass, nothing unusual except for the fact that one of the kitchen stools had been pulled away from the breakfast bar to the counter. Strange. She tried to remember if Hannah, Greg or John had moved the stool before bed and couldn't picture any of them doing it. She certainly hadn't. A horrible thought popped into her head and she let herself dwell on it. Had John . . . no, he wouldn't, not with the kids in the house, and anyway, nothing like that was going on. As always, she was too good at imagining the worst.

Feeling queasy, she moved the misplaced stool back to its usual spot and left the kitchen.

She poked her head into the dining room and saw nothing of any note. The lounge also appeared normal; empty beer cans and her wine glass sat on the coffee table in the centre of the room. Through the ceiling came the drone of John's snoring. No one was here. She must have imagined the sound of the door banging shut.

Lily lowered the tennis racket and walked along the hallway, wondering. She'd gone to bed before John, yes. He'd said he wanted to stay up and finish watching the film they'd started. Still annoyed with him from their argument, she'd stormed off to bed without kissing him goodnight. She'd expected him to come up after a while and see if she was OK, but he hadn't. Exhaustion from a heavy teaching week combined with too much red wine had meant she hadn't been able to stay awake to have it out with him – for the second time that night. Obviously, she'd been out for the count and something had happened in the kitchen, something that involved moving the kitchen stool.

Puzzled, she stopped at the bottom of the stairs and looked at the front door. It was closed. The key still hung on its hook. No one had broken in. No one had slammed the door. She'd clearly dreamed the sound.

With a sigh, Lily turned off the light and crept back upstairs.

Cringing at every creak, she tiptoed past her children's bedrooms, warmed for a few seconds by the thought of her little boy and girl tucked up in their beds fast asleep and dreaming. She loved them so intensely it scared her. The second Hannah was born and she set eyes on her beautiful little face, she knew she'd never have a worry-free day again.

A peculiar shiver caught at her body as she slipped into the master bedroom. Lily gave John a dark look and got back under the damp sheet, knowing she probably wouldn't get back to sleep.

Chapter 4

LOVE

Age 7

September 1988

The wind stung Love's cheeks. Icy teeth nipped at her ears like Medusa's snakes. Blinking out tears, she hurried inside the caravan she shared with her mother and sister and slammed the door shut. Glad to be in the warmth, she made herself a cup of mint tea – Mother would never know she'd used the kettle if she washed up – then sat cross-legged on her bed and pulled out the piece of paper. Teacher Hope often asked Love to read the story of the week to the rest of the class because she was the best. Even though Peace was older, Love was better. At the moment they were reading *Charlotte's Web*, a silly story about a pig called Wilbur and his spider friend, Charlotte. The other children seemed to love it, but Love found it boring and predictable. She preferred myths about gods and goddesses who used their special powers to destroy or save people, depending on their mood. She also enjoyed reading the monthly newsletter, which always described interesting stuff going on in the community. Uncle Saviour was always mentioned too, and she loved to read about him. He was so strong and clever. Sometimes she thought he was like Zeus made real. Smiling at the idea, she took a sip of tea then began to read.

Community Newsletter
September 1988
Written by Nobility, ed. Uncle Saviour

SPECIAL NEW CEREMONY

This Saturday, the community welcomes its fifth family with a special new ceremony.

The event, aptly named the Birthing Ceremony, will take place in the barn at midnight on Saturday. Led by our esteemed leader, Uncle Saviour, the Birthing Ceremony will pave the way towards our new family's exciting new life by bestowing upon them their pure names.

Having completed their three-month period of acclimatisation in Uncle Saviour's farmhouse, the new family are excited to begin their journey. Neil (27), husband to Penelope (23) and father to Christina (4) and Samantha (5), says he is excited to join the community: 'Before we came here, we were in a terrible place, both financially and emotionally. Milk Snatcher's savage attack on the steelworks saw me out of a job and struggling to make ends meet. There were no jobs in Flintshire. I tried everything, but with interest rates rising it was impossible. Our house was repossessed last year and we've been sleeping at friends' houses ever since. In May, Milk Snatcher said this: "If a man will not work, he shall not eat." Can you believe the audacity of that woman? She is the reason people are starving. It's not that we don't want to work, it's that we can't.'

I asked Penelope how their family came to us. She said: 'When a friend of a friend told me about the farm, I knew this was where we were meant to be . . . Uncle Saviour's kindness and generosity are astounding. His wisdom knows no bounds. He has literally saved us from a life of homelessness and starvation. More than that, he's given us hope by showing us that not everyone is as evil and immoral as Thatcher. Good people still exist in this world. A happy, wholesome future remains possible for our girls. Indeed, my husband and I cannot wait to learn our pure names and begin our new life here. With Uncle Saviour as our guide, we are confident that we can grow into better versions of ourselves. This is the best life we could ever provide for our girls. A life of peace and harmony. A pure, good life amongst honest, like-minded people who want to help their fellow man.'

Excitingly, Uncle Saviour has announced that white smocks and masks will be provided for everyone to wear during the ceremony: 'White clothing will reflect the purity of these new names,' he says. 'This colour also represents a fresh start for the family. I also think that masks will add a sense of mystery and excitement to the proceedings. Bobby left me a vast collection of Venetian masks, so we'll use these. I know the children especially will adore this added element of theatricality, but I'm sure us adults will too.'

Love rested the newsletter on her lap and slurped her tea. Her mind whirled with all the new words she'd read. She tried to make sense of them, work out what long words like acclimatisation and audacity meant, but it was impossible. Half of her wished Mother was here to tell her. The other half was glad she was off picking blackberries in the bitter cold with Peace. Mother was strange – always trying to encourage her to play with the other children when all she wanted to do was hang around Uncle Saviour.

She thought about going to Hope's caravan and asking her what the words meant, but now that she was all warm, she didn't want to go outside. Besides, the important parts were clear: there was to be a special new ceremony and they'd all get to dress up in masks. Her knees danced at the thought. Love imagined her uncle leading the ceremony and her heart swelled. He was so special and he made her feel special too. Everyone looked up to him, just like people used to look up to Zeus in the olden days.

With a smile, she returned to the newsletter.

UNCLE SAVIOUR SAVES VIRTUE

Last Friday, at eight o'clock in the morning, Uncle Saviour saved Virtue from a broken leg or worse.

Uncle Saviour was feeding the chickens in the farm-yard when he heard a scream. He said: 'It was a scream of pure terror. Luckily, I guessed it was coming from the stables and I was right.'

Despite battling one of his worst migraines, Uncle Saviour ran to the stables where he found Virtue trapped in a corner of Saturn's stable: 'Saturn was in one of her moods. She was rearing up and slamming her hooves back down near poor little Virtue.'

Uncle Saviour threw caution to the wind and leaped over the stable door, putting himself between the mighty horse and the little girl. 'Virtue was too terrified to move, so I picked her up, shouted at Saturn to back off and carried her out of the stable.'

Uncle Saviour assessed Virtue's condition and discovered a nasty cut on her knee. He tended to her bleeding wound with a kiss, just as any loving parent would.

Virtue said: 'Uncle Saviour saved my life and kissed my knee better. He's my hero!'

Love's heart banged against her ribs. She reread the words and her hands shook. Outside, the wind battered the farm in the same way that anger and confusion battered her mind.

With a scowl, she screwed up the newsletter and threw it at the caravan wall.

Everyone knew about Virtue's stupid behaviour and that Uncle Saviour had saved her, but this thing about him kissing her knee was new. And wrong. He shouldn't be giving special gifts like a kiss to Virtue. Virtue was an idiot – a slow, lazy girl who did nothing to deserve something like that. Yes, it showed how good a person Uncle Saviour was, but Love didn't like it. She didn't like it one bit.

Closing her eyes, she played out a story in her mind. The story made her feel better. It began with Virtue being attacked by Medusa's snakes and ended with her being turned to stone.

Chapter 5
HANNAH

Now

The night was horribly dark, the air so still and quiet that being out on the street felt wrong.

All of the houses on Cherry Tree Close were asleep, their eyes pulled shut. Clouds pasted themselves over the moon like stickers in a sticker book, so Hannah and Greg had to rely on the street lights for sight, and there was something wrong with those; instead of beaming strong, steady ribbons of light, they flickered like twitching eyelids. That's what her best friend Lucie's eyes did when she fitted. Froth bubbled around her lips and her whole body shook like it was being electrocuted. It was scary. Almost as scary as walking up the street in the middle of the night without a grown-up.

Hannah's tummy ached. She looked down at Greg's smiling face, torn between not wanting to spoil his fun, not wanting him to tell on her about kissing Jack Pickering, not wanting him to think she wasn't brave, and wanting desperately to turn back home where she knew they'd be safe.

'How much further is it?' she said.

'Not far.'

'I know, but how far exactly?'

'Uh . . .'

'Tell me where we're going, Greg, and I'll work it out.'

'No. It's my quest.'

She snorted. 'Quest? What are you on about?'

'Don't you know what a quest is?'

'Course I do. But this isn't a quest. This is just a stupid walk in the middle of the night to see something that's not real and won't be there when we get there anyway.'

'This is why I didn't want you to come. I knew you'd be like this,' he said, puffing his hair out of the way.

'Like what?'

He shrugged and looked away. Tears shimmered in his eyes. He sniffed and upped his speed, arms swinging sharply by his sides. She walked faster to keep up with him, stomach churning.

Greg turned left at the end of their close and they started up the hill. His friend, Aurora White, lived at the top of the hill, and Hannah wondered if that was where her brother was going. Aurora was a strange girl. She'd come to their house for dinner once and set fire to a piece of newspaper then dropped it on the fireplace where it had left a mark. Mummy had found out and spoken very nicely to Aurora, telling her that it wasn't safe to do things like that. Instead of saying sorry, Aurora had burst into tears, buried her head in her knees, and refused to do or say anything until her mummy had picked her up. She hadn't been back to the house since then and Hannah was glad about it. Aurora always stared at her and made her feel cold inside. She didn't understand why Greg liked her, but he was a bit different so maybe that was why. He didn't have many friends at school or play with other boys at break or lunchtime. Sometimes a couple of boys said nasty things to him and she had to tell them to leave him alone. It made her worry about what would happen next year when she moved to big school.

They left Cherry Tree Close, skirted the new builds belonging to Maple Court, and entered Dogwood Street.

Dogwood Street did not have trees or flowers or nicely mown front gardens. It had mattresses, tyres and empty beer cans. Glass and cigarette ends dirtied the pavement and someone had draped two slimy-looking balloons over a plastic bag. The road was as pocked as a fossil, and it was really noisy. Dogs yapped. Music thumped. A baby wailed. And there was a strange, dirty smell in the air.

'What's that?' Greg said, wrinkling his nose.

'I don't know. I don't like it here. I think we should go back.'

'No way. You *said*. And we're nearly there now.'

'Nearly where?' Hannah grabbed his backpack and yanked him back.

'Hey! Get off!'

'I will when you tell me where we're—'

She stopped as two men appeared in the road up ahead.

Hannah pressed a hot hand to Greg's chest. He stopped walking and followed her gaze up the road to the men. For a few moments, she and Greg stood on the pavement beneath the street light, jaws slack, eyes bulging. Music muffled the men's words but it was clear they were angry with each other. Hannah had never seen a fight in real life, only on TV, so for a moment she was too shocked to do anything other than watch. Greg covered his mouth with his palm and took a step back. A cold, heavy feeling expanded in her chest and she backed up too.

The men began to shove each other's chests. One man raised his arm and took a swing at the other, who ducked, staggered to the side and barked out a laugh.

With a sudden jerk, Hannah grabbed Greg's hand and

dragged him behind a blue car. Not caring about being too rough, she forced him into a crouch inches from the number plate and knelt beside him on the gritty road. Greg raised an eyebrow and she held her finger to her lips then stabbed in the direction of the two men.

More shouting echoed through the street.

Hannah peered around the side of the car and saw the taller one punch the other in the face. The short one stumbled back as another man came running out from between two houses. The shorter man and the new man launched themselves onto the taller man, making it two against one. The taller man started shouting and fighting back, but after a second or two he fell to the ground and the other men climbed on top of him and smashed their fists into his body.

Hannah clutched her throat and looked away. Her jaw clenched. Panic shot up and she stamped it back down; as long as she and Greg stayed hidden behind the car, they would be OK. The man on the ground wouldn't, but there was nothing she or Greg could do about that. They had to stay quiet and stay put in their hiding place until the men went away. If they did that, they'd be fine.

Abruptly, Greg stuck his head out from behind the car to see what was happening. He gasped and Hannah yanked him back.

The sounds of fighting stopped.

Hannah's heartbeat thrashed in her ears. She slowly raised her head to the rear window. The shortest man was pointing in their direction. He said something and his friend turned to stare. One of the men gave the fallen man a kick.

Hannah held her breath. Maybe it was all over. Maybe Greg hadn't given them away.

The men spoke some more and then one slipped his hand into his pocket and pulled something out. Something that

28

glinted in the moonlight. They faced the blue car. One used his T-shirt to wipe blood off his face. The other said something and they laughed. Then they started to walk over, towards the blue car. Towards her and Greg.

An ache erupted in the back of her throat. She looked at Greg. 'They've seen us.'

She grabbed his hand, pulled him to his feet, and yanked him around the other side of the car.

They ran. One of her unicorn slippers flew off her foot.

Feet pounded the ground behind them. One of the men shouted at them to stop. The other laughed, high and excited as a hyena. But both men ran after them very, very fast.

Chapter 6
LILY

Now

Lily Woods could not sleep. It was as if her brain were a book being flicked through by a million invisible hands that refused to take a break. Through her mind fired thought after thought, worry after worry. She tried counting down from one hundred, counting sheep, picturing a golden beach with gentle turquoise waves, remembering good times from their summer holiday on the Costa Brava a few years ago. Nothing worked. A tinny noise rang continuously in her head and she worried that she had tinnitus. When the kids weren't in the car, she always had her music on really loud – had she damaged her ears for good? She pressed her ear hard to the pillow, hoping that would stop the ringing, but it didn't make a difference. Rolling onto her other side, she tried to ignore the sound, but that made it worse. The ringing started to dominate every other thought, so she tried to imagine what their upcoming holiday in Majorca was going to be like and frowned, unable to stop a rush of anxiety – would she and John argue every day like they had for the last few months – would they have anything to talk about – would John storm off and refuse to talk to her like he had last night? The ache in her chest intensified.

Lily focused on his Darth Vader snores, and aggressively switched onto her other side, rustling the covers as much as she could. She knew it was immature, but it was so annoying how easily he slept when she was driven crazy night after night by sleep deprivation. It made her think he didn't care about how much they fought, which made her even angrier. She began to think about Juliet Pickering and the comment John had made about how good she looked for her age, then she relived the argument she'd had with the woman the other day at pick-up; Juliet had asked if Hannah was OK. Said she'd noticed Hannah wasn't smiling as much as she usually did, and she'd snapped at her to mind her business, that Hannah was fine. And Juliet had told her to chill the hell out, and Lily – who never, ever swore – had told her to chill the crap out and then that sweet, young teaching assistant, Miss Mills, had interrupted to ask if she could have a word with her about Greg, and Juliet had given her the evil and charged off, fake breasts motionless as a pair of spherical paperweights. She had tripped on the kerb in her ridiculous stilettos, and the memory now made Lily smile in the darkness of her bedroom. That had been priceless and the look on the woman's tangoed face – perfection. She ought to text Georgie and tell her about it.

With a sigh, she rolled her eyes at herself. She felt embarrassed about overreacting to the woman's comment, and told herself to be civil the next time she saw Juliet. Hopefully Juliet would do the same and they'd move on as two civilised adults should.

Chewing her cheek, Lily thought about what Miss Mills had said about Greg. She said she'd found him in the toilets at lunchtime. At first, according to Miss Mills, he wouldn't say why he'd chosen to eat his packed lunch in the bathroom, but she'd finally found out that the other boys had been mean and his best friend Aurora hadn't stuck up for him so they'd had a big fight and because he hadn't had anyone to eat his lunch with, he'd decided to eat alone in the boys' toilets.

She hadn't spoken to him about it yet, because everything had been so crazy – taking Hannah to ballet and making the meal, picking her up and so on. She vowed she'd talk to him tomorrow. Poor little thing was a bit of an oddball. He didn't fit in easily like Hannah did. Hannah was more of an extrovert. Whenever they went on holiday, she made friends at the pool while Greg usually did his own thing. Last year he'd been fascinated by lizards. Every time he'd seen one, he'd trailed the poor thing and tried to catch it; thankfully he'd failed every time, but that hadn't stopped him from continuing to try. Her little boy was nothing if not persistent. Stubborn as rust, just like his father. Just like her, come to think of it. Stubborn and overly anxious.

Her anti-psychotics. Damn. She'd forgotten to pick them up – again. It was three days now since she'd taken her last pill. That must be why she'd been feeling so dizzy all the time. Tomorrow was Saturday, which meant she wouldn't be able to get them for another two days unless she went to the hospital and sat there for hours on end, and she didn't have the time to do that.

Nausea crept up her throat.

John didn't know. And he wouldn't find out. She wouldn't tell him. He lectured her when she forgot to re-order or collect them. The problem was that failing to take them sent her off the edge in a really bad way. Once, about six years back, she'd forgotten to take them on holiday with her and the result had been catastrophic. John had tried to get her GP to send a prescription through to the pharmacy in Rhodes, but the man had refused – for some ridiculous protocol-related reason she couldn't recall – and so the rest of the holiday had been hell. Dizziness, vomiting, severe anxiety she couldn't control. It was shocking how quickly the side effects of withdrawal had kicked in. She'd even experienced suicidal thoughts, the likes of which she hadn't endured since the year Hannah was born.

She didn't like to think about that time. Not at all. Thinking back was almost like allowing the darkness to creep in.

John was supportive, but every time she forgot her pills, his patience thinned. Now, she hid it from him when she forgot, which she still did from time to time. She really ought to come up with a system, but what with the kids and work and her and John's arguments there didn't seem to be any time to sort one out.

She heard John's voice in the back of her head. *Excuses, excuses, excuses. Just do it.*

She knew he was right. Tomorrow, first thing in the morning, she'd set a reminder on Alexa. That was possible, wasn't it? Alexa was a recent purchase and she was still getting used to it. John was far more into technical gadgets and social media than her. He practically lived on his phone in the evenings, which was another thing that caused tension between them. Another thing that made her wonder whether he was communicating with someone he shouldn't. She was tempted to peek over his shoulder and check, but if he found out she was having suspicious thoughts, he'd probably go crazy.

As crazy as her.

Lily stared at the back of his head. In the past she'd have reached out and gently stroked the nape of his neck, just to feel his skin on hers.

She used to love sharing a bed with him, used to look forward to their morning and night-time spoons, which, in the early days, would often lead to sex. Now, she felt no urge to touch him, only a horrible tightening in her chest that she knew was her old enemy Anxiety.

Chapter 7

LOVE

Age 8

November 1988

When Mother finished reading the newsletter, she looked odd. Sort of pinched and yellow, like a dried-up lemon.

Peace glanced at Love then said, 'What's wrong, Mother? What does it say?'

Their mother didn't answer. Her hand moved to her throat and hovered there, fluttering like a dying fish. She squeezed her eyes closed and dropped her chin to her chest.

Her sister reached for the newsletter, but Love snatched it up, hurried to the tiny bathroom, and locked the door. She didn't need to go to the toilet. She wanted to read alone.

Community Newsletter
November 1988
Written by Nobility, ed. Uncle Saviour

A MIRACLE CURE

Having suffered from migraines for the last decade, Uncle Saviour is suddenly headache-free, and he thinks he knows what cured him. 'Ever since I kissed Virtue's knee and my lips made contact with her blood, I've felt different and my migraines have gone! I feel purer than ever too, and I'm beginning to wonder about the benefits of blood – does it have the potential to do more?'

With this exciting new possibility in our midst, Nobility agrees that anything is possible: 'It's the food we eat, the air we breathe each and every day living here with Uncle Saviour away from the evil pollutants in the outside world – is it any wonder our children's blood contains such goodness?'

As Uncle Saviour always says, blood is life. Perhaps he's on to something that could make our extraordinary path all the more exceptional.

Blood? *Virtue's* blood?

Love read the newsletter again. If blood made Uncle Saviour's headaches go away, that was good. She hated to think of him in pain, but the fact that Virtue's blood had made him better made her feel sick. She wanted to be able to help him. She needed to be special, important, and powerful enough to kill off his migraines.

She reread the text, desperate to know if there was a way to make that happen and there it was – she'd missed it the first time, but it was true, written in black and white – there was hope: is it any wonder our children's blood contains such goodness?

Our children's blood. Not just Virtue's. Hers too.

Dizzy with relief, she flushed the chain and unlocked the door. Peace stood outside the bathroom staring at her. Without a word, she snatched the newsletter out of Love's hand, turned on her heel and snuggled up to Mother on the sofa.

Love watched as Mother pulled Peace in close, watched as her mother absently stroked her sister's mouse-brown hair, listened as they talked about the fact that Virtue's blood had made Uncle Saviour's migraines disappear. She frowned as her mother murmured that it wasn't possible; it was a myth, a dangerous lie, she was worried about Uncle Saviour's state of mind.

When Peace nodded in agreement, Love's heart burned. She couldn't believe the way they were acting. Her uncle was the kindest, greatest person on earth. How dare her mother act like he was wrong? And there was Peace, nodding along, too thick to think for herself.

Trembling, Love stormed out of the caravan into the frost-bitten afternoon to look for Uncle Saviour, determined to tell him that she believed in the blood story and, if he wanted, he could have her blood too.

Chapter 8

HANNAH

Now

Hannah didn't know where she was going, all she knew was that they had to get away. If the men caught up with them, they might do bad deeds. Mummy and Daddy didn't like her to watch the grown-up news because it had horrible things in, but she caught bits here and there and stories had stuck in her head and haunted her ever since. Like the story of the little girl who went missing near here and never got found.

She looked over her shoulder. The men were getting closer. Up ahead lay the bridge and beyond that, a dead end. Behind the dead end stood the woods, which were black. There were no street lights in those trees, which meant the bad men wouldn't be able to see them. It also meant they wouldn't be able to see the bad men.

Greg slowed down. She tugged his hand and pulled him along. 'Don't stop, Greg! They'll get us!'

He groaned and speeded up. Her chest burned and she imagined his did too. Sweat dripped into her eyes and down her back. Greg's backpack thumped up and down as he ran. She thought about telling him to drop it, but that would mean he'd have to stop and they couldn't afford to slow down.

'I – can't – run – any – more!'

'Yes, you can. You have to,' she said.

They ran under the bridge and total darkness fell on them. Hannah's shoulders shuddered and her legs turned to jelly. She tripped and stumbled. Greg held her up and they ran on towards the woods and the blackness within.

'We have to hide,' Hannah said. She could hear the men's footsteps pounding the ground. They weren't far behind and they weren't giving up.

She yanked Greg further into the trees. She was only able to see a few inches in front of her feet as the trees closed around them and blocked the moon and they left the street lights far behind.

'It's too dark,' she whispered, slowing down.

'Hang on,' Greg said. She heard the sound of his bag unzipping, heard him rustling around inside.

A tiny red beam pointed into her eye. 'Ouch.'

'Sorry.' He moved the light away and the beam lit up a wall of moss and stone and tree all jumbled together.

'Quick. Behind that!' Hannah snatched the tiny torch out of his hand and dragged him up and over the bumpy ground.

They crouched down behind the mossy wall and put their hands over their mouths. They were both breathing hard and loud. Too loudly for the silent woods – which suddenly came alive with crackles and rustles. The men were here.

Hannah tried to slow down her heartbeat and stop the blood pumping in her ears, but it was impossible. She hoped the men couldn't hear her.

She turned off the red light. Greg's sweaty hand found hers. Hannah squeezed it tightly.

'I'm scared,' Greg whispered.

She wanted to tell him to be quiet, but didn't dare speak.

The woods went quiet. She listened hard. The trees were silent again. Had the men seen them? Had they seen the red light? Were they staring straight at the spot where she and Greg had hidden?

Her heart tried to break out of her chest. She gripped Greg's hand even more tightly, and he gripped back and shuffled closer to her. She wished he would stay still: even that tiny movement had made a sound that the men might have heard.

It was so dark now. Hannah looked up. Saw nothing. She couldn't see Greg's face, just his outline.

It was impossible to know where the men were. She'd heard them enter the woods and then everything had gone quiet, which made her think they were standing there, not very far away, maybe right behind their wall. If she or Greg made a single sound the men would hear and what then? These men were bad. They'd hurt another man. They'd ganged up on him and beaten him up and chased her and Greg. Only very bad men would do those things. If they caught her and her little brother, did that mean they would hurt them too?

Hannah shook her head, then froze, terrified they'd heard her hair flinging about. She had thick, curly, heavy hair. It had made a sound in her ears, which meant they might have heard it.

She swallowed and immediately regretted it. Even swallowing made a loud sound when everything else was so quiet.

Hannah wondered if her little brother was crying. His hand was trembling in hers. She wanted to tell him everything was going to be all right, but she couldn't speak and she didn't know if that was the truth. The men could be on the other side of their hiding place listening and waiting until she or Greg made a sound.

Greg shifted his weight. That made a noise too. A short, whispery, rustling sound. She squeezed his hand quite hard, trying to tell him to keep still, and he sniffed. Her heart banged. His sniff had been very quiet, but the men might have heard that too.

She felt cross at him suddenly. It was all his fault that this had happened. If he didn't believe in stupid fairies, they wouldn't be out here in the middle of the night being hunted by two nasty men. They would be tucked up in their beds all cosy and safe. She also felt angry at whoever it was who had told him to leave his house in the middle of the night to go to see a fairy. It was stupid and ridiculous and dangerous, and she should never have come with him. She frowned, angry at herself. She was Greg's big sister. It was her job to look after him and keep him safe, but she'd allowed this to happen by being scared he'd tell on her about kissing Jack. If she wasn't such a coward, she'd have let him tell Mummy. Yes, Mummy would have told her off, but that was it. It wasn't such a big deal, it was just that she didn't want to make Mummy mad, not when she was already mad at Daddy all the time.

'Can we go now?' Greg whispered in her ear.

Shoving her finger to his lips, she shook her head, hoping he understood, hoping and hoping and hoping the men hadn't heard his voice, which had sounded horribly loud.

Quivering, Hannah held her brother's hand. Her heart thumped like Thumper's foot in the film *Bambi*. Greg's breathing was too fast and loud and she worried he was going to have an asthma attack. He hadn't had a bad one for a while, but whenever he did, Mummy and Daddy had to use a big pump machine to get air into his lungs so he wouldn't die. If Greg had an attack now, there was no way the bad men would miss it and no way she could help him. She wanted to ask him if he'd packed his inhaler in his bag, but held her tongue. If it was a small attack, his little inhaler might be enough to save him.

41

Her head ached and she wanted to go home. She couldn't believe this was happening. Just minutes ago, she'd been in the kitchen trying to persuade Greg not to leave the house. Why, oh why, had she given in?

Hannah flinched at the sound of the men's heavy breathing. Clenching her teeth together, she listened. The atmosphere had changed. The air smelt of the strange smoky-herby smell from Dogwood Street. There was a rustle, the scuff of feet, a thud.

'Little shits have gone.'

'Not like they could see us anyway. Too dark.'

'No. We need to keep looking. They saw us. They saw what we did. It was light enough—'

'Nah. I'm going.'

'Whatever. Go. Think I give a shit?'

'Come on, Rudge, we need to move Red. We hit him up pretty bad. Probably should dump him outside a hospital. He won't say nothin'.'

'Hey. Wait. My phone.'

Hannah almost gasped. If the man used the torchlight on his phone, he might think to look behind their wall. He might see them.

'Nah, mate. I'm off.'

'Fine. Fuck off then.'

Hannah's chest relaxed. She listened carefully as the men's footsteps scuffed the dry earth and grew quieter and quieter until they completely disappeared. They'd gone, she was sure of it. Moving her hand away from her mouth, she let go of Greg's sticky palm.

'Have they gone?' Greg whispered.

'Yes. Phew. That was close.' She flicked on the little torch and aimed it at the ground. A slimy worm writhed around in a pile of moss right next to her unicorn slipper.

'Ugh.'

42

'They used swear words,' Greg said.

'They're bad men, that's why. Come on, let's go home.'

'No! We haven't seen the fairy yet.'

'Are you kidding me? Greg, we nearly got captured by two evil men who just beat up another man. It's not safe out here. We need to go home.'

'But we're so close!' he whined.

Hannah grabbed his wrist and pulled him out from behind the mossy wall. 'I don't care. We're going home.'

'No.'

'Yes.'

'No. I want to see the fairy.'

'What if they come back? They might bring lots of their friends. They might bring knives!'

Greg stumbled on a root and she held him up. He sniffed. 'We're so close. It's only on the other side of the woods. There's a path. See.'

He pointed to the ground and she found the footpath with the red light. She moved the tiny beam up the path.

'How do you know that it leads there? There are probably loads of paths in here.'

'It takes you to the forest school. I went there with my class.'

It looked creepy, but slightly familiar, and she realised she'd walked this path herself last year on a trip to the forest school. It led to another small close of houses a bit like theirs, quite near Jack Pickering's house. She remembered Jack talking about it. Saying he liked to play army in the woods with his brothers.

She frowned and tried to remember how long it took to reach the other side of the woods.

Greg sat on the ground and crossed his arms and legs. He tried to puff his fringe out of his eyes, but it was stuck to his forehead. 'I'm not going home. Not until I've seen the fairy.'

She chewed her cheek, wondered what time it was. It was still very dark. They couldn't have been gone for that long. If they were quick, they could reach wherever it was Greg was taking them and it wouldn't take him long to realise that there weren't any fairies to see, and then they could run back the way they'd come, get home and be tucked up safe in their beds. Mummy and Daddy would never know they'd left the house. It would be their little secret. Hers and Greg's. For ever.

'OK. But we need to be really quick. If Mummy and Daddy wake up and realise we're not there, we'll be in so much trouble.'

'You're already in so much trouble, sweetheart.' A bright yellow glow fell on her red dot of light.

Hannah gasped. Someone had spoken. A man. A man with a phone light. She swivelled around and shone the red beam up at his face. He was smiling, but it wasn't a real smile. The smile didn't happen in his eyes, only in his dry, cracked lips.

She glanced behind him. He seemed to be alone. The other man must have gone.

He shone his light first at her and then down at Greg.

'Gotcha,' he said.

Chapter 9
LILY

Now

Lily rummaged around in the medicine cabinet, dropping anything she wasn't looking for in the sink; a half-used tube of baby toothpaste – she'd kept it in case her and John had a third, but two had proved more than enough – several packs of painkillers, a condom – they hadn't made love for months – an ancient tub of Vaseline, Peppa Pig plasters, Calpol.

She frowned, yawned so hard her jaw hurt, kept searching, certain she'd bought sleep aid tablets last summer and not finished the packet. They'd worked wonders but the instructions said not to overuse them so she'd stopped taking them as soon as she'd had a few nights' decent sleep.

There was so much out-of-date crap in the cabinet. She really ought to clear it out, but tomorrow she was having hers and the kids' hair cut then taking them to swimming in the afternoon. John would be working all day, holed up in the garage creating some incredible new piece of furniture. He was extremely talented. When she wasn't annoyed with him, she felt proud of his creations and hard work, and sometimes a little envious – teaching was incredibly full on. She was often so exhausted in the evenings that she felt like a zombie, whereas John worked late, still energised and so focused on his work he barely registered her or the kids when they popped in to say hi. He usually ate his dinner in the garage too, claiming he couldn't take a break or he'd never finish what he'd started – which was a load of rubbish. Codswallop. Baloney. Complete and utter crap. When had he started doing that? She couldn't remember. Six, seven months ago?

He could be getting up to anything while she was at work . . .

She bit her lip so hard she felt it bruise. She knew she had to stop thinking things like that. John wasn't cheating. John would never cheat. He hadn't been disloyal in the whole fifteen years they'd been together. Even when he'd been part of a very laddish group, he'd stayed faithful to her.

They'd met the year she'd qualified as a teacher. She'd gone cycling that hot summer's day and decided to stop at a pub she'd never tried before. The Green Man in a little village called Thornhill a fifteen-minute cycle from her house. Behind the bar, with his eyebrow pierced and fringe dyed blonde, had been John Woods. Two years older than her, built like a swimmer, sexy as hell. Nerves had crushed her ability to talk, but she'd snuck a few glances at him while sipping her Coke, and noticed him staring at her. He'd given her a cheeky smile and joined her for a drink, much to his boss's chagrin, but John being John had given his employer a wink and carried on chatting her up, not caring about his boss's reaction. At that time, aged twenty-four, he'd worked part-time as a barman, part-time as a carpenter. She'd fallen for him that day, and stayed in his minuscule flat that night. Back then, he'd been charming and chatty. Now he was quiet and moody. She didn't understand it at all.

Juliet Pickering's tanned face swam in her mind. No. The woman wasn't John's type. John liked petite, natural-looking women like her, not tall, over-made-up women like Juliet. He didn't even like it when Lily got her nails done. Said they looked fake. And yet, there was something about the way he'd said that comment about Juliet looking good for her age. Something about the way he'd looked at her.

It had been at Hannah's parents' evening in November. She'd gone dressed in smart jeans, a jumper, and suede boots. Juliet had worn a skin-tight dress and stilettoes. She'd noticed quite a few fathers gazing at the woman and glanced at John just to check he wasn't doing the same – but he was. It was then, when she caught him looking, that he'd mumbled about her looking good for her age. Then that she'd started fixating on how distant he'd become.

She'd ignored him for the rest of the evening and when he'd finally asked her what was wrong, she'd felt too embarrassed and silly to say anything about it, blaming her moodiness on her period, which, to be fair, probably had had something to do with her acting and thinking like a jealous cow.

She frowned hard then smiled – she'd found the sleeping pills. Relieved beyond belief, she took two instead of the recommended one. She knew it was irresponsible, but she needed the sleep. A good night's rest would make a world of difference to everything. She might even have the guts to talk to John about what was on her mind. She also needed to talk to Greg about the incident at school.

Lily stared for a moment at the purple half-moons under her eyes, then stretched the skin at her temples back towards her hairline making her laughter lines disappear. With a sigh, she released her skin and tried not to dwell on the fact that she and John hadn't laughed together for a long, long time. She hadn't laughed with anyone for a while.

Laugh-a-minute Georgie was on sabbatical in Australia having a whale of a time, and her other friends were always too busy to meet up, not that she made the effort to suggest getting together any more. The idea of trying to find the time to fit in friends always made her feel exhausted, and she worried they'd see the anxiety burning in her head, press her on it and she'd spill her guts about John. She knew talking to someone about her worries would help. When Mum was alive, she'd always talked problems like this through with her, but she wasn't here any more.

Longing to hear her mum's voice made her eyes sting. She knew what Mum would say: talk to John. Communicate. But it wasn't that easy. Still, for the sake of the kids, she would make herself try.

With a heavy heart, Lily turned off the bathroom light and left the room.

Hesitating outside Hannah's bedroom, she put her hand to the door and thought about going in to stroke her little girl's soft cheek. She pushed the door gently and a great creak erupted, making her cringe. Worried she'd woken her daughter, Lily left the door alone, turned, and padded back into the master bedroom where she slipped under the covers, surprised to find John's side empty. She wondered dully where he was and realised she hadn't heard his Vader snores for a while. Maybe he'd gone downstairs for a glass of water.

She rolled onto her side and got comfortable. A heavy feeling descended behind her eyes like black velvet, dulling her mind and muddying her thoughts. She exhaled. Her shoulders and chest relaxed. Her muscles loosened. Her brain softened. All tension melted away like ice under a hot sun. A slight smile teased her lips. She sighed.

Lily never knew whether John returned to the bedroom, because within moments she was so deeply asleep that a blaring siren wouldn't have woken her up.

Chapter 10

LOVE

Nearly 9 years old

July 1989

The barn was burning hot. It provided protection from the blistering sun, but swallowed the heat, roasting them all like chicken. Everyone was half-naked. The women wore floaty blouses. The men were topless, bottom halves covered in denim cut-offs. The children wore cycling shorts and very little else. Even the straw was warm.

The open doors revealed a wavy heat-haze sizzling above the field beyond, the cows motionless, half-dead from sunstroke. Within the wooden walls, attracted by the pong of sweating bodies, flies buzzed through the sludgy air attempting to land on a patch of skin and taste its salty sweetness. Despite their unrelenting attack, most were too hot to bother with the effort of waving them away.

Uncle Saviour gestured for everyone to sit in a circle. With the community up to twenty-five, it was a squeeze, but the adults sat the little ones on their laps to make it work. Hope, dressed in a stripy blouse that barely covered her enormous bottom, passed around flame-roasted cobs of corn dripping with butter and cups of homemade mead. Everyone *ummed* with pleasure, and the flies buzzed with excitement and tried to attack the corn.

Love licked butter off her fingers and smiled at her uncle. Unlike the other children she wore no shorts, just a beetroot-dyed blouse, so the straw beneath her thighs was scratchy, but she didn't care. Community Unity Time was one of her favourite activities. Always held on a Sunday afternoon, it made a happy end to a busy week. Though she cared little for anyone other than her uncle, getting together like this on a weekly basis felt right.

Community Unity Time had actually been Mother's idea, which made Love feel good. Sometimes Mother could be as helpful as the other mothers. She would never be as good as teacher Hope, but Uncle Saviour said mother was getting there. The problem, he'd confided to her, was that Mother was weak.

Uncle Saviour clapped his hands. Everyone fell silent. Even the flies took a break. He beamed at each adult and child in turn, then let out a hearty laugh. 'Gosh, it's hot! Look at us – all half-naked and sweating buckets. What a sight for sore eyes!' Everyone laughed, even Peace, who normally looked like she'd been face-slapped by a trout.

'Anyway, first, I wanted to say welcome everyone. I've been thinking long and hard about the topic of this week's Community Unity Time and finally made up my mind. Any guesses, children?'

Love's hand shot up. 'Acts of kindness?'

Uncle Saviour smiled at her. 'Close, but no. Anyone else?'

Love frowned. She hated getting it wrong. She thought hard, but Virtue's hand flew up. 'Courage?'

He shook his head.

Grace's butter-greased finger stabbed the air. 'Purity?'

Uncle Saviour gave her one of his biggest smiles. Love's stomach hurt. She tried to catch her uncle's eye, but he had moved on.

'Well done, Grace, what a clever girl you are. Yes, today I thought it would be a good idea to share ideas about purity.'

Uncle Saviour stood up and walked into the centre of the circle. He always liked to stand up when he talked. Love enjoyed gazing up at him and watching his jaw move as it delivered such clever, important messages.

He clapped his hands, grinned down at everyone, whirled in a circle. 'Let's kick things off, shall we? Purity – did you know the word means freedom from adulteration or contamination? And doesn't that definition define us and everything we strive for and strive to be? I remember when my sister first came to live here five long years ago. Charity here – my own little sister – didn't recognise her own brother!'

Mother nodded, a blush darkening her already pink cheeks. 'What can I say? The brother I'd known was a different man. And here I was, presented with a smart-talking farmer who lived off the land and talked my ear off about all these fancy new ideas.'

Uncle Saviour's laugh boomed. Love adored its full, earthy sound.

'And that's what I'm getting to,' he said. 'I wanted to tell you all about how I ended up on my feet instead of in an early grave.'

The tone in the barn shifted on the word 'grave'. Nobody liked to think or talk about death. It was a dark, horrible topic. A few weeks ago, her uncle had sat her down and told her how everyone died in the end. People were not built to last. One day, everyone she knew would die. She would die too. It had been difficult to understand the idea at first, and then the fact had hit her and she'd felt like she couldn't breathe. Why did she have to die? And what happened when she did? Uncle Saviour had said that she would simply stop

51

being. Stop learning. Stop eating. Stop thinking. Stop . . . being alive. The thought was so frightening she'd started to cry, but he'd wiped away her tears and said he knew a way to stop her from dying, to stop all of them from dying, and in his eyes, she'd seen the truth. Uncle Saviour was special. He knew how to save her. He knew how to save them all. She didn't want to die. No one did. She would do anything to live for ever.

Uncle Saviour's eyes darkened and he stopped smiling. For once, he lowered himself to the ground and sat amongst everyone while he talked. He spoke of his terrible childhood, of strict Catholic parents and the hypocrisy they and their religion preached. His voice turned gruff as he described a lazy, jobless father who ignored him, and a mother who drank too much and called him every name under the sun until her throat was hoarse, often hitting him for good measure. He said he had craved kindness and the love of family, but that he'd been denied it at every turn. At school, he was bullied, at home he was ignored or screamed at, at church he was made to feel like a constant sinner even though he did not think he had done anything wrong. Mother nodded along. She never spoke of her time growing up, but Love could see that she had experienced the same sort of treatment. Love stared at her mother, but felt no need to comfort her; instead, she longed to pat Uncle Saviour's shoulder and wipe away the tears shining in his eyes.

Uncle Saviour wiped his cheeks with his fingertips and said, 'I was close to death when Farmer Bronson found me. Half-crazed with addiction, I'd stooped so low as to snatch old ladies' bags in order to fund my habit. It was on one particularly hot July day like this that Bobby Bronson caught me stealing and dragged me back here to the farm – kicking and screaming like a baby I might add.' Uncle Saviour did a comical impression of a tantrummy baby.

Everyone relaxed. All of the children – apart from Peace – giggled. With a soft voice, he described Bobby Bronson's unending patience and kindness, how he had shown him a new way to live.

'Bobby spoke of purity, about living off the land, giving more of yourself to others, being kind to the environment as well as to strangers. He did not speak of worshipping one God or sticking rigidly to the words of an ancient book full of hypocrisy. Instead, he talked about fostering a love of common cause and an appreciation of your fellow man. Bobby believed in shedding worldly possessions and sharing with others, and talked at length about a set of ethics taught to him in his youth that has stuck with me for ever. Lately, I've been thinking a lot about this ethos. We already practise much of what it entails in our everyday acts of kindness and our quest to be as good and pure as we possibly can, but lately I've been thinking we need to do more. Since discovering that the purity we've nurtured in our children could very well make us stronger, I've been unable to stop thinking that another goal could actually be attainable.'

Love's hand shot into the air. Her mother patted her lap, as if to tell her she shouldn't be asking questions, but she ignored her. 'What is Bobby's ethos called?'

Uncle Saviour gave her one of his brightest grins. He smiled at everyone and said, 'Bobby called it Communalism, but I thought we could give it a name ourselves. Make it our own. Please, turn to each other, discuss, and then we'll share ideas.'

Excited chatter filled the barn, but it was cut off when Peace shouted, 'What's this other goal you can't stop thinking about?' A frown drew her eyebrows together. Her voice sounded mean.

Everyone stared at Peace. Love glared at her.

Uncle Saviour raised his eyebrows. 'Ah – good question. Any guesses, children?'

'Just tell us,' Peace said, earning a harsh look from Mother.

Uncle Saviour stood and took centre stage again. He rubbed his hands on his thighs as if nervous, then stepped out of the circle between Mother and Peace, knelt behind them, and rested his hands on their backs. Love stared, wishing he would rest his hand on her.

Grinning at everyone, he waited until he had their full attention, then his eyes flashed. In a serious voice, he said, 'Bobby's ethos, if practised wholeheartedly, using every possible method to attain absolute purity, could, I believe, give the follower the ability to outlive anyone else, perhaps even to live *for ever*.'

He paused and scanned the room. Love scanned the room too. Every eye in the barn was on her uncle. Her breath hitched as she replayed his words in her head. The idea of living for ever was incredible.

Uncle Saviour nodded wisely. 'Indeed, I like to think of this final stage – the stage a person has to reach in order to achieve this goal – as Total Illumination. In order to reach it, the person has to become totally pure-hearted. Clean and good to their very core.'

'That's not possible,' Peace muttered, just loud enough for people to hear.

Love imagined kicking her sister's ankle to shut her up, but she didn't need to.

Uncle Saviour took his hand off Peace's back, stood up and moved back into the centre of the circle. He looked down at Peace and held his arms wide. 'Life is what you make it, dear Peace. If you choose not to open up your heart and mind like your father before you, that is entirely up to you, but I choose hope and eternal happiness. I choose to believe in life, love and all things good. We all get along beautifully here and I'm so thankful for just a little bit of it, this bond, this devotedness that creates a fellowship in the heart, a family of our own making that stretches beyond genetic make-up. I don't know about you, dear Peace, but I need it. In all honesty, I think we all need it.'

Peace stared at her knees, clearly embarrassed for being so stupid.

Love stuck her hand in the air and said, 'I think we should call it Eternal Life.'

Every eye landed on her. Uncle Saviour's face lit up. 'Why, Love, do you know what? I like that name. I really, really like that name.'

Love flushed with pride.

He turned to the community and grinned. 'What do you think everyone?'

Everybody erupted into cheers and whoops and raucous applause. Several children jumped to their feet and ran around the inner circle crowing like cockerels. Peace picked at her sandals. Tears trickled down her sister's cheeks, but Love didn't care; she only cared about what Uncle Saviour thought.

She beamed up at him, and he bent down and whispered to her that she was his Special One. Her heart skipped. She grinned so hard her cheeks ached.

He turned to the rest of his flock and said, 'Now, let's put on our masks and dance around the fire to celebrate!'

Chapter 11

LOVE

Age 10

December 1990

Fine white powder sprinkled the land. Snow dusted the cara-vans and the stables as well as Uncle Saviour's house and the ancient hall that hardly ever got used. Sugary snowflakes floated down from the black sky in no hurry to touch the ground.

Guided by the candles in their hands and light emanating from the farmhouse, the community hurried towards the barn. A raw squeal fractured the quiet of the night, as did whispers and giggles. The gift was so heavy that it had to be carried in two wheelbarrows that had been tied together. Excitement enveloped the group like a force field. The only person missing was Uncle Saviour.

Once inside the barn, people set to work. Cream candles were placed next to the walls, one every few feet to give enough light and provide as much warmth as possible. The girls were handed red or silver tinsel to put in their hair and the boys were given wreaths of ivy to wear on their heads. Everyone wore their white ceremony smocks under-neath lamb's wool fleeces that they would soon shed. While

56

the adults laid a crimson rug over the straw-covered floor, the children added decorations to the Christmas tree. Love had made a bauble out of a blown chicken egg upon which she'd carefully painted ten red hearts. She tied a thin piece of string around the painted shell then stood on tiptoe and tied it to the uppermost branch of the tree, hoping Uncle Saviour would notice her decoration first if she tied it in such an obvious place. Satisfied with her work, she turned around and watched her mother. Unlike the other mothers, Charity stood back, her narrow body pressed into the shadows of the barn, rubbing her forearms with the palms of her hands. It was as if she wanted to disappear. The other mothers bubbled with pride and excitement. The gift had been teacher Hope's idea and Love thought it was a great one. Uncle Saviour did so much for everyone – he was so selfless, so pure and kind – he deserved this. He also needed it.

She turned her back on her mother and scanned the group of children. They all looked as thrilled as Love, but Peace was frowning, just like Mother. Love narrowed her eyes. Peace didn't want to do it, but she was spoilt and ungrateful and selfish. Peace had reacted exactly the way Love had expected her to when Hope had first suggested the idea at the mothers and daughters book group last month.

She blanked out Peace's ugly face. Her stupid sister was not going to spoil this moment.

With quivering fingers, she tightened the scarlet tinsel that secured her ponytail and smiled. Her tummy fluttered with excitement; she imagined Uncle Saviour's face when he saw his surprise. He would be so shocked, then pleased – better than pleased – over-the-moon happy! She grinned, remembering the surprise he'd given her for her eighth birthday. That had been the happiest day of her life. When she'd first laid eyes on her golden-haired boy, she'd felt like her heart would burst with love – not for the foal, but for Uncle Saviour. Jupiter was perfect, just like her uncle, who had known exactly what she wanted and given it to her, just like that. He was the best grown-up in the world. The purest and the cleverest.

'Now, line up sensibly please, children,' Hope said in her teacher voice.

Everyone lined up. Love made sure she was at the front of the line. She wanted to see Uncle Saviour's reaction up close. She peered around. Peace hung at the back looking moody as ever. Love frowned at her then focused on Nobility, who was wheeling in Uncle Saviour's marvellous gift. As well as writing the community newsletter and being the tallest, blackest man she'd ever seen, Nobility was gifted in woodwork. Love stared at his big brown hands. He was such a large man, even bigger than Uncle Saviour, though not as clever or good, of course. No one was as bright or nice as her uncle.

The children gaped in wonder at the wooden sculpture; it was an excellent copy of real-life Uncle Saviour. It even had his thick beard.

Nobility stood back and grinned at the mothers. 'I hope he likes it.'

'He'll love it,' someone gushed.

'He'll like the next bit more,' Peace said, her tone dark.

Everyone looked around at her sister. Love swished her hair and said, 'Ignore her. She's selfish.'

The children shifted uncomfortably, but no one contradicted her. Already, the other kids knew not to get in her way. She smiled to herself. They were all scared of her, she could feel it deep in her bones, like rich, sticky treacle melted through sponge cake. The knowledge warmed her, excited her too. They knew she was Uncle Saviour's favourite, so they knew she could say and do no wrong. She smirked at Peace then faced the front, unable to stop jiggling her legs – not from fear or needing a wee, but from sheer excitement.

The rest of the community trickled into the barn and stood at the back, behind the line of children. Mother hid behind them, a meaningless shadow merging into the wall. Teacher Hope withdrew a needle from her sewing kit with piggy fingers. Love thought she looked like a sow with her stuck-up nose and fat pink cheeks, but she was a good person and a brilliant teacher. Hope picked up a little blue petri dish and knelt at the front of the line beside Love.

The stage was set. If it hadn't been so freezing, it would have been perfect.

Dressed only in her white smock, Love shivered uncontrollably. She rubbed her hands together and tried to still her dancing legs, wanting to be calm and controlled like Uncle Saviour always was. To her surprise, Grace, Nobility's youngest daughter, who was only one year younger than her, started to cry.

Nobility's large head whipped around. He glared at his daughter. Grace sniffled and tried to stop crying, but she couldn't.

Love scowled at her and hissed, 'Stop blubbing. You'll ruin everything. Don't you want to make Uncle Saviour happy?'

Grace looked around at the other children, but everyone stared at their feet. She looked at her father, who looked away.

'Love's right,' Nobility snapped, 'stop being such a baby. It's only a tiny prick. The pain will be over in less than a second.'

Grace looked at the needle in teacher Hope's hand and shuddered. She tried to back away, but Nobility reached out and grabbed her wrist with his huge hand. 'I'm warning you, Grace. Don't. You're embarrassing me.'

The girl sniffed and choked down her tears. 'Sorry, Father. I'm being ungrateful. I'm OK now.'

In a loud voice, Hope said, 'If only every child was like you, Love.'

Love smiled at the compliment. She knew she was better than the other children, but it was nice to hear someone say so.

'He's coming!' someone cried.

The barn went silent. Every head turned in the direction of the door. Uncle Saviour appeared a moment later dressed in his woolly fleece and long johns. His face lit up at the sight of everyone gathered there.

'Hello, everyone. What a pleasant surprise.' His gaze fell on the line of children and trailed up to the wooden sculpture. 'Oh – wow.'

'HAPPY CHRISTMAS, UNCLE SAVIOUR!' everyone bellowed, making the candles quiver.

Uncle Saviour strode towards the statue of himself. His hands roved over its smooth, fine surface. He stared for a long time at his face reflected in wood then turned slowly. Tears glittered in his eyes. Love's heart raced. He glanced at her then up at everyone else. 'Thank you for this gift. It's wonderful.'

'Nobility carved him,' Hope said.

Uncle Saviour beamed at Nobility. 'I never knew you were so talented. Thank you, Nobility. I love it.'

'We've got another surprise for you,' Hope said.

'Really?' He took in the needle in Hope's hand, the hand-made quill at her side and the blue petri dish. A huge grin took over his face. Love thought she had never seen him look so happy.

Nobility stepped forward. 'We all want to help you reach Total Illumination as quickly as possible.'

Uncle Saviour nodded. He opened his arms wide and

raised his voice, 'Thank you, all, for this wonderful gift. It is clear to me that we have all evolved in our understanding of what it means to become pure. We have bypassed our earthly, human fears and opened our hearts to each other. Together, we will become purer. Together, we will complete our journey. Together, we will reach Total Illumination.'

Applause roared inside the barn. Love's heart rose with the sound, her pulse clattering along with it. Her cheeks ached from smiling. She held out her index finger to Hope who stabbed the fleshy tip with the needle. Blood beaded to the surface. Hope held out the blue dish and Love squeezed three droplets of her blood into the bowl. As she squeezed, she smiled up at Uncle Saviour, adoring the light shimmering in his eyes and the heavy rise and fall of his strong chest. He was as excited as her. This was a new step in the right direction. As he always said, blood was life, and she wanted to live for ever. She wanted Uncle Saviour to live for ever too, because he could help her get what she wanted.

'Thank you, dear Love,' he said when she withdrew her finger.

Hope handed her a plaster, which she stuck over the tiny cut.

She watched, unable to believe it was happening, as Uncle Saviour took the dish from teacher Hope's hand and brought her blood up to his lips.

Chapter 12

HANNAH

Now

The man grabbed Greg's ladybird backpack and lifted him off the ground. Greg screamed, turned his head and sank his teeth into the man's arm. He swore and dropped Greg, who stumbled into her. He also dropped his phone and the light went out.

Knowing this was their only chance, Hannah seized Greg's hand and dragged him along the footpath further into the woods.

The trees seemed to grow taller and thicker, the shadows darker, looming close and towering over them like mythical giants with deformed bodies. The woods were so dark, the branches and roots so twisted. It was like the trees didn't care about the path that had been stamped between them; roots crawled across and snagged at their feet; thorny plants invaded the trodden path and ripped at their clothes. Hannah's remaining unicorn slipper flew off her foot, snared by an invisible claw that uncurled out of nowhere.

Greg whimpered as they ran. She gripped his little hand in hers so hard she thought she was probably hurting him but didn't want to let him go. If she did, he might fall behind and the man would catch him. Poor Greg was so small and young. He wouldn't know what to do. He'd probably blurt out that they'd seen those men hitting the other man. But Hannah wasn't stupid. She knew that was why the man was running after them. He knew that they'd seen him hurt someone. He had to stop them going to the police and telling them what they'd seen. Like *The Client*, which she'd watched over Daddy's shoulder one night when she was pretending to watch the Disney channel on the iPad. Hannah knew she shouldn't have been watching it but she couldn't tear her eyes away. She'd only stopped watching when Mummy had caught her and told her off. Daddy had told Mummy to relax and the look Mummy had given Daddy had sent chills down her spine. But those chills had been nothing compared to the horrible prickles of fear she felt now.

She focused on the red light, which waved from side to side as they ran. The path seemed quite windy but it wasn't hilly, so they could move fast, despite the nasty roots and thorns that kept trying to get at them. She knew her feet would be dirty and sore when she stopped. But they weren't hurting yet and she couldn't stop. She couldn't even slow down. The man's heavy feet were coming after them. Every now and then he shouted something, sometimes 'stop', sometimes a swear word. Hannah tried to block out his voice and concentrate on running and pointing the little torchlight at the path. The path seemed to be going on for ever; if they could get to the other side of the woods before the man caught them, they could scream and bang on someone's door, they'd hear and come to help.

Greg had said the place he needed to get to was on the other side of the woods. He'd said it wasn't far. So why was it taking so long?

As if he was reading her mind, her brother said, 'We're – near-ly – there!'

Hannah dragged Greg forward, unable to believe her eyes as the trees opened like a pair of curtains at the cinema to reveal a wooden fence and a kissing gate and beyond that, street lights and pavement and . . . yes – houses!

'Go!' Hannah said, letting go of Greg's hand.

Greg bounded forward, backpack bouncing on his back, and whipped in and out of the kissing gate. Hannah ran after him, struggling with the gate, which bashed back and hit her knee. She glanced behind and hesitated as a dark figure flew after her. The man roared and reached out but his fingers skimmed the ends of her hair. She sprinted after Greg, grabbed his wrist and yanked him across the little close of houses.

Greg tripped and fell to his knees. He screamed and she whirled around at the sound of feet slamming the concrete.

'Don't move,' the man panted.

He shone his light from Greg's face to Hannah's, withdrew a knife from his back pocket, ripped her mini torch out of her hand and threw it away.

Hannah sank to her knees and pulled Greg's face into her chest. He was crying and shaking all over.

She held in her tears and lifted her chin. She knew it was up to her to get them out of this. Though she was terrified, she didn't really believe a grown-up would hurt her. That sort of thing happened in films, not in real life. She tried to think of something clever to say.

'Please don't hurt us,' Hannah said. 'We didn't see anything. I promise.'

The man tutted at her and crouched down, bringing his eyes level with hers. Aiming his phone light at the ground between his knees, he said, 'Nice try, sweetheart, but you wouldn't've run if you'd seen nothin'. Now come 'ere.'

He wrapped his hands around Hannah's and Greg's necks

and forced them to their feet. 'Let's find us somewhere a little cosier for our chat, shall we?'

Greg was crying and sniffing and looking at the ground. Hannah tried to hold his hand but the man yanked them apart roughly and steered them back towards the kissing gate and the woods.

'Please, sir,' she tried again. 'We won't tell anyone. I promise. We shouldn't have left our house in the first place. If our parents find out, we'll be in so much trouble, so we won't say anything. We just want to go home.'

'Too late for that. And switch off the waterworks, kid. Don't you know boys ain't supposed to cry?'

He guided them towards the kissing gate, pushed them through and steered them into the woods. A clack-clack sound cut the quiet and he froze. Hannah looked in the direction of the sound but couldn't see anything through the gloom of the trees.

'What the fuck is that?' he said. He pocketed his knife, wrapped one thick arm around Hannah's throat and dragged Greg alongside the wooden fence by the scruff of his neck. Greg whimpered and the man shook him roughly to quiet him. Her brother fell silent. Hannah longed to comfort him, but the man had forced her face to the ground so all she could see was his large trainers and the orb of light from his phone that bobbed on the ground a few feet in front of them as they walked.

The clack-clack stopped and so did the man. He seemed to be listening, trying to work out where the sound was coming from. Hannah tried to say something but he tightened his pressure on her throat and she swallowed her words and blinked back tears.

'Enough with this shit,' he muttered, whirling them around and dragging them back to the kissing gate.

The strange noise started again. This time it sounded nearer.

The man stopped and fumbled in his pocket for his knife, and an idea popped into Hannah's head. It probably wouldn't work, but she was getting desperate. The man might be the most evil man in the world. He might actually be taking them into the woods to kill them. This night might be the night she and Greg died and they were too young to die. NO. She couldn't let the man hurt Greg. She couldn't let him hurt her. Not tonight. Not ever.

With a dreadful scream, Hannah stamped on the man's toes as hard as she could. At the same time, Greg twisted around and whacked the phone out of his hand. The man swore, but didn't let go of either of them.

'Fuckin' kids. If either of you try that again, I'll cut off your ears. You – on your knees – find it!' He shoved her to the ground. She scrabbled around on the dry soil, looking for his phone.

'Hurry up,' he said, 'or I'll cut him.'

Hannah's heart slammed against her ribs and she crawled forward, hands searching, finding only dried mud, leaves, sticks and sharp, painful stones. She felt his heel on her bottom and fell hard onto her stomach as he kicked her forward. 'Keep lookin'. Be quick. I need that phone.'

Clack-clack. Clack-clack. Clack-clack.

There it was again, that weird sound.

'I can't find it,' she said. Her voice was wobbling now. Fear stuck in her throat, blocking her airway like a gobstopper.

Greg was whimpering again and this time the man ignored him. 'I'm giving you three more seconds to find my phone.'

Hannah gasped and frantically swiped her hands across the dark ground. Tears would have blinded her if she'd been able to see, but it was too dark.

'Three.'

It was as though the trees had swallowed the moon and the stars. She could smell the man's sweat and the strange smoky smell from Dogwood Street. She pictured him with a wolf's head, sinking his teeth into Greg's small, white neck.

'Two.'

She searched faster and harder – and her hand touched something that felt right. 'I've got it!'

She whirled around and held up the phone to him. His hand found hers and snatched the device off her. 'Good girl.'

He turned the torch back on and aimed it directly at her face. 'We're going back into the deep, dark woods, kids. Get going.'

Hannah tried to move to stand up, but he shook his head. 'You're crawling, sweetheart. Go.'

She tried to catch Greg's eyes but he held his hands over his face as if he was too afraid to look. She was reminded again of the film she'd watched over Daddy's shoulder. The little boy had lost his ability to talk after he'd seen the bad man lock his brother in the car and threaten him with a gun. If they made it out of this alive, would Greg lose his voice too? It was a terrible thought. But it wasn't as bad as Greg dying.

With a shudder, she crawled along the footpath following the man's light, trying to think of another way to escape, but no ideas came. Her brain was black, as black and bottomless as the night around them.

Unable to do anything but obey, she tried to crawl as slowly as possible. The deeper into the woods they went, the worse it would be for them. She didn't know how she knew it – she just did. If they got really far into the woods, no one would be able to hear them scream.

'Are you going to kill us?' she said, twisting around to look up at the man.

He shoved her with his foot, forcing her to scrabble forward. She didn't want to cry; she wanted to stay strong and be a brave, clever sister. A sister who was bright enough to come up with a plan and save her little brother, but she felt like a dog on its way to be put down. It wasn't up to her. Her life was in this evil man's hands. Greg's life was in his hands too. She was just a ten-year-old girl and this was real life. This wasn't a film where everything had a happy ending. Deep down, she knew things didn't work like that in the real world. Princesses didn't get rescued by handsome princes. Little girls got killed by evil men.

'Right. This is far enough,' he said.

He pushed Greg to his knees. Greg crawled over to her and Hannah wrapped her arms around him and looked up into the man's shadowy face. He pointed the light at the ground in front of them, tilted his head and blew out his cheeks. For a second, Hannah thought he was going to let them go. He looked thoughtful, almost kind. Flipping the knife through his fingers like it was a toy, he drummed the fingers of his other hand on a tree.

Hannah hid Greg's face in her chest, and thought about Mummy and Daddy.

She looked at the knife then up at the man's eyes. His eyelids hung low and heavy like a cartoon dog whose name she couldn't remember, but he continued to weave the blade very quickly through his fingers. Knees cracking, he crouched down in front of them and held up the knife. 'Look, I don't know what the hell you're doing out in the middle of the night. I don't know if you're running away or what and I don't care. What I care about is you keeping your traps shut. You saw something you wasn't supposed to, and now you're a fucking liability. My fucking liability.'

Greg jumped at his use of the bad word and began to cry.

'Point is,' he said darkly, 'I need to know you won't talk.' He pointed the knife at Hannah then Greg.

'We won't,' she said, 'will we, Greg? We promise.'

'Uh – no. We won't.'

The man's eyes narrowed. His lip curled. 'If you do talk, I'll find out where you live, come over at night and kill your parents.'

Hannah's stomach hardened. She tried to shuffle backwards, but he reached out, grabbed her shoulder and held the knife to her throat. 'Don't fucking move.' He drew the metal blade lightly across her neck, making it tingle. His teeth grinned. He looked mad. Not like a human being at all. More like a Halloween mask.

A loud rustle whispered through the trees.

He flicked off his phone light, plunging them into darkness.

PART TWO

Chapter 13

LILY

Now

Lily was wrenched out of her deepest sleep in years by John shaking her shoulders.

'What are you doing?' she said, frowning hard, heart slamming against her ribcage. Her cheeks were damp from crying. She squinted up at the bedroom light and glared at him.

'The kids are gone,' he said. His face was the palest she'd ever seen it.

'What d'you mean?' She pushed herself out of bed and lost her balance when her feet hit the carpet. Panic uncurled its claws.

'They're not in their rooms.'

'*What?*'

'I couldn't sleep so I went down to do some work and when I came up, I checked on them. They aren't there.'

Lily pushed past and hurried out of their bedroom. She strode into Hannah's room and stared at the empty bed. Panic sliced through her drowsiness like a guillotine. Her heart thumped. Her eyes darted around the room. It was empty. But it smelt of her. It smelt of Hannah. A strange dream simmered in her mind's eye, toxic and mocking. She shoved it away, turned and ran out of the room, along the landing into Greg's bedroom. His bed was also empty, his sheet on the floor in a messy heap. Something stabbed at her chest.

She looked at John. 'Have you searched the whole house?'

'Yes. They're not here.'

'Back garden?'

'Yes.'

'Then where are they?'

'I don't know.'

'You've called the police?'

'No, I—'

She clenched her jaw and bit back every word she wanted to scream. 'Do it. Now.'

She flew past him, ran down the stairs and grabbed the front-door handle. Expecting it to be locked, she jumped with surprise when it opened and glanced at the key hook: the key was still there. Of course it was. She'd seen it earlier when she'd gone downstairs to check, which meant . . .

Her gut lurched.

John appeared at the top of the stairs. 'They're sending someone now. You'd better get dressed.'

'Did you lock the door last night?' she said, stomach twisting.

'What? *Yes*. Of course I did. I always lock it.'

'But you'd had a lot to drink. Maybe you forgot.' Her words hung in the air like toxic gas, the accusation clear. She immediately regretted it: blaming John wouldn't help them find out where Hannah and Greg were. It wouldn't help her get her babies back. She needed to get a grip. Stay calm. But something was pressing on her lungs and it was hard to breathe.

John stared at her for a moment then looked away.

74

She hauled on a jacket from the coat rack, yanked open the front door, and ran outside into the velvet-black morning, screaming her babies' names until she could taste blood on the back of her tongue. Lights came on in people's windows. Mr Saxon was at his door within seconds, navy dressing gown gaping open to reveal a pallid torso.

'What's all this racket about, Mrs Woods?' he said, marching down his drive.

'It's the children. They're missing. You haven't seen or heard anything, have you?' Lily said, looking past him at his open door, a horrible idea leaping into her mind. Most children were taken by people they knew. She ran through every terrible kidnapping story she'd ever heard about on the news – it seemed to be happening more and more these days. Children – girls mainly – went missing. Taken. Stolen. Kidnapped. Years later they somehow escaped, having been locked inside somebody's house hidden from civilisation, being abused for years and years with no one finding them. Sometimes they never escaped. Sometimes they turned up dead or were never found. Only a few years ago, a little girl had gone missing not far from here. She remembered the mother's eyes – how lost they'd been – and how she'd had a terrible thought. Thank God it wasn't my baby. And then an even worse one straight after: how is that woman still alive? I'd die if that happened to me.

She took a step closer to Mr Saxon. Fishy body odour wafted towards her. Why was it that only he'd come out to see what all the fuss was about? She scanned his eyes. He was staring at her. She tried to read his thoughts. Couldn't.

Predators liked to get involved sometimes, didn't they? Liked to get in on the case. Observe their victims' friends and family. Watch them suffer.

Mr Saxon was an odd man. A loner in his sixties, not too

75

old to— No, she couldn't finish the thought. But wasn't that what these sorts of men were like? Strange and quiet. Hermits who kept themselves to themselves? Men you'd never suspect, because they blended into the background?

She found herself glaring deep into his red-rimmed eyes. Words hissed from her lips before she could suppress them. 'Have you seen them? Have you seen my children?'

'What? No. Of course I haven't. I was merely coming out to see why you were making such a racket!'

Was he protesting too much? Being too defensive? She stared at his left eye, drawn by the way the lined skin had started to twitch. His right hand clenched. Unclenched. Clenched again.

'I'm going back to bed. I expect your children are playing a churlish prank. Now, please keep the noise down if you wouldn't mind, Mrs Woods. I need my sleep far more these days than I used to, you know.'

She glared at him, unable to believe how little he cared. He looked away, unable to meet her eye. He turned, but she reached out and grabbed his arm, surprised to find it stick-thin beneath her fingers. 'Don't. Wait. Can I just—'

'Unhand me, woman!' he said, snatching his arm out of her grasp and striding away with jerky steps.

She stared after him as he marched up his drive, disappeared inside his house and slammed the door. She heard him twist the key in the lock and felt something inside her tip. Her knees buckled. Firm hands found her shoulders. John pulled her around to face him and guided her into the house without a word. She let him steer her into the lounge and sit her on the sofa. A cup of tea was placed in her hands. An arm wrapped around her back.

She felt sick with fear.

This couldn't be happening to them. But it was.

Chapter 14

PEARLINE

Now

Ripped from sleep far too early, DI Pearline Ottoline reached for her phone. 'Ottoline.'

'Sergeant Cross here. Initial Responder. Trouble in Dogwood.'

'Go on.'

'Victim DOA. First impressions are that he was beaten to death.'

'Area taped?'

'Yup.'

'Rudge's crew?'

'Probably. The body's right outside his door.'

'OK. I'll make some calls. Be there in about twenty minutes.'

Christ. Connor Rudge was bad news.

She exhaled through a surge of stress and adrenaline. Cross had better be handling things properly. He'd seemed smart when she'd met him briefly at last year's Christmas do and her DS, Sam Dibbs, knew him from college and said Cross was good. Dibbs had to be right. Being the Initial Responding

77

Officer at any crime scene was an immense responsibility. Cross would play a crucial part in maintaining the integrity of the scene. If Dibbs said he was good, he probably was. She trusted her DS like a brother, but that didn't stop ants creeping across her shoulders. Rudge was an abusive drug-dealer who needed to be behind bars. If Cross screwed up, evidence that might nail Rudge to the wall might never make it to court, and that, ultimately, would be on her.

She shook her head. *Christ almighty*. By now, she ought to be able to put her trust in another professional's ability to do the job right. But she was the way she was; her father had made sure of that. As if conjured by a dark witch, a childhood memory shot upwards and the room's shadows bent themselves into her father, dark, threatening and ever-present, just an inch away from destroying all the progress she'd made.

Frowning hard, Pearline pushed the horror away. There was nothing to be gained by driving a stake through an already cracked wall. She needed to be present. Focus. *Be the cop you know you can be*. The past couldn't control the present. She could handle this. Helping people who couldn't help themselves was her domain. She did it well. Most of the time.

As she made to end the call, Cross said, 'Ottoline – I've just found out – there's kids involved.'

She jerked upright. 'How?'

'Rudge's wife, Crystal, says she saw two kids running into the woods. Boy and a girl, she thinks. Says they witnessed the whole thing. Rudge and his mate followed the kids into the woods.'

'Grimstone Woods?'

'Yup.'

'When?'

'About twenty minutes ago.'

Chills trickled down her arms.

The Hart case slithered up over the frail wall she'd constructed in her mind, entwining with Cross's words like barbed wire.

Two missing kids. Sweet Jesus.

She heaved herself out of bed. Anger tightened her jaw; fear loosened it.

Through gritted teeth she said, 'Cross, make that ten.'

She hung up and made quick calls to Crime Scene Manager, Phillip Verne, and detectives Dibbs, Fielding, Hill and Cusp – her murder squad. Finally, she called in extra uniforms from the surrounding areas. The more feet on the ground and eyes in the streets and trees, the better.

Pearline only lived a short drive from Dogwood Street, so she slipped into a blue blouse and grey trousers, and knotted her white-blonde hair into a bun. No time for make-up. No time to eat.

She drove to the crime scene at high speed, trying and failing not to think about Isabelle Hart. If she failed again, she'd have not one, but three lost children on her watch. Not one, but three families' lives destroyed.

Pearline raced up Maple Hill towards Dogwood Street savaged by memories she wished she could forget.

Four years ago, seven-year-old Isabelle Hart, a pretty child with auburn hair and skin nearly as white as her own, had been walking the Harts' miniature Schnauzer in the field behind her house. Faye Hart, the girl's mother, was weeding in the back garden and her boyfriend was watching football in the living room. It was normal for Isabelle to take the dog for a walk on a Saturday afternoon. She'd been doing it since she turned six, which was part of the problem. Routine made life easy for predators. It was only when the dog appeared back at the house without Isabelle that Faye Hart realised her daughter was missing.

During that time, for months afterwards, and every year around the date of Isabelle's disappearance, the press went berserk, and rightly so. The entire nation was bombarded with Isabelle's face. So-called witnesses came forward, but were either fame-seekers or mistaken, and every line of enquiry came to a dead end.

Pearline received her terrible fifteen minutes of fame, calm in the face of the camera, but drowning beneath the surface. She'd worked tirelessly, shunning all other aspects of life, dedicating day after day and night after night to the case, but after a year, every lead had been exhausted and she'd been forced to accept that there was no fairy-tale ending for Isabelle. She was gone, most likely dead. There had been no reasonable hope that new information would come to light, so the case remained open, pending annual review, and Isabelle Hart remained gone.

Pearline had failed her. She flinched. She could hear her father's voice, the vicious onslaught that followed. Recoiling from the memories, she chewed the inside of her cheek until a piece of flesh came away in her teeth.

She'd moved from Missing Persons to Major Crimes, but she wouldn't let herself forget.

Two more children were missing. There was no room for error. Now was the time to be at her very best. Failure was inconceivable.

With a shiver, she turned the Honda into Dogwood Street and pulled up a few yards from the tape.

Chapter 15
LOVE

Age 11

September 1991

Rain fell from the darkening sky. Love tucked the newsletter into her apron pocket and peered up at the purple clouds. Movement caught her eye and she jerked with surprise. Uncle Saviour was pounding on the door of their caravan. He rarely visited. His shotgun was slung over his shoulder. He must have been hunting again. Uncle Saviour was a brilliant hunter. He was terrific at everything.

Love stood up and hurried towards him. Chickens scattered out of her way fleeing for their coop, desperate to escape the sudden downpour.

She was wet through and shivering by the time she slipped into the warmth of the caravan.

Excited to tell Uncle Saviour how pleased she was about the new part of the Birthing Ceremony, she opened her mouth to pour forth all of her positive thoughts, but stopped short at the sight of Uncle Saviour looming over Mother. He was standing very close to her with his hand resting on the barrel of his shotgun. Her mother frowned up at him and folded her arms across her chest. Her back was pressed into the kitchen counter. She made Love think of the weak, scared deer her uncle had just been hunting.

Without looking away from Uncle Saviour, Mother said, 'Go to your room please, Love. Uncle Saviour and I need to talk.'

'But I—'

'Now,' Mother said.

Love gave her mother a hard stare then left the tiny kitchen and stomped into the bedroom she shared with Peace. She immediately pressed her ear to the peeling wallpaper. The caravan was small and the walls were paper-thin, so she could hear every word that followed.

'You've changed, Charity,' Uncle Saviour murmured. 'You used to be so bright and open, so supportive. There was a time when you thought the world of me and my dreams for the community. You trusted me. I trusted you. I thought I still could, but now . . .'

'I'm sorry, Saviour, but this new direction, it seems, well – you know what I think.'

'But you've seen the benefits for yourself. I'm better. Purer. I've never felt brighter. I need this – we all need this. It's what we need to reach Total Illumination. And it's not like anyone's going to get hurt—'

'I'm sorry but I don't agree. I want to believe. I do. Every day I try to be as open-hearted as possible, but this . . . this is wrong.'

There was a long, stony silence. Rain hammered the caravan. Love thought about their words, what they meant. Shame thrummed in her chest; Mother was so ungrateful, so unkind, so selfish. After everything Uncle Saviour had done for them, how she could go against him was beyond her understanding. He was perfect, the purest man on earth.

Anger curled her nails into her palms. Love fought the

desire to storm out of the room and scream at Mother to apologise and change her stupid mind.

Gritting her teeth, she pressed her head against the cold glass and watched the rain plummet from the grey sky, turning the land into slush. She wished, for a long moment, that the rain would turn Mother into slush, teach her a lesson. There was nothing so impure as betraying Uncle Saviour's trust. Nothing.

Finally, in a tight, quiet voice, her uncle said, 'Then I am afraid we shall have to agree to disagree, *sister*.'

The caravan door squealed open. A split second later, it slammed shut. The caravan shook.

Love winced. She glared through the wall at her mother, longing to go after Uncle Saviour and comfort him, but now was not the time. At the new Birthing Ceremony, she would express her feelings through a shining smile and rapt attention. There was little she could do about Mother's strange response, but she could show Uncle Saviour that she was nothing like her. She was strong and devoted. She was only eleven, but her grasp of the situation was leagues above and beyond Mother's. She would never betray him like his own sister had.

Chapter 16
PEARLINE

Now

Being early morning, it was still dark but street and crime lamps morphed Dogwood Street into an uncanny mix of glaring light and utter darkness. Support officers had cordoned off the area outside Rudge's house and were guarding the scene. CSI Harrison was snapping photographs of the body and CSM Verne was making notes. No music came from behind the beige bricks; her colleagues would be inside writing down names. Everyone in that house was now a suspect or a witness to what appeared to be a murder.

Pearline scanned the street. Four police cars were parked up, lights flashing blue, looking like shiny new toys compared to the battered cars of Dogwood Street. Neighbours watched from twitching curtains and a lone street light flickered as if it was about to die. The air was thick with the not-so-innocent perfume of marijuana. Warranted uniformed officers were knocking on doors and taking statements, asking residents if they'd been awake, had they seen anything? Uniforms swamped the area; eight officers were searching the woods for the children.

Pearline frowned. Her feet itched. She longed to join the search, but that wasn't her priority at present. She scanned the scene once more. Everything seemed to be in order, but she needed to find lines of enquiry to follow.

Dibbs joined her at the tape. Anxiety creased his ebony forehead. The sight of him eased the pressure in her chest. An urge to have him hold her came and went like lightning; there then gone; electric but not appropriate, now or ever.

He frowned. 'You OK? You don't look too good.'

'I'm fine. Thanks.'

She glanced at the blue Kia Soul parked outside Rudge's house and did a double-take: on the pavement a yard or so away from the car lay a small slipper. Child-size. She stared at it and placed a hot hand on her stomach. Glanced at Dibbs. His face had blanched. He'd seen the slipper too.

Verne ducked under the tape and loped over to them. He wiped a hand across his forehead and flicked an eye at the slipper. 'Oh – you've seen it. Good.' He looked away from the soft pink unicorn and gestured to the body on the road.

Christ. The man had been beaten blue. His body looked twisted, his mouth frozen in a cruel smile. His eyes were open and staring; the whites mazes of ruptured capillaries, the skin around the sockets puffed up like stuffed courgette flowers. Blood sprinkled his T-shirt like red confetti.

She stared, aiming for dispassionate and removed, but bile stung the back of her throat. She'd seen a few battered bodies in her time but never grew immune to it – no one did really, unless they themselves were sociopathic. The only way to cope was to assign the horror to a mental dumping ground and try to crush it whenever it resurfaced. That, of course, was easier said than done. Sometimes a bloody carousel of images cycled through her mind at night and the only thing that made it stop was turning on the bedside lamp and googling photos of puppies.

'I've called someone from the lab to come to assess the blood splatter,' Verne said, giving her an odd look.

'Any ID on him?'

Verne handed her a bagged driving licence. The name read Brett Kirby. The photograph matched the dead man on the ground.

'Good. Any sign of a weapon being used?'

Verne shook his head. A damp curl flopped over his bloodshot eyes. 'No. See there? Those marks clearly indicate punch wounds. This man was beaten very badly. It's unclear whether the cause of death was from the beating he endured or from the hit to the head he sustained when he fell.'

Blood puddled out from the man's head, blackening the concrete. She felt her gorge rise.

'Any self-defence wounds?'

'Plenty. He put up quite a fight, but I believe he was outnumbered two or more to one.'

'Why so?'

Verne pointed to a small triangular imprint on the dead man's right temple. 'This appears to be a ring indentation, indicating one perpetrator. See here?' Verne indicated a bruise on the right side of the man's mouth. 'Unless the attacker took off his ring to deliver another punch, I suspect this bruise was caused by a second individual.'

'That tallies with what Crystal Rudge said,' Pearline said.

Dibbs nodded. 'Cross said she saw Rudge and one other running after two children.'

She armed sweat off her forehead. 'Anything else?'

Verne smiled grimly. ''Fraid not.'

Dibbs rubbed his jaw. His eyes betrayed fear, the very same fear she felt. Fear for the utterly innocent. For children. Fear, maybe, that she wasn't up to the task.

'Can you keep watch here?'

Dibbs nodded. He frowned at her. 'You sure you're OK?'

86

She'd talked to him about the Hart case. He'd suggested therapy and she'd snapped him down. Still, her heart beat faster at the soft concern in his gaze. She couldn't help feeling touched by his worry, and fearing that he was right. She was a jumble of nerves today. Trust Dibbs to see the cracks in her facade. That was the problem with him; he was too perceptive. He understood her too well.

She straightened her spine, glanced around, hoping it wasn't too obvious to anyone else that she was struggling.

'I'm OK, thanks.'

He held her gaze a moment longer. His eyes scanned hers, deep and knowing. 'Let me know if you need me.'

She nodded, wanting – just for a second – to open up, but holding back. It wouldn't do any good. If she divulged her fears now, she'd probably break. With two children missing and a man lying dead at her feet, breaking wasn't an option.

Dibbs gave her a long look then joined Verne.

Tight-chested, Pearline turned her attention to CSI Harrison, the crime scene photographer. Being the way she was, she'd made it her mission to take in as much information as possible about the role of each and every individual who contributed to a crime scene investigation. By talking to colleagues and reading everything she could, she'd acquired an extensive awareness of the fundamental part each person played. Pearline needed to feel in control of the investigation. Knowing exactly what each player should be doing, when and how they should be doing it, also meant she was quick to spot inconsistency, incompetence, or mistakes. Human error, sadly, was more common than it should have been. Sometimes, frustration at others' mistakes made her insides hurt.

She watched CSI Harrison for a few minutes. He'd progressed from mid-range photos to close-ups of individual pieces of evidence. Just as he should, he was using a tripod and professional lighting techniques to achieve optimal detail and clarity. These pictures in particular would provide the forensics lab with views to assist in analysing evidence. If this man did his job properly, every photograph would be included in a photo log that documented the details of each photo, including its number, a description, and the location of the object or scene, the time and date the image was taken, and any other descriptive details that might be relevant. The thoroughness and accuracy of the photo log was essential; without it, the pictures of the scene would lose a great deal of their value. But mistakes were often made, details missed. In the investigation into JFK's assassination, FBI photographers hadn't recorded descriptions of their photographs. As a result, investigators were later unable to distinguish between the entrance and exit wounds of the bullets; a vital factor in determining the position of the shooter. Human error, pure and simple. She couldn't stand it, and yet she knew perfection was an impossibility. No one was infallible. Everyone made mistakes, including her. Even childhood beatings hadn't cured her of that. She often found herself running through the Hart case, wondering if she'd missed anything, made any mistakes.

Her heart fluttered strangely, like a trapped butterfly. She pressed her palm to her chest. *Christ, Get a grip.*

Clenching her jaw, Pearline told herself that she wasn't spiralling into the realms of control freakdom. Scrutinising the process helped. If she checked people's work and maintained a high standard in herself and others, crucial evidence was far less likely to leak through the gaps and create a huge bloody puddle.

Harrison snapped a close-up of the victim's right eye. It resembled a chewed-up plum. A shiver played about her shoulders. Rudge was as brutal as he was immoral. Would he hurt those children?

Resting a hand on her abdomen, she gave Harrison a nod of approval then moved to stand beside the sketch artist.

Pearline was pleased to see that details such as the distance from Rudge's door to the body had been indicated in the drawing. The woman was talented and precise, exactly as she should be.

A second woman was making notes on her tablet. Pearline approached the note-taker, and introduced herself, not familiar with this investigator, a petite strawberry-blonde who looked like she was just out of university – not that this meant the young woman wasn't experienced. Pearline had learned many years ago not to judge a book by its cover.

The woman extended her hand. 'Investigator Sky Lark. Good to meet you, Chief Inspector Ottoline. I've just completed my walk-through. Want a glance at my notes?'

Pearline nodded. 'Definitely. Quick as you can please.'

Lark raised an eyebrow, but didn't comment. She nudged her glasses up her nose and swiped the screen, then handed Pearline the tablet.

She scanned the notes as quickly as she could, pleased to see that the CSI was highly skilled in the art of scientific observation.

Scene
    . . . Saturday 3rd June, street light in front of 29 Dogwood Street is flickering. Unicorn slipper, child size 13, to the rear of a sky-blue Kia Soul reg. KYA 5IN parked on pavement in front of 29 D. Weather humid: 21 DC. Victim male, Caucasian, red hair, 25–30 yrs, lying in road opposite 29 D on back, eyes closed, left cheek on tarmac, right arm across chest, left arm parallel to side of body. Victim wears white T-shirt, blue jeans, white Nike trainers. Blood on T-shirt, hands, jeans and trainers. Bruises and cuts visible on victim's face and arms.

She'd read enough. The woman's notes were thorough. As far as she could see, the young investigator had missed nothing. And, just as she'd hoped, Lark had noted the unusual presence of the child-sized slipper.

Relieved, Pearline handed her back the tablet. 'Good work, Lark. I'll leave you to it.'

She approached Dibbs and nodded, keen to hide the panic skewering her heart. 'Where could these kids have gone?'

He glanced towards Grimstone Woods. 'They might be hiding in there. Maybe they made it out – what's beyond these woods?'

'Fields mainly on the west side, houses on the left. You can walk through and come out onto Birch Close.'

'So maybe they know someone who lives there?'

'Maybe. But why are two little kids out at two in the morning in the first place?'

'Runaways?'

'Possibly. I'm also thinking this area has its fair share of criminals. Could be another bad-on-bad. Maybe someone kidnapped these kids and they got away? Or they cut them loose because their parents refused to pay?'

'Could be.'

'Maybe they were playing out late and their parents decided to teach them a harsh lesson and lock them out for the night; they saw Rudge beating the crap out of someone, and legged it?'

'If that's the case, chance is these kids live nearby. Maybe house-to-house visits will come up trumps.'

'We can but dream,' she said, fighting to sound calm.

Dibbs sighed and rubbed his jaw. He raised his hand then let it drop.

She fought to slow the frantic pounding in her chest and hurried towards Rudge's house.

* * *

A young uniformed officer met Pearline at Rudge's front door. 'All three men claim not to know the whereabouts of Connor Rudge or Mike Gibson. They said Rudge and Gibson left the party at approximately 2 a.m. We tried speaking to Mrs Rudge but she's not very forthcoming. She did corroborate the others' story though, saying that she, her son, and the three in there never left the house.' He paused, raked a hand through his hair. 'Shall we let the others go?'

'Got their details?'

'Yep.'

'Good. Yes, do that.'

He nodded and led her into the lounge where beer cans abounded but, unsurprisingly, there was no evidence of marijuana, bongs or any other drugs. Three men sat on Rudge's faux-leather sofa looking spaced out and stinking of cannabis. She didn't recognise any of them. Mrs Rudge sat on a tub chair with her son on her lap. As she stroked his hair, her fingers trembled. Her mascara was smudged, face pale, collar bone so pronounced above her vest that it resembled an excavated bone. Her right leg jigged while the fingers of her free hand tapped her thigh. Their eyes met and Pearline gave her a tight smile.

The officer spoke to the three men, who grabbed their bags and left as quickly as they could without running. She itched to rip open each man's bag and search it, but she wasn't here regarding drugs. She was here to process a murder and find two missing children.

Pearline perched on the edge of the sofa and withdrew her notepad and pen from her pocket. She scanned the woman's face and body for signs of injury, but found none. They were probably under her clothes.

A sharp pain flashed along her side and the past resurrected itself in her mind with unsettling clarity. As always, the same memory splintered her thoughts and she recoiled from the vision of her father looming over, belt in hand. She had always felt so small and weak. Helpless. But she wasn't helpless now. She couldn't afford to be, not when children's lives were at stake. Nevertheless, no matter what she did, the terrified child she'd once been still lived inside her, just as it still lived in Crystal Rudge. The difference was that her abuser was dead and rotting; Crystal's wasn't.

With a shudder, she dragged her thoughts from the past and looked at the woman's scrawny neck. She wanted to put an arm around the young woman, persuade her to seek help, prosecute and leave her abusive husband, but domestic abuse was a complex labyrinth, and she wasn't qualified to point the woman in the right direction or know the correct things to say. She certainly wasn't one to judge either, not when she'd kept quiet about her father's violence for so many years.

She sighed inwardly. She knew a little about psychological manipulation and the terrible hold abusers yielded over their victims. Leaving wasn't simple. The practical, physical elements involved in escape weren't easy to overcome, but breaking and escaping the psychological confines was even harder. Also, Crystal Rudge wasn't contending with just anyone. She was up against a drug dealer with eyes and ears all over the South West. Escaping would be a lot harder for Crystal than most. But, maybe, if she did her job well and caught Rudge, Crystal's biggest problem – him – would go away for good, and she and her son could start fresh, some-where safe, far away from Rudge and this mad, sick life.

Pearline extended her hand, relieved to see it was steady. The woman hesitated, then took it.

'Hello, Mrs Rudge. I'm Detective Inspector Ottoline.'

'Call me Crystal.'

Pearline nodded. 'I'm told you called it in.'

Crystal Rudge began to nibble her nail. 'Yeah. Uh, can I put Tyler to bed first?'

'Yes, of course, but tomorrow Tyler will need to talk to a specially trained detective to give his account of events.'

'Oh. OK. Sure. Of course. Tyler, honey, run up to bed now, there's a good boy.'

The boy nodded, averted his gaze from Pearline, and looked at his mother. He looked healthy. She saw no sign of malnourishment or injury, but his eyes weren't as alive as other children's. This life was already eroding his childhood, scrubbing away at the boy's innocence and happiness. The child knew what his father did for a living. Even though he probably tried to hide from the knowledge, he knew his daddy was one of the bad guys. Connor Rudge wasn't like other daddies. His daddy did bad things.

Just like mine.

Her heart clenched as the little boy gave his mother a hug then ran out of the room.

Pearline waited for the sound of his footsteps to die then said, 'My colleague said that you saw two children being chased into the woods. At what time was this?'

'I dunno. About one, two maybe.'

'It's important I know the time. Think carefully, Crystal. Was it closer to one or two?'

She chewed her lip. 'Two, I think. It's hard, I was pretty hammered.'

Still are.

'Look. I just wanna say quickly that I'm sure my Con won't hurt them kids. I mean, he's got Tyler. He likes kids. But I was worried cos there are some right nutters out there – you know crazy perverts who go kidnapping little kids to do God knows what to 'em and—'

'Who chased them exactly? Can you tell me their names?'

Crystal looked like she'd been slapped. 'Uh, yeah, sorry. OK, so it was my Con and Mike Gibson.'

Pearline stared at the young woman. She could smell the

booze wafting out of her skin. See the veins in her eyes. 'How old were these children, roughly?'

'The girl was bigger. I dunno. Eleven, twelve maybe? The boy was small. Five or six? Not sure. Maybe older. He looked about Ty's size. Yeah. Maybe seven or eight.'

'Can you describe what they looked like? Hair colour? Clothing?'

'The boy was wearing a green onesie. The girl had big hair.'

'What colour was the girl's hair?'

'I dunno. Brown, I think. Black maybe?'

Pearline gritted her teeth. 'And the boy's?'

Crystal shrugged. 'I'm sorry. It was dark.'

'Did they have anything with them?'

She chewed her lip again. 'I think the boy had a bag. Oh yeah – he did! It looked like a ladybird. I remember thinking how cute it was.'

Pearline jotted the information down on her pad.

She looked at Crystal. 'Do you have any pictures of your husband and Mike Gibson?'

Crystal nodded. She withdrew a pink phone from her pocket, unlocked it, opened the gallery and handed the phone over. Pearline stared at the photograph of two men lounging on the Rudges' sofa, rollies in hand. Crystal stood on tiptoe and pointed over Pearline's shoulder. 'The muscly one's Mike. And that's—'

'Your husband,' Pearline said, staring at the man's dark, soulless eyes.

Crystal let out a booze-heavy sigh. 'Yeah. That's him.'

'Can I keep hold of your phone for the time being?'

'Uh, yeah. Sure.'

Dibbs poked his head around the door and gestured for her to come. Pearline thanked Crystal Rudge and dashed out of the room.

'They've just found another body,' Dibbs panted.

'Who?' she croaked. *Please, not one of the children.*

'I don't know.'

She bit her lip. 'Where?'

'The woods.'

Chapter 17

LOVE

Age 12

November 1992

Uncle Saviour stood in the centre of the barn, breath misting, naked.

Love frowned. Candles dotted the large space, but did nothing to temper the chill. She wondered if his skin was goosed up like hers. Hoped and wished it wasn't.

Uncle Saviour was pure. Soon, if she behaved well, she would be pure too.

She smiled. Stared at him. Absorbed every detail.

His skin shone like melty marble chocolate, some light, some dark, some in-between, clouded by shadows and hair, lightened a touch by firelight. Every member of the community wore a mask, but he didn't. He was bare from head to toe, open, bold, braver than them. He led, they followed. His chest rose and fell slowly, powerfully. He was strong. They were weak, but his strength and purity could fix that.

She almost squealed with excitement. Anticipation bounced up and down her spine like a yo-yo. She couldn't wait to witness the new part of the Birthing Ceremony. It made complete sense, but Peace didn't like the sound of it. Mother wasn't so sure either, which Love thought was a betrayal of the highest order. But Charity was weak, that was what Uncle Saviour said.

Love cringed as a hot hand of shame squeezed her heart. She did not understand why Charity had argued with Uncle Saviour, not when everything he said and did was so pure. Her mother's behaviour made her angry.

But Peace was even worse than Mother. She openly badmouthed the new part of the ceremony to anyone who would listen.

Love scowled at her sister. She felt like spitting, or tearing something up. Not a piece of paper or anything simple like that. Something more alive. Something that could scream.

If her stupid sister continued to talk to other people about her bad opinion of the new part, she would ruin everything. Eternal Life Community was perfect. Uncle Saviour was the only one in the entire world who could help them reach Total Illumination. If Peace didn't understand that, she needed to be made to understand soon, before she spoilt things for everyone.

Love blinked. Focused on Uncle Saviour. A sheen glossed his bare chest. Behind him stood the two new adults, both dressed in outsider clothes, faces unmasked. The fair-haired man carried a little boy in his arms. The child was asleep. He looked peaceful. A white rag dangled from his mouth and he wore a pale blue matching top and trouser set.

Uncle Saviour strode to his place on the red cross in the centre of the two circles. He raised his face to the ceiling rafters and stood for a moment, not saying anything. The whites of his eyes gleamed like marbles. The muscles in his arms and chest stretched and expanded. His shadow swelled large and wide. Kissed by flames, his outline glowed.

The barn fell silent, but Love could hear the pounding of

her heart. She licked her lips and her tongue grazed the inside of her mask.

Her uncle lowered his gaze and stared at each adult, all of whom were on their knees in the outer circle, faces masked. Every person in the barn watched him, glorying in his purity as he gazed upon the children in the inner circle and beamed at each child, pausing on Love to smile at her for the longest.

He gestured for the new couple to go down on their knees. They obeyed. Like him, they were maskless. They would receive their masks once the new part of the ceremony had been completed. Love looked at the man – he had a smile on his face. The woman didn't look quite as content. A plum-coloured bruise dirtied her cheek and she could not take her eyes off the sleeping boy.

Uncle Saviour raised his arms.

'We welcome you to Eternal Life Community, dearest ones, and to our Birthing Ceremony where we shall help you commence your journey on the road to Total Illumination by bestowing upon each of you your pure name.'

This was the part where Uncle Saviour gave them a kiss on their foreheads and whispered their new names into their ears. They would then stand up and shout their names and everyone would applaud. After Uncle Saviour's speech, which Peace said went on for too long, a great feast would be shared in celebration of the new people and their new names. This family had been living in Uncle Saviour's house for the last three months so that they could grow used to the community's routines and ethos. They had not yet been permitted to mingle, so the party after the ceremony was a joyous occasion where everyone got to know the new people and welcome them into the community properly.

But Uncle Saviour did not give them a kiss. Instead, he beckoned to one of the adults kneeling in the outer circle, who stood up, walked forward, and handed him a long-handled scythe. Uncle Saviour held the scythe aloft, turning in a slow circle to make sure that every adult and child in the barn glimpsed the long, curved blade.

Love frowned. A few adults and children were fidgeting. They ought to be as still as stones during this part. This was the new part Uncle Saviour had been telling the community about for the last few weeks. She glared at the new woman, who had gone very white and begun to tremble. Only the weak and disloyal tremble in the face of the journey to Total Illumination. That was what Uncle Saviour always said.

'With this blade, on this very night, I offer those who are new to us the chance to be birthed with a higher level of purity than I have ever been able to offer before. Indeed, now that I have reached the stage of Total Illumination, I am able to transfer some of my strength through this blade with two simple cuts and a kiss. By giving you these cuts, I am freeing you of any lingering ties to the outside world and any ties to the evil within it. By giving me your blood, you are revealing your undying devotion to our journey and thus marking your first step on the road to salvation.'

He paused and looked around the barn, stepped closer to the inner circle and said, 'Members of Eternal Life Community, say it with me: *To be free, you must be cut. To be pure, you must give blood. The end justifies the means.*'

After a beat of silence, everyone repeated Uncle Saviour's words, 'To be free, you must be cut. To be pure, you must give blood. The end justifies the means.'

The atmosphere in the barn felt stiff and cold. Love looked at her mother, whose chin touched her chest. Love's heart burned and her fingers curled into claws. It was as if Charity didn't want to watch what Uncle Saviour was about to do. Love wanted to run across the circle and yank up her mother's chin to make her behave, but she had to be still.

She had to be present and focus on this big occasion and all that it would mean to their community, just as her mother should.

If Uncle Saviour noticed Mother's behaviour, he didn't let on, but Love knew that he never missed anything. She smirked. Mother would be told off for her behaviour. She wouldn't make this mistake again.

Uncle Saviour took a step towards the brown-haired woman, who stared up at him and tried to smile. Tears dripped down her pale cheeks.

He smiled down at her, patted her shoulder, and stared into the new woman's watery eyes. In his loudest, purest voice, he said, 'To be free, you must be cut. To be pure, you must give blood.'

Her mother looked away. So did Peace.

Behind her mask, Love grinned.

Chapter 18

PEARLINE

Now

Darkness swarmed in on them like a pack of wolves. Their torchlights did little to brighten the gloom as she and Dibbs hurried after a uniformed officer through Grimstone Woods to a second body.

Christ. What were they about to see? A dead man or a dead child? She dreaded to think. Two murders and two missing children: this day was turning into a nightmare. She only hoped this second body didn't belong to one of the children. If it did . . . no. She couldn't go there. Not yet. Not until she'd set eyes on the body.

Dibbs strode ahead, holding branches out of the way. Ahead of Dibbs walked their guide, his strides long and fast.

She aimed her light on the ground, careful to avoid roots. She'd walked these woods in daylight several times. Walking helped. It was one of the few things that did. Alcohol made her depressed, food comforted but didn't ease the constant ache in her shoulders. Walking through nature – admiring its untampered wildness while being cut off from the noise and grime of technology – was the only thing that offered her any kind of peace. But these woods weren't peaceful or beautiful now. Darkness changed everything, morphing beauty into danger, shadows into ghouls, trees into gravestones. Pearline never avoided walking under ladders. She didn't touch wood, avoid black cats or strain her back to pick up random pennies, but as she pounded the path her body stiffened, not from exertion but from dread, for she felt certain that something uncanny had happened in these woods. A terrible event had taken place. Her bone-white skin prickled with the certainty of it.

The stifling dread could have come from the knowledge that Isabelle Hart had gone missing not that far from here. During the hunt for the little girl, the woodland on the outskirts of Cruxley had been searched. Woods were a common dumping ground for the murdered. Any place with dense trees or foliage was an ideal choice to hide a body, and the woods beyond Cruxley covered a lot of ground. Of course, nothing had been found.

Pearline considered the obvious differences here. Rudge had chased these children, possibly because they'd witnessed him and his friend kill Brett Kirby. As far as she knew, the two kids had not been taken. They had been – *were possibly still being* – chased.

If she'd been a religious person she'd have been praying. Her father had tried to beat the sin out of her, and she'd tried to do all she could to appease him, but any wispy belief she'd held in an almighty being had died the second she'd told Mrs Hart they needed to move the case to annual review. Disbelief. Yes, the woman's disbelief had been the worst part of it. The young mother's disbelief, her rage and fear and utter devastation, were tattooed onto Pearline's brain. When she tried to sleep, Faye Hart's face screeched behind her eyelids like knives on china. That much grief – seeing it in someone else, knowing you could do nothing to ease it – was impossible to forget. And the failure excavated the bones of the lost little girl that she'd once been, the lonely, beaten kid she'd tried for so many years to bury.

She shook her head fiercely and earned a concerned glance from Dibbs, which she didn't acknowledge. Sweat plastered her blouse to her stomach and back. Her trousers clung to her legs like an extra skin. She wiped her upper lip and walked faster.

As she walked, she moved the torch slowly from left to right, scanning every inch of visible woodland. Déjà vu swept over her. *Sweet Jesus.* She'd been here in this precise spot, in this exact position, sweeping the very same torch across the very same trees.

Déjà vu. Already seen. She'd studied the peculiar phenomenon during her psychology degree back when she'd harboured dreams of becoming a criminal profiler. According to science, déjà vu was a neurological anomaly. But the word 'anomaly' had always struck her as strange. She'd never been able to fully invest in the idea that déjà vu was meaningless. It couldn't just be a mental blip of electrical discharge, not when it felt so real. But it wasn't real. She didn't believe any of that precognition/prophecy crap. Not any more.

This bout was lasting a long time. Too long. She'd lived this exact experience before. Travelled this path. She must have.

She stopped moving the torch, and again, she'd done that before.

With a shudder, she strode on, but déjà vu's tentacles clung on wetly, turning her skin cold. That was when the uniformed officer stopped walking and moved to the side, and she saw it; a body.

Déjà vu vanished and absolute clarity returned.

A body. She stared at the corpse. Big, not small. Not a child.

She could breathe again, but for how long?

Pearline crouched beside the dead man and held up the photograph of Rudge and Gibson.

The horror of the man's injury was almost too much.

Saliva flooded her mouth. *Christ.*

The skull was split open into a gory mess so grotesque it almost looked fake; however, despite the fact, there was no doubt that the body belonged to Connor Rudge. Blood obscured the eyes, but the mouth and nose were Rudge's, and the middle finger of the right hand bore a blood-stained gold signet ring.

In the same instant, she wanted to throw up and cheer. Instead, she moved away from the body, and called in a Crime Scene Co-ordinator and a second Crime Investigation team, while Dibbs organised for the area to be taped.

She fell into thought, trying to recreate what might have happened here. Rudge was dead, skull cracked open like an egg. Someone had attacked him. But what had happened to the children? Where were they now?

She crouched down and scanned the area. Leaves, sticks, moss. Her heart jumped as something pink caught her eye. Oh God. It was half-hidden by a fallen tree. She gestured at Dibbs and mouthed, 'What's that?'

He hurried in the direction she'd pointed, directing his light onto the item. He turned back to face her, teeth white as pearls, eyes grim. 'It's the other unicorn slipper.'

Chapter 19
LOVE

Age 16

July 1997

Love watched Uncle Saviour's farmhouse from afar. The large building bathed in a powerful ray of sunlight that seemed to epitomise the radiance and purity of the man within. Scattered around the farmland roamed the community's fifty or so chickens and two enormous turkeys who pecked at the threadbare grass with savage urgency. Outside the big house, Gilly and Gabby, the two bearded goats who provided some of the community's milk, stood atop the wooden bench as if determined to prove they ruled the roost. Beyond the house in another pasture stood the community's cows and, beyond that, stretched the patchwork countryside, which looked indescribably pure beneath the clear blue sky.

While the sight of her home should have filled her with peace, Love's chest felt as though it had been injected with acid.

Since the first Blood Birthing Ceremony five years ago, Uncle Saviour had invited her to the big house every Sunday morning for tea and cake. On her sixteenth birthday, he'd started to confide in her about his plans for the community, all of which were spectacular and made complete sense.

Every day she glowed with pride at the fact that the purest man on earth had chosen her and her alone to dispatch his secrets to. Indeed, he invited her and only her. He never invited her mother or Peace or any of the other adults or children in the community. Uncle Saviour told her she was his Special One and that if she continued on her current path, she would reach the stage of Total Illumination even more quickly than he had. That was what she needed, what she craved. The thought of dying made her feel like screaming and ripping her own skin off her face. She'd do anything to gain eternal life. Anything at all.

But he hadn't invited her last week, or the week before, or today. He hadn't even looked at her for three whole weeks.

Her stomach felt like it was being squeezed by demons. Her heart burned. She frowned and rubbed her tongue over her front teeth, wondering if she'd done or said something wrong at their last meeting. He'd kissed her and she'd jerked away, surprised but not in a horrible way – more in shock. She hadn't been able to believe that her deepest, darkest desire was finally coming true. When she was around Uncle Saviour, her tummy twirled with butterflies. Sometimes she dreamed about him kissing her and imagined what it would feel like.

The kiss, though short, had been incredible. She'd felt like she was kissing salvation itself, that by touching Uncle Saviour's lips, she was gaining more purity, more strength, bringing herself one step closer to eternal life. But maybe her reaction had upset him. After the kiss he'd turned his back on her and said he was tired, that he needed to think, so she'd drifted back through the farm feeling confused yet excited.

Now, she wanted to make things right, but she didn't know how to.

With a sigh, Love trudged back to the caravan. She stopped outside at the sound of raised voices. Sensing trouble, she stood beneath the window and strained her ears.

'It's too dangerous. I can't.' Love recognised the woman's high-pitched voice instantly: it was Faith, the brown-haired woman who often had bruises on her face and wrists. She said it was because she had a rare skin condition that meant she bruised easily, but Mother and Peace thought that Fervour hit her. Love knew that her mother had tried to tell Uncle Saviour about her suspicions once. He'd told her that Fervour's and Faith's relationship was private and that outside interference was not to be tolerated within the community, that it was a sign of impurity. He'd also warned Mother to stop meddling in others' affairs and said that if Faith felt Fervour's behaviour was impure, she'd speak to him for guidance.

Faith had been birthed at the first Blood Birthing Ceremony along with her husband, Fervour, and her son, Zeal. She, her husband and her son bore the Birthing Cross on their chests, as did every member who had joined Eternal Life since that night. Love often felt jealous of those who had been given the chance to offer their blood to Uncle Saviour's lips, but she knew that her blood would be of no good to her uncle because they shared the same bloodline. She had given her blood once, when the community had presented Uncle Saviour with his sculpture, but that had been the only time. He didn't need her blood to build the strength he required to maintain his purity and thus help them reach the stage of Total Illumination; he needed the blood of others and, it was becoming increasingly clear to her through what he alluded to during their private meetings, he required the blood of those young enough to possess the purity of innocence. And he needed more than just kiss-blood every now and then; he yearned for a decent, constant supply of blood. Without it, his migraines returned and he grew weak, which threatened his chances of eternal life, and thus everyone else's. Only the totally pure could live for ever.

The problem was that the community was still too immature in its thinking. Too afraid to go beyond the conventional and take unorthodox measures to achieve its end goal.

Uncle Saviour knew they were not yet ready to give more of themselves. He feared they were too narrow-minded to understand that to attain what they all craved – a long, if not *eternal*, life – certain sacrifices must be made.

Love's heart hammered. People's simplicity made her mad. Uncle Saviour was patient, still hopeful that eventually people would embrace the truth, but she had her doubts.

She tuned in to the voices inside the caravan, tensing at her mother's words.

'You can. *We* can,' Mother said, 'you, me, Zeal, Peace and Love. We can do it together. Tonight.'

'But what if someone sees us. What if they tell?' Faith said.

'No one will see. We'll do it at midnight, when everyone's asleep. No one will stir, not after the ceremony and all that drink.'

'But where will we go?'

'It's OK. I've got a plan and I've already stolen the keys to the van.'

Love swallowed a gasp: her mother had stolen something. Stealing was an impure act. Why had she stolen the keys? What were they talking about?

'Are you sure no one's going to need it this afternoon? No one's going into town for anything?'

'I've checked the board. There's not another trip planned until Friday.'

'But what if Hope goes into labour, there's an emergency, and she has to be rushed to hospital?'

'She won't. She's not due yet and many births are late,' Mother said.

'But—'

'Look, Faith, do you want Zeal to grow up here?'

Faith didn't answer.

'Do you want him to turn into an abuser who thinks it's fine to beat his wife?'

'No.'

'Right. Then it's now or never.'

'Will he come after us?' Faith said.

There was a long silence.

'Charity, will he come after us?'

'Probably, but don't worry. I know how we can disappear.'

'Are you sure?'

'Yes. I want Love and Peace to grow up far away from here where they can make their own decisions and choose who they want to love. Eternal Life isn't what it used to be. Saviour's following a dangerous path. He's lost his way. He's only going to get worse; I know it. I'm surer now than I've ever been in my whole life. I've made up my mind. I'll never forgive myself if I keep the girls here. Any day now one of the men will decide they want Peace or Love and there will be nothing I can do to stop them. Nothing at all. If Saviour approves the marriage, it will go ahead, regardless of my opinion, regardless of the fact that they're barely out of childhood.'

Love almost snorted; what her mother was saying was ridiculous.

Charity sniffed. In a weepy voice, she said, 'And you must have heard the rumour? The one about a child?'

Faith didn't reply. Love's heart banged. What was Mother talking about? Surely Uncle Saviour hadn't . . .

Her mother carried on. 'Look, we need to leave now, before it's too late. Are you with me?'

'Please say yes, Faith. Please.' It was Peace's voice now.

Love jumped. Her skin began to crawl. Understanding dawned: Mother and Peace had been planning this for a long time. Planning it together, in secret, behind her back.

For a moment, she felt strange, as if she were standing outside her body watching herself. The sun was on someone else's head burning someone else's hair and skin. The hard ground was under someone else's feet, the smell of manure in someone else's nose. Salty tears touched someone else's lips. Someone else's fingers moved to someone else's pounding chest.

For the first time in her life, she didn't know what to do. With a guttural sob she launched herself away from the caravan as if she had been possessed.

Chapter 20

PEARLINE

Now

Early dawn light silvered the trees, turning Connor Rudge's body the colour of ash. She couldn't help picturing Isabelle Hart's small body left in a similar place, abandoned to the vermin that roamed the woods, ants crawling across her eyes. If she knew what the missing children looked like, she'd be imagining them here too, lifeless and blood-drenched like the corpse in front of her.

The second crime scene team was setting up camp. Lamps were positioned around the body, photographic equipment assembled. Light glared through the shadows, and people spoke in muted voices. A sketch artist started drawing; another taking notes for their first walk-through.

Pearline watched through a haze of fear, unable to pull focus from the tightening sensation pressing down on her chest. How the hell were they going to find these kids? They didn't even know who these two children were. Finding the child's slippers felt like a tiny piece of luck, as it indicated that the girl had been in this very spot of the woods, but that still didn't help them identify the lost girl or where the hell she'd gone.

Christ almighty. She could feel herself teetering. Her heart hammered, erratic and frantic. Her chest constricted. Pearline turned from the body and walked away. Hoping she was out of sight, she sat down heavily behind an oak and hung her head between her knees. She just needed a minute. One minute. That was all, and then she'd be able to focus again.

Crunching leaves made her glance up. Dibbs crouched beside her. He hesitated then placed a smooth hand on her forearm. She sucked in air, blinked back tears, and stared at her shoes. Embarrassment and shame pinched.

'I'm OK. I just need a minute.'

'Look at me,' Dibbs said.

She shook her head.

'Please.'

Pearline looked up.

'You can do this, Pearl. You're the best person for the job. You're quick, smart and annoyingly good. Don't doubt yourself for one second. You hear me?'

She swallowed. She opened her mouth to argue, and he said, 'No ifs or buts. You're a bloody machine. If I had a child missing, there's no one else I'd want trying to find them.'

She forced herself to meet his gaze.

He stood up and extended his hand. Pearline took it and he pulled her up and gave her a quick hug. In her ear, he whispered, 'We got this.'

She pulled away and gave him a tight smile. 'Thanks.'

He nodded and returned to the scene. Watching him go, she inhaled a long, deep breath. After releasing it, she followed him back to the body with his words on repeat in her mind. She hoped Dibbs was right. If he believed in her, she ought to as well. Still, her stomach churned and her father's viciousness flashed in her mind like hazard lights.

Focus. Do your job. Be the machine you know you can be.

The photographer snapped glaring light into the trees. Pearline's eyes locked on Dibbs' and, to her relief, her investigative brain kicked back into gear.

'Are you thinking Gibson killed Rudge, then ran off with the kids?' Dibbs said.

'I don't know. It just feels . . .'

'Too easy?'

'Maybe. Nobody mentioned anything about Rudge or Gibson carrying the kind of weapon that could do damage like that.' She gestured to Rudge's cracked forehead. 'That's not been caused by fists or feet. Then again, one of them could have had a hidden knife. But what kind of blade could deliver damage like that? And why would Gibson kill his buddy? Deal gone wrong? Argument about the kids? Maybe Rudge wanted to let them go, Gibson didn't?'

Dibbs scratched his jaw, as perplexed as she was.

Pearline approached Liz Hitchcock, the second Crime Scene Manager. She shook Liz's hand, and jerked her head at the body. *Christ. What a mess.* 'What could have done that to his skull?'

Liz knelt down and peered closely at Rudge's head. She inspected the bloody wound for a long time before looking up at Pearline and shrugging. 'Hard to say at this stage. There's too much blood. But I'd hazard a guess at some sort of sharp blade. Certainly nothing blunt. You'll have to wait for the post-mortem.'

Pearline scratched the back of her neck. Her hand came away wet with sweat. She looked at Dibbs. 'Where would Gibson take the children? Where would he hide the bodies? What do we know about any places this man frequents? Any other relatives in the area? Property, vehicles under his name?'

'Shouldn't take long to find out given he's been arrested before.'

'Good. Get the team on it. Gibson's our top priority.'

Dibbs nodded and left the scene. His long legs carried him away quickly and soon he was lost in the trees. Uniforms were still searching, but had yet to find anything. Soon the woods would be fully searched and then she would know for sure that the children had left these trees – of their own accord or by force, dead or alive, it was impossible to say. So far, no other blood traces had been found, but the dark inhibited the search. Now that light was dawning, at least blood trails or smears would be easier to see. And footprints, though with the ground so dry they'd be harder to track.

Her phone rang. 'Ottoline.'

'There's been a call from a John Woods of 6 Cherry Tree Close, Grimstone. Says his children, Hannah and Gregory, are missing.'

She couldn't speak for a second. She ended the call quickly, then rang DS Fielding and told her and DC Hill to go directly to 6 Cherry Tree Close to interview Mr Woods. When she could, she defaulted to colleagues she trusted most for enquiries like this one, and Fielding and Hill were two of her best detectives. Fielding was also a family liaison co-ordinator and Hill a family liaison officer, so she couldn't have chosen anyone better.

Before she hung up, aware she was in danger of patronising the experienced officer but unable to stop herself, Pearline told Fielding not to mention that the children had been chased into the woods. The parents didn't need to know that detail yet. It would only serve to terrify them all the more.

Chapter 21
LILY

Now

This was all her fault. She should have checked the front door or at least gone into the children's bedrooms and checked on them. What had held her back? Three steps and she'd have been in Hannah's bedroom, her hand on her little girl's cheek feeling her baby-soft skin. Another five steps and she'd have been in Greg's bedroom, making sure he was there and safely tucked up in bed. But she hadn't done that. She'd not bothered. She'd told herself they were fine to save herself the minuscule effort of going into their rooms. She was a lazy, selfish—

'I'm getting a cup of coffee. Want another one?' John murmured, turning to leave the room.

Something about the way John said those words made her snap up her head and stare at his retreating back. She began to wonder what he was thinking. What he knew. What, perhaps, he was hiding?

No. That was ridiculous. Downright crazy.

She placed her cup on the coffee table, unable to believe the darkness opening up in her imagination. John might have been acting oddly, but there was no way he'd ever do anything to the children. Even if he was planning to run away with Juliet Pickering and take Hannah and Greg with him, he wouldn't do something as horrible as this. He didn't hate her. He might not love her any more, but he didn't want to destroy her.

Dizziness swirled behind her eyes. She tried to think of anyone who did hate her. If there could be anyone who held a grudge against her, and who might be insane enough to do something like this. Like their neighbour, Mr Saxon. They'd lived in the same close for six years and they weren't friends. Not even close. They weren't exactly enemies, but she knew he hated having them as neighbours. Several times he'd complained about the noise. Once he'd left a rude note on their door complaining about the number of parcels they had delivered to their house and how disturbing he found it. On another occasion, Greg had accidentally kicked his football into the man's back garden. Instead of giving it back, he'd ripped a hole through it and placed it on top of their wheelie bin.

Lily twisted around on the settee and whipped open the curtain. There, watching the house from his bedroom window, was Mr Saxon.

'John – wait,' she called.

He strode back into the room. 'Yeah?'

'Look. Mr Saxon. He's watching the house. I really think he might have something to do with this.'

John looked out of the window. 'No, he's not. No one's there.'

Sure enough, the old man had gone and his bedroom was dark.

She frowned. 'He was there. Watching us. When I spoke to him, he was acting weird. D'you think I should tell the police?'

'I don't think it's a good idea to go pointing the finger

at our neighbours just because you think they're weird,' John said.

'But I've got this feeling about him.'

'Lil, he's always given you the creeps and he's a grumpy neighbour, but it's probably not more than that.'

'But what if it is? What if you're wrong?'

John sighed and rubbed the back of his head. 'Look, if you feel the need to mention Mr Saxon to the police, do, but I very much doubt he's done anything wrong. Did you know he's got lung cancer? I bumped into him the other day and he told me. I feel sorry for the man. He's clearly on his last legs and I don't think he has any family left. I highly doubt he snuck in here in the middle of the night and managed to carry Hannah and Greg from the house without either of us hearing something and waking up. Do you?'

She opened her mouth to answer, knowing he was making more sense than she was, but wanting to argue, prove her point, just in case, but there was a sharp knock on the door. John left the room to answer it.

She turned around and checked the window again. Mr Saxon's light was off. He'd gone. Like always, John was probably right.

A man and woman followed John into the lounge and introduced themselves. DC Hill was in his late twenties. Mini craters pocked his cheeks and he clearly needed more sleep. As if to compound the look, he yawned long and wide then rubbed sleep out of his eye. Towering beside him was an elegant, older woman with soft eyes.

Detective Sergeant Fielding smiled gently. 'It might be a good idea to sit down for a moment.' She had a motherly voice that seemed to suggest everything was going to be OK, but panic bit at Lily's throat like raw chilli. She thought about bringing up Mr Saxon, but held her tongue.

John sat beside her and rested a hot hand on her knee. The pressure irritated and comforted at the same time. She caught his eye, saw her fear and confusion mirrored there. In that moment, strange though it was, she felt closer to him than she had in months.

'I know this is an extremely difficult time for you both. I want to assure you that we are doing everything we can to find Hannah and Gregory. The quicker we can work through these questions, the better. Some questions might seem unnecessary, but there are reasons I need to ask them. Let's begin with your children's full names, ages, hair and eye colour, and any identifying features,' Fielding said.

Lily spoke quickly. 'Hannah Elouise Woods and Gregory Finn Woods. Greg's full name is Gregory, but everyone calls him Greg, even his teachers. He's seven, small for his age, brown hair – the same as Hannah's, eyes are lighter, more hazel. Hannah's ten and—'

'What sorts of identifying features do you mean?' John interrupted. She shot him a look.

'Moles, scars, that sort of thing,' Fielding said, tapping away at her tablet.

DC Hill prowled around the room like a tiger, picking up pictures of the kids, having a stare, and replacing them at the wrong angles.

Lily cleared her throat. The situation felt surreal, like a terrifying dream with her sitting in the corner watching everything progress and wishing she could make it stop. 'Um, Hannah's got a kidney-shaped birthmark on her right hip. I can't think of anything for Greg.'

'Hannah's hair's pretty wild,' John added.

'OK, that's good. Thank you. Now, let's move on to time-line. When did you realise your children weren't in their bedrooms?'

Lily looked at John. Guilt flushed her neck. Would better

parents have realised sooner? When she'd heard the door slam, she hadn't investigated it properly. She'd been lazy. Careless. If she'd checked that the door was locked, would Hannah and Greg still be missing?

John scraped a hand through his hair. 'Only about half an hour ago. I was working in the garage because I couldn't sleep. I came up and thought I'd pop my head in, have a look at the kids. They're so cute when they're sleeping.'

'I heard the door slam at around 2 a.m.,' Lily said, rushing out the words, 'I went downstairs to check. I was worried we were being burgled or something—'

'Why didn't you wake me?' John said.

'I took my tennis racket. I know how much you need your sleep.' She regretted the hardness in her tone, especially when Hill and Fielding exchanged glances. What were they thinking? That John and Lily were unstable parents? Too caught up in their marital problems to notice when their kids went missing?

John patted her leg, as if to tell her it was fine. She wanted to scream at him to take his hand off. She'd done nothing wrong by going to check herself. She only wished she'd checked the door . . .

'Were the doors locked?' Fielding said, right on cue.

'I didn't check the front or the back door,' Lily said, holding her hand to her throat. 'Oh God, why didn't I check?'

John patted again. She stopped herself from whacking his hand away, just.

Fielding added notes to her tablet. 'Did anything look amiss? Is anything missing from the children's bedrooms or the rest of the house?'

Lily looked at John. They hadn't checked. *Shit*.

'Shall we take a look?' Fielding said, reading the situation with remarkable speed

'When I went downstairs, I noticed that the kitchen stool

119

had been moved to the counter, but that was it.' She looked at John. 'Did *you* move it?'

He shook his head and stood. 'I'll check Greg's room. You check Hannah's.'

'That would be good,' Fielding said. She looked at her partner. 'Can you go with them? I need a minute.'

Fielding pulled out her phone and Lily hesitated, wanting to know what she was going to say, but John tugged her arm and she hurried after him out of the room up to Hannah's bedroom.

Standing in the doorway, Lily assessed the room from a distance, heart pounding. There was no sign of a struggle. The room was neat as always. One of John's nicknames for Hannah was Little Miss Tidy.

She stared at the bed. There was no way Hannah and Greg would run away. They were happy children, weren't they? Hannah had lots of friends. Greg had Aurora and his imaginary fairy friends. She took them to clubs outside of school. Hannah adored ballet, though not as much as art. Greg sort of liked his swimming. Yes, Miss Mills had told her about the incident at school, but that was a one-off. If that sort of thing had been happening a lot, she'd have heard about it by now. Greg was usually good at telling her things. Not so much with Hannah lately. Her little girl seemed less talkative. Had she missed something? Come to think of it, Hannah wasn't that smiley any more, but surely that was just because she was growing up. Children grew up so quickly these days. Too quickly.

She'd always made sure that if they used the internet, they were sitting right next to her, just in case they entered some hellish chat site and got bullied – or worse. Hannah desperately wanted a phone, but Lily had said she couldn't have one until her eleventh birthday. If that made her stricter than other parents, she didn't care. Phones were terribly antisocial.

And Hannah was never out of her sight long enough to need a phone.

Oh God. She needed to focus. Concentrate. Be quicker. But her brain was blitzed salami.

'Mrs Woods? Are you OK?' DC Hill's face swam in front of her eyes.

She swiped tears from her cheeks, nodded.

'Try to search logically,' he said. 'I'd suggest starting with the back of the door then moving to the wardrobe then the chest of drawers.'

She nodded again and checked Hannah's pink bunny hook. Her dressing gown was still there. Check. She hurried to the wardrobe.

'Don't rush. Take your time,' Hill said, looking around the room. 'Oh – what was Hannah wearing when she went to bed?'

'Nothing,' Lily said, clutching her throat, 'she sleeps naked when it's this hot. Greg does too.'

'OK. What was she wearing *before* she went to bed?'

Lily glanced at the end of Hannah's bed, at the white wooden frame where Lily always laid her pyjamas, ready to put on in the morning. They weren't there. They weren't on the carpet at the end of the bed either. What had she been wearing? Think, think. She pictured Hannah curled up on the sofa after dinner watching TV. It was a light bulb moment.

'Her pyjamas. Pale pink leggings, a white T-shirt with a pink heart on the front, and her unicorn slippers. She always drapes her pyjamas over the end of the bed and leaves her slippers here,' she pointed to the near side of Hannah's bed, 'but they're gone.'

'Unicorn slippers?' Fielding said, making her and Hill jump.

'Yes. Why?' Lily said.

John appeared at Fielding's side. 'Greg's frog onesie. I think it's gone.'

121

'What?' Lily pushed past John and dashed into Greg's room. She'd hung it up for him on the back of his bedroom door before reading his bedtime story. She knew she had. She might have been tipsy, but she remembered doing it as clearly as if she'd done it two minutes ago. But it wasn't there.

Not willing to trust that John was right, she yanked open the wardrobe doors and rummaged through Greg's clothes.

John's hand was on her shoulder. 'It's not there. I've looked.'

'Yes, but—'

Fielding stepped into the room and held up her tablet for them to see. 'Does this look familiar?'

Lily stepped closer and stared at the two photographs. One showed Hannah's unicorn slipper on the pavement next to a blue car. The other showed a slipper on what appeared to be a ground of earth and leaves.

'Yes,' Lily said, 'they're Hannah's.'

Fielding withdrew the tablet. 'What I need to tell you now will be hard to hear. Earlier this morning, at about two o' clock, two children were reported to have been seen in Dogwood Street. According to a witness the children went into Grimstone Woods.'

John gasped. Lily grabbed his arm. 'Are they hurt? Where are they now?'

'I'm afraid right now we don't have answers to those questions. Officers are searching the woods and surrounding area as we speak. We're doing everything we can to find them. I've sent photographs of Hannah and Gregory to everyone involved, along with their physical descriptions. So are we to assume that Gregory is wearing a—'

'Frog onesie, yes,' John said, sitting on Greg's bed.

'And Hannah?'

Lily stared. Her head was being crushed. Air was being sucked from her lungs.

Hill spoke. 'Pale pink leggings and a white T-shirt with a pink heart.'

'What about her feet? Her poor feet,' Lily said.

Fielding said something she didn't hear, then turned and left the room.

DC Hill gently grasped Lily's elbow and guided her to Greg's bed. Barely aware of anything, Lily perched on her son's mattress and stared sightlessly at the golden-haired fairy with shimmery silver wings she'd stuck on his wall last summer.

John gasped. She spun around, heart pounding, certain for one terrifying second he'd found Greg lying dead under the bed, lips blue from an asthma attack they'd never heard him have.

'What is it? John? John!'

John held a slip of paper in his hand. His face was colourless. His fingers shook. 'It's a letter. To Greg. Telling him to go to someone's house.'

'What?' She made to rip it out of his hand, but DC Hill held up a gloved palm. 'Don't touch it. Give it to me.'

John handed the paper to the detective and met her eye. She swallowed. 'Who does it say it's from?'

Her husband shook his head. 'There's no name. It just says *from your secret friend.*'

Chapter 22

LOVE

Age 16

July 1997

Love sat in the middle of the cow field and stared unseeingly at her mother's caravan. Above her, the sun was a yellow conker in the flawless sky, but she was unaware of the beauty that lay above and beyond. She was in her head, her thoughts wild and frantic, buzzing manically like bees in a jar. Once, when she was a little girl, she'd caught a bee and trapped it in one of the empty glass jars her mother and the other women used for their home-made blackberry jam. For a while, she'd watched it whizz around, bashing itself into its little glass cage again and again and again, amazed by its pathetic determination, its self-sacrifice. She'd always thought it strange how a bee would kill itself to protect its queen. How it lost all ability to prioritise self-preservation when faced with a threat. How it stung a person, then died. To live then die. Just like that. The act itself was pure, but stupid.

Love had known, even then, that she would never do anything as foolish and illogical as that, and she'd done what any clever child would do, but most would never dream of doing: she'd released the bee from its pointless existence. It was going to kill itself sooner or later anyway. What she'd done was merciful. She'd simply speeded up the process.

What was the point in being alive just to die? Life was for living. For eternity, otherwise being born was pointless. A purposeless, stupid, insane thing that made no sense.

Love was all about sense. It made sense to do anything you could to live for ever. Becoming pure in order to achieve eternal life was right. Logical. There was no point in death. Dying was for the weak and the cowardly. Sometimes sacrifices had to be made to get what you wanted, but you got others to make them for you. She would never be a worker bee. She was born to be a queen. The queen.

Love pictured her mother's face. She rested her palm on her chest and focused on her body. She could feel a pulsing sensation in her hand, but couldn't tell if the beat was coming from there or her heart. All Love knew was that her heart was beating slowly. Very slowly. She felt calm because she knew what she had to do.

Love rose to her feet and walked across the field. Trailing her fingertips over the cows' sweaty backs she weaved between their thick bodies, her body lithe and supple as a nymph's, her feet light as feathers on the dry grass. A smile teased her rosebud lips and sunlight sparkled along her raven hair transforming it into liquid silk. She felt a kind of peace she'd never known; a tranquillity that freed her mind and body of any earthly worries, for she knew now beyond a shadow of a doubt that Total Illumination was within her grasp. And her grasp was in her control and hers alone.

Excited as a new-born foal, Love gambolled across the farmyard and skipped up to Uncle Saviour's house. For a few seconds, she stood on the porch and admired the inscriptions of the names that had been carefully penned into the life-sized sculpture of her uncle. Hope, who had a talent for French script, acted as scribe, adding new pure names every time a member joined the community. Thirty-three names now graced the sculpture.

Saviour
Charity Love Peace
Nobility Kindness Virtue Grace
Courage Hope Verity Devotion Joy
Honour Beauty Mirth Harmony Truth Belief
Valour Promise Humility Passion
Fervour Faith Zeal
Diligence Duty
Freedom Liberty Choice
Loyalty Bliss

Love stared at her name, which stood between her mother's and Peace's on sculpture Saviour's naked chest. She looked at her mother's name and then her sister's. She didn't feel any change of heart, only a burning resolve to do the right thing. She traced her name with her index finger, imagining that the blood with which her name had been scribed was seeping through her skin into her veins. Visualising the blood inside her made her belly tingle low down. With a spring in her step, she opened the door and entered the farmhouse.

She knew that she had not been invited but at that precise moment, she didn't care. She felt freer than ever, buoyed by a blissful certainty and devotion that propelled her up the creaking wooden staircase along the floorboards towards Uncle Saviour's study, which was where he spent a lot of his time when he wasn't giving speeches or socialising with the community.

On hearing a noise, Love stopped outside Saviour's

bedroom. The door stood ajar. She could hear a strange sucking sound coming from inside the room.

Without thinking, she pushed the door and stepped inside. Her mouth dropped open and Love stared at the scene in front of her, too shocked to move.

Chapter 23

LILY

Now

Lily perched on the sofa. Despite the unbearable heat, she felt cold all the way through. Cold and hollow. John paced in front of her, his face hard as granite. They hadn't said a word to each other since Fielding had told them about the discovery of Hannah's slippers. The fact put paid to Lily's suspicions about Mr Saxon, but made her throb with fear. According to Fielding, Hannah and Greg had been seen on Dogwood Street, which she knew was a rough part of town. For some reason, they had entered Grimstone Woods. Dogwood Street wasn't far from here at all, less than ten minutes' walk. The woods sat right behind the street. A forest school sat at the heart of those woods. Both Hannah and Greg had visited it on school trips. She remembered having to sign the permission slips, and Greg's excitement at the thought of seeing a tree fairy.

Lily snatched up an invisible key and tried to lock the door to a host of terrifying scenarios. It was too early to think the worst and yet she couldn't quite turn that key. Image after image pushed through the gap and flooded her mind. Greg curled up in the foetal position as an asthma attack stole air from his little lungs; Hannah trying to struggle away from a hooded figure, unable to break free, crying, begging for him to let her go.

If only Mum were here. She'd know what to do.

Mum's dead. You've already lost her. You're going to lose Hannah and Greg too.

For a few seconds, she couldn't breathe. If they were OK, they'd have turned up by now. Something awful must have happened.

Having now searched Hannah and Greg's rooms and the house from top to toe, they knew Greg's ladybird school bag was missing too. Add to that the strange letter John had found under Greg's pillow and that the door had been left unlocked, the key still dangling from its hook, and it was only possible to draw one conclusion: her children had left the house of their own accord. They had not been kidnapped in the night but they – or at least Greg – had been lured away by a temptation too wonderful to resist, possibly by the words of his best friend, Aurora. There was no one else she could think of who would have written a letter like that, so she had told DS Fielding that and the officer had sent someone over to check Aurora White's house, but Greg and Hannah had not been there.

Lily bent over the letter, which Fielding had bagged in clear plastic. The message was written on a cream sheet of A5 paper bordered with little daisies. The words were in pencil in a surprisingly neat hand. Despite the paper not being lined, the writing ran in a straight, controlled line across the page. Greg's reading was above average for his age, but his handwriting was all over the place. These letters were nicely rounded and level. Not joined though. It would be remarkable for a seven-year-old to be able to join their letters in such a neat style. Having taught four to eleven-year-olds for over a decade, she was one to know. What Lily didn't know was what Aurora's handwriting looked like, but the girl was very smart. Gifted and Talented. Brightness didn't always correspond with fine motor skills and neatness, but very often, especially with girls, it did. The police might have already questioned Aurora about the letter, but what if she'd been lying? What if Aurora knew more than she was letting on?

Shivers plucked at Lily's ribs. Her heartbeat quickened as she reread the letter and imagined Greg doing the very same thing.

Dear Greg,
I want you to come tonight, but you will only be able to see her at two o'clock in the morning. Make sure your mum and dad are asleep then leave your house. Don't tell anyone. You know where I will be. I can't wait for you to meet my fairy! You are going to love her so much. Throw this letter away!
Your Secret Friend x

If that was why her children had left the house at two in the morning, she was shocked at Hannah. She wouldn't have put such silliness past Greg, who had been obsessed with fairies since the age of five and still believed in Santa, but Hannah? Hannah was sensible. At least, she used to think she was. Why her little girl would do such a reckless, dangerous thing was beyond her.

The knowledge brought a sour taste to her tongue and made Lily think she didn't know her daughter at all – which, unarguably, was her own fault. Work was always crazy; teaching full time and paying enough attention to two children was hard. Sometimes, she didn't know how people made it look so easy. Some mums seemed to be able to fit in reading books and keeping fit too. She hadn't the foggiest how they found the time or energy to do that. She hadn't been to aerobics for a good eight months. Lately, life was manic, but lots of people found the drive, which meant she was lacking. She'd always feared she wouldn't be a good mum even before Hannah was born, and severe anxiety sunk in its heinous teeth. Exercise was meant to help with anxiety of course, but she just couldn't find the motivation to squeeze that in on top of everything else. And her worries about the widening fracture between her and John took her focus off the kids too. But that was no excuse. Something must be wrong with Hannah to do such a silly, dangerous thing and leave the house in the early hours of the morning. She thought she'd taught Hannah how to stay safe. Without scaring the life out of her, she'd tried in lots of little ways to communicate the possible dangers she could face. Had Hannah done this to get attention? Was something going on at school that Hannah hadn't told her about because she was too busy marking books or arguing with John? And Greg, with this letter hidden under his pillow. Was he hiding things from her because he didn't think she'd care?

Her brain ached. Every muscle in her shoulders folded into a knot. She licked her lips. Even her tongue seemed to be trembling. The letter was so odd, and hateful. She wanted to rip it apart and watch it burn, but it was evidence now. Hannah and Greg's life might depend on it.

'You still think Aurora wrote it?' John said.

She looked up. Focused on his ashen face. 'What?'

'The letter. Think it was Aurora?'

'Yes. It must be. She lives a couple of streets past Dogwood. Greg's walked there before. He knows the way. They must have decided to take a shortcut through the woods.'

John shook his head. 'The question is, if they were going

to Aurora's house, why aren't they there? They should have got there ages ago.'

Fear speared her stomach.

He sat down on the other sofa and put his head in his hands. 'I can't stop thinking the worst.'

Lily didn't reply. She hadn't the energy to comfort him. Her thoughts kept veering down a deadly path where no hope remained and she might as well be dead. Life without Hannah and Greg was no life at all.

She looked away from him. Photographs of her babies covered every surface of the lounge. Pictures of them as newborns, toddlers, on the beach on holiday, smiling, laughing, holding hands, running and playing together. Hannah's most recent school photograph was in her hands and she didn't know how it had got there, didn't remember moving or picking it up. The glass was smudged. A tear rolled off her chin and splashed onto Hannah's heart-shaped face. Hastily, she wiped it away with her finger, but the glass remained smudged. She turned it upside down and rubbed it dry on her jeans, checked it. Now it was better. She could see Hannah's face again. See her smile, her slightly embarrassed expression. She relived the conversation they'd had about it. Hannah didn't like the picture, and Greg had teased her about it, and she'd jabbed him in the ribs and they'd wrestled on the ground for a while until Greg accidentally poked her in the eye and she started crying. Lily held the photo to her chest, crushed it against her bones. Hideous thoughts surfaced: was Hannah crying now? Was she scared? Hurt? The idea was unbearable. Too much.

Fielding entered the room and shook her head. 'I'm afraid there've been no sightings of Hannah or Greg. Officers are speaking to the children in Greg's class, trying to ascertain whether one of them could have written the note. I've sent

132

an image of it to the team and once I've finished up here, I'll take it for DNA testing.'

John grabbed her hand. She let him crush it in his sweaty fingers. The world seemed to tilt.

'What now?' she said, telling herself to focus. *Do something. Be helpful.*

'We'll keep searching, extend the search area. Right now, we need to turn our attention back to the letter, as it seems clear that Aurora White didn't write it,' Fielding said.

John stepped forward and bent over the note. But Lily held back. Her gut told her the police were wrong. There was no one else who would write like that to Greg.

'Aurora. It has to be,' Lily insisted. 'She's very bright. She and Greg always play imaginary games about fairies. She even has a fairy house in her bedroom, and figurines. Greg told me about them.'

Fielding held Lily's eye for a moment before gently saying, 'We've already spoken to Aurora. She says she didn't write it. Right now, I'd like you both to have a think about any others who might have written this letter to Greg.'

Lily wanted to scream at Fielding and Hill to go to Aurora's house now and speak to her again. 'Greg doesn't have any other friends,' she said, 'it has to be Aurora who gave it to him. She's bright enough to write something like that too.'

John squeezed her hand and gave her 'calm down' eyes. She tore her palm out of his grasp and stood up.

Fielding took a step towards her and said, 'It's important that we consider other possibilities. Please have a think about anyone Greg has contact with, in or out of school, who may have written this letter, including adults. There's always a chance it was sent by someone older. The writing looks rather controlled to me, though of course, I'm not an expert.'

The idea that an adult had written the letter seemed absurd.

Why on earth would an adult tell a child to leave their house at two in the morning to go and see a fairy? It didn't make the slightest bit of sense. Lily fought the urge to roll her eyes, and folded her arms. John was looking at her, silently begging her to calm down, but she ignored him and spoke quickly. 'Like I said, Greg doesn't have any other friends really. None that he talks about anyway.'

Fielding looked at John, who nodded. 'Even at swimming, he doesn't talk to the other kids. He's a bit . . . eccentric.'

'How so?' Fielding said.

John shrugged. 'I don't know. I mean, I guess it's just that he gets obsessive about things. Like the whole fairy thing.'

'That's why it has to be Aurora,' Lily said, 'she's obsessed with them too.'

Fielding nodded and tapped notes into her tablet. She looked up. 'Any problems at school?'

John shook his head, but Lily said, 'Just one thing. The teaching assistant told me he ate his lunch in the bathroom because a couple of boys in his class were being unpleasant.'

'What's her name?'

'Miss Mills.'

'And when did this incident occur?'

'I think she said it happened on Tuesday.'

'Do you know these boys' names by any chance?'

Lily shook her head. John was looking at her. She caught his eye. He looked mutinous, furious she hadn't told him what the TA had said about Greg.

Fielding smiled tightly and picked up the letter. She glanced at John then touched Lily's shoulder lightly. 'That's enough questions for now. We'll head back to the station and contact you the second anything comes up. Hold tight and keep thinking. If anything comes to mind, tell us. Here's my direct number.' She handed Lily a card.

Lily nodded, feeling more helpless than she'd ever felt in her whole life.

John saw the officers to the door then turned to her.

Lily dragged her hands through her hair, down her face, pulling down her eyelids so hard they hurt. She was beginning to think that maybe she needed to do something. Maybe . . .

'Why didn't you tell me about what the TA said about Greg?' he said.

Lily shrugged. 'Does it really matter now, John?'

He stared at her for a while then turned and took himself off into the kitchen, away from her.

Lily sat on the sofa and put her face in her hands. She was so confused, so frightened. What if Aurora had lied to the police? What if the police had missed something?

She wanted to scream. Her children's lives depended on the actions of strangers, and there was absolutely nothing she could do about it. Or was there?

Chapter 24

PEARLINE

Now

Disease infused the air, seeping into her skin the moment she stepped into the reception area of Midsomer Langton Community Hospital.

Pearline tried to focus on the here and now, rather than allowing the past to creep up as it often did in places like this. Hospital corridors made her think of paths to death. Of Purgatory and Hell and the reprimands her father used to shout when she failed, yet again, to live up to expectations.

Pearline flinched as a memory lashed up from her subconscious like the whip of her father's belt.

Jesus, you need to see someone.

She counted down, focused.

There was a team of thirty detectives working on the investigation into the children's disappearance. Right now, her team was in full swing doing house-to-house enquiries and talking to Greg's classmates and teachers. Fielding had brought in a letter written to Gregory Woods instructing him to leave his home at two in the morning, which provided a strong line of enquiry she'd asked Dibbs to run. She was putting strategies in place as quickly as possible, but it still might not be enough.

With sick in her throat, Pearline rushed to the morgue.

Even as adrenaline fired her up, dread pulsed like an abscess, dragging her down. Five minutes ago, Crystal Rudge had identified her husband's body. At first, she'd seemed unmoved by the discovery. A few minutes later, she'd collapsed. Too distraught to make it to the women's bathroom, Crystal had vomited down herself, and needed assistance from a nurse to make it to the sink before she did so again.

Death, like people, was never black and white, good or bad; it was coloured by ambiguity and perspective, subjective to its core, and horribly conclusive. The dead could not speak. Someone might have rid the world of Connor Rudge, but that someone was a murderer. The prime suspect now was Gibson. Everything was being done to track him down. His rap sheet listed arrests for shoplifting and possession of cannabis. Nothing violent or paedophilic. Yet Gibson had chased the children into the woods with his so-called friend, who was now dead, and two small children were missing. It made logical sense that he was their man. But something niggled, something she couldn't put her finger on.

Pearline took a step towards the morgue table. The lights in the room were too bright, the smell too medicinal. She wasn't usually squeamish, but the savage crack splitting open Rudge's forehead was hideous, made worse in the glare of artificial lighting. Holding her breath, she swallowed a wave of nausea and leaned in to inspect the body, which had been stripped, the wounds cleaned to allow for closer scrutiny.

The blood-splattered clothing had already been sent to the lab for testing, though she suspected they wouldn't find any blood belonging to the attacker on Rudge's clothes. By the look of him, Connor Rudge had been unable to put up any effective defence against his killer, which suggested he'd been taken by complete surprise. Perhaps Gibson had attacked without warning? Dealt a swift, strong blow, then taken Hannah and Gregory with him by force.

Janet Weatherby nudged a pair of steel-grey glasses up her nose. She was a slim woman in her mid-fifties whom Pearline had met before, and held in high regard. An expert in her field, she emanated a quiet confidence that briefly shuttered the blinds on Pearline's mounting panic.

'Unlike the first victim, who was beaten with fists, this victim was clearly attacked with a weapon. See the damage here,' Janet pointed a gloved finger at the wound on Rudge's head, 'this was caused by the blow of a metal blade.'

'Can you hazard a guess at the type of blade?'

'Oh yes. See the length of this cut?' She trailed her finger down from the centre of the scalp to the eyebrow area. 'This, coupled with the depth of the incision, indicates that the injury was created by a long, curved blade.'

'Curved?'

'Yes. And the curvature suggests a blade at least twenty inches in length, though it's hard to be precise. The striking angle also indicates that the attacker was two to four inches taller than their victim – or,' she smiled lightly, 'they were wearing heels.'

'Twenty inches? What sort of weapon has a blade that long?'

'Well, given that I can estimate it to be half an inch wide at its broadest section, my best educated guess would be a scythe.' Janet Weatherby gestured for Pearline to join her at her desk. She bent over her laptop and enlarged a window to reveal an image of a farmer's scythe. 'Long-handled, I believe. The shaft – or snaithe to use the technical term – is most likely about sixty to seventy inches long.'

'Christ,' Pearline said. She stared at the image for a long time. Her heart beat harder.

'Any defensive injuries?' Pearline said, looking at Rudge's hands.

'See the bruising on the knuckles? My best guess is that those minor injuries were caused by hitting his victim. However,' she turned Rudge's right hand over so that it was palm-up, 'see that bruise running down the length of the palm?'

'Defensive? The scythe's handle making contact?'

Janet smiled. 'Precisely right. This man attempted to shield himself from the blow by raising his hand, but the scythe struck nevertheless.'

'Just once?'

'Oh yes. My feeling is that the attacker managed to land a blow to this man's head regardless of his attempt to defend himself.'

'That's a lot of rage,' Pearline said.

'Yes, and, I would think, great determination to kill.'

'So, what's your best guess at the killer's height?'

'Judging by the angle of impact, taller than five foot nine. The victim here stands at five foot eight, so I'd say five ten to six foot. And strong. The killer managed to crack the frontal bone. They only struck once, and that was enough. It was a killing blow.'

Pearline nodded. Inside, she winced. According to police records, Mike Gibson was only five foot seven inches tall. If Janet was right, Gibson might not be the killer after all.

Chapter 25

LOVE

Age 16

July 1997

Uncle Saviour's bedroom was a vista of white: white walls, white bedding, white carpet, white desk, white chair, and white wardrobe. A canvas of purity. The smell of something sweet and chemical tinted the air. Hot light streamed in through the windows warming the room and spotlighting the little girl on Uncle Saviour's double bed.

Beneath the mask, the child's eyes were closed, so Love could not see their colour, only a pair of pale, twitching lids. Her flat chest rose and fell steadily. This made Love think she was asleep, which was just as well. The girl looked peaceful, like she felt no pain. That was important. It wouldn't be right for her to feel any pain. She had not chosen to give her blood to Uncle Saviour. She had been chosen by him because she was pure.

'You did it,' Love said, trying to keep her tone matter-of-fact.

'Yes. I'm sorry I didn't tell you. I wasn't sure you were ready,' he said, dusting himself down; a pointless act given that he only wore boxer shorts.

Love's tongue tasted bitter. She bit back what she wanted to say. In spite of herself, her tummy fluttered. She pulled her gaze up to his.

'How old is she?' she said.

'Seven. Innocence in its prime, a moment away from turning. Purity personified.'

She nodded. Her heart pounded. She had to control her feelings. He could not know the way her stomach clenched or her inner voice raged.

'How long has she been here?' she said.

'Nearly three weeks.'

'Did you get her yourself?'

'No. I had Nobility and Fervour do it.'

'They knew before me?' She hated the hurt in her voice.

He smiled sadly. 'Yes. I needed their help. I wanted to tell you, but as I said—'

'You don't trust me.'

'It's not that, my Special One. I just, well, when you reacted the way you did to our kiss, it made me wonder if you were ready for the next stage.'

'I was surprised, that's all. I wanted to explain, but you didn't give me a chance.'

He walked across to the wardrobe and pulled on a pair of denim cut-offs and a white shirt. Not bothering to do up the buttons, he approached her slowly. He stopped a yard away. Blood smeared his lips. Love glanced down at the girl's thin white leg and the inch-long cut that had been sliced into her inner thigh. A thin line of blood trailed down onto the white towel beneath her small body.

'What's making her sleep?' Love said, licking her lips.

'Sleeping pills. She'll have a headache when she wakes, but nothing more.'

Love scanned her uncle's face. He looked incredible.

Younger and brighter. His skin seemed to glow like firelight, more radiant than the light spilling in at his back.

'Is it working already?' she said, taking a step closer to him. The air around him vibrated with energy.

Uncle Saviour's lips stretched into a smile. His eyes sparkled like a thousand glistening rain droplets touched by sunlight. 'Yes. I can feel her blood mixing with mine. I can feel myself becoming stronger. Purer.'

Love's lower lip trembled. Her ribs ached with longing. 'When can I—'

'Not yet. But soon. I promise.'

'But I—'

His look silenced her. She knew when to stop. Even Uncle Saviour had his limits. Perhaps it was that he still didn't think she was ready. But she was as ready as she'd ever be. She felt like she'd been born ready. This was her destiny. His and hers. Together, they would ascend. Together, they would lead others to salvation. Together, they would lead those worthy into Total Illumination, into heaven as it were, on earth. The kind of heaven where you didn't die. A paradisiacal state where you lived for ever in peace and harmony and love.

She took a step forward and bit her lip. Gazing up into his eyes she reached out her hand and trailed the very tip of her index finger over his bloodstained lips. His lips were hot and full. She could feel their vitality pulsing against her finger. Behind him, sunlight poured in through the windows, but he was brighter.

'I'm ready,' she said, lowering her voice and closing the distance between their bodies.

He smiled down at her, but said nothing. She closed her eyes and parted her lips, willing him to kiss her, but after a few seconds, her finger touched only air and she heard him walking away. She opened her eyes, heart thundering. He had returned to the girl on the bed. With gentle fingers, he parted the slit on her thigh and lowered his lips to the blood.

Love lingered in the bedroom, unsure what to do. The room was stuffy and tinged with the scent of blood. For some reason, she felt dirty. She wanted to scream and rant at him. To tell him she was ready and that she was still here, waiting to do his bidding, but she did not want to displease him. She needed to show Uncle Saviour that she was ready. That she could be trusted. Part of showing him meant displayed self-control and behaving in a mature, adult fashion. She was only sixteen. That was why he doubted her, but she would show him she was wiser and cleverer than her age suggested.

Without a word of parting, she turned away from the sound of Uncle Saviour sucking blood from the unnamed girl, and exited the bedroom. As Love hurried along the landing, her ears rang and her teeth ground against each other so hard she could hear them crunch. Her heart pounded, but she knew what she had to do. Nothing was going to stop her. Not now. Not ever.

As she walked, Love realised she was not surprised by her decision or the quickness with which she'd arrived at it. Nor was she surprised by the way in which she planned to execute it. The only thing that surprised her was the unfettered excitement twittering in her breast like a clutch of birds about to fly free from their cage – a cage they had been trapped in for a very long time. In fact, as she dashed across the farm, Love felt more alive than ever – more alive than the grass or the trees or the sun or the sky or the blood in her veins. She was life. She was life and she was going to prove it to Uncle Saviour. She was going to live for ever.

Chapter 26

LILY

Now

Lily pressed Bob's soft fur to her nose. Her mum had given the teddy bear to Hannah on her third birthday. He was a golden-haired bear with brown eyes and a heart-shaped nose. Hannah had been obsessed with re-runs of *Bob the Builder* at the time, hence the teddy's name. She'd loved him as soon as she'd laid eyes on him. Since that day, she'd slept with the bear every night, even taking him to friends' houses for sleepovers. Bob was her comfort blanket. Her anchor and silent best friend. When arguments with friends threatened to make her cry, Bob was always there to offer a sympathetic glance and a soothing cuddle. Last Christmas, Hannah had asked for the White Musk perfume from The Body Shop, and now, before she went to school, she stood in front of the mirror in her bedroom and spritzed herself before turning to her pillow where Bob took pride of place, and spraying him with a healthy dose of the stuff too.

The teddy bear smelt of Hannah. In a sense, he was Hannah. And her mum, who she'd already lost.

She couldn't lose Hannah as well.

Lily buried her nose in his tousled fur. She couldn't smell him enough. Couldn't put him down. The thought of never smelling Hannah's hair or skin again made fresh tears burn. She held Greg's blanket to her face. Her little boy's smell was here. In this blanket in this room. She imagined the house without Hannah and Greg. Thought what it would feel like to never hold them or kiss them again.

Lily stood and reluctantly placed Bob back on Hannah's pillow. The burning in her chest seemed to amplify. She ran down the stairs, into the kitchen.

'We need to do something.'

'Like what?' John looked up at her from his phone. He was still in his pyjamas. He sat hunched over the kitchen bench with a coffee cupped between his calloused hands.

'Like – I don't know – go out and look for them or something!'

'The police are already doing that. They've got cars everywhere. A helicopter's out there too.'

'They need to speak to Aurora again, but they won't.'

'Lily, you need to trust them. The police know what they're doing,' John said, rubbing the back of his neck.

'Not everyone can tell when kids are lying. There's no one else who would've written Greg a letter like that. They need to push her to get the truth, but they'll be too scared to do that. She knows something, I'm sure of it.'

'Why don't you ring Aurora's mum then – what's her name?'

'Felicity.'

'Yeah, ring Felicity and ask if you can talk to Aurora on the phone.'

Lily dragged her hands down her face. 'She'll just lie on the phone. No. I need to go round there. Question her face-to-face.'

'We just have to stay calm,' John said.

She glared murder. 'Calm? John – our children are missing. They're out there, somewhere, terrified. Maybe hurt. How can you possibly tell me to stay calm?'

He put out his hands as if he didn't know what else to do.

She turned to the kitchen window. The dawn sun was glaringly bright. A brutal ball of fire in a too-perfect sky.

'I can't believe this is happening,' she said.

John didn't say anything. She glanced around. His head was in his hands again.

'John?'

'Yes.'

'I need to do something. I can't just sit here doing nothing.'

He looked at her. Sighed. 'I know. I want to do something too, but Sergeant Fielding told us to stay here in case the kids turn up.'

'But they're not going to, are they?'

His lower lip trembled. Tears filled his eyes. 'I'm sorry. I'm so sorry, Lil.'

'For what?' she said.

'For being a crap dad and an even crapper husband. If I wasn't a moody bastard all the time, you'd have woken me up when you heard the door and—'

'And what? You'd have checked the door?' She waited, heart clanging against her ribs.

'No. You're not listening. I'm not saying that. I'm trying to—'

'Don't. I don't want to hear it,' she snapped, striding out of the room.

Running upstairs, Lily stopped outside Hannah's bedroom. Her heart was racing so fast she feared for a moment that her body wouldn't be able to cope. She bent over and put her head between her knees. Heard footsteps behind her. Felt John's hands on her shoulders. 'Breathe. It's going to be OK.'

146

She let him guide her into Hannah's room. He sat her on the bed and crouched down in front of her, placing hot hands on her knees. 'Lily? Lil, look at me. I'm going to ask you something and you have to tell me the truth, OK?'

She looked up and blinked out tears.

John's eyes were gentle. 'Have you forgotten your pills again?'

Anger flared inside her and she pushed his chest, making him fall back onto his heels. 'You're asking me that now? Are you insane?' She knew she was acting crazy, but the pounding in her head and the stress was like poison feeding her inner bitch.

'I'm sorry,' he said, standing up, 'but I need to know. You're acting a bit—'

'Emotional? Worried? Who wouldn't be given the situation, John?'

She strode past him, ran back downstairs, slipped on her trainers and yanked open the front door. Without a word, she stepped out into the hard sunlight and slammed the door. If John wasn't going to do anything, it was up to her. He could stay at home and wait for Hannah and Greg – who were never going to come. She would go out and look for them and she knew where to look first.

She unlocked her red Mini Cooper, slid behind the wheel and released the handbrake with trembling fingers. If she got in trouble, so be it. She couldn't care less.

Reversing down the drive, Lily checked the rear-view mirror. Mr Saxon watched her from his front garden, hand raised to shield his eyes from the sun. She yanked the car around and glanced up at the house. John stood in the doorway. She could only make out his silhouette, felt a stab of guilt as she imagined the look on his face. Shoving it back down, she slammed her foot on the pedal and accelerated out of Cherry Tree Close, not caring that she was driving fifty in a thirty, not caring about anything except Hannah and Greg.

Yes, John was right about the pills. Being off them was dangerous. But she'd run out. There was nothing she could do about that. It was her fault. She'd forgotten again. But she would function OK. She had to.

If she were a better mother, Greg would have told her about the letter. He'd never have left the house. Neither would Hannah. Lately, she'd not given her babies enough attention; she'd let her fears about John skew her priorities. But she'd never do that again. She would help the police find them. She wouldn't give up; she'd fight this anxiety, keep her shit together.

At the T-junction Lily caught a glimpse of a police car turning up ahead. The sight did little to persuade her that they were doing everything they could quickly enough. Politics and paperwork and ethics would slow them down. Nothing would slow her down. Not even being off her pills. She wouldn't let it.

Chapter 27
LOVE

Age 16

July 1997

Love walked into the stable barn intending to brush Jupiter's long golden mane until the coast was clear. Most of the community were in the ancient hall putting up decorations and laying out gifts for Hope's Baby Ceremony, but Peace and Mother were still inside the caravan. She'd spied them through the window talking animatedly, their faces pink with excitement as they discussed their plan. When, she wondered, did they plan on telling her? From what she'd heard, they wanted her to go with them, so it made little sense to keep it a secret.

She shrugged. It would be their loss not hers. She was going to make sure of that.

Standing in the centre of the stables, she inhaled the heady aroma. She'd always enjoyed taking care of the horses. Though the smell was rank, she took comfort in its familiarity. The community kept two: a white and brown girl called Saturn, and Jupiter, her special golden boy. Jupiter was her only friend apart from Uncle Saviour. Jupiter was solid, reliable and he couldn't answer back.

She'd never clicked with any of the other children, not even her sister, but that was hardly surprising considering Peace's character. If Love had to describe Peace in five words, she would choose weak, selfish, greedy, jealous and stupid. They didn't look anything alike either. Peace was short and stubby-limbed with mousy hair, whereas Love was tall, slim and black-haired, with beautiful hazel eyes, far more similar in her looks to Mother than Peace.

In class, Peace revealed little talent for anything other than chatting and distracting their teacher, Hope, who was so close to having her new baby that class had been cancelled for the time being. In contrast, Love was good at everything, which was probably another reason the other children disliked her – not that they made it known. They kept their distance because they knew she was tough. She'd shown them eight years ago when Peace had put a spider in her hair in the middle of the lesson, causing her to scream and embarrass herself. Not long afterwards, Love stayed up until she was certain Peace was sound asleep then placed a dead, maggot-infested mouse she'd found in the barn on her sister's pillow. Mother had banned her from social time for a whole month, but the look on Peace's face and the fear in the other children's eyes had been worth it.

She smiled. She was excited to meet Hope's new baby and learn its pure name. She liked the name Care for a girl and Strength for a boy, and hoped it was a boy because Hope already had three girls. The baby would be cut on its chest and give a little of its blood to Uncle Saviour at the next Blood Birthing Ceremony signalling its commencement on the journey to Total Illumination.

Love scratched the back of her neck, suddenly hot with irritation at her mother and Peace. To distract herself, she leaned over and picked up the horse brush, scratched Jupiter's nose the way he liked it, then drew the brush gently but firmly through his mane. He nuzzled her hand and pushed his shoulder into hers as he often did – his sign of affection, and she smiled and pulled an apple out of her pocket. It was her mid-afternoon snack, but she wasn't hungry. Holding the shiny green apple up to Jupiter's lips, she smiled as he bit it out of her hand in one go and gobbled the fruit down with a toss of his head and a delighted tail swish. With a laugh at his babyish behaviour, Love dropped the brush on the hay-strewn ground and patted his shoulder.

A moment later, she heard a girl's laugh followed by a man whispering *be quiet.*

Love immediately ducked down behind Jupiter's stall and listened to the sound of two people smashing their lips against each other's. The nasty, sucking sounds made her feel sick. Peeping over the stable door, she gaped at the people who were kissing; the girl was Hope's middle daughter, Devotion, who was only fourteen, and the man was Fervour, Faith's husband, who was even older than Uncle Saviour and not half as good-looking. He looked like a pug dog and his hair-line was receding. It was ridiculous. No, more than that, it was wrong. Fervour was married to Faith. This kind of thing was not allowed. It was a sign of impurity. They should both know better. Especially Devotion. Only last month Hope had taught a lesson on the impurity of adultery. But Devotion was weak, like so many of them. Weak and selfish. Too weak to devote herself to the cause, too selfish to follow a few simple rules and commit herself to their glorious journey.

Love shook her head bitterly. First Mother and Peace, and now this. Then a smile tickled her lips: Faith deserved this; she was planning to leave too and she was going to take Fervour's only child with her. Well, good. It served her right. If she was going to abandon the community and go against the rules of the purest man on earth, Faith deserved to suffer the consequences of her husband's disloyalty.

Love watched Devotion and Fervour kissing. She frowned and chewed her hair, part-disgusted, part-curious. She imagined kissing Uncle Saviour and a sultry sort of heat drifted down her body and pooled in the very pit of her abdomen, making her feel warm and tingly.

'I don't think – I mean, I'm not sure I'm ready,' Devotion panted, pulling away. Her cheeks were as red as cherries, but she wore a hard frown.

'Kiss me. You know you like it,' Fervour said, pulling her face back to his.

They kissed for another few seconds then Devotion yanked her head away. 'I'm sorry. I just – this is wrong. I can't.'

'Yes, you can. Don't think about anyone else. Just think about us.' He rested his hands on her waist and stared into her eyes. 'Look what you've done to me. I want you. I need you.' He glanced down at himself and Devotion followed his gaze, jolting at the sight of the bulge in his trousers. Love jerked with surprise too. Surely not? Devotion was only fourteen.

Anger boiled Love's blood. She dug her nails into her palms and fought the urge to charge through the stable door and slap them both around their thick heads.

Devotion took a step back. 'No. I'm sorry, Fervour. I'm not ready. I'm scared.'

Good, Love thought, relaxing a little. *Good*. Devotion wasn't as stupid as she thought.

Fervour closed the space between them. 'Don't worry, my sweet. I'll show you the way. I'll be extra gentle. See?'

He trailed one hand across the waistline of her dress and up towards her small breasts.

Devotion gasped and jerked backwards. Her heel clanged into a metal bucket and she fell onto the dusty ground, her smock dress riding up to reveal a pair of thin, coltish legs that made her seem even younger than she was.

She laughed awkwardly and tossed her hazel curls out of her eyes. Reaching up, she said, 'I'm such a clumsy fool. Help me up?'

But Fervour didn't help her. Instead, he seized her extended wrist, pushed it to the ground beside her head and knelt astride her hips.

Devotion opened her mouth to scream, but Fervour slammed his hand over her parted lips. He was smiling, clearly enjoying her fear.

With a small frown, Love pulled a piece of hair into her mouth and began to chew.

Chapter 28

PEARLINE

Now

Once in the office, Pearline updated the team on Janet Weatherby's summation then joined Dibbs at his desk.

The room was too hot. A lone fan on its last legs did a half-hearted job of combating the heatwave while the open windows served to welcome more humidity. People's shirts were patched with sweat, their foreheads lined, minds bent on saving the lives of two innocent children. Hannah and Gregory's faces were pinned to the wall, as was Mike Gibson's.

Strewn beside Dibbs's laptop lay sweet wrappers, peppermint creams being his most popular choice. Swiping the mess into the bin in one smooth motion, Dibbs handed her a copy of the letter the Woods had found in their son's bedroom. 'As you'd expect, the parents are in a state. Both are convinced that Gregory's best – and only – friend, Aurora White, wrote it, but Felicity White, the mother, says Aurora's never laid eyes on that letter or even written a letter to Gregory before. Obviously, she could be lying, but officers swept the house and no one was there except for the mother and daughter.'

Pearline reread the letter and looked up into his concerned eyes. 'How far have they got with his other classmates?'

'Team's nearly visited them all. No luck.'

'OK. We need someone to speak to his teacher.'

'Already on it. She's being interviewed right now.'

Pearline smeared her forehead. 'OK. The letter may well be a dead-end, seeing as Rudge and Gibson chased the kids into the woods, but we need to know who wrote it.'

'I agree.'

Dibbs reached over and touched her hand. 'Hey, how you holding up? You eaten anything?'

'I'm fine.'

Not moving his hand from hers, he opened his desk drawer, pulled out a peppermint cream and offered it to her. 'Sweet treat?'

She shook her head. 'Not hungry.'

He unwrapped the sweet one-handed, popped it into his mouth, and eyed her. 'Talk to me if you need to. Promise?'

She looked down at his hand on hers, felt her chest loosen a little. 'I will. Thanks.'

Dibbs smiled, stood, and left the office quickly.

She watched him go, shocked to feel a stab of sadness. He liked her a lot, more than she deserved. If things were different and she wasn't such a mess . . . no. It was a stupid idea. They were colleagues, nothing more. And Hannah and Gregory Woods needed her complete focus. She couldn't waste any time on thoughts of her own happiness when two innocent lives were at stake.

Trying to ignore the tension knotting her shoulders, Pearline reread the letter Fielding had shown her when she'd returned from the Woods' house. The note indicated why the children had left their house at two in the morning, but not where they had been headed, which in itself was probably an irrelevance given what had occurred since their departure

155

from Cherry Tree Close. Still, the letter shouldn't be discounted. If Dibbs had any luck, he'd call immediately. The original letter was in the lab for testing, but the results wouldn't be back for a while.

Chapter 29

LOVE

Age 16

July 1997

Love watched Devotion struggle. Fervour pinned her hands above her head and forced her thighs apart with his knee. His receding hairline shone.

Beyond the stables, the farmyard was abandoned. The chickens sheltered in their coop and the goats slept beneath the picnic bench. The majority of the community remained inside the hall making arrangements for Hope's Baby Ceremony.

Across North Devonshire, afternoon sunlight flooded down from the pristine sky, dominating the land and drying out the dirt enough to make it crack like a pair of chapped, bloodless lips. Nothing moved and nothing changed. Dust floated, meaningless and mindless in bars of brilliant, white light. Excited voices floated from the hall as the community prepared to celebrate the much-anticipated birth of Hope's fourth baby.

Outside, all was pure, untouched by the evils of man. Inside, human depravity oozed like a putrid sore.

Love dragged her gaze away from the farmyard, longing, for a brief moment, to be one of those ignorant dust motes.

'Stay still,' Fervour growled, slapping Devotion hard in the face.

The stupid girl was sobbing. Love scratched her ear and wondered why she wasn't screaming for help.

She frowned and yawned so hard her jaw cracked. The stable was too hot and it was making her sleepy. What Fervour was doing was wrong, but she found herself searching for the right course of action. The answer wasn't obvious.

Fervour yanked up Devotion's smock dress. She shrieked and he clamped his fist over her mouth, freeing one of her hands, which she used to scratch at his cheek. He slapped her and she stilled and turned her head to the side. Her body went limp and she stopped struggling. For a second, Love thought she had fainted, but then she saw Devotion blinking and tears glistening in her wide eyes.

Love scratched the back of her neck and wondered what to do. Abruptly, an idea popped into her head and she smiled. This was actually great. She could use Fervour's impurity to her advantage.

No guilt accompanied the idea. Fervour was attacking an underage girl. He was impure and deserved to be punished and what she had in mind was not a particularly harsh punishment. Besides, if Uncle Saviour caught wind of what one of his most-trusted members was up to, he'd go for his shotgun quicker than she could say Total Illumination. She tried to picture such a turn of events playing out. She didn't think Uncle Saviour would actually shoot Fervour or use his scythe, but he would certainly make an example of him, and once her uncle had shamed him, exile would be a certainty. Lately, her uncle had drawn up a list of reasons for exiling someone from the community. He said it would always be a last resort, but that he would not hesitate to banish a member if they committed a level one impure act. One of these acts was rape. Another was disloyalty, though he was yet to clarify what that included.

Devotion's body was rigid, her dress bunched up around her waist, pale pink knickers on show like a doll.

'That's a good girl. Now just relax.' Fervour removed his hand from her mouth, lowered his lips to hers and slid his fingers up her exposed thigh.

Love waited a beat, watched the dust motes drift in the sun. Excitement thrummed in her chest. She swished her hair and stepped out of the stall. 'Fervour, stop.'

His expression was priceless. His jaw dropped open and he gawked at her like a puce-faced fish, eyebrows up near his receding hairline, eyes wide, mouth wider. Devotion's eyes slid up and latched onto hers, hope brightening them in a way Love found irritating. Behind her, Jupiter nuzzled her neck, unaware of the drama unfolding in his house. Absently, she scratched his chin then moved closer to Fervour and Devotion, amused to see Fervour frantically scrabble to his feet and attempt to hide his erection.

'It isn't what it looks like,' he said, as Devotion rolled onto her hands and knees, pushed herself to her feet, and darted across the stable to stand beside her saviour.

She felt Devotion's body pressing against hers, how much it trembled. She looked at the girl and said, 'It's OK. I'll deal with him. I won't tell anyone what happened. I promise. Go to the hall and act normal. I'll talk to you later.'

Devotion nodded gratefully and ran out of the stable without a word or a glance in Fervour's direction.

The stupid girl had beat a lucky escape and she knew it. Love had done her a huge favour. Devotion wouldn't realise yet, but she owed her big time, and Love would collect at a later date, probably when the girl was least expecting it.

'She wanted it. She—'

'Shut up,' Love said, taking a step towards him, relishing a delicious tingle in the base of her spine at his fear. 'I saw the whole thing. You were going to rape her. She's only fourteen. Add to that the fact you're married and I'd say you're totally and utterly screwed.'

Her words knocked the wind from his already sagging sails. He stared at her and frowned, unable to decide how to proceed.

Enjoying herself, Love smiled and said, 'The way I see it, you've got two options. One: confess to Uncle Saviour and suffer the consequences.' She paused and let the unsaid work its magic.

Fervour's ugly face blanched. She could see the cogs in his small brain whirling. Spinning out of control.

How would Uncle Saviour deal with such a severe transgression? Fervour was close to Saviour. Closer than most. The fact that he had so badly betrayed Saviour's rules and trust would make him angry. Very angry. And Fervour knew it. She could see it in his eyes – the fear of being banished, but more than that – the terror of Saviour withdrawing his chance at eternal life.

She gave it another few seconds for the terrifying truth to sink in and swallow him whole like Jonah and the whale. When she was satisfied that he was about to wet himself, she continued.

'Two: you do what I ask, whenever I ask it, and I'll forget the whole thing ever happened.'

He frowned hard. 'What about Devotion?'

'She'll keep silent about it. She won't want anyone knowing what she's been up to with a dirty old bastard like you, will she? And I mean,' Love laughed, 'she's not entirely innocent, is she?'

'No, she's bloody not.'

160

'So, do we have a deal?' Love extended her hand to his. She didn't want to touch him, but this was how you sealed the deal. Hand on hand. Flesh in flesh. Blood to blood.

'What exactly is it you want me to do?' he said.

'I'll let you know.'

His throat bobbed up and down as he swallowed with obvious difficulty. He didn't have a choice and he knew it. He was hers now and she'd use him to her heart's content. She already had ideas, some of which linked to her mother and Peace.

With a heavy frown, he took her hand, held it for a beat too long. 'You're not going to mention any of this to Saviour?'

Love held his gaze with eyes like steel. 'Not if you keep your end of the bargain, no.'

He snatched his hand out of her grasp as if she'd burned him, and rubbed his palm on his trouser leg. With a quick nod, he turned and hurried out of the stable, and Love returned to Jupiter, unable to stop smiling as idea after idea raced through her mind like bloodhounds after a fox.

Chapter 30

LILY

Now

If Mum was alive, she'd have a fit if she knew what you're about to do. She'd tell you to turn around and drive back home. Be with John. Do what the police tell you to do. Be sensible. And she'd be right. John's right. What you're doing is crazy. John needs your support. Go home. Turn around. Now.

But Lily couldn't listen to that voice. She felt wired and twitchy. Her hands jerked on the steering wheel and she clamped them down tightly as a memory surfaced of baking fairy cakes with Greg and Hannah when they were three and six. Greg had licked the bowl clean and Hannah had told him off. As revenge, he'd smeared cake mix down her nose, she'd grabbed the icing sugar and soon the whole kitchen was a powdery white mess, but they'd all been in stitches, covered head-to-toe in the stuff when John came into the room. To her surprise – and the kids' – he'd grabbed a handful of icing sugar and thrown it up in the air, then stuck out his tongue to catch the sugary mist as it fell. Hannah and Greg had tried to copy him and touched tongues by mistake. She'd laughed so hard her ribs hurt.

If she never got them back, she'd never laugh again. Or smile. Or . . . she couldn't complete the thought.

With a lump in her throat, she swerved her Mini onto the road that led to Aurora's house. She'd been hoping to see police officers here, but there was no one around. Juniper Avenue was deserted except for a fat white cat that stared at her from the brick wall that ran between number 25 and number 26.

Running up the path, Lily knocked on the door of number 25. She'd dropped off Greg here plenty of times in the last three years. He and Aurora had hit it off in the first week of reception. She'd not hit it off with the girl's mother, Felicity, but they got along well enough whenever their paths crossed. Felicity worked as a cleaner and dinner lady at the kids' school, Grimstone Primary. The woman was always polite and pleasant, if a little closed off. But maybe that was her own fault – she could have made more of an effort to develop a friendship with the woman. Perhaps if she'd done that, none of this would be happening.

Felicity opened the door. She wore her staple outfit: leggings and a baggy T-shirt. 'Lily – I'm so sorry about Hannah and Greg. The police have been here and—'

'Hi, Felicity. Look, I'm so sorry to turn up like this, but I need to speak to Aurora.'

'Oh. Uh, but the police—'

Lily entered the house. 'Where is she?'

'She's in her room, but—'

Knowing she was being rude, but not much caring, Lily ran up the woman's stairs and pounded her fist on Aurora's bedroom door. Felicity was three steps behind her. Aurora's narrow face appeared and Lily entered the room without asking.

'Aurora, I need to ask you a few questions about Greg. OK?' She stared down at the girl, who was dressed in Teenage

Mutant Ninja Turtle pyjamas. Half of the room was a shrine to the Turtles, the other half to fairies.

'OK,' Aurora said with a little shrug.

'Lily?' Felicity said, a stronger tone in her voice than normal.

Lily glanced around. 'I'm sorry, Felicity, but I have to do this. You'd do the same if it was Aurora missing. I need to ask Aurora a couple of questions then I'll be out of your hair. I promise.'

The woman's voice softened. 'Yes, yes. I'm sorry. Of course. Aurora, answer all of Mrs Woods' questions, all right? Just like you did with the police officer.'

Aurora nodded, her one green eye and one blue eye never leaving Lily's. Lily sat down on the girl's bed and patted the mattress beside her. 'Come and sit next to me, Aurora. We need to have a talk.'

But the big-eyed child took a step back. 'What do you want to ask me?'

Lily took a moment to gather her thoughts.

She told herself to stay calm. Aurora was a smart girl, but she was only seven. Lily didn't want to upset her, but needed the truth. She cleared her throat. 'Aurora, Greg is missing. Do you know where he might be?'

Aurora frowned and shook her head. 'No, Mrs Woods. I haven't seen Greg since yesterday at school.'

'He didn't come to your house very early this morning?'

'No. Why would he do that?'

'Because you told him to.'

Aurora scratched her head, the image of confusion. Either she was a very good actor or she genuinely didn't know what Lily was getting at.

'Why would I tell him to come to my house early in the morning?'

Lily stared hard at her, trying to work out if she was pretending to be so puzzled.

Aurora bit her lip. 'He's not even my friend any more.'

'What do you mean? You're best friends. You've been best friends for years.'

'We broke up. Greg was mean to me. He wouldn't eat lunch with me. He wanted to eat it with someone else, so he's not my friend any more.'

'This is the first I've heard about this,' Lily said.

'And he likes her more than me. He says she gives him special notes and that she has a fairy at her house.'

A fairy at her house. Lily leaned forward. 'Who is she? Who is this girl?'

Aurora shrugged and rubbed her blue eye. 'I don't know. He won't tell me. I know she's in our class though.'

'Aurora, can you tell me the names of every girl in your class, please?'

The girl perked up at this. 'Of course. I've got an eidetic memory.'

Lily didn't know what one of those was and she didn't care. She snatched her phone out of her pocket and opened the notepad. 'Start with the girls he speaks to the most.'

'He doesn't speak to anyone except for me,' she said.

'But – oh, never mind. Just tell me their names.'

'There are seven girls in my class including me. We're way outnumbered by the boys. There are fifteen boys, if you include Trevor. He's more of a toad than a boy. Anyway, the girls are: Sasha Brown. She's got brown skin like her name. Posie Gibson, who sounds like she's pretty because her name's a flower, but she isn't. Jessica Smithy, who's really pretty. All the boys fancy her. Eve Remington who's dyslexic and has to have one-to-one help from Miss Mills. Then there's Clara Richards. She's a bit chubby and some of the boys call her

165

nasty names like Miss Piggy. The last one is Fatima Chatterjee. She's OK.'

Lily held her gaze. 'And you're sure you don't know where he is? You promise?'

Aurora nodded. She sniffed. 'I want Greg to be my friend again. Please tell him that I forgive him for being mean to me.'

Lily gave her a quick hug. She'd interrogated enough children in her time to know when one was telling the truth. 'I will. I promise.'

Lily thanked Felicity and hurried out of the house. She needed to get back to John, tell him about Greg's special friend and persuade him to help her contact the six girls' parents. Two of them on the task would be more efficient. And she and John would push harder than the police to find out the truth. The letter felt so important. They needed to know who'd manipulated her seven-year-old son into leaving the safety of his home in the middle of the night. But would John support her in this? So far, he'd done nothing but provoke her inner bitch, which she felt guilty for, but couldn't control. Of course, he was right about her pills. She wouldn't be able to get more until Monday. Today was Saturday, and the pressure in her head was building, the anxious tightening in her chest worsening with every passing minute.

Trying to reassure herself that John would be willing to help hunt down the other six girls, she swerved out of Juniper Avenue and sped back home.

Chapter 31

LOVE

Age 16

July 1997

The hall was a thing of beauty.

Love's heart expanded at the buzz of human bees busying about in their collective endeavour to turn the dull into the splendid. She smiled, felt a sublime happiness glide through her limbs. This was her hive. She was one of these bees. Not queen bee yet, but that time would come.

Usually, the old building looked as ugly as Fervour, with its rickety chairs, pocked table, cracked walls, and pine flooring scratched to within an inch of its life; but now, it was a caterpillar transformed into a butterfly. Concealing the floor were four handwoven blankets darned from butter-yellow wool, decorated with flowers of every colour. These treasures were the result of five months' worth of labour from the most artistically talented women of the community. The table was decked with handmade birds' nests and twirling ropes of ivy crafted by Hope's daughters. Candles lit these centrepieces as well as the tired walls, which had been revived with two colourful drapes: bedsheets that had been tie-dyed and sewn together. The nasty chairs were now padded with pretty cushions created by Love, Peace, and their mother. These were beetroot-dyed pillow cases stuffed with sheep's wool. There weren't enough chairs to seat the whole community, so people had brought some from their caravans to make up the numbers.

She watched her mother handing out daisy crowns to the girls. She wasn't smiling and grooves knitted her forehead. Love longed to run over to her traitorous mother and tell her that she knew about their plan to run away at midnight. But she wouldn't. She had a far better idea. Still, she chewed her cheek, unable to believe Peace or her mother hadn't told her about it yet. They were, after all, planning to take her with them, which made her think that the only reason she hadn't been let in on their secret was that they didn't trust her. Love smiled. In that case, they'd be right. They shouldn't trust her. Not one little itty-bitty bit. But they would have to tell her at some point.

Saviour was talking to Nobility. He looked her way and winked, hitched the shotgun higher up his shoulder. He held the scythe in his right hand and kept turning it, making Nobility flinch every time the curved blade spun too close. She grinned back and waved, earning a sly glance from Peace.

Fervour was sulking in the corner, not bothering to help. Love caught his eye and raised her eyebrow. He looked away quickly, heat burning his cheeks.

She allowed herself a chuckle at that and jumped at a sudden pressure on her elbow. It was Peace. 'We need to talk.'

Love stared blankly at her sister. 'About what?'

'Not here. Home.'

Love was surprised Peace still thought of their caravan as home considering she was about to leave it.

Saying nothing, she followed her stubby sister out of the hall, across the farmyard down to the caravan they'd lived in their whole lives. Their stained, yellowed, beautiful home.

168

Inside, she was greeted with their family smell: rosemary sprig soap, their mother's favourite. Peace flicked on the lights and walked into the small living space. Love sat on the bench sofa opposite her sister. Peace's daisy crown was wonky, her face paler than normal, piggy eyes slits pressed into doughy flesh. Love saw her own reflection in the window behind her sister's face and liked what she saw. She looked calm, collected and . . . normal.

'What's so important that you have to bring me here to tell me?' she said.

Peace licked her lips. A nervous gesture, Love thought.

'What would you say if I was to tell you that Mother's not happy?'

'I'd say I don't know what you're talking about. She seems fine to me.'

Peace hesitated. Looked at the door then back at Love. Licked her lips again. 'Well, she's not. And neither am I.'

'Oh no. Why?' Love said. It was important to act like she cared.

Peace blew out a long tunnel of air. Her breath was sickly-sweet as if she'd been eating overripe strawberries. 'Mother – well, we – don't like it here any more. Things are changing. Going downhill. It's just . . . we don't really feel safe and—'

'You don't feel *safe*?'

Her sister fidgeted with the hem of her dress. Licked her lips. 'This blood obsession Uncle Saviour's got. It feels wrong. And there are rumours flying around about a girl. A stranger. Mother doesn't like it. Neither do I.'

'What girl? I don't know what you're talking about.'

Peace lowered her voice and leaned in. 'Apparently, Saviour's taken someone. She hasn't chosen to be here. She's been taken. Stolen.'

Love raised her eyebrows, trying to look as shocked as possible and a touch horrified for good measure. It was rather ironic that Peace was acting so terrorised by the crime of stealing when she and mother had done the same thing by stealing the keys to the van. 'That's awful. Stealing is a terrible thing to do. I can't believe Uncle Saviour would do something like that. Are you sure?'

Peace nodded, face grim. 'He's been getting worse. Haven't you noticed? First with the blood birthing, then with the voluntary blood giving from community members, and now this. It's crazy if you ask me. Mother thinks the same. She thinks the power's gone to his head. It's making him lose the plot.'

But nobody's asked you, have they?

'What do you think?' Peace said. It was clear from her voice that she was desperate for Love to agree. In that moment, Love almost felt sorry for her. Her poor, stupid, naïve sibling. Death was calling for Peace, just as much as it was calling for her mother, but Love knew how to help them. She knew exactly what to do and how to get it done.

'So, what are we going to do about it?' Love said.

Peace's face relaxed. She smiled and leaned in even closer. Reaching out, she grabbed both of Love's hands, which were ice-cold despite the mugginess of the night. 'We're leaving. Tonight.' She paused. Waited for the enormity of her words to sink in.

Love widened her eyes and gasped in the perfect imitation of surprise. 'Really? How?'

Peace told her their plan, spilling out the words so fast Love found it hard not to laugh. Peace was afraid but excited, pathetically so.

'Great,' Love said, smiling. 'At midnight, we'll sneak out of here, run to the van, get in and drive off. Simple as that?'

'Yes. Just make sure you don't tell anyone. Faith and Zeal are coming with us. If Fervour finds out—'

'I know,' Love said, 'he beats her, doesn't he? It's terrible.'

'Yeah. And Saviour knows he does and doesn't do anything to stop it.' She looked down at her knees. When she looked up at Love, tears dribbled down her cheeks. 'I know we haven't always seen eye-to-eye and sometimes we fight like cat and dog, but I do love you, you know. You're my sister and I always will. I'm so glad you're coming with us. I was worried you were too caught up in Saviour's fantasies to realise what's really going on. What with him making you his little pet and all.'

And you're too caught up in your own ego to realise that the purest man on earth is the only one who can ever know the truth. The only one who can save us.

Peace leaped to her feet. 'I'm so excited for this new start. Aren't you?'

Instead of voicing her real thoughts, Love nodded and smiled, and allowed her sister to pull her to her feet, link her arm through hers, and lead her back to the hall with a big grin on her gullible face.

Chapter 32

PEARLINE

Now

Pearline suppressed the urge to fist-pump the air. Mike Gibson had been found. They'd just brought him in.

Finding Gibson was a huge piece of luck – possibly monumental – but she kept her excitement under wraps and reminded herself that if Janet Weatherby was right about the killer's height, Gibson wasn't their man.

She called Fielding over. 'As Dibbs isn't here, I want you in with me. Gibson's in the custody suite. He was found at his friend's house, a Daniel Foe, who said he's been hiding there since around two-thirty this morning. Mr Foe's girlfriend gave the same statement. Says he turned up alone, no kids with him. A neighbour heard banging on Foe's door and saw Gibson, alone. Neighbour also says a time of about two-thirty in the morning.'

If two witnesses saw Mike Gibson at two-thirty and he'd been holed up there since then, there was very little time window in which he could have taken Hannah and Gregory. Gibson most likely wasn't their guy. But that didn't mean he hadn't seen or heard something that could assist the investigation.

She heaved herself out of her chair and they headed for Interview Room 1.

Sitting down in the small, stale room, they waited for Mike Gibson.

Fielding perched on the edge of her chair, back straight as a ballerina's, face void of emotion. She dusted an imaginary crumb off her pristine white shirt, sat up straighter.

The room was too hot. But that was good. They wanted Gibson to sweat.

Five minutes later, Mike Gibson sat down heavily and stared at the wall, avoiding eye contact. The custody officer gave her a nod and left the room.

Fielding rested her elbows on the table, leaned forward, and stared icily at Gibson's hooded eyes.

The young man had the physique of a welterweight boxer. He wore over-the-knee combat shorts and a camo vest top. A sleeve tattoo swallowed his right forearm. *Rough* was the word that sprang to mind. *Child-killer*, not so much. The kid was barely a man himself and, despite the tattoos, he looked like he was about to wet himself. But perhaps she was being optimistic, which was more Dibbs's domain than hers.

Gibson could have changed his clothes since Rudge's murder, but it smelt and looked like he hadn't. Sweat and dirt wafted off him in one nauseating swell that made her wish she was wearing a mask.

'I want to wait for my lawyer,' he said.

She mirrored Fielding's ice-cold stare. 'Mr Gibson, two small children are missing. This is an urgent taped interview because I need you to answer immediate questions as there is a threat of life to children. Right now, all we want is to know what you know about those youngsters. We need answers quickly. This may very well be a matter of life or death for ten-year-old Hannah and seven-year-old Gregory, the two innocent children you and your friend chased into Grimstone Woods last night.'

He paled. Looked down at his wrists. Shook his head. Mumbled.

'Speak up, Mr Gibson. We can't hear you.'

Mike Gibson looked up. His eyes were wet. 'I didn't do nothin' to them kids. Once they was in the woods, I didn't see them again. I swear.'

'So, you're admitting that you and Rudge chased two children into Grimstone Woods?' Pearline said.

'Yeah. I didn't do nothin' to them though.'

'And what time was this?'

He shrugged. 'What time? I dunno. Late? Gone midnight for sure.'

'Do you own a scythe, Mr Gibson?'

'A *what*?'

Pearline stared at him until he began to shift about in his seat. Fielding stared too. The young man looked down at his bruised knuckles. He was hiding something. Guilt emanated from him, rife as his sweat.

'Mr Gibson. Mike. May I call you Mike?'

He hesitated then nodded.

'Mike. You've got siblings, haven't you? Two little sisters, Posie and Petal. That's right, isn't it?'

'Uh, yeah. Hey – they're OK, aren't they?'

'Yes, they're absolutely fine. Did you know that Posie is in Gregory's class?' She paused, let it sink in. The implication of her words: that he might have something to do with the boy's disappearance.

He smeared sweat off his forehead. 'Look. I already told you. I didn't do nothin' to them little kids. I got sisters, like you said. I'm not like that.'

174

'For all I know, you could have waited until Rudge was out of the picture, then done something terrible to those children.'

Tears filled his eyes. 'I didn't, I swear. I chased them, yeah, but that's it.'

'There's something you're not telling me.'

'No, there ain't. Honest.' Guilt flickered in his features.

'You saw something didn't you, Mike?'

'No. I—'

'Don't waste our time, Mr Gibson,' Fielding said. 'We've been doing this too long to be fooled by someone like you.'

Gibson flinched as if stung. He looked up at the ceiling and tried to blink back tears, but one fell anyway.

He darted a shameful look at Pearline. 'I'm sorry. I was scared. I'm sorry.'

'Sorry for what? What did you do, Mike?' Pearline said softly. 'Remember, all I care about is finding Hannah and Gregory before it's too late.'

He sniffed. 'It's not what I did. It's what I didn't do.'

'Tell me then. Tell me what happened. Don't miss anything out. Tell me everything.'

He exhaled. The toxicity in the air was off the Richter scale. 'OK. Right. So when we got in the woods, Rudge wanted to carry on looking for them but I didn't so I said I was leaving but then realised I'd be in the shit with him so I went back and saw him running after them. I started running after him and then tripped and fell over. I got up and thought about going back to the party, but decided to stay, see if I could find him. Make sure he knew I hadn't left, you know?'

Pearline nodded. She did know. Connor Rudge had been a frightening man.

'So I listened real careful and heard this strange sound.'

'What sound?' Fielding said.

175

'I dunno. It was like something being whacked against the ground.'

'Go on,' Pearline said.

'I carried on and fell over this tree and grazed my knees – look,' he bent over to show them and Pearline waved her hand.

'That's not necessary, Mike. We don't need to see your knees.'

'Oh.' He straightened, eyes clouding. 'I heard a scream. It sounded like a kid. I was scared. I didn't think Rudge would hurt them. I didn't want him to. He was just going to scare them. I mean, he hits Crystal a bit, but that's it. He's never laid a hand on his kid. His dad used to beat him so he's always sworn—'

'The children. Mike, tell us about the children.'

'Uh. Yeah. Right. So there was this scream then everything went quiet. I was so scared I nearly pissed myself.'

'And then?'

He swallowed, smeared the beads on his upper lip. 'I crouched down and looked out from behind a tree. I could just about make out four people.'

'Four?'

'Yeah. Two small. The kids, I think. One was tall. Holding some sort of stick with a blade stuck on the top.'

That fits with Janet Weatherby's identification of a scythe.

He sniffed. 'The other was big, but not as big as the other one.'

'Male or female?'

'Couldn't say. Too dark.'

'Then what happened?' Pearline said.

'I got a bit closer. I could see something on the ground. It was Rudge. His head – oh God . . .'

'What were the two adults and children doing?'

'Not sure. I freaked out. When I looked up, the one holding

the stick was gone. The shorter one grabbed the kids and left.'

Christ. Her pulse ramped up. Beat so hard her chest hurt. 'Are you saying this person left the woods with the children?'

Gibson swallowed. 'Yeah.'

'What do you mean by "grabbed"?' Fielding said.

'Yes – did the children go willingly or did they struggle?' Pearline added.

'I don't know. I'm sorry. God, I'm so sorry. I was too freaked out by seeing Rudge like that.'

'Think carefully – did you hear a vehicle of any kind?'

'I can't remember. I don't think so. I was too fuckin' scared. There was my mate lying on the ground, not moving, and I didn't know if that crazy dude was gonna come back with that big stick and finish me off, and—'

'What did you do?' Pearline said.

He licked his lips and hung his head. 'I went over to Rudge, just to check he was dead, and, uh, his face was so mashed up that I freaked out and turned and, uh, trod on something.'

'What? You trod on something? What was it?'

He swallowed. Wiped his lips with the back of his hand. 'Oh shit – I'm sorry. I know I shouldn't of, but I took it. I wasn't thinking straight and just picked it up. I was scared my fingerprints were on it so I took it with me. There was nothin' I could do to help Rudge, and them kids were gone with that fuckin' psycho, so I,' he shook his head in shame, 'I took it and legged it to Foe's house.'

'Took what?' Fielding snapped.

'What? Oh. A mask.'

'A mask?' Pearline glanced at Fielding. 'Where is it now?'

Gibson sniffed. Guilt flushed his cheeks. 'At Foe's, under the sofa bed.'

Chapter 33
LILY

Now

Lily drove too fast. Her head throbbed. She wrestled a packet of painkillers out of the glove compartment and choked them back. She started to imagine Hannah and Greg and a whole host of scenarios splintered her thoughts. They were being held to ransom – locked in someone's basement – chained to a wall – forced to pose naked while some bastard pervert took their pictures before posting them on an obscene child porn website . . . or – no – she couldn't let herself continue. She'd fall into an abyss of despair and never be able to pull herself back out. And she needed to have all cylinders firing. They had to track down whoever wrote that letter. She felt it deep in her gut. Deeper than before. Yes, it didn't make much sense, but none of this made any sense. Yesterday, she and John had had problems, but the world had made sense. Today was a nightmare come true.

Lily yanked up the handbrake and scrambled out of the car. She left the engine running. She wouldn't be staying for long. Once John understood how to help her, they could leave together to find the other girls in Greg's class.

With a steadying inhalation, she hurried inside the house, and froze, heart somersaulting nastily.

A woman was sitting in her kitchen. A woman with long black hair in a skin-tight T-shirt and butt-hugging shorts.

Juliet Pickering.

Juliet was in *her* kitchen, sitting at *her* kitchen bench opposite *her* husband, one orange hand outstretched on the counter as if it had been resting on top of his.

'What the hell's she doing here?' Lily said, staring murder at Juliet Pickering's tangoed face. She'd seen a car outside her house. A fancy white thing. Juliet's new car, she realised.

John looked pained. 'I should have told you. Ju—'

'I knew it!' Lily laughed. It was a high, manic laugh. She laughed again and clapped her hands. 'Well done, John. Well done for completely and utterly ruining our lives.'

John frowned and got up. Juliet frowned too. They both stared at her as though she'd done something wrong, as if she was crazy, not them.

Fighting a savage need to hit one of them, Lily glared at Juliet and stabbed a finger at her inflated chest. '*You*. Couldn't you have had the decency to wait until I was fully out of the picture? And you—' she whipped her head in John's direction, 'how could you? Hannah and Greg are missing! I needed you and here you are, sneaking around with her the second I leave the house. I knew something was going on. I just knew it!'

'No. Lily, it's not like that. It's not what you think,' John said, taking a step towards her, hands up as if she were a caged animal about to attack.

Juliet was looking at John and nodding. They were both looking at her, acting as if she was stupid.

Juliet stood up and reached out a hand, wafting too-sweet perfume all over the kitchen. 'Lily. This has nothing to do

179

with anything like that. This is merely because I've been seeing John. He—'

'Shut up. Just shut the hell up. Stay away from me. Both of you!' Lily turned and ran out of the house. She could hear them running after her, calling her name, but she didn't slow down or look back.

Reversing down the drive at a crazy speed, she whipped out of the close, tears so thick she could hardly see, chest jabbering so fast she felt as if she was about to have a heart attack.

Swiping angrily at her eyes, she pulled up at the side of the road, cut the engine, smashed her fists against the steering wheel, and cursed until her throat burned. Embracing the anger was all there was: she needed rage to keep her going and beat back the misery threatening to swallow her whole. Hannah and Greg were missing. Sod John and his tangoed tart on the side. Sod them both. Now, it was crucial she focus on her children. There was no time for self-pity. Speed was everything.

With jerky hands, she grabbed her phone and went on Facebook. John was supposed to be helping her do this, but she didn't need his help. She would do it on her own.

She was friends with two of the mums in Greg's class. One of them she knew practically lived on Facebook. A boy called Arthur Darling's mother, Rebecca, who was also a member of the PTA and a general busybody. With frantic fingers, Lily messaged both of them, briefly explaining the situation and asking if they had contact numbers or addresses for any of the girls in Greg's class. Her heart thrummed while she waited, but she didn't have to wait long. After a minute, Rebecca replied saying she had Mrs Chatterjee's address. It was a long, probing message. Lily ignored the woman's questions.

Heart erratic, she drove to the Chatterjees' house.

Chapter 34

LOVE

Age 16

July 1997

'Quick now, girls,' their mother said.

Each of them held a bag stuffed with as much as it would carry.

'Farewell, old Mr Cara,' Peace said. Mr Cara was what she used to call the caravan when she was learning to talk.

Love feigned a smile at her sister and followed them out into the farmyard. The night was lit by a globe of silver moon, the air tinged with the scent of the roast chicken dinner from Hope's baby ceremony. It had been a magical evening full of fun and laughter. Uncle Saviour had given a short, heart-warming speech to kick off the night's festivities, and then everyone had let down their hair, danced and drunk and had a brilliant time. Uncle Saviour had lifted her into the air in the middle of the hall and she'd thrown her head back and screamed with abandon, not caring about Peace's look of bewilderment. Peace could look on and rethink her conversation with Love all evening for all she cared. It didn't matter. She was still going through with the plan, wasn't she?

She was tipsy from downing half a bottle of elderberry wine. It tasted disgusting, but she might need a little extra courage for what was to come next.

'I can't believe we're finally leaving,' Peace squealed.

Finally? Love frowned at the back of her sister's head. Imagined stabbing it with a needle. How long had she and Mother wanted to leave Eternal Life? A lot longer than she'd thought by the sound of it.

'Shush, Peace,' Mother whispered.

Love looked askance at her mother. She felt nothing but disappointment and anger. No love. Had there ever been love between them? What she felt for Saviour was love, but she didn't think she'd ever felt anything like that for her mother. Certainly not for Peace. Was that weird? She supposed it was, but had never really considered it before. One thing was for certain though: she didn't like the idea of Mother leaving Eternal Life, which had to mean something.

'Stop!' Peace said, freezing and holding up her hand.

Mother froze and Love copied. Up ahead, Nobility was sitting on a deckchair outside his caravan. Love could hear her sister's and mother's panicky breathing. Smell their fear. She grinned. Perhaps she hadn't needed a helping hand after all. Maybe fate was on her side.

'It's OK,' Peace whispered, 'he's asleep. This way.'

She scurried forward and they followed.

'Are Faith and Zeal meeting us at the van?' Love said.

Her mother nodded and slipped her hand into Love's, giving her the widest smile she had in years. Tears glistened in her eyes. 'I love you, Love. I know I don't show it enough, but I do. I really do.'

Love felt something move inside her, just for a split second, and then it was gone. On robot mode, she echoed the sentiment, 'I love you too, Mother.'

Hand in hand, they hurried in between the caravans and ran the final fifty yards to the van. Mother glanced back at the farm, clenched her jaw, and turned back to face the vehicle. She raised her hand and waved a key at the girls. 'Faith and Zeal should be here any second. Then we're off and we can say *sayonara* to this terrible place.'

The night was hot and still, the air soundless. Peace exhaled a whoosh of relief, and Mother smiled at her. A second later, a squealing noise came from the back of the vehicle. It sounded as though someone was scraping their fingernails across metal.

Mother and Peace recoiled as if struck. Fear stained the air. They looked around, frantically trying to locate the source of the strange sound.

Fervour stepped out from behind the van. Love smiled; he was playing his role. They couldn't leave now, not with him obstructing their escape. She snuck a glance at her sister and swallowed the urge to giggle at the shock on Peace's face.

Leaning casually against the driver's door, he wolf-whistled at their mother. Peace gasped and shrank back, stepping on Love's foot. Love tried not to grimace when her sister slipped her hand into hers. Her mother's grip tightened on her other hand.

'Looking mighty fine tonight, Charity,' Fervour said, raking his eyes up and down her mother's body, which was mostly hidden by the dark.

'Where's Faith? What have you done to her?' Mother said. Her voice was steady, but Love could feel her hand trembling.

'In bed, fast asleep,' he stepped away from the van, 'being a good girl like I told her to.'

'Is she OK?'

Fervour raised his eyebrows, all innocence. 'Why wouldn't she be?'

'Because you're an evil dickhead who likes to beat on women, that's why,' Peace said.

He clutched his chest and said, 'Such hurtful words. Such lies. You ought to wash her mouth out with soap, Charity.'

'She's not lying and you know it.'

Fervour shrugged. 'Whatever. Now, be a good girl and hand over that key and I'll pretend none of this ever happened. It'll be our little secret.' He held out his hand and closed the last couple of feet between them.

'Saviour doesn't know?' Mother said.

'And he doesn't have to. Not if you give me the key now.'

'What's stopping you from telling him?' Love said, playing her part.

Fervour looked at her. She saw a flash of surprise in his eyes that he concealed with a smirk. 'A favour for a favour, isn't that how the saying goes?' His eyes lingered on her mother's breasts, and she felt disgust and anger ripple through her. He'd better be play-acting. Her mother wasn't a sex toy for him to use whenever he felt like it.

'Get out of the way, Fervour. I don't care if you tell Saviour. He can hunt us down for all I care, but we're leaving tonight and you're not going to stop us,' Mother said.

Love was surprised by her mother's courage. For a second, she almost admired her, then she remembered her betrayal and how much Uncle Saviour had done for her – for all of them.

Fervour stood his ground. He held out his hand and tutted. 'Cut the shit, Charity. You're not leaving. Not now, not ever. Give me the key. Now. Before I lose my patience.'

'Get out of the way,' Peace said. 'There are three of us and just one of you. We might be women, but together we're strong.' It was the cheesiest thing she'd ever said. Love stifled a laugh.

Fervour sighed long and low as if he was the weariest, most put-upon man in the world. 'You asked for it.'

He lashed out with both hands and grabbed Mother's throat. Peace launched herself at him, battering her small fists into his back. He didn't seem to notice and threw her off with ease.

'Love! Do something!' Peace screamed, scrambling to her feet.

Love gave him a feeble push as he manoeuvred her mother into a headlock. Despite the poor light, she could see Mother struggling to breathe. Peace leaped onto Fervour and wrapped her arms around his throat; and he threw his head back, smashing his cranium into her nose. She gasped and fell to the ground, clutching her face.

Fervour snatched the key out of her mother's hand and let her go. She staggered backwards, grasping at her throat. Love thought it was all over, but Mother barrelled into him with a roar of pure rage, knocking him back. He almost fell, but managed to right himself. With a noise that sounded more animal than human, he lunged forward, grabbed her arm, and threw her into the side of the van. The impact of her body left an indent in the metal and she fell to the ground. Fervour strode forward and grabbed a fistful of her hair. Love darted forward; suddenly afraid he was going to kill her. 'Stop! That's enough.'

Fervour twisted around to look at her. 'I'm not sure your mother's learned her lesson yet.'

Peace screamed as Fervour knelt down beside their semi-conscious mother, rolled her limp body over, and positioned the bottom half of her leg over his knees. He looked up at Love and Peace, smiled, and placed one hand on the back of her ankle and one hand above the back of her knee.

'Don't,' Peace begged. She began to cry. Sobs wheezed out of her and she sank to her knees and buried her face in her hands.

Love shook her head. She didn't want this. He was taking it too far.

But she couldn't say anything to stop him, because her sister and mother couldn't know the part she'd played. They had to trust her. She wanted to lead them all one day, to save them, and saving everyone depended on earning their trust, so she said nothing and sank to her knees on the dry grass beside her sister.

Fervour's mouth stretched into a smile. Love knew he had made up his mind to teach Mother a lesson she would never forget.

With a gentle sigh, Fervour snapped their mother's leg in two.

The scream could be heard for miles.

People came out of their caravans to investigate the source of the scream. Fervour told them to go back to sleep, that Charity had had an accident.

Once everyone's curiosity had been satisfied, he drove their mother to the hospital and Love helped Peace back to the caravan where she tucked her into bed and whispered what she thought were soothing words. When Peace had cried herself to sleep, Love left the caravan and walked across the yard to Uncle Saviour's farmhouse.

As always, the door was unlocked. She mounted the stairs, stripping her clothes as she went, shedding her baby skin like a snake, her chrysalis like a butterfly.

At the bedroom door, she knocked twice. When there was no answer, she entered the room. The room was pitch black. The air smelt of him. Of purity itself.

Naked to the waist, she crawled up the bed and pulled back the sheet from his hot, damp body.

The lamp came on, making his face glow. He didn't look at all surprised. With a lazy smile that made her groin tingle, he seized the back of her neck and pulled her on top of him.

Love couldn't sleep. Her body tingled with pleasure and her mind ran in circles. The sex had not lasted long, but the sensations Uncle Saviour had given her still vibrated through her groin, making her smile like the cat with the cream.

Beside her lay her lover.

Uncle Saviour.

The purest man on earth. The only man who could help her attain eternal life.

She stared at the rise and fall of his hairy chest, watched the rhythmic flare of his nostrils. Semen glistened on his abdomen like a slug's slime, disgusting but strangely exciting. He had pulled out at the last moment and sprayed himself all over her stomach. He'd wiped her clean, but she still felt him on her, a slight stickiness below her belly button.

Love thought about the blood in his veins, the child's blood. He'd told her he gave the girl sleeping pills to help her sleep, but had not said where he kept her. Where was the little girl? The house had more bedrooms. Five or six. Not many to search until she found what she craved. For she did crave it, suddenly and absolutely. It was as if losing her virginity had opened a hunger inside her, a hunger to become the very best, purest version of herself that she could.

Visions too blissful to imagine danced behind her eyes as she pictured pure blood mixing with hers and visualised her organs glowing gold as the blood of the innocent filled her with the purity she needed to reach Total Illumination.

Smiling, Love slid off the bed and pulled on her dress to hide her nakedness. The moon slipped through the curtains, casting her shadow on the wall. Her head swelled large and black. She shivered with anticipation and crept out of the room. She didn't want to wake Saviour.

The floor creaked as Love tiptoed to the room opposite Saviour's. It was empty. Swallowing disappointment, she tried the next room and the next and the next. No luck. There was one more bedroom to try. Staring at the door, she wiped sweat from her palms onto her dress. A key stuck out of the lock. It was a sign. The child was in there. She could feel the girl's innocence and purity buzzing in the air like a swarm.

Love hovered outside the room, savouring the moment. But she could not wait another second; her body hummed, chest quivering as she twisted the key, unlocked the door, and crept into the room.

A lamp beside the bed made the little girl's face glow. She was a pretty child with long blonde hair and delicate features. Doll-like. Her eyes were closed, lips parted. A white sheet covered her small body. Her chest rose and fell with every other second. She looked relaxed, content. A pink teddy bear lay on the bed, its head resting on her shoulder.

Darkness pervaded the room, but lamplight held it off, making the angelic creature on the bed shine like a star in the night. A guiding light. One that would provide her with what she wanted most: the chance to live for ever.

With clammy fingers, Love peeled back the bedsheet to expose the girl's thigh. There were two tiny cuts there now. One had scabbed over, but the other looked fresh.

Love knelt beside the bed and gently peeled the scab off and flicked it away. Blood beaded to the surface of the girl's milky skin. The child frowned and gave a small moan, but did not wake. Relieved, Love placed her fingers either side of the bead of blood and gave a gentle squeeze. More blood

188

came, vibrant and pure. Pleasure sizzled in her chest and she lowered her lips to the scarlet nectar and dipped the tip of her tongue into the small pool of blood. The taste was not unpleasant; it was rich and metallic and full of life. Exactly as she'd imagined.

The child moaned, but remained asleep. Love smiled and tasted the blood again. Already she could feel its magic invigorating her body like rain on a dying rose. The sensation was truly exquisite. Finally, she felt she was alive, and Saviour had made that happen.

She kissed the child's cut a few times to catch all of the blood. When the blood no longer wept from the wound, she covered the girl with the sheet.

For a while, Love stood beside the bed and focused on the energy flooding her veins. It was remarkable, and Saviour had been keeping this to himself. She frowned, tilted her head, and stared intently at the little girl's pale neck. Beneath that layer of milk-white skin ran a vein filled with blood. Lots of blood. One stab and that scarlet nectar would flow from its source like lava from a volcano.

Swallowing, Love licked her lips and pressed a hand to her racing heart. She pictured herself going downstairs into the kitchen, selecting the sharpest knife and, returning to this room, to the child. She let the fantasy play out; imagined the gush of blood, the rush she would experience when she lapped up the blood and purity infiltrated her body by the bucket-load.

Entranced by the idea of speeding up her journey to Total Illumination, she turned to fetch a knife and stopped short as a fact splintered her plan: such a cut would kill the child. Saviour would not be happy. She didn't want to displease him.

Still, she hovered by the bed, staring at the girl's neck, hungering for more. She felt torn; desperate to achieve her goal, to live for ever – but, according to Uncle Saviour, she would reach Total Illumination if she took the child's blood in small doses across time, just as he did.

It was a hard decision to make.

Take all of the blood now, or eke it out over time. Displease Saviour, or remain his favourite.

Why was life so full of decisions?

She tried to imagine his reaction when he found the girl dead and drained of pure blood. He'd know it was her. He'd look at her and shake his head. Disappointment would mist his eyes and she'd lose everything she'd worked for these last few years. Someone else would become his lover and that person would rise to become queen bee of Eternal Life. The very thought brought bile to her throat. Her decision was made.

Ignoring the burning desire to open the girl's jugular, she turned from the bed and left the room. The key clicked as she locked the door.

She lingered for a few seconds, nodded, then walked away, head high, proud of herself for making such a sensible decision. Draining the girl would have been rash. The sort of thing virgin Love would have done. But she wasn't a virgin any more. She was an adult – a princess of sorts – and soon she would be queen.

With a secretive smile, Love returned to Saviour's bedroom and slid into his bed.

Chapter 35

LILY

Now

The Chatterjees were as helpful as possible, but Fatima knew nothing that could help Lily find Hannah and Greg.

She slid back into the Mini and rested her head on the steering wheel. The exchange between her, John and Juliet cycled around and around her mind leaving a trail of thorns and poison. She could remember little of what was said, only snapshots of John's and Juliet's lying faces, the way they'd stood so close together, the horror in their eyes when she'd caught them, and the horrific pounding in her chest as her blood pressure soared and all of her fears became real. John had destroyed their relationship. There was no going back from this, not for her, not ever. He didn't deserve her forgiveness and he'd never get it. She thought forward to what would happen after this, to their family, and an ominous tunnel loomed large and oppressive.

She retched into the glove compartment, bringing up a string of bile. Shivering with rage and grief, Lily dried her mouth on her T-shirt and told herself to shut down all emotion related to John. Hannah and Greg needed her. They were everything. John was nothing. He could rot in hell for all she cared.

She knew she was lying to herself. Her heart felt like it had been cleaved apart, but she forced the wrenching pain away. Exhaling shakily, she yanked at the rear-view mirror and stared at her face. The shadows under her eyes were deep. Veins spiked the whites of her eyeballs. Her eyelids were puffed up and swollen from crying. Self-pity throbbed in her chest. She stamped down on it; there was no time for that. Hannah and Greg were all that mattered. She had to pull herself together and find them. Terror sliced at her nerves as she got out of the car and ran up the gravel drive of 9 Dew Drop Lane.

A teenage girl answered the door, a Keira Knightley look-alike dressed in skimpy silk pyjamas. She barely looked up from her phone. 'Yeah?'

'I'm Mrs Woods. My son's missing. He's in Jessica's class. Can I come in?'

'Sure.' The teenager backed out of the way. Without glancing up from her phone, she said, 'Mum! It's for you!' then ran up the stairs leaving Lily standing in the hallway.

A little girl who was the miniature image of her sister appeared at the top of the stairs.

'Jessica? Hi. I'm Mrs Woods. I've come to speak to you about Gregory. He's my son. I know you're in the same class and I wondered—'

Mrs Smithy appeared in dirty dungarees and gardening gloves. A twig was stuck in her hair. She pulled off her gloves and smiled. 'I'm Jo. How can I help?'

Lily explained as quickly as she could. The woman said that the police had paid them a visit about an hour ago, but Lily begged. Jo gave in quickly and told her daughter to answer Lily's questions. Jessica ran down the stairs and perched on the bottom step.

'Greg gave me a love letter, yeah, but I never writ him back.'

'Wrote,' her mother corrected.

'I have a boyfriend. I don't need another one. One's plenty.'

'Have you ever seen Greg exchanging notes with anyone else?'

'Nope. Not even with Aurora, and she's his best friend.'

Lily sighed and dragged a hand through her hair. Dizziness made her sway. She hadn't eaten anything since the previous night, but it was more than that. Withdrawal was wreaking havoc with her brain.

Jo Smithy's concern was touching. She helped Lily into her living room and sat her down on a squishy sofa packed with cushions. 'Wait there a second. I'll get you a glass of water.'

'What's wrong?' Jessica said, stroking her arm.

'I'm just tired.'

'Tired and worried about her son,' Jo said, returning with water and a pack of Hobnobs. 'I wish there was something we could do.'

Lily tried a biscuit. It tasted like chalk. She downed the glass of water, hand shaking. 'There is one thing you might be able to help me with.'

'What is it?'

'Do you have contact numbers or home addresses for these girls?' She showed Mrs Smithy the list on her phone.

'Yes! We invited all of the girls in Jess's class to her birthday party last year. Sent invites in the post. Hang on a minute. Let me grab my phone.'

Chapter 36
LOVE

Age 18

March 1999

Love chose March for its daffodils. She cared little for their six petal-like tepals and puckered trumpets, but liked what they suggested. In truth, their brightness and enduring popularity would help send an important message on this special day to hers and Saviour's flock: yellow represented light and hope, illumination and ambition. This shining colour conjured up the light of life in order to cancel out the darkness of death. In many people's minds, these showy little flowers were life-affirming and positive. Using them on her wedding day made sense. If the community thought of this transcendent colour when they thought of her, it might lessen their view of her as a cold fish, and imprint her in their limited brains as golden. Of course, it might not, but people's views had already shifted. Increasingly, they watched her with wary eyes that spoke of respect. They sensed her power over Saviour, her ability – in spite of her years – to sway his mind, coax him to her way of thinking. Some of the adults even feared her, which was good.

She smiled and adjusted her crown. The way the daffodils

partitioned the dark ivy pleased her a great deal. She also liked the contrast between her stark black hair and the yellow flower. Light versus dark versus light. It was perfect.

Mother had made the crown. Peace had contributed nothing to the wedding other than a dour expression.

Love glanced up. In the mirror, tears fell from Mother's eyes and dripped onto her white smock. Her mother now walked with a limp, but held her chin high – something Love could not help but admire her for. It was clear that Mother was frightened of Fervour, but she hid her fear well.

Love turned to her reflection and studied her dress. The garment was white for purity, embroidered with tiny yellow hearts – a nod to her name and a good way to reinforce the message of hope. The dress also boasted a corset that cinched in her waist and a full, dome-shaped skirt. Teacher Hope had made the wedding gown, and Love would be for ever thankful for the woman's skill with a needle and thread.

Everyone else was to wear their ceremonial smocks today. This was another crucial choice she'd made. To be a queen, you had to stand out. A leader didn't join ranks and blend in. Queen bee was greater and cleverer. She deserved recognition for her efforts, so she needed a magnificent dress.

She glanced back at the woman behind her. Mother was still crying. She didn't know if her mother was weeping out of happiness or sorrow, but she didn't really care. She was going to marry Saviour today, and she was going to do it with a smile on her face.

Love applied a deep red lipstick to her lips and met Charity's eye in the mirror. 'How do I look?'

Her mother ignored the question and gazed into her eyes. 'Are you sure about this?'

'About what?'

'Marrying him.'

'What, marrying the purest man on earth? Hmm, let me think . . . yes. I'm sure. I'm more than sure. I'm ecstatic.'

She watched her mother's eyes die, and felt a strange sort of delight. Charity was weak, but she was strong. She was going to lead the community on their journey to Total Illumination, and she was going to be worshipped for doing so. In contrast, her ineffectual mother would slip back into the shadows where she belonged. She'd do as she was told, no more, no less. Some people were made for great things. Her mother wasn't. But, as Saviour said, it was useful to keep your doubters close.

She rose from her chair and performed a spin. In a hard voice, she said, 'How do I look?'

Charity's chin wobbled, but she smiled. 'You look beautiful.'

Love knew she did. She looked stunning, the best she'd ever looked. She couldn't wait to see everyone's reactions. Saviour's jaw would drop; the other men's too – especially when they saw her cleavage – and the women would look on with false smiles and hearts that griped with envy.

With a happy sigh, she led her mother out of the room, down the landing and the stairs, out into the courtyard where a yellow ribbon of silk created a meandering path across the farm to the barn. She'd chosen the barn for her ceremony because it held such fond memories. She'd seen the first blood-birthing there, imagined her first sip of human nectar beneath those rickety wooden rafters.

Everyone waited for them inside the barn. Mother was to be her only attendant as she made her way along the yellow silk path.

On either side of the path lay clusters of daffodil heads, their yellow sprays wide open like screaming mouths. Above her head, the sun glistened gold in a pure, cornflower sky. A cold breeze plucked at her skin and cooled her flushed cheeks. Charity walked behind her, checking that the train of her dress remained free-flowing. They did not talk now. The time for conversation was over. In truth, it had never really begun. But at least Mother was keen to please. Since her attempt to leave the farm, she'd been more helpful and agreeable. Just the way she should be.

Feeling like a queen, Love entered the barn. She smiled and paused a moment, allowing everyone to drink in her beauty and all that she promised. Hers and Saviour's eyes locked and he trailed his gaze up and down her body, eyes wide with delight. Fervour stood beside Saviour holding a bird's nest, upon which lay her wedding ring.

Love glided through the centre of her flock, who all raised their heads to watch her. They had been kneeling for a long time now and must have been cold in nothing more than their thin smocks, but not a frown could be seen. Everyone, it seemed, was happy for them. But where was Peace?

Love looked over her shoulder at Charity and hissed, 'She's not here. Where is she?'

Peace was supposed to be at the front with Saviour and Fervour. Love had decided to have her sister pass her the wedding ring. Force Peace to witness her triumph up close and personal. Maybe if she finally accepted that Love was better than her, she'd fall in line and become a useful member of the community.

But Peace was missing.

Rage like no other flooded her body, blinding her, turning her mind black. She saw herself in her wedding dress dragging Peace by her hair to the well in the woods, grabbing her neck, throttling the life out of her impudent body, then pushing her into the dark stinking cavity.

'Here,' her mother said, 'she's here.'

Every eye turned to the barn entrance. Peace stood there

in her white smock, a stupid smile on her face. 'Oops. Sorry I'm late everybody!'

Peace was drunk. She swayed, hiccuped, burped, and made her way down the aisle, shuffling past Love, who had to use every ounce of self-control not to strangle her.

People watched in horror as Peace planted a kiss on Saviour's cheek, then turned and curtsied to Love.

A child giggled. No one else moved. Saviour leaned over to Peace and whispered something in her ear, something that wiped the drunken smile off her sister's ugly face.

Love felt she could breathe again. The atmosphere relaxed and a gentle breeze lifted her hair and tickled her neck. With a wide smile, she completed her bridal walk and joined hands with Saviour at the altar.

Nobility cleared his throat and the ceremony began.

Love thought about asking Saviour what he'd said to Peace, but decided that, in the end, it didn't matter. All that mattered was that her sister was in her lesser place, and that she was about to become queen of Eternal Life.

Chapter 37

PEARLINE

Now

Luck, it seemed, was on their side. Mike Gibson hadn't been lying. They found the mask under the sofa bed in Foe's house, just as Gibson had said they would. It was now in the lab for testing.

Clearing her throat, Pearline beckoned Dibbs and DS Cusp over, pulled up two chairs, and slid a photograph of the mask into the centre of the desk. It stared up at them with vacant eyes and they stared back with tired, haunted ones. The mask was designed to cover the whole of the wearer's face with holes cut in for the eyes and nostrils. A jester-like pattern split the mask into four diamonds: the right eye surrounded by a crimson diamond, the left by a black one, and the spaces between filled with gold diamonds. Creepy, to say the least.

'This mask – why?' she said.

'It's a Venetian mask,' Cusp said. He was new to the team, twenty-eight, bright-eyed, keen to impress.

'I know what it is,' Pearline said, 'just not the reasons for it or behind it.'

Cusp leaned in for a closer look. Dibbs did too, bringing with him a manly smell she liked more than she cared to admit.

'I've been there. To Venice. When I was in my twenties,' she said. 'They sell them everywhere.'

'What's their history, symbolism et cetera?' Cusp said.

'I don't know. That's what I want you to look into in a minute, but first, let's say the person who killed Rudge was wearing this mask. Why would he or she be wearing it?'

'For fun. Fancy dress party. Heard a commotion, came outside to have a look,' Dibbs said.

'To hide. They knew they were going to commit a crime and needed a mask, just in case they were seen, or,' Cusp said, 'it could be ritualistic.'

'Yes,' Pearline said. This idea had occurred to her so she was glad it had occurred to Cusp as well. She'd heard of masks being worn during rituals. Certain tribes wore masks. Satanists too. She called Hill over.

'Cusp, take this picture,' she handed him the photograph of the mask, 'find out everything you can about this sort of mask – it's origins, the works. See if any mask-wearing satanists or the like have been practising their art in the county recently. Dibbs, keep running the letter. Hill, as a starter for ten, get a list together of every identical Venetian mask sold, borrowed or stolen in the last year, then try to trace every purchase.'

The mask, just like the letter, provided a priority line of enquiry. It might be nothing more than a costume piece as Dibbs suggested, but the level of violence involved made her think something more sinister might be at play. And there was, she thought with a shiver, a certain insidiousness about masks. Whenever she thought about masks, she pictured the killer from the horror film *Scream* or the cannibal from *The Silence of the Lambs*. Her references might have sprung from fiction, but when it boiled down to the limescale, masks were bloody creepy and they usually meant bad news.

Pearline sat at her desk. Now that all of the fast-track options were in place, writing out a list of theories around what could have happened, covering everything that could possibly have occurred was the next step.

She shifted in her chair and scratched her neck, pinched the skin between her eyebrows.

When she'd finished scribbling like a maniac, she read what she'd written. Circled three words that seemed important. MASK. SCYTHE. COLLABORATORS. Two 'unknowns' were involved and they were collaborators. One of them – if Gibson's story was solid and she believed it was – was a tall individual who'd used a scythe to kill Connor Rudge. The other 'unknown' was involved but not the killer. According to Gibson, the children had left Grimstone Woods with the smaller unknown individual at approximately 2.30 a.m. They had exited onto Birch Close, and to all intents and purposes vanished into thin air.

Where did they go from there? What were they doing now? Everything, of course, depended on the kidnapper's intentions, but she listed possible answers.

1. Walked the children to someone's/the unknown's house in Birch Close or nearby
2. Drove them further afield to an unknown location
3. Are still driving them to a further location
4. Doubled-back into the woods – UNLIKELY – we would have found them by now
5. Killed them and fled

Pearline nibbled the end of her pen. Two unknowns had come into contact with the children in the woods, and Gibson

201

had seen Hannah and Gregory leaving with one of them. The fact that the kids had not turned up suggested two likely conclusions. One: they had been kidnapped. Two: they had been killed.

This also meant that in all likelihood, Hannah and Gregory Woods had been taken by a murderer. According to Gibson, the two unknowns were together. She thought about updating the Guvnor in person, but decided to send another email instead. Detective Chief Superintendent Patrick Dent was an arsehole. Talking to him would only slow things down.

She sighed. Reread the list. Ran through the case. Graded the list on the most likely scenario to the least likely. She sighed again, trying to lessen the pressure in her chest.

A shadow fell on her desk and she looked up. Without a word, Dibbs took hold of her hand, uncurled her fingers one by one, and placed a Wagon Wheel on her palm. 'Eat.'

'Wagon Wheel? Really?'

He always kept a stash of something unhealthy in his desk. She knew he was particularly fond of peppermint creams. Wagon Wheels were a new one. If she ate like that every day she'd be obese, but Dibbs was one of those lucky buggers with the metabolism of a racehorse – and the muscle definition to match.

He half smiled. 'Sugar's good for the soul. Eat.'

She raised an eyebrow, expecting him to leave, but he tapped his foot. Reluctantly, she unwrapped the wheel and took a bite. 'Satisfied?'

'All of it. You look as washed out as an old cloth.'

She snorted but took another bite, surprised to find the pressure in her chest easing, the sugar working magic in her veins.

'Good,' he said. With a small smile, he walked back to his desk.

She rolled her eyes at the fluttering sensation in her

stomach, finished the ludicrously sweet snack, then updated the team.

The press still knew very little, but they were beating at the door, so-to-speak. Soon, she would need to make a statement about the two murders and the missing children, but would put it off for as long as possible.

DS Cusp appeared at her desk looking worried. She raised an eyebrow.

'As you said, I've widened the field of enquiry and looked outside Dorset at related cases that have taken place in the last five years. So far, I've found two reports that may be of interest. None mention masks though.'

'Send the reports to me, then dig deeper. Go back another five years.'

Cusp nodded and ran back to his desk. She'd never seen him so animated and wondered when she'd lost that youthful kind of energy. A long time ago. Longer than she cared to admit. Before she'd failed Isabelle Hart, that was for sure.

Giving herself a mental kick, she rang Lily Woods's mobile. Fielding had said that Mrs Woods would prefer a call to a meeting, which was good because it saved time.

Lily Woods answered before the second ring.

'Hello?'

'Mrs Woods?'

'Yes. Who is it? I'm busy.'

'It's Chief Inspector Pearline Ottoline. I'm leading the investigation into your children's disappearance. I'm sorry we haven't spoken before now. Are you at home?'

'No. I'm trying to find out who wrote the letter that made my children leave home at two in the morning.'

'It would be best if you stayed at home with your husband, just in case—'

'In case what? Hannah and Greg stroll in and ask for ham sandwiches?'

'I know it's unlikely they'll just turn up but—'

'Have you seen the letter?' the woman said.

'Yes. And we're looking into it.'

'So you don't know who wrote it yet?'

'No, we're trying to discover who wrote the letter.'

'Look, I think I can help. I need to. If I talk to every girl in Greg's class, I'll be able to find out who sent it to him.'

'OK, but I want to assure you we're doing all we can to find Hannah and Gregory. It really would be most helpful if you stayed at home. We're taking the letter seriously and—'

'But Aurora didn't write it. I've already asked her. It has to be one of the other girls in his class. Not Fatima Chatterjee or Jessica Smithy – I've already spoken to them. I'm on my way to Clara Richards' house now.'

'Mrs Woods, please listen to me. This is a police investigation. You can't go around people's houses interrogating them. You need to go home. Let us do our job. I know this is a terribly stressful situation, but I promise you we're doing everything we can to find Hannah and Gregory.'

Lily Woods went silent. Pearline thought for a moment she'd lost her, then the woman said, 'I'm sorry, Inspector Ottoline, but I can't. I have to do something.' She hung up.

Christ. Pearline stared in disbelief at her mobile, and wondered if the woman was unstable. Either way, Lily Woods was playing cop, which was going to end badly.

Chapter 38

LILY

Now

Lily threw her phone onto the passenger seat. Part of her knew DI Ottoline was right: she ought to be at home with John, waiting just in case Hannah and Greg came back. But she couldn't do that. The police cared about finding her children, of course they did, but they didn't care as much as she did. They wouldn't be willing to break the law to find out the truth. To the police, her kids were strangers. They wouldn't be willing – or able – to do whatever it took. But she would.

Her thoughts strayed to John and her knuckles turned white on the steering wheel. For the hundredth time, she shut him down. Locked him away. Hannah and Greg were all that mattered. John meant nothing.

Lily slowed the car to a stop and blinked away a daydream of killing a hooded stranger with her bare hands.

Clara Richards lived on the outskirts of Grimstone in a beautiful thatched cottage at the very end of Waterfall Lane. Lily stared at the house, readying herself to interrogate another unsuspecting child.

Doubts pushed forward, but she pushed them back and told herself that the inspector was wrong. There was no stopping now. Every girl in Greg's class had to be questioned. If that didn't provide answers, she'd go around every house in Grimstone, starting in Birch Close, and bang on every door. Sneak around the back and break into people's houses if she had to. There was no way she was going home and sitting idle when her children were out there. She didn't care if the police prosecuted her for interfering. Hannah and Greg were all that mattered. To hell with John and Juliet. To hell with the police.

Her phone beeped. It was another text from John. *Where are you? I'm worried. Please call.* He'd tried to ring twice. Sent five texts. She'd ignored both calls and hadn't replied to any of his messages.

A shiver crisscrossed her shoulders and she pressed her hand to her breast. It felt like her heart was trying to pummel its way out. She pictured it, bloody and raw with tendril-like arms and hideous blood-red fists pounding and pounding and pounding against her chest. Her mouth went dry and a sour taste coated her tongue. Grabbing a half-empty bottle of Evian, she downed its stale contents. On wobbly legs, she got out of the car and hurried up to the thatched cottage.

Clara answered the door. Lily recognised her instantly. She was the only overweight girl in Greg's class.

'Hello?'

'Hi, I'm Gregory Woods's mum. Can I come in please?'

Clara nodded and stood back so Lily could enter the cottage. Lily wondered where her parents were and thought how strange it was that they would let their seven-year-old daughter answer their front door alone, but the moment she reached the hallway, she became aware of a rhythmic banging coming from the room above.

The girl followed her gaze. 'Mummy and Daddy are

wrestling. They always wrestle on Saturdays. They'll be down soon. They don't wrestle for long.'

Feeling sick, Lily smiled at the girl, then followed her into a small, dark lounge. An unpleasant charity shop smell lingered in the air. Clara knelt beside the coffee table and proceeded to line up her My Little Ponies in a neat row. Every now and then she reached over to a pink bowl and plucked out a few chocolate buttons.

'It's actually you that I need to speak to,' Lily said. She could still hear Clara's parents upstairs. She heard the woman cry out, wondered if she was climaxing. Grimaced.

Clara looked at her. She had such sweet, innocent eyes. Innocent like Greg's. And Hannah's. Untouched by evil – until now.

'Did you write a letter to Greg?'

Clara ate more chocolate buttons. 'No. No one in my class likes him except for Aurora. And Mrs Edwards and Miss Mills. The boys bully him and the girls think he's weird.'

Lily let the sharp pain in her chest fade before saying, 'Are you sure? No one passed him a note? Not even a nasty note?'

'No.'

Footsteps thundered down the stairs. A flustered woman with a sex flush appeared in the doorway.

'What are you doing in my house?' she panted. In the next breath she screamed, 'Ryan!'

More footsteps hit the stairs.

'It's OK, Mummy. It's Gregory's mummy.'

'I'm sorry,' Lily said as a huge, red-faced man appeared. 'Clara answered the door and you two were busy . . .'

The man cleared his throat and lifted his chin. 'What do you want?'

'My children are missing. I wanted to see if Clara had seen them.'

'Have you?' the parents said as one, looking at their daughter.

Clara shook her head and returned her attention to the last few chocolate buttons.

'There you have it,' the woman said coldly. 'I'll see you out.'

She slammed the door at Lily's back. Lily stared through flooded eyes at her car, gave herself a mental shake, and hurried away from the cottage. For some reason she'd thought such a pretty home would house lovely people. What a stupid thing to think. You couldn't judge a book by its cover and you certainly couldn't judge a person by their house.

Chapter 39
LOVE

Age 21

May 2002

The weekly meeting took place in Uncle Saviour's living room and began promptly at four in the afternoon. Love had tried to liven up the achromatic room with a few colourful throws and cushions, but it still needed work. She loved white for the purity and innocence it represented, but colour was life, a mantra that she tried to reflect in her clothes. Today she wore a yellow cotton dress, a grass-green cardigan she'd knitted herself, and a beetroot-dipped hairband – a rare gift from her mother.

A large table dominated the left half of the vacuous space offering ample room for the five most-trusted community members. The room smelt of the four freshly baked apple muffins in the centre of the table. Love had already eaten hers.

'She's not adapted yet. She needs more time,' Charity said.

Fervour snorted and Nobility rolled his eyes to the ceiling.

'More time? She's been here for five years, Mother. She stopped giving a whole year ago. How much more time do you think she needs?' Love looked at her mother. She had aged a lot in the last few years. Grey streaked her hair and deep wrinkles lined her forehead.

'I agree,' Uncle Saviour said, placing his hand on Love's ripe belly, 'we've invested enough time and energy. It's time to let her go.'

'I'm afraid of what will happen to her,' Charity said, focusing on Love more than anyone else. 'She's just a child. A sad, confused little girl. If we—'

'She'll have to find her way,' Fervour said.

Mother looked down at the table. She could never look him in the eye. Not since that night. She and Faith never spoke any more either, a fact that pleased Love. Faith was dangerous. She was unhappy because of her situation with Fervour and that unhappiness had rubbed off on her mother. To try to instil contentment in Faith, Love had told Fervour that if she ever saw a bruise on Faith again, she would tell Saviour about his attempted rape of Devotion. As far as she knew, he'd never laid another hand on her, but the woman still moped around the farm like a lost lamb. Sometimes Love felt like slapping her herself, but she wouldn't. She wanted to help her husband maintain a harmonious, happy community in which its members felt safe and loved. Any kind of discord would ruin that balance and affect everyone's chance of reaching Total Illumination and gaining eternal life. That was why it was essential to let the eleven-year-old giver go.

Saviour shook his head. His gaze bored deep into her mother. 'Charity, listen to me carefully. Last night, she tried to run away. It's not the first time she's done that. She's unhappy here and she's not pure any more. We've tried to teach her our ways and show her what's possible, but the girl simply can't adapt. She won't allow herself to embrace us, which leaves us with one option. Release her.'

'How? Where?'

Nobility caught Saviour's eye. Saviour said, 'That's none of your concern. Just know that we will deposit her in a location far enough away from here that no one will link her to us.'

Love nodded and placed her hand over her mother's. It was ice-cold. 'Yes, Mother. Don't worry. This really is for the best. Finally, she'll be at peace.'

Charity looked from Saviour to Nobility to Fervour. Her gaze landed on Love. Her eyes were bloodshot. Her lips quivered. Ripping her hand out from under Love's, she said, 'Nothing I say will make you change your minds, so what's the point? I know you're lying to me. You're not going to let her go. You're going to kill that little girl and dump her body far away from here. The sad thing is that you've convinced yourselves you're doing her a favour, but I'm telling you, what you're planning to do is the most impure thing you could. Killing her won't release her. It will release you from the responsibility of looking after her, nothing more, nothing less.'

Fervour's hands clenched. His jaw worked like a meat grinder.

Everyone's eyes were on Saviour. Love felt odd. Her mother had never spoken out like this. As if sensing her consternation, the baby in her womb kicked and punched like a demon.

'You're wrong,' Saviour said through gritted teeth. 'We're not going to kill her. I can't believe you could even think I'd allow something like that.'

Charity sniffed. 'Tell yourselves what you like. I know what you're going to do to that innocent little girl. A child who never chose to join us in the first place.'

'Mother—'

'And you,' her mother spat, stabbing a finger at Love's face, 'you're going to let it happen. You could put a stop to this, but you won't, will you?'

Love looked at Saviour. He looked as if he was about to cry. She herself felt about as close to crying as she'd ever been. She thought Mother had evolved, that she was totally loyal to the cause, but she had been mistaken. Charity was as bad as Peace. The last five years had clearly been a lie.

Saviour sighed. 'If you choose not to believe us, that's your failing, Charity. I'm very sorry you feel this way. I – *we* – have done everything in our power to bring you into the fold, and you repaying us like this makes me feel . . .'

'Sick,' Love said. She pushed herself up from the table. Her mother did the same.

Charity stared at Love. In a low, trembling voice, she said, 'I hope you find what you're looking for. I really do.'

Love opened her mouth to respond, but her mother turned and limped out of the room.

Love dashed after her. On the porch, she seized her arm. 'What the hell's wrong with you?'

Charity laughed. 'Me?'

'Yes, you. I thought you were on board. That you under-stood—'

Charity reached out, squeezed Love's hands and searched her eyes. 'Love, do you really believe you've found a way to live for ever? Do you really think that's possible?'

Love tore her hands away and stared at her mother, speechless, so angry she thought her skull might explode.

Charity looked past her, towards the meeting room. She lowered her voice and said, 'It's all a myth. A cruel,

212

dangerous myth designed to control us. People believe it because they're terrified of the idea of death. That's why you believe it, why I tried to believe it for a time – but drinking the blood of the innocent won't keep you alive. Nothing will. In the end, everyone dies. It's a part of life. A necessary part. If people didn't die, there would be too many of us in the world. We need to die so that others can live, don't you see that?'

'All I see is a weak, sick person who's too scared to open up her mind and embrace an extraordinary way of living,' Love spat.

Charity's eyes glazed over. A tear shivered on her lip. 'I feel sorry for you, I really do. And it's all my fault. If I hadn't brought us here all those years ago . . .'

'If you hadn't brought us here, life would be pointless. Because of Saviour, life has meaning. Why can't you understand that? Don't you want to live for ever?'

Charity laughed hollowly. 'And get older and older and more and more fragile until I can barely lift a finger?'

Love frowned. 'No. It won't work like that. Look at Saviour – he's old but he looks younger than he is. A lot younger, and he's so full of life. Pure blood does that.'

'And what about in fifty years' time? Sixty? Seventy? Do you truly believe children's blood can prevent old age?'

Love rolled her tongue around her gums. This was something she rarely considered. She found it a futile exercise. It irritated her that her mother was trying to stab holes in her logic; what right did she have to attack her beliefs?

'I think you need to leave,' she said.

To her surprise, her mother nodded. She met her eye and said, 'Yes. You're right. I think I do.'

Love watched her limp out of the house. Love didn't feel sad to see her go. Anger reddened her cheeks, but relief eased the tightness in her chest. Charity was weak. She'd always been weak. She'd never understood the benefit of pure blood. She never would.

She waited until her heartbeat slowed, then returned to the meeting room and sat in her chair.

'Ignore her, my love,' Saviour said, leaning across to stroke her cheek. 'We've tried everything we can to make her see sense. All we can do now is give her time to think. Let her come round to the idea.'

Love scowled.

Fervour shook his head. His legs jiggled restlessly. 'I know she's your blood, but she's not with us. She needs to go.'

Saviour glared at him. 'Don't. Blood is blood. Don't push your luck.'

'Sometimes I think he's right,' Love murmured.

'Shall we get back to business?' Nobility said.

They all nodded. Love was grateful to him for changing the topic. She couldn't lose herself to her emotions. If she allowed herself to go down that road, she would not be strong enough to take part in these meetings, let alone make the tough choices she'd need to make. And this meeting was extremely important. In a sense, the community would live or die by the decision they were about to make and its subsequent execution. There were already whisperings in nearby towns and villages about Eternal Life. Negative whisperings. Ignorance bred fear and fear bred rumour. Saviour had brought up the idea of spreading the word; welcoming more people into the fold, but Love thought it was a bad concept. A dangerous one. People needed to come of their own accord, free of preconceptions. The world was constructed of hypocrites and cynics, people too afraid to open their eyes, hearts and minds to alternative ways of life. Those consumed by fear were dangerous.

'We are agreed, then? Release the girl?' Nobility said.

'Yes. I'm happy to do it,' Fervour said. He was trying to hide his excitement, but it was clear in the wildness of his eyes.

'That's settled then,' Saviour said, banging his palm on the table. 'It needs to be quick and painless. Ideas?'

Fervour tilted his head to the side as if deep in thought. He licked his lips.

Love felt a sudden need to stop Fervour from releasing the girl. She trusted him about as far as she could throw him. Though she still held Devotion over his head and felt she could control him to a certain extent, what he did beyond her line of sight was something she couldn't control.

She rested her hand on her bump. Delivering another member into the fold would progress her standing within the community and move her so much closer to attaining eternal life. But for those positive effects to occur, the baby needed to survive. It needed to prosper. She had a recurring nightmare of Fervour creeping into her room and strangling the baby while she lay pinned to the bed by invisible manacles, unable to save the screaming infant. Fervour was useful at times, but he was a sadist. He would enjoy the process of releasing the giver, and that was wrong. There was no way he would ever become pure; he was too damaged. A tarnished penny could never be wiped clean.

She kept her thoughts to herself, however, and never spoke badly of him to Saviour. Her husband, she'd learned, was a complex man. She had to play him carefully, make him think her ideas had originated in his mind. If he ever suspected she was trying to tell him what to do, he became hostile and distant. Most of the time, he was loving and respectful – the perfect partner – but her miscarriages had hit him hard, and sometimes he sought comfort in the arms of other women

215

in the community. It hurt her a little, but he always came back to her, and she didn't think he'd strayed since this pregnancy had moved beyond the first trimester. Adultery was wrong, yes, but the pressure Saviour was under was immense. And besides, she wasn't queen bee yet. Of course, one day she would be, and when that day came, she wanted Saviour by her side.

One day she would be ready to lead, but she was not ready yet. She was still too emotional, too anchored by her own impurities. Over the last few years, the giver's blood had helped her gain purity, but she needed to be far purer to reach Total Illumination. Of course, even when she transcended to the final stage, she would continue to drink human nectar in order to sustain her transcendence. Saviour said that the attainment of Total Illumination inspired a unique feeling in the self; a feeling of glowing from the inside out; a radiant purity that, once achieved, could be felt and seen by all. She couldn't feel it yet. In time, if all went to plan, she would. She had to.

'I'll do it,' she said.

'But Saviour said—' Fervour spluttered, looking at her husband.

'A woman's touch will ease the process,' she said in a hard, cold voice.

'Are you sure?' Saviour said.

She nodded. Nobility looked relieved, Saviour impressed. 'Great. OK. Have you considered how?'

'Yes. And I'll do it tonight.'

'What?' Fervour said. His cheeks burned with anger. 'Shouldn't we discuss this?'

She wanted to laugh in his face.

Saviour placed his hand on Fervour's shoulder. 'If Love's decided on a method there's no need for a discussion. I trust her completely. Don't you?'

216

'Yeah, but what about the body?'

Ignoring Fervour's question, Love said, 'I'm going to have a lie down.' She gave him a bright smile and patted her bump. 'This one's doing the tango in here.'

Chapter 40
LILY

Now

Lily pulled up beside a row of council houses on Fir Road. After Sasha Brown she'd go to see Posie Gibson. Last stop would be Eve Remington.

She hurried up a gritted path to number 37, rapped her knuckles on the scarlet door and waited. No one answered. The windows were black and there was no car parked out front. Her heart sank.

She knocked again and an elderly woman with green hair peered over the garden fence.

In a voice worn to a crackle by years of smoking, the old woman said, 'They're away. Gone to Cornwall of all places.'

'When did they go?' Lily said.

'Hmm. Now let me see . . .'

Lily waited, fighting the desire to scream at the old woman to hurry up.

'I think it was yesterday evening. Oh yes! Yes, it was. I remember because I had to clean up a nasty little present one of their cats decided to deposit on my doorstep.'

'Do you know when they'll be back?'

The woman shrugged. 'Nope.'

'Do you have their mobile number by any chance?'

'Nah. I don't mingle with the likes of them. Good day to you.' She flapped her hand then disappeared inside her house.

Lily felt angry at the Browns for not being home. She knew she was being irrational, but couldn't stop the violent swirling of her thoughts. The shuddering sensation beneath her chest bone was getting worse.

Feeling increasingly desperate, Lily drove to Posie Gibson's house on Sycamore Drive.

Chapter 41

LOVE

Age 21

May 2002

The giver's hand felt pathetically small in Love's palm. She looked down at the girl's white-blonde hair and felt a strange kind of dread. But the most logical course of action was to release the child from her own warped feelings; it was impossible, after all, to let her out into the world. Having lived within the community's walls for several years, she would be like a tame animal released into the wild to fend for itself. She would ultimately flail, suffer, and die. Though the girl did not realise and though she had not accepted their ways, she would not be happy anywhere now. The child was in a grey zone; neither with Eternal Life nor with the impure people who roamed the land beyond the community. The girl was, in a sense, already dead.

But taking a life was a new action. The knowledge that the giver would never breathe again because of her was . . . destabilising. When she was sixteen, on the night she'd first tasted the child's blood, she'd considered killing the girl in order to reach Total Illumination more quickly, but back then she had been foolish and naïve. There were consequences to actions, repercussions that were hard to predict. She did not want to regret this action. She couldn't let anything muddy her mind, not when it came to this.

Love inhaled the fresh night air. The temperature was mild and pleasant, the earth scented with mildew.

The girl looked up and gave her a questioning look.

Love had told her that she was to be released, but that was all. The child had asked no questions. Indeed, the girl barely ever spoke. Her words had dried up a long time ago, just like the place Love was taking her to.

Dew kissed the grass. The light from her torch made the droplets of water glisten. The moon was a scalpel, the stars fireflies sparkling in an ocean-deep sky. Not long now and they would arrive at their destination and Love would be free of the ugly feeling twisting her chest. It felt like someone was inside her, jiggling her heart while standing on her lungs. Crushing and wobbling. It was a horrible sensation. She tried to name it and failed.

'When is your baby going to come?' the girl said suddenly in a small, flat voice. She stopped walking and inclined her head. A frown squeezed the ghostly skin between her eyebrows. Her cheeks were flushed, her white dress not as white as it once was.

Love considered ignoring the question, but not many people had shown an interest in her pregnancy. Not many of the women liked her. They respected her, yes, but they didn't like her. She lacked Saviour's natural warmth and contagious personality. Last year, she'd overheard Virtue say to the other young women that she was a cold fish, and that she could not understand why Saviour had chosen Love for his wife. Far from upsetting her, Virtue's criticism confirmed what she'd always known; she was a cut above the rest. She was brighter and purer and prettier. Being better than others inevitably drew jealousy. Marrying Saviour magnified that jealousy, but it also magnified other things. Like power and purity.

She exhaled. 'It could come any day now. I'm eight and a half months along.'

'Is it a boy or a girl?'

'I don't know.'

Love tugged on her hand and they carried on walking towards the trees. Not far now. She felt a tremor vibrate down the centre of her chest and frowned.

After a couple of minutes, the girl said, 'If the baby's a girl, what will you call her?'

Love spoke immediately. Her words rushed out, 'Starlight maybe. Or Serenity. I like the name Song too.'

'They're nice names. I like Serenity best.' The girl's voice was a touch more alive.

Love stopped walking and crouched down. She pulled the girl around to face her and aimed the torch at her chest. Light divided the girl's face, making her look half-dead.

'Why won't you join us?' Love said.

The girl blinked. A tear rolled down her cheek. She stared at the blackness behind Love and said, 'You won't understand.'

Love sighed. 'Try me.'

'I can't stay here when I know—'

'Know what?'

More tears rolled. 'When I know my mummy and daddy are out there. I miss them.'

Love shook her head. 'But they're not living the right way. If you go back to them, you'll never be pure. You'll die, like everyone else.'

'All I want is to be with them again.'

'Don't you like it here?'

The girl's eyes flitted to Love's, then away. In that fleeting glance, Love saw all she needed to. The child hated it here.

She hated them. Her. Everything the community stood for. She was not one of them. No matter what Love said, she would never belong. She was too simple-minded. Too tainted by her life before.

The pressure in Love's chest eased.

'Please, just let me go,' the child begged. Tears streamed down her cheeks. 'I want to go home.'

Love's hands began to shake. She stood up and yanked the child towards the trees.

Chapter 42
PEARLINE

Now

Pearline rubbed her eyes, which were gritty from staring at her screen.

On her watch – which numbered two years in Major Crimes – human killings in Dorset related to cult-like activity numbered zero. Five years ago, in Sherborne, three ponies were mutilated in what was suspected to be a satanic act, but the case was never solved and there was no mention of masks. Other than that, there was nothing of interest.

She leaned back in her long-suffering chair, ignoring its squeal.

Dibbs could be right; a fancy dress party at someone's house. The perp had been wearing a mask simply as part of their costume; nothing more sinister had been at play. If not a fancy dress party, perhaps some sort of fetishist affair where participants wore masks to heighten sensations and offer themselves anonymity. Someone might have been walking home from the party. Or popped out for a smoke or fresh air – not that the air was fresh right now given the heatwave

– heard a commotion in the woods, and gone to investigate. This was plausible.

In all likelihood, their killer owned a scythe, which opened up another line of enquiry. She'd tasked two detectives with the job of gathering a list of scythes sold or stolen in the last year and tracing every purchase. It was a longshot, but there was still a chance the search could yield results.

Pearline rubbed her forehead. Would someone, if they were at a fancy dress party or even a more deviant affair, carry a *scythe* around with them as part of their costume? It seemed unlikely. But perhaps the person carrying the weapon had taken it from the house in which they'd been partying/lived when they'd heard said commotion, thinking they'd use it for protection in the event of things turning dangerous.

Why anyone except for a farmer, and an old-fashioned one at that, would own a scythe posed another question. But, if she pursued this line of thinking, questioning people who lived within earshot of the woods – asking them specifically about whether a party was going on in the area that night – might provide an answer. As yet though, house-to-house visits had given them nothing. No one seemed to have heard or seen anything.

Cusp approached her desk. He was hot and grim-faced. 'Nothing much to go on, I'm sorry to say. I've emailed you a report. Whittled it down to the most relevant info, but basically, the type of mask the killer may or may not have been wearing is called a volto or larva. There are six other types of Venetian masks. You'll find details about those in the report too. Volto means *face* in Italian. Larva means *ghost* in Latin. It's commonly worn with a tricorn and a cloak. Far as I can find, there are no links between this type – or any type of Venetian mask – and rituals. These days people wear them to masquerade balls and fancy dress parties.'

'Right. Give me a potted history. And by potted, I mean mini cactus on your kitchen windowsill.'

Cusp gave a curt nod. 'It's said that the Carnival of Venice originated from a Venetian victory in the twelfth century. In honour of this victory, people started to dance and gather in San Marco Square. Apparently, this festival became official in the Renaissance. Masks have always been an important feature of the carnival. One scholar argues that covering the face in public was a Venetian response to one of the most rigid class hierarchies in European history. During the carnival, people could dress as they liked, instead of according to the rules that were set down in law for their profession and social class.'

'And I bet you can buy them everywhere?'

'Yep. When I searched "buy Venetian volto mask" there were one hundred and seventy-eight thousand results.'

Shit. 'That's going to take Hill a hell of a long time. OK, keep looking into incidents that might be related. Broaden the search to include the rest of the country.'

Chapter 43
LILY

Now

There was an elephant on her chest, and it was dead and rotting. Lily sucked in air and tried to stay calm. Heinous ideas bombarded her, creating explosions of pain deep inside her body. John was having an affair and Hannah and Greg were missing. Both were her fault; if she'd paid more attention to all of them, given more of herself, focused less on her own needs, none of this would be happening.

A tiny voice said she was being irrational. Being off her pills was making her lose perspective.

A louder voice insisted that she was a selfish bitch and deserved what was happening to her, that Hannah and Greg were gone and nothing she could do would bring them back.

The voices tussled; her mum's voice joined them, and it was loving and kind. She told her to go home. Reassured her that the police would find her babies. That she still loved John and he still loved her. Only together would they get through this. He was suffering too. He wanted them back just as much as she did. Even if he'd made a terrible mistake, she needed him now more than ever.

Lily sat still for a while. The voices warred and a headache built at the base of her skull, spreading into her temples. One sentence, louder and clearer than the rest, boomed out. *Don't stop until you know.*

She dragged hot air into her lungs.

Clinging on to her last thought, she opened the car door and hurried outside into the scorching sunlight.

Posie Gibson's house was a red-brick terrace in one of the nicest parts of Grimstone. Flower pots bordered the doorstep and a pig-shaped hanging basket dropped from the wall beside the door overflowing with pink ballet girl fuchsias.

After a few seconds a middle-aged woman answered the door. Her panda eyes made it clear she'd been crying.

'Hello?' The woman was well-dressed, in casual grey trousers and a white blouse. She looked fragile.

'Mrs Gibson?'

'Yes? Are you – oh – you're Gregory's mum, aren't you? Why are you here?'

'My children are missing. I'm trying to help the police find them. I need to talk to Posie.'

'Oh. Oh. Of course. Yes. The police have already spoken to her, but please, come in. God – I hope my son's not caught up in this. No, of course he isn't. He wouldn't—'

Lily stepped inside a neat, clean hallway. The woman's words stopped her cold. 'What do you mean?'

Mrs Gibson clutched her face. Tears glimmered in her eyes. 'The police have been here to speak to Posie about Gregory and to look for Mike. They found him a couple of hours ago. He's been arrested. They won't tell me what it's about.'

Two little girls appeared on either side of her, clutching each leg.

'That's odd.' Lily stared at the woman, trying to tell if she was hiding anything. Mrs Gibson wiped her tears away and gestured to the little girl on her right. 'Here's Posie. Ask her whatever you need to. Answer all of Mrs Woods's questions now, Posie.'

Posie looked alarmed. Mrs Gibson looked down at the other little girl and said, 'Go to your room and play for a bit please, Petal.'

The little girl turned and ran upstairs.

The house was clean and smelt of fresh laundry. Mrs Gibson led them to the kitchen, sat down at the table, and pulled her daughter onto her lap. Posie was a plain child with a habit of sucking her hair.

Lily sat down opposite the pair, unable to still her trembling hands. 'Do you know Aurora?'

'Yes. She's in my class. She's Greg's best friend.'

'Great. Well, Aurora said that Greg has a secret friend who passes him secret notes. This friend told Greg that she has a fairy living at her house. Do you know who this friend might be? Have a really good think before you answer.'

Posie shook her head. 'I don't know. Greg doesn't have any other friends. The boys don't like him. I know he believes in fairies cos he always writes about them in his stories. Aurora believes in fairies too. I don't. Fairies aren't real. Only stupid people believe in fairies.'

'Tell me a bit about Aurora. What's she like?'

Posie wrinkled her nose. 'She's weird. She tells lies for attention.'

'What sorts of things does she lie about?' Lily said.

'Fairies. She tells everyone they're real, and they're not. And Father Christmas.'

'Does she lie to the teachers?'

Posie frowned and stuck out her tongue. After a moment, she nodded enthusiastically. 'Yes! She lied to Miss Mills on Friday about having a headache. She did it so she didn't have to read to her.'

'Miss Mills, the teaching assistant?'

'Yeah. She's really nice,' Posie said.

'How do you know Aurora was lying?'

'She wanted to carry on making the *Titanic* boat. We were all building it together. It was really fun.'

'Was Greg building it too?'

'He was . . . and then he went out for a bit.'

'Do you know where he went?' Lily said, leaning forward.

'I think he went to the toilet, but he was gone a long time. I know because when he came back, Hughie made a joke about him doing a *dump*.'

Mrs Gibson said, 'Posie, don't use that word, please.'

'Sorry, Mummy.'

Lily steeled herself. 'Posie, you're not the first child who's told me no one likes Greg. Can you tell me why?'

Posie looked at her mother as if for permission. Mrs Gibson glanced at Lily worriedly then nodded at her daughter.

In a chirpy voice, the girl said, 'Because he's a *gaylord*. That's what Hughie and the other boys say. Mummy, can I go play now?'

Chapter 44

PEARLINE

Now

The team were done with house-to-house visits in Birch Close. Not a single person was aware of a party – fancy dress or not – taking place in the vicinity the previous night and no one had seen two children fleeing the woods or any suspicious activity in and around the area; most people had been sound asleep. No witnesses had come forward. No one had seen or heard anything, except for Mike Gibson.

She looked up from the pile of statements on her desk, sighed, and mopped her face with her handkerchief. Despite the blinds being shuttered, the too-hot sun was turning the office into a microwave, making tempers short.

Pearline shook her head in frustration. No CCTV footage in the area, no witnesses, nothing. Results still weren't in for the mask. The letter line of enquiry was also a no-go. Every child in Gregory Woods's class had been spoken to, including his teacher. The school kept good records of contact details for next of kin. There was one exception: Miss Mills, the Teaching Assistant in Gregory's class. Attempts were being made to locate her, but she wasn't at her listed address. Her mobile had gone straight to automated voicemail.

Her heart thudded. If they didn't find the children soon, chances were they never would. They could be being whisked across the country right now. She'd put out an APW a few hours ago, but that may have been too late.

She thought about what they had so far. The killer – who was very likely linked to the children's disappearance – was tall and strong, Rudge had been murdered with a scythe and the perpetrator, for some unknown reason, had worn a Venetian mask. Gibson had witnessed the children leaving the woods via Birch Close with a second smaller individual.

With hot fingers, she called Forensics about the mask again. No luck. They were still waiting on the results.

Squashing the urge to tell them to work faster, she hung up. *Christ.*

Her thoughts stuck on the mask. One fingerprint. That was all they needed. One tiny little print. Of course, it had to be in the system, otherwise it would be useless. Even if Rudge's murderer hadn't had anything to do with the children's disappearance – which was highly unlikely but still a possibility – there was a chance he or she had seen where they'd gone.

Speculation, speculation, speculation.

A clanging headache erupted, beating down on her temples like a boxer's fists. Isabelle Hart's innocent little face came again and Faye Hart's grief-stricken eyes tracked through her thoughts like an assembly line in hell. Lily Woods and her husband were going through hell right now. Only she could ease their pain, but how, when she didn't have a single beat on where Hannah and Gregory were?

She clenched her fists and stared at her white knuckles, turned whiter still as the bones popped against the skin, and felt herself descending into her age-old enemy, pessimism.

This was when she needed Dibbs to balance her out, pull her up.

Her phone bleeped, making her jump, and she answered Cusp's call.

'I've found something,' he said. 'Sending it now.'

She opened Cusp's email and read the article. It told a horrific tale about a cult based in North Devon led by a man called Anthony Finch who called himself Uncle Saviour.

She spoke quickly. 'This case rings a bell. I can't believe I didn't remember it before. What was it – eight, nine years ago? OK. Good. But where's the link?'

Cusp cleared his throat and spoke quickly, 'I've tried to get in touch with Detective Inspector Barnes, but no luck. He's on holiday in Peru. Someone who worked the case is going to call me back asap. I managed to speak to the journalist, Tammy Clarkson, who said that *masks* were found at the scene, and guess what? These masks were *Venetian*.'

Her heart skipped a beat. *Good God.* 'Wow. Right, find out more. Get me everything you can on that case.'

She hung up and reread the article Cusp had sent. Uncle Saviour. Anthony Finch. A gut feeling was rippling through her body. If this cult had used Venetian masks then . . .

A call came through. Pearline's heart leaped. It was Linda Bead from Forensics.

Speaking fast, Linda said, 'We found a partial print on the mask matched to a convicted felon called Anthony Finch.'

Pearline's jaw dropped. Anthony Finch. She couldn't believe it.

With a silent cheer, she punched the air. Partial, but admissible in court. This was the piece of luck she'd been desperate for. The mask wasn't a bad omen now; it was a godsend. A terrifying one yes, but one that could help them find Hannah and Gregory.

It was almost too good to be true. 'Any other prints?'

'None that're on the system, apart from Mike Gibson's of course.'

'OK. Thanks.' She hung up, called Dibbs over, told him about the print on the mask and handed him her phone.

He scanned the article Cusp had found and paled.

She nodded and called everyone closer. 'We need to research cult leader Anthony Finch, known to his followers as Uncle Saviour. I need to know everything there is to know about him, his cult and its members. This man's print is on the mask. It's a partial, but there, and definitely his.'

Her heart pounded. It was coming together. Luck, it seemed, was on their side.

For now.

Chapter 45
LILY

Now

Lily drove to the last girl's house trying not to think about the fact that a child had called her son a gaylord. Greg was clearly being bullied. Miss Mills had told Lily about it, and instead of acting immediately on the woman's warning, she'd told herself it could wait until the weekend. She felt like slamming her forehead onto the steering wheel until she passed out, but she couldn't do that. There would be time to punish herself later. All that mattered was finding her babies.

Still, the urge to hurt herself raged and she bit her lower lip until it bled. An instant of relief was followed by stomach-turning confusion and guilt.

What are you doing? Hold it together. You have to find them.

She concentrated on the road and drove faster.

Eve Remington lived in a tiny yellow cottage a ten-minute drive away in the Georgian village of Grovehill, just outside the catchment area for Grimstone Primary. Lily vaguely wondered how she'd managed to get in. Grimstone had an

235

outstanding rating from Ofsted and was always heavily over-subscribed.

Her phone rang and she glanced down to see John trying her again. Ignoring it, she pulled up outside the cottage and got out of the car. Eve was the last girl on her list. If this girl didn't know anything about the letter, there was little more she could do.

Oh God, oh God. She has to know something. She has to.

Fear constricted her airways and a wave of dizziness sent her sprawling onto the pavement. She shook her head and blinked back tears. The sun burned into her back. Her head swirled. She wanted to stay there, lie there for ever, let the darkness pull her down, take her away from this horrific world, but she couldn't do that.

With a groan, Lily pushed herself to her feet and staggered up the path to the yellow cottage.

Peering up at the windows, she feared no one was in. The curtains were drawn shut in every window, there was no car at the front of the house, and the area was silent. Strangely so.

A shiver zigzagged her shoulders and she looked around. Behind her lay the narrow road. Open fields stretched beyond, home to clumps of cows. It was a beautiful spot, if remote. Just the sort of place you might hide two children.

Lily stared back up at the house. A jackdaw landed on the top left windowsill and examined her. She imagined the black bird swooping down and plucking out her eye.

With a shiver, she rapped her knuckles on the door, waited three seconds, then knocked again, louder and faster. Again, no sound came from within. She knocked five more times, heart racing, hands clammy.

Finally, the creak of footsteps announced a presence inside the cottage.

After a lot of scuffling, an elderly man wearing a navy cardigan answered the door.

'Hello, dear. Are you here to ask about those missing children?'

'Uh – yes I am. Is Eve here?'

'The police popped by earlier. Are you with them? Good on you, dear. You do such good work.'

Lily forced a smile and hurried into the cottage. 'Are you Eve's father?'

'Oh no, dear! I'm far too old for that! I'm her grandfather. Poor little mite's mother – my daughter, Harmonica – passed away three years ago. God rest her soul.'

'I'm so sorry.'

He nodded and called up the stairs to Eve, who came running down dressed in a fairy outfit. Lily stared. Bile sloshed in her gut. Maybe this little girl was the one. Maybe *she'd* written the letter to Greg.

'Cup of tea? Lemon cake?' he said.

'No. I'm fine thank you.'

'All right. Let's go sit in the living room, shall we, dears? Eve, this nice lady wants to talk to you about those missing children. Answer all of her questions, poppet, OK?'

'Yes, Grandpa.'

Eve smiled at her, and Lily focused on the girl's big brown eyes rather than her fairy dress.

'Eve, I'd like to start by asking you about your friendship with Greg. Are you friends with him at school?'

'Sort of. He likes fairies and so do I. So does Aurora.'

'Really? That's good. And do you talk to Greg about fairies?'

'No. Maybe. Sometimes. Aurora doesn't like it when I talk to him. She thinks I'm trying to steal him away.'

'Did you eat lunch with Greg last week?' Lily said.

The old man shifted on the sofa. Lily glanced at him. He looked down quickly and brushed imaginary dirt off his trousers.

Eve's eyes grew wet. 'Am I in trouble?'

'No, poppet, of course you're not,' her grandfather said, giving Lily a frown.

'No, you're not in any trouble, Eve. Why do you think you are?'

The girl shrugged and fiddled with her glittery wand. 'Because, um . . .'

'Because what?' Lily said, leaning forward.

'Because I spied on him when he went to the loo.'

'What do you mean?'

'Well, Greg went to the loo and he was gone a really long time. Aurora told me to go to the loo as well and spy on him. She said he had a secret friend who he kept seeing during the lesson when he wasn't s'posed to.'

'Who was it? Did you see the secret friend?' Lily said, trying to keep the excitement out of her voice.

Eve sighed. She waved her wand about and said, 'No.'

'Oh.' Lily's heart sank. She blurted, 'Did you write Greg a letter telling him to come and see a fairy at your house?'

'The other officer already asked her this, dear,' the old man said, shifting in his seat.

She stared hard at Eve. 'Eve – the letter. Did you write Greg a letter?'

Eve shook her head. 'No. I couldn't see Greg's secret friend, but I heard her say something to him. They were in the library behind the door.'

'You heard her? What did she say?'

'I can't remember. I think she said the word *letter*. I'm not sure.'

Lily wanted to rip the wings off the girl's back and stamp on them. 'What do you mean you're not sure? Either you did hear the word letter or you didn't. Which is it?'

The old man flinched and moved as if to stand.

Lily blinked tears of frustration out of her eyes. Eve was

just as useless as the other girls. She didn't know anything either.

'I think I should show you out now, dear,' the old man said sternly.

Lily swallowed and nodded. Despair made her light-headed. Pushing herself to her feet, she lost her balance and stumbled into the coffee table. The old man's eyes widened, but he said nothing and turned to lead her out of the room.

'Hang on,' Eve said, tugging Lily's T-shirt, 'I think I know who Greg's secret friend is cos I know her voice.'

Lily turned, not daring to hope, but doing so in spite of herself. 'Really? Who do you think it is?'

'Actually, I *know* it's her.'

'Who?'

'Miss Mills, our class helper. I know her voice really well cos she helps me a lot with my writing and numbers. I didn't tell Aurora cos I like Miss Mills and I didn't want Aurora to be horrible to her too.'

'Eve, did you tell the police about this?'

'No.'

Her grandfather stepped forward. 'Why ever not?'

Eve shrugged. 'I forgot.'

Lily rang the police and asked the person on the line to pass on a message to Chief Inspector Ottoline to call her back, then drove home as fast as possible. She needed to tell John. Miss Mills – the teaching assistant in Greg's class – had something to do with this. She found it hard to believe such a lovely-seeming young woman could be involved, but looks were deceptive; she'd thought she could trust John and she'd known him for years.

As she approached the front door, nausea swept around her gut, threatening to rise. She didn't want another confrontation, but Juliet's car was still parked out front. The gumption of that woman was unbearable. And John . . . he may have been cheating, but really? Letting the woman stay in her house while she was out trying to find their children . . .

She could feel herself choking up, but held it together by running through Eve Remington's words. Miss Mills. If she could just find Miss Mills.

Steeling herself, Lily opened the door and shouted John's name. He appeared in the living-room doorway. 'Thank God. I was so worried. I've been trying to contact you—'

Juliet appeared behind him. She gave Lily a pathetic wave, her face pinched and tight. Lily ignored her and strode up to John. She told him about Miss Mills and John gawped at her, then glanced around at Juliet, who had begun to fumble around in her handbag.

'What are you doing?' Lily hissed at Juliet.

'Looking for my phone. I think I've got—'

'I can't believe she's still here,' Lily said, glaring at John so viciously her eyeballs ached.

'I think I've got—' Juliet tried again.

Lily cut her off. 'Get out of my house.'

John tried to pull Lily in for a hug. She resisted, flinching away and storming up the hallway to the door. 'Get. The. Fuck. Out.'

She opened the door. Dizziness came. Nausea hit.

Juliet stared at John as if expecting him to leap onto his white steed and gallop to her rescue, but John was staring at the wall, shoulders slumped.

Lily glared from him to Juliet, to the woman's tangoed face and melon chest, to the fake worry pinching the skin between her pencil-thin eyebrows. A vision of her stabbing Juliet's breasts with kitchen scissors flashed into her mind and she shook her head, glared at her. 'Are you deaf? I said GET THE FUCK OUT OF MY HOUSE.'

Still, the woman remained, digging around in her bag as

though she belonged there. Lily strode away from the door and reached out to grab Juliet's arm. 'Right. If you won't go, I'll make you go myself.'

John lunged between them and held up his hands. 'Wait, Lil, wait. Hear me out.'

She laughed, shook her head, stabbed her finger into his chest. 'Hear what? How you two've been shagging behind my back? How you've been fucking someone else? How you've been—'

'STOP,' John's voice boomed. His face was red, contorted, chest rising and falling too fast.

She glared at him, bit her lip. In a low, quivery voice, she said, 'Get out. Both of you.' She turned and headed away, not knowing where she was going, just knowing she needed to create distance between them.

'Lil, wait. Please. Juliet's my counsellor,' John said, following her into the hallway.

Lily snorted over her shoulder. 'Good one, John. Try the other leg.'

'It's true,' Juliet said, hurrying forward with her hand outstretched, a berry-red phone in her hand. 'I've been treating your husband for a few months now.'

'What?' Lily looked from Juliet to John. He was unable to meet her eyes, but nodded.

Relief and fear swarmed in her chest. She looked at Juliet. 'Why?'

Juliet thrust the phone into Lily's hand. 'He can tell you about that later. First, you need to see this.'

Lily took the phone and stared at the address. The name at the top said Sarah Mills. She looked at Juliet. 'You're friends with her?'

'Not friends exactly. She's come round a handful of times to help Tyler with his reading. He's dyslexic. The last time she came round I meant to give her a thank-you card and

241

gift, but I forgot, so I got in my car and tried to catch up with her – she was on her bike. I beeped at her to stop, but she didn't so I followed her to her house in Birch Close, jumped out, and gave her the present and card. That's why I have her address.'

'Have you got her phone number?' Lily said.

'No. We only spoke at school pick-up. Everything was arranged there. I asked for her number, but she said she'd lost her phone and was in the process of getting a new one.'

'Ring the police. Now,' John said.

Lily shoved her hand in her pocket, grabbed the card Sergeant Fielding had given her, and dialled the number. The line was busy. She left a message.

'Shit,' Lily said, looking at John. 'It's engaged.'

'Try again,' he said.

She did. The line was still busy.

'Dial 999,' Juliet said.

'There's no time for that!' Lily spun around and ran out of the house.

John ran after her. He didn't even put on his trainers. He got in the passenger seat and slammed the door shut, looked at her, and put his hand on hers. 'I'll ring. You drive.'

They left Juliet Pickering standing in front of their house in the shattering sun. Lily gave the woman a final glance.

Juliet wasn't her enemy. She was her saviour.

242

Chapter 46

LOVE

Age 21

June 2003

Despite the curtains being drawn shut, the bedroom was a furnace, the white walls expelling heat like an open fire. Love lay on her back on the bed atop a red towel, her cheek mashed into her shoulder as pain ripped her apart. Every particle of her body hurt. She had never known so much pain.

'Your mother's still sulking,' Saviour said darkly, stroking Love's sweaty forehead.

'She said she'd come. Where is she?'

Hope knelt on the bed, making the mattress sink about a foot. She dabbed Love's face with a cold sponge. 'Fervour's gone to look for her. Don't worry, my darling. He'll find her.'

Another contraction tore through her back and clawed its way across her side. She exhaled through the pain, then glanced at Hope. 'I can't believe you've been through this five times.'

Hope smiled knowingly. 'You're already fully dilated. It won't be long. None of mine progressed this quickly. You're lucky.'

Lucky? Love gritted her teeth, more against Hope's words than the next contraction. She didn't feel lucky. Her mother wasn't here and she was being ripped apart. Three hours now. That's how long she'd been contracting. Three bloody hours. And her mother hadn't come to check on her, not once. Peace wouldn't come – they barely said two words to each other these days – and Hope was doing her best, but she needed Charity. She couldn't explain why, but she did. She needed her mother by her side. Needed to hear her mother say she was not going to die, because that was what was so terrifying – the all-consuming thought that she was going to be killed giving birth to her first baby.

She couldn't die. She wouldn't. If she died now, everything would have been for nothing.

Desperate to focus on something other than the pain, Love thought about the new giver. Another little girl, this one from Somerset. She hoped this child would accept her new life.

Pain shuddered through her body. She crushed her head into her shoulder and moaned.

Saviour stood up. 'I can't bear this. I'm going to find Charity. If I have to drag her by her hair, I'll do it. She will be here for the birth of her first grandchild if it kills me. And Peace. She should be here too.'

Love looked down at the sleeping baby in her arms. She and Saviour had already decided to name him Rigour. The baby's face was swollen and ugly, but he would be a positive addition to the community.

Right now, his tiny body was swaddled in a turquoise blanket her mother had knitted. The blanket smelt of Charity; of rosemary soap and weakness.

She looked up. Her mother was hanging from an apple tree.

The clouds parted and sunlight lit her up like a Christmas tree decoration. She seemed to glow. Her skin and hair shone like polished glass, but Mother wasn't pure. She was impurity itself. An impure rag doll dangling from a branch by its neck, lips parted, spit dry.

Rope was her poison. Rope, a tree, and a chair. Love remembered playing hangman with her mother and Peace as a child, and her baby-free tummy quivered.

Charity's final message was scrawled in blood upon her white smock:

ALL A LIE

The smock mocked and the words hurt. Each letter seeped into Love's heart like poison.

Peace was on her knees, screaming. Faith was trying to comfort her.

Fervour climbed the tree. He cut through the rope and Nobility and Saviour caught her mother's corpse.

Everyone had come to watch, even the children. Some were weeping. Others were staring in horror. A few whispered behind their hands, eyes bright, nodding as if they'd known this was going to happen all along.

Peace pushed herself to her feet and stumbled towards her. Raising an accusing finger, she stabbed it at Love's face, punctuating each word with a jab. 'You did this. You killed her. You killed our mother.'

'Don't listen to her. She's in shock,' Faith spoke quickly, snatching a glance at Saviour.

Saviour and Nobility stopped in their tracks. Saviour held Charity's upper body, Nobility the lower. They were both sweating buckets. The late afternoon sun was hot and glaring.

'I'm not in shock,' Peace spat. She whirled around, stabbing her finger at everyone watching. 'All of you are to blame for her death.'

'She's not in her right mind,' Saviour said, staring at Love.

Love stared back at him. She wanted to scream, but she could not show weakness in front of her worker bees. This was her moment. The moment she had been waiting for.

Calmly, she turned to Faith and handed her the baby.

She looked at Peace and smiled. 'In a sense, you're right. I did kill our mother.'

A gasp rippled through the crowd. Inside, Love laughed. She had their attention. Every eye fixed on her face.

Peace looked confused. Her eyes narrowed.

'I killed our mother because I refused to follow her. I chose Eternal Life instead,' Love said.

Her sister gawped like a fish and flailed for a retort, but Love didn't give her a chance. Strolling over to Saviour and Nobility, she stared down at her mother's body. She felt nothing. Only excitement. The thrill of an audience hanging on her every word.

'Charity was my mother, but she was weak. Like her husband before her, she was a traitor.' She lowered her voice and turned to face her audience. 'Want to know a secret?' She paused, held them. 'On the night of Hope's baby ceremony, my mother tried to steal the van and leave our beloved home. Tried to force me to go with her. Peace too.' She stole a glance at Peace. Her sister's face was stony, eyes glazed over. She knew she'd lost. If she said anything now, Love would tell them the whole truth: that Peace had been more than willing to steal the van and leave with their mother.

'Of course, I didn't want to leave. I have always been totally devoted to our path – to our gracious leader, my beloved husband – but I was only sixteen years old and I was scared. I was confused. I'd been made to believe for my whole life that my mother was devoted to the cause. I thought she was days away from reaching Total Illumination. To say this came as a shock to my system, is an understatement. I was horrified. I tried to persuade her to stay and explained how if she took the van and Hope went into labour, there would be no way to get her to the hospital in time, but did she care?' She left the question hanging. She shook her head, forced tears to drop.

She glanced at her sister. 'Peace was terrified too. It was only because of Fervour that we are still here today. If he hadn't come along, my mother would have forced us into that van and driven us to who-knows-where to live amongst the faithless masses out there, with nothing to live for but death.'

She sighed, wiped her tears. She appealed to each and every member with her most sincere gaze. Saviour's eyes were on her, digesting every word. 'We gave her one final chance. We welcomed her back into the fold. Allowed her to become a member of the council. We trusted her. I trusted her. It breaks my heart to see that everything was a pretence. My mother was a confused, weak woman. She was not one of us, and she knew that. Charity knew she could never uphold our values. She could never become pure enough to reach Total Illumination. That's why she did this unspeakable act. She did this to punish herself, but she also did it to make you question your beliefs. To frighten you. Charity was frightened so she wanted to make others feel the same way.

'I'm glad I know the truth. I'm not happy she's gone, but maybe it's better than her being around and causing more damage.

'I know I might seem a little distant at times, but ultimately all I care about is helping every one of you attain eternal life. It's all I've ever wanted. I'm only sorry my mother could not become pure enough. She tried, yes, but she gave up. I will never give up. I'll never give up on any of you. If you're ever having doubts, come to me. Come to Saviour. Talk to us. All we want is for everyone to be happy on their path to Total Illumination.'

It was the most she'd ever spoken in public. For a while, the clouds floated, the birds twittered, and her audience remained captured by her words, stunned into silence. Love smiled at each and every member, pausing to smile at Saviour for the longest. She could see what they saw: a strong, brilliant, pure-hearted young woman with raven hair who promised them an exceptional future. Their future leader and queen.

The applause began with Hope. It spread and built to a glorious chorus that made the birds explode from the trees. All the while, Love felt Peace's eyes burning her skin. Smiling gently, she turned and walked over to her sister. Peace shook with rage.

In a low voice, Love said, 'If you know what's good for you, you'll let it go.'

Her sister's eyes were red and swollen. A vein pulsed in her throat.

Before her sister could turn away, Love enveloped her in a hard hug. She held onto her for a long time before letting go, and Peace didn't struggle; she knew she was fighting a losing battle. Love held her gaze, pleased to see a pair of deadening eyes and the sagging posture of someone who was beginning to accept defeat.

With a smile, Love took her newborn baby in her arms, carefully unwrapped him, and dropped the blanket on the ground. A pool of green blood. Tainted and impure, like her dead mother.

Saviour gave her a wary nod as he and Nobility carried the body back towards the farm.

Love kissed baby Rigour's forehead and smiled to herself. Tonight, she would lead the community's first Passing Ceremony where they would burn her mother to ash, and though tears would drip from her eyes, they would be as fake and meaningless as the words Charity had written on her smock.

Chapter 47
PEARLINE

Now

With the team looking into Anthony Finch's cult, Pearline focused on another line of enquiry. So far, they'd interviewed all of the children in Greg's class, his headteacher and classroom teacher, but they'd been unable to trace the boy's teaching assistant, Miss Sarah Mills.

Grimstone Primary School had an address for the young woman, but the address had been falsified. An elderly woman named Mrs Edith Hawthorn lived at 13 Herring Road, Grimstone. Sarah Mills must have stolen the woman's utility bills and submitted them to the school when applying for the role. Apparently, she'd told Human Resources that she rented a room from Mrs Hawthorn, but the old woman had never heard of her. The contact number Miss Mills had given was also a no-go, and she'd provided fake documents in order to obtain a DBS check.

Pearline suppressed a groan. This woman had gone to great lengths to hide her address and real identity. Why? What was she hiding? It seemed unlikely that the young woman could be involved in the children's disappearance, but forging an address and providing fake details raised questions that needed immediate answering.

Mrs Edwards, Gregory's teacher, sat in front of Pearline in the airless meeting room clutching her handbag to her chest as if it was a life vest. She was a bird-like woman with masses of curly black hair and bulbous eyes. Though she had already been questioned, Pearline wanted to speak to her again in case she could provide more information about Miss Mills.

'How long have you worked with Miss Mills?' Pearline said.

The woman looked directly at her. She spoke quickly with a slight accent that Pearline thought might be Turkish. 'Three years. She's an excellent TA. Bright, enthusiastic. Incredibly helpful. Stays late to help me prepare resources for the next day. I really don't understand how you can think she has anything to do with Gregory and Hannah's disappearance?'

Pearline ignored her. 'Do you have her mobile phone number? Or any other contact details for her?'

'No. She's a private young lady. Have you tried Human Resources?'

Sweet Jesus. 'Yes. The address she gave was false, as was her phone number.'

'Oh dear. I am shocked. You just never know with some people, do you?'

'No. You really don't. Have you ever noticed Miss Mills communicating with Greg at a time when you wouldn't usually expect her to?'

'Not really.'

'What do you mean, *not really*?'

'Well . . . I did see her eating lunch with him a couple of times. I thought it was to cheer him up. He's socially awkward. Sometimes I think he's a little lonely.'

'Seen her giving him anything?'

'Like what? A present?'

'Yes. Or a note. Remember anything like that?'

The woman shook her head.

'Is Miss Mills close to any of the staff?'

'I don't think so. She usually stays in the classroom at lunchtime and eats her lunch there while doing odd jobs for me.'

'All right. Thank you for coming in. If anything else occurs to you, call me straight away.' Pearline handed the woman her card and walked her to the door.

Mrs Edwards turned. Her eyes glistened. 'Good luck. I'll be praying for you and poor little Greg and his sister. He's a lovely little boy.'

Pearline watched the woman hurry away. As soon as she was out of sight, she allowed herself to sag.

Cusp ran up the corridor. 'Lily Woods left a message asking you to call. She said it's urgent.'

'Call her back. Find out what it's about. Let me know if I need to handle it.'

'On it. Oh, and the Guvnor wants you.'

'Now?'

'Yeah. Sorry.'

Pearline sighed. Now was not a good time. She'd already sent the Super an email briefing him on this crucial development. Meeting now would only pull her away from the investigation, but Detective Chief Superintendent Patrick Dent often did this. Stepping in at a vital moment when everyone was up to their eyeballs and offering spectacularly useless and often patronising advice was his speciality. Dibbs liked to call him Pat-a-cake, which worked on a level she couldn't explain.

Dent's office was on the next floor up. His room smelt of the musty cologne he wore to hide his halitosis – which didn't work. It actually made it worse. A baby palm tree stood in one corner of the room, a red watering can on the carpet beside it. A fan whirred from the middle shelf of the bookcase, pushing his few strands of remaining hair onto his bald patch. Motivational signs plastered the walls. The worst was one of a rainbow arcing over a mountain. Above the rainbow were the words: *Climb high, not low. Be a rainbow, not a colour.* Not for the first time, she wondered if the man had painted it himself.

Standing opposite Dent's desk, she glanced at her watch, hoping he'd get the hint. He didn't.

He bridged his fingers and danced them against each other. 'I responded to your email but you didn't reply.'

Christ almighty. 'Oh. I didn't realise,' she lied; his email had not required a response as far as she was aware, so she hadn't wasted any time on it.

'Hm,' he said. 'Now, you're trying to find this Miss Mills individual and investigate a cult leader by the name of Anthony Finch?'

'Yes. Like I told you—'

He held up his hand for her to stop speaking. She gritted her teeth and waited for the inevitable nuggets of wisdom to trickle forth.

A knock on the door interrupted them. Dent frowned at the intrusion, but barked to come in. It was Cusp, red-faced and short of breath.

'It's Mrs Woods. She thinks Miss Mills has taken them, and she knows where she lives. She's going there right now. I told her to go home, but she wouldn't listen.'

'Damn. Where's she going?'

'11 Birch Close.'

PART THREE

Chapter 48

LILY

Now

They pulled up at number 10 Birch Close. Sunlight poured onto the houses and front lawns, making everything too bright, almost fake-looking. Juliet had texted John to explain that to reach number 11, you had to follow the cut between number 10 and 12 until you reached a red-brick wall with a door built into it.

Lily stopped the engine. Adrenaline buzzed through her veins like a thousand dragonflies. John got out of the car and she followed him down the cut quite a way, hot sun burning her head. They stopped at a high wall with a heavy door built into it, and stared at a Beware the Dog sign. They exchanged a look and John leaned over and picked up a rock. No words were needed. Dog or not, they were going in. If a Rottweiler was prowling behind the wall waiting to attack, Lily doubted a rock would protect them, but it was better than going in empty-handed.

John tried the door, but it was locked. He assessed the height of the wall. 'I think I can scale it. When I'm at the top, I'll pull you up.'

She nodded, hoping he was right. The wall was at least seven feet high. John shoved the rock into his pocket and jumped up. His fingers brushed the top layer of brick. He tried again and managed to grip the surface, then slipped and dropped back to the ground with a grunt.

'Hurry,' she said.

John backed away from the wall, then ran forward and tried to step-jump to the top, but failed to make it. Lily felt panic pulling her down.

'There's no time. Give me a foot up,' she said quickly. 'I know I won't be able to pull you up, but I might be able to unlock it from the other side.'

He nodded and created a step with his hands, and she used his shoulders to climb onto the makeshift rung. John held her feet in place as she grabbed the top of the wall and managed, with difficulty, to pull herself up.

Crouching low on the wall, Lily looked at the pink cottage that stood less than five yards away. Light leaked from between loosely drawn curtains, making the tiny old house look strange and whimsical, like something out of a fairy tale.

The drop from the wall to the ground was high, so Lily lowered herself carefully, dropping to the grass the moment her arms were fully extended.

Whirling around, half-expecting to be attacked by a dog at any moment, she scanned the lawn, but it remained eerily still.

'Hurry,' John said.

Shocked into action, Lily turned to the door in the brick wall and tried to unlock it, but nothing gave. 'It needs to be opened with a key,' she whispered.

'Damn.'

'I'll have to go in alone,' she said, glancing at the cottage.

'No – wait! You need to climb back over. There's no way

you're going up to that house on your own. Is there a bench or something you can stand on?'

Lily scanned the yard. There was nothing except for sunlit grass and weeds. 'No. I have to go. Try the police again. We can't waste any more time.'

'No. Wait.'

'I'm going.' She strode away from the wall towards the pink house.

A dilapidated sign said Sugar Cottage. Lily paused and listened, but heard nothing. Fear gripped her muscles. She had nothing to protect herself, no shadows to contain her, no weapon of any kind, but she couldn't wait for the police. Hannah and Gregory could be inside the building fighting for their lives. One more minute and she could be too late.

Every limb shook as she raised her hand. She gently tried the door handle and, to her surprise, it gave.

She looked back. She could hear John's voice, just make out his hoarse, rushed whisper, urging her to wait, but waiting wasn't an option.

Focusing on the door, Lily pushed.

The hinges creaked as she crept into the house, along a dark hallway painted olive green. There was a worn staircase ahead leading to the first floor. To her left, stood a closed door. The paint on the walls was peeling and a patch of damp darkened the low ceiling. A strange, fusty smell pervaded the air.

Lily scanned the hallway for anything she could use as a weapon, but saw nothing, not even a coat hook. Swallowing dryly, she turned the knob of the door that led off the hallway and edged it open.

Chapter 49

LOVE

Age 31

August 2012

Love sat on the farmhouse porch and watched her daughter feed the chickens. Reaching across Saviour's shotgun for the herb trug, she tore off five mint leaves and dropped them in a cup of hot water. She waited a minute, then took a sip, but the water was too insipid to drink.

A summer storm was brewing, turning the sky a dirty, pigswill grey. Wind howled through the caravans, flipping the clothes on people's washing lines upside down and, in some cases, tossing them to the ground like leaves. Despite the gathering clouds, Love felt calm and contented. Her movements were languid as she picked up her mint tea and took another sip. This time the strength was perfect.

Sighing with pleasure, she thought about the new child about to join the community, a seven-year-old boy called Aaron from Weston-super-Mare who Fervour was collecting today. Aaron would be the fourth giver to be brought to Eternal Life. A child's blood only remained pure until ten years of age, then it began to turn. They always took children of six or seven years old because the blood was more powerful than a baby's. Too young, and the blood hadn't had time to purify. Also, six-year-olds were old enough to understand their new situation and grasp the benefits of Eternal Life, but not old enough to pose any major challenges.

Love hoped this new boy would be as adaptable as the last two children, and that in three years' time he would be content to remain a dedicated member of the group and receive his pure name at the Blood Birthing Ceremony.

Like the previous two givers, Aaron was an orphan. Love and Saviour had adopted the second giver, and Love had named her Serenity. With Serenity, they had found that choosing an orphaned child and taking that child's blood with a syringe rather than a cut and a kiss helped to ease the child into accepting their new life. The equation had also worked with the next child, renamed Trust. He had come from an unhappy foster home and had embraced Eternal Life even more quickly than Serenity. Hope – love her – had taken Trust into her ever-expanding nest without a second thought.

If this new giver was not as adaptable, he would be released quickly, no messing about this time. Blood was purer when it sprang from an agreeable source. Reluctance soured the taste.

Love waved at Serenity, who looked up and beamed.

She was glad she'd kept Serenity. After Rigour's cot death when he was two months old – a difficult and unfortunate time – she and Saviour had tried for another baby and suffered through two miscarriages before deciding enough was enough. By that time, Serenity's giving days were coming to an end and she had accepted her new life wholeheartedly. It only made sense to keep her, make her part of their unit. It also set a good example to the rest of the community and further progressed Love's reputation as a dedicated leader of Eternal Life.

Love watched the wind whip Serenity's hair across her enchanting face. The girl had grown into a real beauty; a doll turned real, with luscious auburn hair and flawless porcelain skin. She had a short fuse, but was bright, with a sly streak Love adored. Every boy and man in the community lusted after her, but she was only sixteen. Love wouldn't let her marry for at least another two years, and she'd have a helping hand in deciding who it was when the time came.

With a happy sigh, Love scanned the farm and watched her worker bees busy about their duties.

Everything worked perfectly. Hope and a dwarf woman named Delight acted as the community's teachers, with Serenity serving as a teaching assistant. The men worked the fields and vegetable patches, while the women presided over the herb garden, the cooking, cleaning, and tending to the little ones. As far as possible, clothes and accessories were handmade, meaning little expenditure and an organic way of life. Visits to town were minimal, and only then for medical supplies and the like. Such necessities were purchased with money earned from sales of handcrafted goods at the local market. With a near self-sustaining farm and Saviour's inheritance from Bobby Bronson, the community needed little money. Eternal Life was like a human beehive, with blood for nectar, a superb little ecosystem that ticked along like clockwork.

Love took another sip of mint tea and grimaced. The tea had gone too far and turned bitter. She placed it on the ground and kicked the rocking chair into a gentle rhythm.

Despite the wild wind, drowsiness descended. Her mind teetered on the brink of sleep, and her thoughts dipped in and out of the last decade. A smile teased her lips. Over the years, bias against blood-supping had eased, just as Saviour had hoped. Only the senior council members – herself, Saviour, Nobility, Hope and Fervour – extracted blood from the givers and had direct contact with them during their preliminary years under the farmhouse roof, and blood-supplemented water was circulated to the rest of the community every week. Some members remained uncomfortable when talk of a giver arose, so most avoided the conversation and drank their purified water, grateful not only for its special properties, but for the fact that they could feign ignorance regarding its source.

As such, Eternal Life was the purest, happiest place on earth. The farm provided an egalitarian home that sheltered the needy, provided a family for the lonely, and fostered a climate of love. Families continued to trickle in as word about the community spread organically. She felt proud to play such a fundamental role in its development and preservation. Indeed, it was largely because of her diligence that such order and sanctity reigned. Because of hers and Saviour's unending devotion to Eternal Life's end goal, every member felt loved and valued. Each man, woman and child knew that their lives would be long, fruitful and harmonious, and what could be better than that?

The only thorn was her sister. Peace was as prickly as a hedgehog, a demon sucking the life and soul out of everyone she looked at.

Saviour strode past Serenity and ruffled her hair, hopped onto the porch, picked up the shotgun, and grinned at her. For several seconds, Love thought about how well he wore his age. Though in his fifties, his skin was almost entirely line-free, his hair barely touched by grey. Pure blood worked wonders for everyone. Its benefits spoke volumes. People rarely got ill and, though they toiled long and hard, they awoke fresh-faced every morning, bursting with energy for the new day. Even Eternal Life's oldest members could sit on their haunches like African tribesmen and work twelve-hour days with little to no break. Life here was truly exceptional.

Saviour planted a kiss on her temple. There was a time when such a touch would have brought her to her knees, but she felt no physical attraction to him any more and he only slept with other women in the community. Theirs had grown into more of a friendship than a courtship, which pleased her. She had no time or inclination for pleasures of the flesh these days.

Saviour slung the shotgun over his shoulder. 'Fervour and Peace ought to be back with the new giver any minute now.'

'Brilliant – *what*? Peace went?'

'I thought you knew?'

'What made you think that? What made you think I'd ever give permission for her to go?' she said.

'Fervour told me you said she could.'

'Fervour? Why would he lie?' She thought quickly. A couple of weeks ago she'd seen Fervour and Peace chatting and thought it odd, but dismissed it at the time, thinking Peace might have been asking him to buy sanitary products on his weekly trip to town. But it had obviously been more than that. Her eyes widened. They were sleeping together. That had to be it. Peace had wheedled her way into Fervour's heart – and trousers – then twisted his mind. Convinced him to trust her. The idea was disgusting; Peace was more desperate and twisted than she'd thought.

'I don't know,' Saviour said, scratching his beard, 'but I'm sure it'll be fine. She keeps her head down these days, tries to make amends.'

'You're wrong. She hates it here. She hates us. She hates everything we stand for. She tosses her purified water down the sink. I've seen her do it.'

Saviour laughed uneasily. 'You're overreacting, sweetheart.' He reached out a hand to comfort her and she recoiled.

'Don't sweetheart me. You could have just ruined us!' She hated to lose control like this, but fear blackened her temper.

'Me? What did I do?'

'We have to clean up. Now. Just in case,' she said, rushing into the house.

Saviour was two steps behind. Love ran up the stairs into the giver's bedroom. Opening the wardrobe, she reached up and grabbed the tin box that held the syringes, antiseptic, cotton buds, and plasters.

'Get rid of these – burn them.'

'What?'

'GET RID OF THEM NOW!'

'Are you serious?'

'Do I look like I'm joking?' She felt as if she was having heart palpitations.

Serenity appeared in the doorway. 'What's wrong?'

Saviour took the tin and ran out of the room.

'Peace. She's finally snapped.'

'She's gone?'

Love nodded grimly. Unlike her adoptive father, Serenity understood the severity of the situation immediately.

'Run as fast as you can to the well in the woods that I showed you.'

'What about you and Father?'

'We won't be far behind. Wait for us there. Oh – and, Seri – bring the scythe, just in case.'

Serenity nodded and left the room.

Love exhaled through her nose and tried to calm down. She'd planned for this moment, but never believed it would happen. A moment later, sirens split the air.

She yanked on her shoes, sprinted down the stairs, and looked into the living room, relieved to see the contents of the tin ablaze in the grate, dead matches scattered on top. Saviour was nowhere to be seen. But he knew the plan. He would meet them at the well, and together they would make their way to the safe place.

She ran out of the back door and peered around the side of the house. Beyond the entrance to the community stood two police officers, behind them, a police car. One of the officers held Peace by the elbow. Peace raised her free arm and pointed at the farmhouse.

Love's entire body jerked; Saviour was walking up to the fence, unlocking the gate, letting them in. Talking to them. This wasn't the plan. Had he lost his mind? But she knew her husband, and what he was thinking; he'd burned the syringes, so everything would be fine, but it wouldn't. Not when Peace was running her mouth, and not when the evidence was still burning. Saviour was sometimes too egotistical for his own good. He was a charmer, but he wasn't going to be able to convince two police officers that Peace was lying. Not when she had probably told them about the giver Fervour was collecting today. She wondered where he was – in custody already? Would he talk too? She wouldn't put it past Fervour; he'd do anything to save his own skin.

People were starting to gather in the centre of the farmyard, huddling together like sheep. Hope grabbed Trust and pulled him away from the crowd. She bent down so that they were eye-to-eye and spoke urgently. Love could imagine what she was saying. If Trust mentioned his life before the community, they'd be done for. But he was a good kid, and he had completely adapted. Love was pretty sure he'd keep his mouth shut.

Saviour beckoned to the officers and they followed him through the gateway onto the farm.

Love hoped he would say as little as possible, get rid of them quickly, paint Peace as a deranged, disgruntled member of Eternal Life trying to get revenge for some fabricated crime.

Saviour gestured at the crowd of onlookers. A broad smile

lit his handsome face. He looked radiant in that moment, utterly perfect. Love began to think everything was going to be OK.

And then chaos swooped down on wings of madness.

Chapter 50
PEARLINE

Now

Pearline hit the siren, adjusted the mirrors, and sped to Birch Close. Dibbs sat beside her, legs jiggling.

'Let me get this straight,' he said, 'Mrs Woods finds out who wrote the letter luring Gregory out of his house and takes it upon herself to drive to this kidnapper's house *on her own*—'

'Not on her own. Her husband's with her apparently.'

'Well, yeah, but still – come on.'

'I know. Crazy, but if I had kids and found out where the kidnapper lived, I think I'd do the same.'

'But you're a professional. She's not.'

'I'm sure she knows that deep down, but right now she's not thinking rationally. She's scared. Losing her mind with worry.'

'I know. I get it. I just don't like it. What if this scythe-wielding nutter's there and decides to attack her?'

She chewed her lip. The same idea had crossed her mind. In a way, she wanted Lily Woods to be wrong. 11 Birch Close wasn't where they'd find the kidnappers. Mrs Woods would get there and discover a sweet old couple rather than a murdering, kidnapping pair of unpredictable strangers, and when she and Dibbs arrived, everything would be fine and no one would be injured or dead.

She sped up Maple Hill, took a right, a left, then another right, and pulled up outside 10 Birch Close. A man and woman stood on the pavement outside arguing with each other. It was Mr and Mrs Woods.

Pearline strode across to the harassed-looking pair. The despair in their eyes was to be expected, but she still felt winded by it.

'Mrs Woods? Mr Woods? I'm DCI Ottoline.'

'They're not there – they've gone,' Lily Woods said. 'The door was unlocked so I went in. Nobody's there.' She rattled out the words through trembling teeth. Her face was colourless, eyes swollen.

Pearline bit back the need to lecture the woman on the danger she'd put herself and potentially her children in, and said, 'Go straight home. We need to check the property properly. I'll send an officer to your house to update you. Please don't get involved again. I assure you both that we are doing everything possible to find Hannah and Gregory.'

'So you know it was Miss Mills who gave Greg the letter?'

'I can't discuss that right now I'm afraid. All I can say is that we are looking into her. Please, let us do our job. Go home.'

'But—' Lily Woods tried to speak, but her husband wrapped his arm around her shoulders.

'Let them do their job, Lil. We might've missed something. There could be a clue in the house that helps the police track them down.'

Lily Woods opened her mouth as if to argue, then nodded meekly and allowed herself to be guided back to the red Mini Cooper parked a few yards up the road.

'Right,' Pearline said, looking at Dibbs. 'Question now is, search or Forensics?'

'Search. I know it's risky, but the children could still be in there.'

She nodded. 'I agree. We need the premises searched right away.'

Without hesitation, she called in POLSA. The specially trained search team would wear PPE to search the premises so they would do the least damage possible to the forensic examination that would follow. Next, she arranged for a CSI to come and photograph the premises prior to the POLSA team going in. The CSI would also take photographs of any items found during the search, so that they could document exactly where and how each item was found. It was a lengthy process, but quicker than a full forensic discovery, which could take weeks.

Christ. Calling in POLSA first rather than a forensic discovery team increased the chances of evidence being destroyed. But the children could be in there.

She hoped she was making the right decision.

Lily and John Woods were right. There was no immediate evidence that any children had ever been in the cottage. From the rumpled appearance of two beds, it looked as though two people had lived there, or at least slept there recently. POLSA had also discovered a handful of clothes in a woman's size 10, mostly from Tesco. There were no photographs on the walls and few decorative accessories. The house appeared lived in, but unloved, as if the resident – or residents – cared little about making the place feel like a home.

There was nothing for them to do at the premises now, so she and Dibbs made to leave.

'Detective, wait!'

Pearline turned at the front door. A member of the POLSA team ran down the stairs into the olive green hallway.

'I think you need to see this.' In his gloved hand he held a piece of yellowed paper.

'What is it?' she said.

'Some kind of birth certificate.'

The man handed her a latex glove and she hastily pulled it on. She took the paper, scanned it, and hurried towards Dibbs.

Rereading the document, her heart bucked. Once, twice. Fresh sweat broke and streamed down her back. Searing sunlight burned her eyes.

She tried to sound calm, but failed. 'Dibbs. Take a look at this.'

Dibbs strode over.

'What is it?' He peered over her shoulder at the piece of paper.

Blood Birthing Certificate

Today, on 23 September 2002 Serenity Finch, age 6, was birthed into Eternal Life Community.

Witness Uncle Saviour

Their eyes locked. Dibbs paled. 'Uncle Saviour. The cult leader. How old is Miss Mills?'

'Twenty-four.'

'Shit.'

She nodded. Her heart beat hard and fast. 'If Miss Mills is Serenity Finch . . .'

'Oh God.'

'I know.'

* * *

271

When she got back to the station, a crowd of journalists waited, pens poised, cameras ready.

Pearline hurried inside the building and rang Hill to tell him to make the Woods aware of the essential facts of the case, knowing it was vital the parents know before the press.

A statement had been drawn up for her. She barely had time to empty her bladder then she was standing in front of the voracious pack. Memories of giving statements during Isabelle's case erupted as she began to speak, and her hands shook, but she ploughed on, determined not to break.

They had a strong suspect, and that gave her something she'd been missing for a long time: hope.

Shit, shit, shit. There was no vehicle registered under Miss Sarah Mills' name. According to Mrs Edwards, Gregory's teacher, Miss Mills had mostly travelled to work via bicycle, but had occasionally been dropped off in a green car. There was, however, no car registered to the Birch Close address. The house belonged to Anthony Finch, and had been left to him in a Mr B Bronson's will. Bobby Bronson had owned the farm where the horror took place some nine years ago. The farm was long-abandoned, but also registered under Anthony Finch's name. A local detective had confirmed that no one was using the farmhouse and that no one had been seen on the premises. Uniformed officers had searched the area to check it remained unused.

CCTV footage was being viewed in an attempt to find out the green car's registration, and everyone in Birch Close was being re-questioned to discern as much as possible about the individual who lived in 11 Birch Close. So far, neighbours said that they only ever saw one woman – in her twenties, attractive, with long red hair – coming in and out of the property, and that she kept to herself. One resident thought she had started living there about five years earlier.

According to Birch Close residents, only one person lived there, which suggested that the second rumpled bed had been used by a guest who'd recently visited the house.

There were no more properties listed under Anthony Finch's name.

Evidence seized from 11 Birch Close was in for testing, but she would have to wait. Pearline bit the quick of her thumbnail and winced. Tracking down cult members was their current play: every remaining detective was on it.

Dibbs ran over to her desk. 'We got one. He's in Exeter Prison. He was arrested for attempting to kidnap a minor around the time of the event at the farm. He's killed inside since then so his sentence was extended to fifteen years. Warden says he's willing to talk.'

'Brilliant – let Hill know so he can update the Woods.'

She grabbed her phone and hurried with Dibbs to the car. It was an hour's drive. If they burned rubber, they could be there in forty.

Chapter 51
LILY

Now

Lily opened her eyes. An acrid taste filled her mouth. Her gums and lips were sandpaper-dry and her head thumped. She tried to orient herself. Above her was a ceiling; rough white bumps. Beside her was John, looking exhausted and worried.

'You passed out the second we got home,' he said, helping her to sit up.

'What time is it?'

'Five.'

'What? I've been asleep for an hour? Why didn't you wake me?'

'You stirred then went back to sleep. I thought you needed the rest.'

'You should have woken me up.'

'DC Hill was here. He left about fifteen minutes ago, but he filled me in on everything. Why don't you freshen up? Have a shower? I've made some sandwiches. You must be starving. That's probably why you fainted.'

She gritted her teeth. 'You should have woken me up, John.'

He held up his hands. 'Look. I'm sorry. I did what I thought was best. Are you going to have a shower?'

'No.' She swung her legs over the side of the bed and stood up. 'Just tell me everything DC Hill said.'

'You sure you don't want a shower fir—'

'No. I don't want a bloody shower! I want to know what's being done to find them.'

'All right. I'm sorry. Just try to calm down. I'll fetch you a cup of tea, then we can talk.'

'I don't want a sodding cup of tea, John! Just tell me!' She felt like she was going insane; why wasn't he telling her? 'Oh God, has something happened? Have they found them? Are they—'

'No. It's not that. It's . . . *OK*. They're still missing. You were right. They think that teaching assistant has taken them. They're doing everything they can to track her down and—'

'What aren't you telling me?' She stared hard at him. He wouldn't look at her. 'John? Just say it. Whatever it is, I'll cope.'

John swallowed. 'There've been two murders in Grimstone. One in Dogwood Street, which they think Hannah and Greg witnessed. That's why they ran into the woods. And that's where the other body was found.'

Lily couldn't breathe. *Murders.* She sat back down on the bed. Tried to think, make sense of everything. Head pain splintered her thoughts. She dashed out of the room.

'Lily? Wait,' John said, following her.

Grabbing painkillers from the medical cabinet in the bathroom, she downed four and looked at John. She couldn't think about the murders, about what that could mean. 'What's being done to find them? Did it seem like they were doing absolutely everything?'

'Yes. From what DC Hill said, they've got a team of about

275

thirty officers trying to trace this woman. Inspector Ottoline has gone to Devon to speak to an old acquaintance of Miss Mills.'

'Devon? Where in Devon?' Lily said, heading for the stairs.

'Wait – where are you going?' John rushed after her.

She turned halfway down the stairs. 'Where in Devon, John?'

'Why? It's not like you're going to go there. We've been told to stay here. They might need to contact us.'

'I can't stay here. I have to do something.'

'Lily, will you just listen to yourself. You're not a police officer. You can't go charging off trying to find them yourself. You're being ridiculous. Come into the kitchen. Have something to eat and drink. You're not being rational.'

'I'm not being rational?' She stopped at the bottom of the stairs and glared up at him. 'How can you just sit around doing nothing when our kids are out there with a murderer?'

'I'm doing what the police have told me to do. We both should. Just think for a moment. If the person who's taken Hannah and Greg wants money, we need to be here in case they ring.'

'I've got my mobile with me. If that happens, I'm contactable. You are too. Where in Devon did Inspector Ottoline go? Tell me, John, or God help me I'll—'

He folded his arms and sat down on the stairs. 'You'll what?'

She was shivering uncontrollably. Grief split her in two. She sank to her knees and put her face in her hands. Tears streamed out of her eyes and she sobbed, 'I have to do something. Please, John. Please help me do something.'

She heard his footsteps, felt him put his arms around her. He stroked her hair and held her tightly while she cried.

After a while, she peeled herself out of his arms and took

his face in her hands, kissed his tear-stained lips and wiped his cheeks.

'I'm so sorry, about everything. But please. I have to go. I have to do something to help my babies.' Her voice cracked. She looked up at him.

He nodded. In a voice that was small, broken, and barely recognisable, he said, 'Exeter Prison.'

Chapter 52
LOVE

Age 31

August 2012

The storm gathered strength; wind howled and whistled, whipping hair into eyes; dark clouds rolled in front of the sun, smudging faces and turning the ground close to black. Rain as warm as sweat plummeted in silver darts, making the land slippery and treacherous underfoot. The watching crowd was drenched in seconds. Drenched and mesmerised, as Faith darted out of the flock and pointed at Saviour and the farmhouse, screaming, wild-eyed. Faith, Fervour's wife, the woman who'd tried to leave the community with her mother and Peace when she was sixteen. Faith, the traitor who'd kept quiet all these years, waiting for her chance to pounce.

Some words the wind swallowed, others it roared. The words *blood* and *children* rang across the farm, and Love winced and dug her nails into her palms, willing the woman to shut her impure lips. But terror emanated from every pore of Faith's frail body, and the police officers turned to face her, listening, taking it all in, believing the insane rantings of a delusional woman. Peace may have been the one to tell the police that Fervour was about to take another child, but now Faith was the one spilling her guts about everything that had gone on here, bombarding the officers, screaming and begging and ranting about kidnapped children and syringes and blood. Faith needed to be shut up, forced into silence, but what could Love do? It was up to Saviour now. Their life was in his hands. If he didn't stop Faith, she'd take them all down, every single one of them. He needed to silence Peace too. She was trying to join in, back Faith up. Her head bobbed up and down eagerly like a nodding dog as she joined ranks with her fellow traitor and spouted lie after lie, twisting the truth and painting her and Saviour as devils.

It was agonising to watch. And Saviour just stood there, doing nothing, letting the two women fill the officers' heads with nonsense.

Love shrank back behind the house as the officers turned to look in her direction. She waited for ten seconds then stole a glance. The officers were heading her way, led by Peace and Faith. Saviour was following them. Panic flared inside her skull: the syringes would not have burned yet.

Saviour suddenly ran out ahead of the small group and held up his hand. She heard him say, 'Don't you need a warrant to search the property?'

Faith ignored him and tried to move past, but Saviour lashed out and hooked his arm around her throat.

Love's heart somersaulted. Everything was changing, going wrong. It was all happening so quickly. And yet this was what needed to happen. The woman – both women – needed to be silenced.

The police officers grabbed batons out of their belts in one swift movement and advanced on her husband, who glanced over his shoulder – back at the house – back at her. Their eyes met and she read his intention, and battled a primitive urge to scream at him to stop, knowing he was right; this was the only option that remained if she and Serenity were going to escape. He was doing the right thing, taking what she realised had always been the one and only action that remained.

Panic subsided and curiosity flooded her veins; and she watched, saliva collecting on her tongue, heart rocketing as her husband transcended and became more radiant than she'd ever imagined possible. Now, he was purity itself; his shadow eclipsed the sun and the stars and everything found within this mortal planet; his purity absolved them all. His blood had been purified and cleansed by the nectar of the innocent: he was ready to make this sacrifice. Ready to save her.

Drool pooled at the edges of her lips and she allowed herself a smile.

Arm hooked around Faith's throat, Saviour turned to his audience, enamoured as ever by their unflinching attention, and bellowed, 'FOR MY FAMILY. FOR ETERNAL LIFE. THIS IS MY SACRIFICE FOR YOU. THESE TRAITORS MUST BE SILENCED BEFORE THEY DESTROY US ALL. NEVER FORGET, THE END JUSTIFIES THE MEANS.'

He was the purest he'd ever been. Not a man, but an element as perfect as gold. A weapon built for good.

His flock gasped above the wind as he withdrew a knife from his pocket, flicked out the blade, held the silver shard aloft for all to see. It sparkled, kissed by a beam of white light that fired down from a sky too bruised and dark to create such luminescence.

Everyone gasped again, but this time the sound was swallowed by a backbiting wail of wind that made the distant trees bow down like Saviour's disciples, the grass flatten itself against the earth, and the police officers blink and hesitate a beat too long.

Love exhaled as her husband raised the knife to Faith's

throat and plunged the short blade into her neck. Blood gushed forth, scarlet and brilliant, streaming down Faith's dress and puddling at her feet. Her hands grasped frantically at her pouring throat, and her knees buckled. Still, she choked and clutched, reaching out to Saviour as if blinded to the fact that he had just killed her.

Love wondered if it hurt as much as childbirth. She thought it probably did. But it was a great deal shorter, which was a significant mercy.

Faith dropped to the ground. Love scanned the crowd for Faith's son. Zeal stared at his mother's body, but said nothing. He was mercifully pure, unlike his dead mother. Hope wrapped an arm around his shoulders and pulled him in close.

Love turned her attention to Peace. Now Saviour would deal with her traitorous sister. He would silence her and hand himself over to the officers. He would take the fall to protect the flock, and she would be for ever grateful for his sacrifice, and glad that he had been the one to do it, rather than her.

A moment passed where no one did anything. The officers seemed frozen with shock and too terrified to approach Saviour, who still wielded the knife and had the shotgun on his shoulder. They looked at each other uncertainly, and then Peace's wits returned in one heady jerk and she lunged forward and ripped the shotgun off Saviour's body. Saviour was shocked, too slow to react, and as the officers darted forward, Peace raised the gun. Saviour stumbled backwards and fell to the ground beside Faith's body. His arms rose in a cross in front of his face and he tried to speak, but Peace shot him in the centre of his forehead and his skull burst open. Its contents spilled over the stone courtyard. Blood mingled with old corn, dust, dirt, strands of swirling straw and chicken excrement. Saviour did not move. His eyes were glass, his sacrifice absolute.

Peace did not hesitate. She dropped to her knees, turned

the gun around to her throat, aimed a glassy stare in Love's direction, then pulled the trigger. Her face exploded.

A hush fell. The scent of blood travelled on the whipping wind.

It seemed Peace had taken care of everything for her. An unexpected, but fortuitous turn of events.

Love licked her lips. There was so much blood. Enough to bathe in. She wanted to scoop it up and watch it drip through her fingers, but she also wanted to scream.

Rain fell and the wind wailed. The sheep trembled. The police officers stared down at the three bodies. Two traitors, one saviour.

Saviour would not live for ever, but she still could. So could Serenity.

Wind and rain lashed blood across the farm. Love inhaled a lungful of metallic air and glanced past Saviour's corpse at her bewildered flock. Then she slipped on Saviour's mask and ran to the well to join her daughter.

Chapter 53

PEARLINE

Now

HM Prison Exeter was a red-brick Victorian building with four residential wings, an imposing structure built to withstand the test of time. The inner walls were painted an insipid shade of yellow aside a grey concrete floor, the smell a cross between that of a school and a hospital. Despite the heat of the day, the air was cool and dank.

Pearline felt dirty the second she entered the prison. The warden met her and Dibbs at reception and handed them a file.

Warden Jones was obese and greasy as a pork pie, but his eyes shone with intelligence. 'He's a sly one. Be prepared for mind games. I trust him about as far as I could throw him. As you can tell, I'm no athlete.'

She thanked him for the file and read as she walked. Dibbs scanned the notes over her shoulder. A chill worked under her skin as they followed a guard along a bleach-scented corridor and entered a room with no windows.

Pearline and Dibbs sat and waited. No evidence of foul play at the farm had ever been discovered, but this man had been arrested attempting to kidnap a child. Since his incarceration, he'd killed an inmate. If such a man had been a top player in Anthony Finch's so-called 'community', she dreaded to think what might have occurred there over the years that remained undiscovered to this day.

Dibbs flicked her a nervous smile and she nodded back. What they got from this guy could make or break the investigation. Stress burbled in her abdomen and she rested her hand there to soothe the muscles, but the action did little good. *Keep it together. Christ, you're better than this.*

A moment passed and she felt light pressure on her shoulder. Dibbs, his hand warm and gentle. 'We've got this.'

She said nothing, but touched his hand. Their fingers brushed. The touch was charged. There were things to be said between them, but now was not the time. Pearline wondered if she'd ever find the time or if she would resist the pull of him for ever. Still, the brief contact eased the pressure in her chest and she let out a long sigh. Dibbs's leg stopped jiggling.

Steps thudded outside the room and two guards led a bald, pug-faced man inside. From the inmate's bowed head, it would have been easy to infer shame or defeat, but the smirk that played on his lips suggested otherwise. *Here we go.*

'Good afternoon, Mr Anderson. I'm Chief Inspector Ottoline and this is Detective Sergeant Dibbs. Thank you for agreeing to speak to us.'

'Call me Fervour,' he said in a rough voice, dragging his gaze across her breasts. Spittle gathered at the corners of his mouth and his naked skull gleamed like a boiled egg.

She sat straighter, felt Dibbs tense. 'As you may already be aware, we're here regarding the disappearance of two children. We have reason to believe that a young woman called Serenity Finch may know their whereabouts. We know that you were part of a group called Eternal Life Community which was led by Anthony Finch. What, if anything, do you know about Serenity Finch?'

The man blinked slowly, licked his cracked lips. 'I've met her. She was at the community. She was a teenager when I got arrested.' He smiled, leaned forward.

Christ. He's enjoying this.

'Is she related to Anthony Finch?' Dibbs said.

He took his time answering, and yawned long and wide, revealing a split uvula that reminded her of the devil's fork. He smirked. 'Yeah, but not by blood.'

'If not by blood, how?'

Fervour's mouth twitched. 'Saviour and Love *adopted* her. I don't know where from.' He made quotation marks around the word 'adopted'.

Pearline and Dibbs exchanged a glance; had the cult adopted or in fact *abducted* Serenity? Fervour seemed to be implying the latter. He'd been arrested for attempting to abduct a child on the day of the farm murders as a result of a cult member called Peace reporting him to the police. That same woman had later taken two police officers to the farm and killed Anthony Finch, then herself. If this man had been guilty of attempting to kidnap a child, it didn't seem too much of a stretch to imagine that the cult had abducted children successfully before that incident. *Sweet Jesus.*

But they weren't here to look into Serenity's past; they were here to investigate the disappearance of Hannah and Gregory. That, above everything else, took precedence in this moment. If this man could tell them anything that might lead to Serenity Finch's current whereabouts, he was useful. If not, they would leave and move on.

She gave Dibbs a nod.

'By Saviour, you mean Mr Finch?' Dibbs said casually.

Fervour nodded.

'And Love?'

'I never knew her original name. I joined after them. Scary bitch, mind.'

Pearline said, 'What's a blood birthing certificate?'

Fervour scratched his nose. Again, he took his time. 'Like a birth certificate, but it means more. When someone joined the community, Saviour gave them a new pure name at a christening ceremony of sorts.'

'Was Serenity six when they . . . *adopted* her?'

He smirked, but nodded.

'What was her previous name?'

'I don't know.'

'Have you had any sort of communication from her or anyone else who might know her since your arrest nine years ago?' Pearline said.

'No. I tried to reach out, but the community split after the incident. No one ever wrote me. Not even my son. I've been in here ever since. And, as I'm sure you know, Saviour killed my wife that day. Not that I care. Faith was a treacherous bitch. Just as bad as Peace.'

Pearline swallowed a lash of hatred and cleared her throat. 'Your son? Do you have an address for him?'

'Nope. Like I said, he doesn't want anything to do with me.'

'What's his name and age?'

'Does it matter? Aren't you trying to find Serenity?'

'Yes, but your son may be able to help us.'

He sighed and scratched his neck. 'Zeal Anderson.'

'Was Zeal his cult name?' Dibbs said.

Fervour scowled. 'It wasn't a *cult*. It was a community. A good place where good people came together and lived in harmony.'

'Until they didn't,' Pearline said quietly.

He glared. She held his gaze until he looked away. After a tense silence, he sighed. 'His original name was Andrew.'

'Andrew Anderson?' Dibbs said.

'Yeah.'

'And just to clarify, you have absolutely no idea where he lives?'

'I already said I didn't.'

'Do you have any idea where Serenity Finch might have gone or who she might have gone with?'

'Oh yeah. She'll have gone with Love.'

She felt Dibbs tense.

'Are you're absolutely certain you can't recall Love's real name?' Pearline said.

'Like I said, I never knew it. She was a member way before me.'

'You're sure?'

'I said I was, didn't I?'

Pearline thought he was telling the truth. She waited a few seconds then said, 'Where do you think Love might have taken her?'

'Beats me. I know Saviour and her had a place ready in case something happened, but they kept it secret.'

Pearline swallowed a sigh.

Dibbs said, 'Are you sure Love never mentioned anywhere?'

'I'm sure.'

'Love and Saviour never went anywhere to get away for a break? There's nowhere they travelled to from time to time?'

Fervour laughed. 'Eternal Life didn't work like that. Once you joined, you didn't leave. No one did. There was no reason to.'

'What did Serenity look like?' Pearline said.

He licked his lips and smoothed his palm over his bald head. 'Fit. Red hair. Leggy. Huge tits. Totally fuckable.' He winked at Dibbs, whose hands curled into fists on his lap.

Pearline recoiled inwardly but remained expressionless. Despite the lurid description, his words matched the

287

photograph of Miss Mills provided by the school. Miss Mills/ Serenity Finch was a tall, attractive redhead. To be absolutely sure, she slid the school photograph of 'Miss Mills' across the table. 'Is this her?'

He looked down and stroked a finger down the photograph. When he looked up, he was smiling. 'Hell yeah. She's all grown up, but that's her all right.'

His eyes flicked up to Pearline's breasts. Dibbs slammed a hand onto the table and eyeballed him. 'Look at her like that again and I'll—'

'You'll what?' Fervour grinned. 'Arrest me?'

Pearline ignored the impulse to smash her fist into his jaw and stood up. 'Right. Thank you for your time. I think you've given us everything you've got.'

Dibbs hesitated and tried to catch her eye, but she hurried to the door.

'Wait a minute,' Fervour said.

She turned around. 'What is it, Mr Anderson?'

'Don't you want to know where Love hid the body? The cops never found it. Never even suspected it was there.' He leaned back, eyes glinting.

'What body?' she said.

Chapter 54

LILY

Now

Memories assaulted her like fists.

Hannah being born. Exquisite happiness followed by months of terrible anxiety. Greg's birth. A wonderful couple of years filled with playgroup and mum dates and a lot of anxiety but the functioning kind managed by pills. Mum's death – thankfully in her sleep after another bout of pneumonia. The funeral. Grief blending with having to go back to work. The struggle of trying to manage it all. Birthdays and Christmases. Wonderful times and stressful times. Making love to John in the Hilton in London on a rare weekend away when Georgie had looked after the kids. Watching *Les Misérables* at Piccadilly Theatre and being moved to tears. Hannah screaming with delight on holiday when they went to a waterpark. Greg getting sunstroke and being very unwell, scaring her to death. Ups and downs. Highs and lows. John and her reminiscing about life before the kids, remembering their first few dates, their first kiss.

Life was busy and stressful, but full. Hannah and Greg and John made it so, and she wanted it all back.

And then John had grown distant and anxiety had reared its head and the pills hadn't seemed as effective. Her worries about their relationship had blurred the last six or seven months. She'd lost focus. Taken her eyes off the kids. Let herself become buried in fears of an affair. Again, anxiety had warped her judgement and she'd lost sight of what really mattered, which was them. Hannah and Greg and John. Talking to them, being with them, loving them.

With a trembly sigh, she drove through the prison car park and pulled into a space. Keeping the engine running for the air conditioning, Lily pushed her hair off her cheeks. Scanning the car park for a police car, she saw none. Her heart sank; she might have missed Inspector Ottoline. Her plan was to follow the inspector and – that was where her plan stopped. Panic gnawed. She didn't really know what she was doing, only that she had to do something. John was probably right; driving to Exeter Prison was an irrational thing to do, but the police could miss something vital that she might just happen to notice. What if, for example, the police questioned someone, then drove away from their house and the kidnapper left after the police had gone, but Lily was there to see them leave – to follow them and see where they went? She might follow that person to the place they were keeping Hannah and Greg. The police couldn't keep watch on everyone and everything. The more people helping to look for her babies, the better. She was doing the best thing she could – she was offering the police an extra pair of eyes and ears, even if they didn't want her to.

You're wrong. You're crazy. You need your pills. Go home and be with John. Stop being so irrational. This is crazy. It's your fault Hannah and Greg left home. They never would have left if you'd been a better mum. If you hadn't been obsessed with telling yourself John was having an affair, you'd have paid the kids more attention and Greg would have felt like he could confide in you about the letter so he never would have left the house. It's your fault they're gone. Your fault. You're a terrible mum. You've always been a terrible mum. And you're a selfish bitch for going on this ridiculous goose chase rather than staying at home with John when he needs you. You're not the only one suffering. John is too. Turn round. Drive home. Stop being such a—

Lily smashed her hands onto the steering wheel over and over again and screamed. When the pain in her palms grew too intense, she stopped and rested her head on the window. Her brain felt as if its hinges had grown loose and was about to detach from her skull. The space behind her eyes hummed and vibrated. She squeezed her eyes shut and massaged the knots in her neck, counting down from twenty. When she opened her eyes, her chest felt calmer, her head less like a rattle. She looked up: the big blue door to the prison opened, and Inspector Ottoline strode out followed by DS Dibbs, the tall, handsome detective she and John had met at Miss Mills' house.

Her heart skipped a beat. Thanking her lucky stars for this stroke of good fortune, she ducked down behind the steering wheel and watched the two officers walk across the car park. They were walking fast, but not fast enough. Lily wanted to scream at them to run to their car, that every second was precious. But she stayed silent and hidden, watching as they opened the doors of a very clean, black Audi A3. She waited until they were pulling out of the space, then put the Mini in reverse and drove after them, keeping a safe distance behind so they didn't notice her following.

Chapter 55
LOVE

Now

Beyond the caravan walls, the woods lay as still as the dead.

Inside the camper, Love stroked the children's heads. Beneath her fingers, their hair felt soft and soothing, but another migraine was building and dark thoughts buzzed around her mind like maddened bees; none of this would be happening if it wasn't for Peace. Saviour wouldn't be dead; she and Serenity wouldn't have been forced to leave the community and flee to that nasty little cottage, holing themselves up like hermits, living a half-life where she only spent short stints with her daughter and longer periods alone tending to the ungrateful giver in this caravan, luring givers to them rather than venturing out to collect them; she wouldn't suffer from these ghastly migraines and awful fatigue, which were the result of the loss she forced herself to suppress day-in, day-out. If Peace wasn't already dead, she'd string her up to the very same tree from which their mother had hung herself. The bullet to her throat had been too quick and easy. Peace should have suffered, just as she had these last nine years.

'What are we going to do?' Serenity said warily.

She looked at her daughter, her beautiful, clever daughter. The only person left from Eternal Life apart from herself. For nine, long, hard years, they'd struggled to survive. Money she'd taken from the farmhouse stash had enabled them to get by. On the black market they'd purchased false documentation, fake qualifications, and a DBS check for Seri so that she could work as a teaching assistant and earn more money. Fortunately, she and Saviour had taken measures to make sure they had a safe-house ready in case anything disastrous happened, so she and Seri had fled to the pink cottage, but in order to be safe, they'd stolen a caravan and Love had mainly lived there, while her daughter lived alone in the cottage. Life had been pretty dismal, but they'd worked together and continued on their path to Total Illumination, knowing that one day, when they found a way, they would build a new community that would be even purer than Eternal Life.

Indeed, no matter how exhausted she was or how much her head hurt, Love was not ready to concede defeat to the impure; she'd never be ready to do that. Still, things were far from ideal and the plan had gone awry.

If Serenity hadn't killed that man in the woods, they never would have needed to come back to the farm. Police had swarmed Birch Close and because of that, they'd had to flee. They couldn't remain in the cottage, not when every resident in the area was being questioned. Sooner or later, the police would have come knocking, demanding answers. But she wasn't angry at Seri. Her daughter had done what she thought best. And everyone made mistakes. Even her. She had made a mistake when she'd let her guard down with Peace. It was a mistake she'd never make again.

Being back at the farm was bitter-sweet, but it was the perfect place to dispose of unwanted goods; even when disaster had struck nine years ago, and the police had searched the farm, they'd failed to find the first giver's body. The well was a charm she intended to use again. And, the more Love thought about it, the more she liked the idea of going back to the farmhouse, of reliving those early days in the place she'd first tasted pure blood, lost her virginity to Saviour, and gained her first true glimpse of eternal life.

'Mother?' Serenity said.

'Let me think.'

Serenity chewed her lower lip; worried, and rightly so.

Love had agreed that using the lure of a fairy to persuade the boy to come to them of his own accord was a good idea. Serenity had been wrong before, but Love had given her a second chance and she'd chosen well. Her daughter had worked hard to get to know Gregory Woods. Harder than before. She was convinced that he was the right choice and had put forward a compelling argument: he was an oddball obsessed with fairies, being bullied, and unhappy at home because his parents argued a lot. Seri had been right about this one. Love knew it. It was just a shame that his older sister, Hannah, had come with him.

Pain sliced through her skull and Love winced. Taking a sip of purified water, she frowned at Seri. 'Neither of us could have foreseen his sister joining him or those men chasing them through the woods. I can see why you thought it a good idea to silence the witness, but I need to stay away from the cottage for a while. You need to return soon though, so you don't arouse suspicion. The police will still want to question you.'

'I'm sorry, Mother.'

'Don't apologise. Focus on rectifying your mistake.'

Serenity nodded. 'What shall I say when the police come knocking?'

'Say you went camping. You won't have an alibi, but there

will be no reason to suspect you. I don't think we have anything to worry about. There's no way the police can find out that you told Gregory to go to Birch Close, is there?'

Seri hesitated. 'I don't think so.'

'Good.'

Her daughter nibbled her nail and clung to the scythe like a lifeline. Since Saviour's death, it had become something of a comfort blanket to Seri. His demise had hit her hard.

Love gestured to Hannah. The girl was sedated. Both children's heads rested on her lap. 'We have to release this one.'

'I agree. We don't have a choice. She's too old and stubborn to adapt,' Seri said, a little too quickly.

Love frowned. There was something about the eagerness of her words that stirred memories of Fervour. She didn't like it. Releasing a child was not something enjoyable. It was a necessity, nothing more. But she hadn't the strength to perform the release, so it would fall to Serenity.

'I agree. Do it now, as quickly as possible. Then you can return to Grimstone and act like nothing happened. I'll stay here, keep out of sight. You can come and visit in a couple of weeks when everything's calmed down.'

Seri nodded, eyes solemn. 'Yes, Mother. Of course.'

Love braced herself for her daughter's reaction. 'I want you to release the other one too.'

Seri's whole body jerked and she looked down at the scythe, colour draining from her beautiful face. Love had warned her against it, but Seri had allowed herself to bond with the giver. As a result, she was reluctant to release the child, but this giver would never adapt to their way of life, no matter what they did or said.

Seri's eyes were on hers. 'But you said—'

Love injected acid into her tone. It took energy she didn't have. 'We don't have a choice. Accept it. Move on.'

Seri opened her mouth to argue. Love held up her hand

295

and gave her a look. 'Don't. Take them both straight to the well. Do it quickly and cleanly like I've taught you. I don't want them to suffer any more than necessary. Got it?' She looked at Seri and raised her eyebrows. Her daughter nodded and blinked rapidly.

Love smiled. A rock had been lifted off her chest. 'Good girl.' She lay back in the bed.

Relieved to rest her aching muscles, she closed her eyes. Contentment warmed her heart. She'd raised an extraordinary child and trained her well. Seri was a good worker bee willing to do anything for her queen. Her daughter would get the job done in a swift, orderly manner, just as she had with the first giver all those years ago.

In a gentle voice, Love said, 'Let me know when it's done.'

She raised her glass. Serenity hesitated, then clinked her mother's glass with her own. Together, united in their purity, they downed the last of the blood they'd extracted from Gregory Woods. Licking her lips clean, Love blew her daughter a kiss, then closed her eyes and pretended to drift off to sleep.

As soon as she heard the door close, she grabbed the boy's ladybird backpack and snuck out of the caravan. She knew a shortcut through the woods that would take her directly to the farmhouse.

As she slipped through the trees, she fingered the small key, held it against her lips, relieved she'd kept it. She felt more excited than she had for a long time. Just thinking about walking through those lofty rooms, reminiscing about the old days when Eternal Life was in full swing brought tingles to her skin.

With energy she rarely possessed these days, Love walked back home.

Chapter 56
PEARLINE

Now

'Sorry I lost it in there,' Dibbs said.

She nodded, secretly pleased he'd stood up for her. 'It's fine. Next time remember to bring your sword with you though, OK?'

Dibbs drove while she touched base with the team, from whom there were no new developments. She tasked a couple of detectives with hunting down Andrew/Zeal Anderson, updated the Guvnor, then hung up. They were on their way to the farm to check out Fervour Anderson's story about the body. Neither she nor Dibbs harboured much hope that he was telling the truth, but Dibbs argued that scoping out the place where Serenity Finch grew up might give them a greater sense of the person they were dealing with. He'd also made the point that other ex-cult members probably still lived in or near the area and that if they stuck around Devon for a bit longer, they'd be better situated to pay them a visit if the team tracked any down.

'It shouldn't take long to trace more members,' Dibbs said,

popping a peppermint cream in his mouth then offering her one.

'I hope not. But if something bad was going on there, they'd have changed their names as soon as possible after the event. The team have been on this for a while now, and haven't found anyone else yet.' She took a sweet. Then another. The sugar helped almost immediately.

'Maybe. But no evidence of kidnapping or murder was found. Everyone stated that the woman who killed Anthony Finch then herself was delusional. Each and every member of Eternal Life claimed they knew nothing about blood being taken from children, or Fervour Anderson's plan to kidnap that boy. They all said he was doing that on his own, that he'd brought shame on the community, and they wanted nothing to do with him.'

'Yeah. I'm just flicking through the file to see what members said about Saviour killing that woman,' Pearline said.

Dibbs speeded up to seventy and adjusted his mirror to block the lowering sun. 'What did the members of Eternal Life believe in?'

'It doesn't say, though by the name of the cult, I think we can hazard a guess. But here's the thing: no one would say *anything* about the rituals they practised or how the community functioned other than the fact that they *worked together as one united, harmonious family to provide a natural way of living for each other and their children.*'

'Sounds perfect,' Dibbs said dryly.

'Too perfect.'

'And zero evidence of foul play,' Dibbs said, pulling onto a dirt road.

'Nothing. Not even a spot of blood.'

'So Fervour Anderson's lying about this body to waste our time? Or terrible things happened on this farm that never came to light?'

A shiver rippled down her arms. 'It's worth checking out the scene. Places shape people's minds too.'

Dibbs arched an eyebrow. 'That's profound.'

Somehow, she managed a smile. 'It is rather, isn't it?'

He grinned.

'What?' she said.

'You're beautiful when you smile.'

'I thought you said I look like an old cloth?'

Turning away, she looked out of the window, blinking fast to push back a sudden sting of tears. When she'd smiled, her cheeks had ached, and she knew why: smiling was something her face didn't usually do. The muscles were unused to the action.

Pearline dabbed at her forehead with her handkerchief then surreptitiously wiped her eyes. The fact that smiling made her face hurt triggered an intense sorrow. After her father passed, she'd managed to build a life for herself. For a few years, she'd felt happy, positive about the future, but that feeling was gone. Now, she was back to the miserable, failure of a person her father had beaten her into.

She could not fail another child. Another parent. She wouldn't.

What if they're already dead?

'We're here,' Dibbs said, making her jump.

Chapter 57
LILY

Now

Lily turned the Mini onto a dirt road and slowed to a crawl. Up ahead, the unmarked police car indicated left and disappeared. She inched up the lane, wincing at the crunch of gravel under the wheels. They were some way from the closest village, surrounded by fields. Long grass and weeds blinkered her view until she grew close to the turning. Bringing the Mini's nose a couple of feet from the side lane that the inspector had taken, she got out of the car and quietly shut the door.

She pocketed her keys and crept around the bonnet. Crouching low, she peered past the end of her car. The police car was parked up in a large, gritted space which she assumed was a parking area for what appeared to be a farm. Beyond a silver gate, were buildings – a big white house to the right, a barn, stables and another couple of ramshackle buildings that looked like they might be used for storage. Behind the farm and to the left lay a patchwork of fields. In the middle distance to the right of the farmhouse lay an expanse of woods. The land had an empty, wild feel, as though it had been left to its own devices for a long time. There were no animals that she could see, and no people, other than DI Ottoline and DS Dibbs, who climbed over the gate – DS Dibbs with ease, the inspector with less athleticism and a groan as she landed on the other side of the fence.

Lily wondered what on earth they were doing at an abandoned farm. Had they worked out where the kidnapper was keeping Hannah and Greg? Were her babies here?

Palpitations thudded under her breastbone. She should be in there with them, to help if help was needed. The more hands on deck the better, especially as there were just two detectives. But she couldn't be seen. Not yet.

She waited until the officers disappeared inside the stables, then sprinted to the gate and clambered up. Her jeans snagged on something sharp at the top and she ripped her leg free and dropped awkwardly to the ground. A sharp pain rang out in her ankle, but she tested it and found it was nothing more than a twist. Frightened the officers would emerge from the stables any second, she ran across uneven ground towards the barn, running behind the back of the stables.

Safely behind the barn, she crouched in tangled grass and gulped air. Her heart was pounding, her body soaked in sweat. Resting a palm against her chest, she peeked around the back of the building and waited for the officers to leave the stables, which they did, walking quickly in her direction. Drawing back, Lily listened to their footsteps, heard them trying doors, rattling a chain.

'Locked,' DI Ottoline said.

'Damn.'

'Hang on – chain's loose. I think we can – yes.'

Lily crawled around the side of the building in time to see DS Dibbs follow his partner into the barn. They appeared moments later, and again Lily yanked her head out of sight.

'Let's try the well, then double back to check the house

301

and the other buildings,' Pearline said. 'I'm beginning to feel like this is a huge waste of time. There's no body here. Anderson's screwed us.'

'Dead creepy, isn't it?' DS Dibbs said as they began to walk across the farmyard.

The inspector muttered her agreement and they moved out of earshot, heading towards the woods that stretched beyond the farm.

The word 'well' cycled around and around in her pounding head, as did the word 'body'; had DI Ottoline meant there's *nobody* here or there's no *body* here? Lily almost screamed at them to stop, wait for her, but bit her tongue. If they knew she was here, they'd send her packing and she'd have to go home and do nothing, be of no help to anyone. If that happened, she'd go insane.

With shaking fingers, she texted John to tell him she was fine, but the text wouldn't send. Frowning, she pocketed her phone and waited for the officers to disappear behind the farmhouse, then ran across the yard to the first of two dilapidated buildings. A padlock held the door fast. There were no windows, making it impossible to look or get inside. She put her ear to the peeling wood and listened. Nothing came from inside. Outside, the air was hot and still, the smell of old manure strong. The sun was beginning to lower, the sky to fade.

She peered around the corner of the building. The officers disappeared into the woods. With a sigh of relief, Lily headed for the farmhouse, pinning hope against hope that she'd find it unlocked and some kind of indication of Hannah and Greg's whereabouts within.

Chapter 58

PEARLINE

Now

Pearline pulled out the vague map Fervour Anderson had drawn for them. He'd marked the supposed well with a cross. According to the drawing, the well was about thirty yards or so into the woods in the middle of a clearing.

Dibbs walked by her side peering down at the map as they strode across the farm. She had to walk quickly to match his loping strides.

Recalling the prisoner's words, Pearline felt a shiver of trepidation as his eyes flashed into her mind. The man had a way of licking his lips that made her feel sick. He was not to be trusted, but there had been something in the way he'd spoken that had given her a sense that he might just be telling the truth. Dibbs was more sceptical.

'If there's a body in that well, I'll eat my hat,' he said.

'Do you even own a hat? You don't strike me as a hat-wearing sort of guy.'

He flashed a grin. 'If you finally take the hint and agree to go out for dinner with me, I'll don my grandad cap just for you.'

She rolled her eyes, but her heart flip-flopped. After a beat, the high disappeared and a black cloud rolled across her chest. She didn't deserve someone like Dibbs.

'Hey – you OK?' Dibbs said, touching her elbow.

She forced a smile. 'Yeah.'

He applied more pressure to her arm and she stopped walking and looked up at him, squinting against the sinking sun.

'I mean it,' he said, 'you and me. We could have something.'

She cleared her throat. In spite of everything, her tummy fluttered. 'I'll think about it.'

He grinned. 'You better.'

They carried on walking, the sun still hot on their backs, but descending little by little as dusk encroached upon the countryside.

The farm merged with the woods. Dibbs walked ahead, torch already in hand to search the well. There was a half-trodden path that they followed, using Fervour's map for guidance. Towering trees brought shadows and welcome coolness. Up ahead, the trees cleared and, just as the prisoner had drawn, a well forged out of stone that looked hundreds of years old sat in the middle of a small clearing.

Dibbs stopped and held up his hand. She froze. He lowered to the ground and backed up. She followed, backtracking away from the well out of the clearing.

He glanced over his shoulder at her, eyes wide. 'Someone's coming.'

They beat a retreat, lying stomach-down on the ground a yard or so away from the clearing, hidden – she hoped – by the trunk of an oak tree and fronds of undergrowth. Dibbs's body pulsed with heat. Their arms touched and the hairs on her arms tingled. The squeal of rusty wheels broke the quiet. Fear spread its claws and scraped a long, slow sear of pain across her shoulders as Pearline craned her neck to try to see the clearing. Her eyes widened as a tall figure in white emerged from the trees pushing a wheelbarrow towards the well.

Beside her, Dibbs's breath hitched.

Chapter 59
LOVE

Now

Despite the sheets and dust, little had changed. Love smoothed her hand over the banister as she climbed, anticipation drumming a manic beat, filling her body with energy. She could feel the new giver's blood coursing through her veins, purifying her, making her stronger, better. This was no placebo effect. This was real, as real and incredible as the first time she'd tasted pure blood. Nothing compared to the benefits of human nectar drawn from an innocent source.

The floorboards creaked beneath her feet as she drifted along the landing towards the master bedroom. Cobwebs silvered the corners of the ceiling. Spiders had made their home here where she couldn't.

She sighed with yearning. A longing to return to the farm properly and rebuild the community raised its head with glowing eyes. For years she'd only dreamed of such a thing, but now, being back here where everything began, she imagined she could make it happen. She hadn't the means, but she'd find a way. In this aching day of suffering upon suffering, people craved hope, and hope was what Eternal Life offered.

Hope, love and purity. A long, fulfilling life amongst like-minded people who worked the land, just as nature always intended.

Her hand rested on the bedroom door. The wood seemed to throb. Blinded by memories, she drifted into the room, removed the sheet from the bed, and crawled up the mattress. She was sixteen again, topless, riding her lover, who radiated purity like the sun's glorious heat. She was young again, vital, shining. Saviour was here smiling up at her, admiring her beautiful naked body. They were one, united in flesh and belief and love. Together they would live for ever.

But he was dead.

In one swift blow, the vision collapsed. Love lay back on the bed and stared up at the ceiling. She did not cry. She didn't think she had ever cried for real. Crying for effect, yes. For real, no.

All at once, she felt flat. Empty. Hollowed out like a gutted chicken.

She missed Hope too. Huge, maternal Teacher Hope. The closest thing she supposed she'd ever known to a true mother. Love often wondered what had become of her, but had never tried to find out. Nine years had passed since the community's collapse. She feared that most of the flock had lost their way and returned to the humdrum existence of the impure masses. Even Hope, for all her dedication to Eternal Life, had probably reverted to conformism. The woman valued her offspring above all else; she'd have done anything necessary to keep them with her, even if it meant spurning her journey to Total Illumination. With Fervour in prison and Faith dead, she wouldn't have been surprised if Hope had taken in Zeal too.

Without Love and Saviour to lead, Hope, like everyone else, would have lost focus, dithered and died. Indeed, Nobility had taken his own life; she'd seen it on the local news.

Overdose apparently. Pathetic. Weak – just like her mother. She didn't know what had become of any other members, and couldn't care less. Death would come for them, and it would be their own doing.

Peace's ugly face came and went like a flickering bulb. Black, white, black, white. Dead dead dead.

She smiled, tasted blood. She'd bitten her tongue. She looked at the scarlet liquid on her fingers. Some of that blood was pure, some rotten. She needed more pure blood. She needed it now.

A migraine was building, bashing against the walls of her brain.

Love sat up. Her mouth salivated with the need for nectar.

Desperate to return to the caravan, she got off the bed and strode to the door, then froze at the creak of footsteps on the landing.

Chapter 60

LILY

Now

Lily thought she heard a noise; a squeal, like the sound of mattress springs. Stopping on the landing, she listened. Beyond the farmhouse walls came the distant cry of a bird. A shrill, echoing call a bit like a seagull's. When that ceased, silence pervaded the blank walls, made heavier by the layers of dust that had collected over the years.

She wondered how long the house had remained in this state and why no one lived here. It was a beautiful building. The walls needed a fresh coat of paint, and the carpets a good clean, but once that was done, it would be good to go. She tried to imagine who had lived here and failed. The place felt sterile and too white. Lacking a human touch.

A shiver caught at her neck and she glanced over her shoulder, but no one was there. She frowned, aware she was wasting time and that the officers could be back to search the house any moment. She'd been pleased to find the front door unlocked. Surprised there was no evidence that teenagers had violated the place or that a homeless person had camped here for a while.

Lily walked on and opened each door as she passed, having a quick look inside, checking under the beds. No one was here. Her heart lurched as a horrific thought stabbed like a knife: *I might never see my babies again.*

An image of Hannah and Greg's sightless eyes, blood trailing from their mouths, their hands curled inwards in pain, winded her, and she leaned against the wall. Wave after wave of grief attacked, thumping her stomach.

No. They're alive. They have to be. I can still feel them. They're out there somewhere. Keep going. Don't give up. Not yet. Not ever.

She smeared away tears she didn't know she'd cried. Now was not the time for this. She needed to hold it together.

After a while, the nausea subsided. She exhaled shakily and pushed open the final door. It was clearly the largest bedroom in the house. White as white.

Lily scanned every inch of the room. Her eyes locked on the bed. There was no sheet covering it. The sheet was on the floor in a heap, just like Greg's had been.

Her shoulders tingled and she whirled around, hand at her throat. A tall woman with long black hair stood behind the door. The woman's eyes were blank and staring. She wore a loose white dress.

'Gosh – you scared me!' Lily said.

The woman smiled. Laughter lines appeared at the corners of her eyes. 'Sorry. I didn't expect anyone to be here. I was worried you might be a burglar. What are you doing here?'

'I – is this your house?'

The woman's eyes took her in, trailing slowly from her head to her feet. 'It was my late husband's.'

'Oh. I'm sorry. I know I shouldn't be here. It's just that my children are missing and I, well, I thought they might be here.' She ended lamely, hoping the woman didn't press her.

310

'No need to apologise. I'd be the same if my children were missing. What are their names?'

'Hannah and Gregory. Look, I'm sorry. I'd better go.'

'No, wait. Let me help you. I know the house inside out. I can show you around, show you all the funny little nooks and crannies. You never know, you might find something useful.'

Lily nodded gratefully. 'Thank you. That would be good.'

The woman stepped away from the door and waved her hand around the room. 'As you can see, there's nothing in here. I just popped in to see if I could find an old necklace of mine. Where have you looked so far?'

'I came straight upstairs. I thought . . . I don't know what I thought. Sorry, I'm not making much sense. Um, so I looked in every room on this floor, but found nothing. Then I came in here.'

'Why don't we check the attic next then? Follow me.'

Lily hurried after the woman out of the bedroom and across the landing. It seemed odd that the lady was here, and that made her wary, but Lily had no choice but to follow her. This stranger might well help her find Hannah and Greg. 'What's your name?'

The woman stopped at the end of the landing, stood on her toes and pulled down the hatch. She glanced at Lily. 'Love. What's yours?'

'Lily,' she said, hugging herself despite the warmth.

Love pulled down a metal ladder and gestured for her to climb. Eagerly, Lily scrambled up the silver rungs into the dark.

'There's a pull switch to your left,' Love called.

Lily pulled it and a weak bulb flickered on. The light buzzed, filling the large, musty space with a swarm-like hum. She jumped as a hand squeezed her shoulder. Love pushed her forward and stood by her side to inspect the space. Lily

311

moved away, uncomfortable with how close the woman was standing, and scanned the attic, disappointed yet relieved to find the wooden boards empty save for one item, which Love picked up.

'There's nothing here,' Lily said, turning to go.

The woman didn't move. Lily watched as she brought a turquoise blanket to her nose. The material must have been smothered with dust, but she held it there for a while. The moment seemed personal, so Lily waited another second, then turned and descended the ladder. Shortly after, Love tossed the blanket to the floor, climbed down, pushed the ladder back into its folded position, and shut the hatch.

Lily hovered by her side a moment, wanting to ask her to show her the downstairs rooms, but sensing the woman's preoccupation.

Abruptly, Love's head snapped up. She stared at Lily oddly, then said, 'Wait there a moment. I just need to get something, then I'll show you the rest of the house.'

Desperate to keep searching, Lily turned and stared over the banister at the broad expanse below. The house felt empty. Hannah and Greg weren't here. They never had been. She was wasting time.

She hurried after the woman to tell her that she was leaving, and Love stepped out from the master bedroom and hitched a bag up her shoulder. Lily stopped. Her heart thudded. She stared at the bag. It was red with black spots, shaped like a ladybird.

'Where did you get that?'

Love hesitated. She looked around. 'This? Oh, I found it.'

'Where? Where was it?' Lily said.

The woman hesitated again before speaking. 'Why?'

'It's like my son's bag. He's got one just like that. Where did you find it?'

'Downstairs. In the kitchen.'

'Can I see it?' Lily held out her hand.

'Yes, of course. Here.'

Lily grabbed the bag and unzipped it. Inside she found a packet of crisps, a banana, an inhaler, and one of Greg's plastic fairy toys.

'This is my son's,' she said, looking up, heart smashing her ribs. 'Please can you show me exactly where you found it?'

'Yes, of course. Follow me.'

Lily hurried after the woman, who seemed to be walking infuriatingly slowly. 'Please hurry.'

Love speeded up a fraction. Lily followed her down the stairs, staring at the back of her head, urging her to move faster.

At the bottom, the woman turned left and led her into the kitchen. She walked into the centre of the vast white space then stopped and pointed to a corner of the room. 'It was there, lying on the floor. I thought it was nice so I picked it up. I thought my daughter might like it.'

Lily ran forward and crouched down, frantically scanning the floor for anything else. The woman's words repeated themselves in her head. There was something wrong with Love's voice. It sounded . . . hollow. She turned around.

Love was watching her. There was an odd look on her face. She raised a hand and flicked a strand of black hair from her cheek. A red smear of what was probably lipstick stained the sleeve of her white dress. Lily caught a whiff of something metallic alongside the movement.

The air shifted. Lily cleared her throat. 'What did you say your name was?'

'Can I have it back?'

'What?'

'The bag.'

'No. It's my son's. I need to show this to the police. In fact, I need to call them right away.' Lily wrenched her phone

313

out of her pocket. It slipped out of her hand and spun across the floor under a kitchen cabinet.

The woman withdrew a knife from the wooden block on the counter.

Lily's head began to roar like the inside of a seashell. She stared at the knife, then at the woman. 'What are you doing?'

No response.

Chills prickled Lily's skin. 'The police are here, on the farm. I followed them.'

Love's cheek twitched, but her voice was calm. 'I don't want to hurt you. I don't want to hurt Gregory either. Neither of us do.'

'Where is he? Please. Tell me where he is and you can go. I won't call the police. I'll just go and get him.'

'I need you to go upstairs now. I'll be right behind you.' Her tone was hard, gaze ice-cold.

Lily stared at the knife. She looked into Love's eyes. 'Please. Is Hannah with him? I just want my babies back. Please.'

'Go upstairs. Now,' she said icily, gesturing at the kitchen door with the knife.

'No.' Lily swallowed and tried not to look at the knife.

'Do it or you'll regret it.'

'Why did you take my son? Did you take Hannah too?'

Love stepped forward and held the knife up towards Lily's throat. 'Walk upstairs, slowly. I'll be right behind you. I won't ask again.'

Lily stared from the knife to Love. If she tried to run past, she'd probably get stabbed. If she got stabbed, she'd never be able to help Hannah and Greg.

Obedient as a lamb, she walked out of the room and approached the staircase. Love followed closely, guiding Lily up the stairs, keeping the knife at the base of her spine. Lily glanced around. 'What are you doing?'

Love was silent. Her silence told Lily everything she needed

314

to know: this woman wasn't going to tell her anything. She was going to kill her.

But Lily wasn't going to let that happen, not when her babies were in danger.

Waiting until her foot touched the landing, Lily sprinted down the hallway. The woman's feet thundered after her. She yanked open the master bedroom door, darted inside, leaned her full weight against the door, and looked for a lock. She grappled with the small metal bar and managed to push it into place.

On the other side of the door, Love kicked and smacked at the wood. Lily kept her whole body pressed against the only thing shielding her from attack. The lock was basic and small; it might not hold if someone decided to go full throttle to get inside, and the woman seemed unwilling to give in. She smashed and kicked and tried to stab through; mercifully, the door held, and the woman's breathing grew hoarser and faster and suddenly, she stopped and went silent.

Lily put her ear to the door jamb. There was no sound coming from the other side. It was almost as if Love had vanished into thin air.

Chapter 61
PEARLINE

Now

Pearline and Dibbs lay side by side and watched as the woman they knew to be Gregory Woods's teaching assistant at Grimstone Primary, Miss Sarah Mills – Serenity Finch, former member of Eternal Life Community – emerged from the trees into the clearing. As if mocking their plight, the last rays of sun poured down like liquid gold making the young woman's face glow. Serenity Finch was tall, muscular and toned, with auburn hair and doe-shaped eyes. Her external appearance said nurturer or friend, but inside she was rotten, capable of kidnapping innocent children, and the facts spoke for themselves: she pushed a wheelbarrow, in which lay the bodies of Hannah and Gregory Woods.

Greg's face was obscured by the hood of his frog onesie. Hannah's face was visible above her white pyjama top. Both children were lifeless, but from the colour in Hannah's face and the slight movement of her chest, Pearline could tell she was still alive. But was Gregory?

Christ. Her heartbeat thwacked and sweat slicked her armpits.

Serenity Finch was alone, but armed; a scythe rose out of her backpack. The scythe no doubt that had cracked Connor Rudge's skull. Pearline stared at the weapon, alarmed yet unsurprised to see dried blood on the blade. This woman had killed Rudge, which meant she was very strong. Indeed, her arm muscles strained against the sleeves of her white T-shirt.

Pearline fixed her gaze on the scythe. Why would she bring it with her? Was she intending to use it on the children?

Fingers shaking, she texted for backup.

Dibbs tapped her hand. Their eyes met. She mouthed, 'On my count.'

He nodded, withdrew his baton, and braced to push up from the ground. She did the same, eyes locked on Serenity who had stopped three feet away from the well and was lifting each child out of the wheelbarrow and lowering them to the ground.

With the children arranged side by side, the young woman stood back to appraise her work. She tilted her head and sighed.

Hannah and Gregory lay face down on the hard earth like mannequins. Neither moved. Pearline stared, willing their bodies to rise and fall; Hannah's did; Gregory's didn't. Was he already dead? She looked at the scythe, relieved that Serenity had made no move to retrieve it, but aware she might at any moment.

Dibbs's breathing was fast and shallow, just like hers. She held up three fingers to him, mouthed, '*Three*.'

The woman still had the scythe on her back. Timing was paramount. They couldn't screw up their attack.

Serenity stretched her arms above her head as if she ached. She sighed and turned her face to the darkening sky, closed her eyes, rolled her shoulders, and shook out her arms.

Pearline dropped a finger. '*Two*.'

Serenity stared down at the children and began to sing. *'Ding, dong, bell, pussy's in the well, who put her in? Little Johnny Green. Who pulled her out? Little Tommy Stout. What a naughty boy was that to try to drown poor pussy cat.'*

She sang the song again, this time faster. On the word drown, she bent over Gregory and turned him onto his back. The frog hood fell off his face. Pearline's heart lurched.

It wasn't Gregory Woods.

Chapter 62

LILY

Now

The house hung heavy with silence. There were no clocks in the white room, no way to tell how much time had passed. Surely not too much. Too much meant Love had left the farm and high-tailed it to a distant location where she was keeping Hannah and Greg. Now that Love knew the police were on to her, if her babies weren't already dead, she might be heading off to kill them.

The thought sent a hot wave of terror through her heart.

Lily pressed her ear to the door once more. Nothing. She'd waited long enough. Love had gone. It was safe. Even if it wasn't, she couldn't waste any more time hiding.

Sliding back the lock, she twisted the doorknob and inched open the door. Creaking hinges sent chills down her spine, but she eased the door open wide enough to slip out of the room, and stepped onto the landing. The coast was clear. The woman had gone. Fled to Hannah and Greg.

Lily hurried across the landing. Beneath her trainers, the

floor creaked, but the walls yawned with emptiness and the house remained quiet.

Her phone was the first step. She needed to find it and call the police. It was in the kitchen. When she'd dropped it, she'd seen it slide under the kitchen cabinet to the left of the sink.

Pausing on the stairs, she strained her ears for the slightest sound, but the air was empty, deserted. Dead. The woman had gone.

With a shudder, Lily dashed down the steps, turned left, and hurried into the kitchen. It too was deserted, the white surfaces and walls smothering in their blankness.

On all fours she reached under the cabinet for her mobile. Her fingers touched dust, cobwebs and crumbs, but no phone. A crawling feeling tickled her neck. Prickling with unease, she pushed her shoulder right up against the wood and reached further, fingers spidering across the dusty floor, frantic and urgent. Still no phone. Nothing but dust and dirt: the residue of an abandoned building left to rot.

A loud crunch splintered the air – glass and something else.

Lily whipped her head around.

Love stood a few feet away, hair cloaking her eyes. She tilted her head and smashed her heel into Lily's phone again.

Lily tried to get to her feet but Love knocked her to the ground and straddled her back, pinning her down with her body weight. She leaned low, dug her knees into Lily's kidneys, pinioned her face to the floor, and said, 'See this as a mercy. This way, you'll never learn how they died.'

Lily struggled, but Love was stronger and heavier. She tried to twist and the woman dug her nails into her head and applied more weight, squashing her face against the ground. Her cheekbone cracked. Pain exploded. She stopped struggling. Went limp. Her brain felt sluggish, slow – but . . . maybe . . . if she could appeal to the woman's maternal side, then . . . maybe, just maybe—

Love moved back and raised the knife. Lily rolled onto her back, eyes widening as the blade flashed down towards her stomach. Raising her legs in protection, Lily screamed.

Chapter 63
LOVE

Now

Love cleaned the knife and slipped it back into its block, giving the woman a cursory glance, pleased to see she was going nowhere. Lily's leg bled heavily. She was unconscious, having passed out a couple of minutes earlier.

Love wondered if she needed to worry about her, then realised that there was nothing to fear. Though she'd missed her stomach, the wound to the woman's thigh would be enough. Given Lily's sorry condition, she would soon bleed out and die. No one would find her for weeks, possibly months. Years, if she was lucky.

Love nodded to herself. It didn't matter that the woman's body would be left here to rot. Her dream of starting a new community on the farm was a silly one. This was not the place; there were too many reminders here. Too many links to the past. She and Serenity would find another place, a better, more secure location. As soon as the media circus surrounding the children's disappearance died down, they'd find somewhere to build her new flock. It was time. She was ready, so was Seri. They'd saved up some cash and waited long enough.

Kneading her temples, Love walked back up to the bedroom with the boy's ladybird bag over her shoulder. There was a blue petri dish on the windowsill that she wanted to take back to the caravan. A memento from time's past. The dish had contained Saviour's first public taste of pure blood. It had held her own blood, and she'd been more than willing to give it. To Love, the dish symbolised her commencement of the journey to Total Illumination. She wanted to take the precious object forward and use it again in her new community.

Back in the bedroom, fingers tingling, she bagged the blue dish, spread the sheet over the bed, and gave the room a final heavy look before making her way back across the landing, down the stairs, and out of the house. Locking the door, she pocketed the key and retraced her footsteps across the farmyard towards the woods.

A strange echoing cry made her glance to her left as she entered the trees. It had sounded half-human, half-animal. She debated whether or not to walk to the well to make sure everything was OK. She was sure it was. Lily had said there were two police officers on the grounds, but she'd been lying. The children had been sedated; Serenity would throw them in the well and be done in no time at all. Her daughter might even be back at the caravan by now. Besides, she was tired. Stabbing that woman had taken too much energy and she was thirsting for more of the giver's blood.

Walking on, slowly now, the migraine escalated its attack. At one point it got so bad that she had to stop and throw up. She grimaced at the stench and the pink-stained contents of her stomach mingling with the dirt. Telling herself she'd be able to lie down in the caravan soon, she dragged herself forward, hands on her head, brow furrowed with pain.

The white of the caravan almost overwhelmed her. Inside

were painkillers and she could sip more blood. She might not even mix it with water; the less distilled it was, the purer, and she needed that purity now more than ever.

Just a little way now, just a few more steps. She grabbed the door handle, pressed down and pulled the door open. Not bothering to shut it behind her, she hurried inside her makeshift home, across the minuscule space towards the tiny bathroom. Inside, Love grappled with the cabinet doors, pulled out a pack of painkillers and downed two with a gulp of water from the tap. She grabbed the syringe, left the bathroom, and hurried into the second bedroom where the giver still lay fast asleep.

She perched on the edge of the bed, lifted the giver's arm out from under the bedsheet, found a vein, and placed the needle on the right spot. Her hands were shaking from the grinding in her head. Nausea swelled in her throat. She took a couple of steadying inhalations and froze at the sound of sirens. Had that woman been telling the truth? Were police officers already here? Had they found Serenity and called for backup? Were the police about to arrive in their droves?

Her blood ran cold. If Seri wasn't back yet, something must have gone wrong. Perhaps the police officers had found her. Would Seri lead them here, to the caravan? The question was unanswerable.

She thought quickly. It didn't take long to make a decision. It never did. Not when it was a question of life and death.

There was no time to wait for her daughter. She'd have to sacrifice her worker bee and hope she got out by herself. Serenity was important and useful, but evading capture meant everything. In prison, it would be impossible to locate pure blood, impossible to continue on her journey to eternal life. If she was imprisoned, her fate would be sealed and she would die a miserable death having lived an almost futile existence.

She'd basically be signing her own death warrant, and that couldn't happen. Life was for living, and she had aspirations, dreams of a new community led entirely by her. A group of pure beings untainted by the common man.

She looked at the sleeping child, and her heart twinged. Those veins pumped such sweet nectar around that small body; one small stab of the syringe, one sip and that nectar would be inside her body, offering the purity she needed, but . . . the police were coming. If they found the giver here she could say farewell to freedom and hello to death.

Love scratched her chest in irritation. She could leave now, drive away quickly with the giver, give him another dose of sedative to make sure he stayed silent. This giver was perfect, innocence in its prime, but . . . if an army of police officers was on their way here, the roads would be blocked, they'd stop her, look inside the caravan. There was nowhere to hide the giver in this tiny space. The police would find out what she'd done.

And that couldn't happen.

Her heart dropped. Her fingers ceased their scratching.

All that hard work gone to waste. Much as she yearned to, she couldn't take the new giver with her.

She bit her cheek to stop herself from screaming, then nodded sharply. The police couldn't be allowed to find the giver inside the caravan. She had no choice. She had to leave him here in the woods. And there was no way she could let him talk. If he was alive, he'd spew forth a deluge of lies; what little he'd observed would stream from his lips like impure blood, pelting people's ears with a monstrous version of events coloured by ignorance. Gregory Woods would tell everyone about Seri and the fairy promise and the letter, and that, ultimately, would lead them to her.

There was a knife in the kitchenette. Gregory was asleep. He wouldn't feel a thing. She could slit his throat in the woods, leave him there, and drive away. Yes. That would work. Then, if the police stopped her, he wouldn't be in the caravan for them to find. When they discovered his corpse in the woods, he'd be dead and thus unable to tell them anything.

That was the only positive about death. The dead couldn't talk.

With urgent steps, Love left the bedroom and hurried into the kitchen to find a knife.

Chapter 64

PEARLINE

Now

Pearline tried to make sense of what she was seeing. The child in the frog onesie wasn't Gregory. It wasn't even a boy. It was a girl with red hair. A girl with a thin, pale face, and a button nose. A girl whose face was tattooed into her brain like ink. A little girl she thought she'd never lay eyes on again.

Isabelle.

Faye Hart's lost little girl.

Older, a little taller, thinner. Isabelle. There was no doubt.

Pearline's vision swam. Faye's face came and went, a blur of misery and grief, a flash of blinding hope.

Acid coated her tongue. Her head cried with relief and her heart pounded with fear. She was outside her body; floating, untethered, a whorl of emotion, a vortex of light and shadow. She must be imagining it – but her eyes weren't lying, and the truth was in Dibbs's eyes too. In the gleaming wetness and the urgency vibrating between their bodies.

Isabelle. All this time she'd been alive. She hadn't been cut into pieces and buried in the woods or wrapped up in plastic and dumped in the sea. She hadn't been mutilated or torn apart. Her body was whole, perfect. There wasn't a scratch on her – not one that was visible, at least.

She'd found her. They'd found her. Together. After four terrible, tortuous years – but was Isabelle alive? Her small body was motionless. There was no sign of life. Her skin was ghost-white, lips anaemic. And there was no time to check.

Pearline's pulse spiked – if Hannah and Isabelle were here, where was Gregory? Was he already dead? She may have found Isabelle, but he was still missing. Lily Woods's son was not here. Another mother was missing her baby.

Maybe it wasn't too late to save him too.

She looked at Dibbs, dropped her hand, pushed to her feet, and ran into the clearing. Dibbs kept pace. They emerged as one, batons up.

Serenity Finch stared, eyes wide, Isabelle in her arms. Hannah lay at her feet. The scythe rose out of her back like the devil's pitchfork. The well stood between them, gaping and black.

In a firm, loud voice, Pearline said, 'Put Isabelle down and step well away from the children. Lie down on your stomach and put your hands behind your back.'

Serenity looked at Pearline. Her voice was soft and pleading, eyes wet. 'Please. She forced me. I didn't want anything to do with any of this. They took me when I was just six years old.'

'Are the children hurt?' Pearline said, taking a step towards her.

'No, just sedated,' Serenity said, 'and I wasn't going to hurt them. I was rescuing them.'

'Take off the backpack and throw it over there, then lie down on your front and put your hands behind your back,' Dibbs shouted.

The woman did as Dibbs said. She was compliant. Cooperative. A good sign.

'Not there,' Pearline said, taking another step towards Hannah and Isabelle, 'back *there*, away from the children.'

Serenity shuffled backwards on her knees then lay on her stomach and cupped her hands at the base of her spine. 'Please, I'm saving them. She asked me to kill them. I told her I would, but it was a lie. I was just pretending so that I could help them escape.'

'We've already called for backup. They're on their way,' Pearline said, her words punctuated by a blaring siren.

Dibbs slipped his baton back into his belt and hurried towards Hannah Woods. Serenity's eyes flicked towards Dibbs.

'Why,' Pearline said, slipping her baton into her belt and reaching for her cuffs, 'were you taking them out of the wheelbarrow here, if you were – as you say – rescuing them?'

Tears shone in Serenity Finch's beautiful eyes. She craned her neck up from the ground and sobbed, 'I was going to leave them here. She told me to drop them into the well, but I wasn't going to do that. I was going to leave them here then go back and tell her I'd done it so that she'd drive away. First chance I got I was going to call you, the police, and tell you where to find them. I swear. I'm telling you the truth. I work with children. I love them. There's no way I could hurt a—'

'Enough,' Dibbs said. 'Tell us where Gregory Woods is and we might believe you.'

Pearline approached her. 'We know you wrote Gregory a letter telling him to go to your house. We know your adoptive father was Anthony Finch and that he used to lead a cult that you and your adoptive mother, Love, were part of. We know everything. I'm not going to lie, it looks bad, it is bad, but tell us where Gregory Woods is and it'll help your case.'

Serenity, overwhelmed by tears, turned her face to the ground. Dibbs bent over and lifted up Hannah as Pearline knelt down to cuff the woman. In that instant, Serenity rolled away.

Pearline darted after her, but the young woman was too quick: she pushed herself to her feet, picked up Isabelle, and fled back through the woods.

There was no time to think. Pearline ran.

The woman was fast. *Sweet Jesus. Too fast.*

Pearline ran faster and harder than she had for years, body screaming against the effort. Ignoring the pain, she pushed harder. Remembered running from her father and ran faster. Right now, she wasn't running from him, but after him; he and this woman were one and the same: evil and dangerous, and she needed to save that innocent little girl from a life of terror and solitude. She might never free herself, but she could – she would – free Isabelle. This was it. If she lost her now, she'd never forgive herself.

The trees became obstacles, and branches speared her arms. Roots rose out of the ground like snakes, the sun withdrew and shadows closed in, chasing and smothering her. She blinked out sweat, fought back a surge of blood-curdling terror, and ran so hard that acid scorched her throat.

A cry pierced the trees and she saw the woman go down. Serenity was carrying Isabelle.

No no no. Fear dealt a searing blow as an image of Isabelle impaled on a branch reared in Pearline's mind. She ran on, battled through the trees.

Serenity was trying to pick up Isabelle. There was blood – a lot of it – and it was hard to tell who it was coming from. Blood splattered the leaves on the ground.

Pearline shoved the woman out of the way and dealt a swift kick to her stomach. Serenity groaned and curled into a ball. Pearline knelt down and turned Isabelle over.

The little girl wasn't breathing. Blood poured out of her tiny nose onto her lips, down her chin and onto the frog onesie, colouring the green material brown. Blood glued her hair to her cheeks. Her chest was still, skin white. Too white. Ashen. Shadows haunted her eyelids. It was too late. She must have hit her head when Serenity fell.

Pearline scrambled to turn her over and inspected Isabelle's head, felt for a wound, found no sign of injury. Turning the child back over, she listened to her small chest. Nothing. No rise and fall. No heartbeat. No sign of life.

It's too late. You're too late. She's dead. Gone. It's over.

She couldn't think. Couldn't do anything except stare at Isabelle's pale, unmoving face.

Serenity tried to get to her feet. Pearline whirled around and pushed her back down.

'She's dead,' Pearline said, willing it not to be true.

Her heart thudded hard and slow. Blackness descended over her mind like a pall. A sickening kind of rage seized her muscles.

Serenity's eyes, wide with fear, flashed to Isabelle. 'No. She can't be. I didn't do it on purpose – I never wanted this. Please, I was trying to save her. Over the years, we've become close. I love her. You have to believe me.'

Pearline yanked the woman's wrists behind her back and slammed on the cuffs. Her thoughts were black, so dark she feared what she'd do if the woman uttered another word. Unable to look at Isabelle's body, she hauled the woman to her feet and pulled out her phone. There was a strange whining in her head, like a dog begging to be put out of its misery. She thought about later, when she reported today's events and had to break down Isabelle's death, piece by piece, and a black, choking despair smothered her mind.

Serenity was saying something. Pearline looked at her,

focused on her face, on her voice. The young woman was staring down at Isabelle's body and pointing at it. 'Look.'

Pearline looked down at the girl. Her heart skipped.

Isabelle's eyes were open and staring, but not empty.

Sweet Jesus. She's alive.

Tears leaked down Isabelle's cheeks. She looked at Pearline and whispered, 'I want to go home.'

Pearline couldn't speak.

Her body took over and did what it was supposed to do. Not releasing her grip on Serenity Finch's arm, she helped Isabelle to her feet.

Dibbs thrashed towards them through the trees with Hannah held tightly to his chest. 'You OK? I couldn't find you. I—' He stopped. Took in the scene.

The relief on his face was immeasurable. Pearline felt like throwing herself into his arms, and she could sense he felt the same way. Their eyes met and they smiled at each other. They were both alive. So were Isabelle and Hannah. But what about Gregory?

Chapter 65

LILY

Now

Lily waited until she heard the front door of the farmhouse shut, then opened her eyes. Her thigh screamed and her cheek throbbed. She tried to stand. Stars flashed, and she retched and almost threw up. The kitchen swayed before her. She closed her eyes, knowing she had to move. That evil bitch had her children. Hannah and Greg weren't far away. If she was quick, she could follow Love to her babies and save them. She just had to find a way to battle the pain, push it away.

She exhaled slowly. Pictured Greg and Hannah beaten and bound. Used the horrific vision to drive past the agony.

Breathing like she had through her contractions all those years ago, she reached up, grabbed the counter, and pulled herself to her feet. The movement made her feel like she was being stabbed all over again. Pain burst through her flesh, making her scream. Her entire body trembled as if it had been electrocuted, but she clung to the counter and forced herself to her feet.

Once standing, her legs shook. Somehow, she limped across

the kitchen out into the hallway, leaving a trail of blood in her wake. Whimpering, she tried the front door in case it hadn't locked properly – no luck. Her eyes found a row of hooks attached to the wall. One solitary key hung from the furthest hook. She snatched at it and shoved it into the front door, which clicked. *Go.* She opened the door and staggered outside.

The sun was a hot sliver at the bottom of the dimming sky, the air thick and stagnant. She turned and limped across the front of the house, scanning the farm for any sight of the woman who'd stabbed her, but the area appeared abandoned. There was no sign of DI Ottoline or DS Dibbs. She thought about screaming for help, but didn't want Love to hear. Panic at not being able to find the woman assailed her, and she almost screamed as pain burst up her leg into her back. *Keep going.* Sucking air, she leaned against the wall for a couple of seconds before limping around the side of the house.

Lily stopped: something white flashed in the trees up ahead. Nausea stunned her breathless for a few moments, then receded as another wave of fire flamed in her thigh. *Move.*

Groaning, she limped as fast as she could. Bile rose in her throat but she swallowed it down. Blood trailed in her shadow, soaking her jeans and making them heavy. Unable to hold her bladder any longer, she let go. Hot liquid poured down her leg and slipped inside her trainer, blending with the blood and turning the tongue of her shoe scarlet. Blood seeped into her sock. Pain entered every part of her body, but she fought against it and pushed on into the woods.

The trees circled her, towering and dense, creating a netted canopy of light and dark. Something small scurried up the barrel of an oak, making her neck twitch.

Keep going. Don't stop.

She heard the sound of someone vomiting – saw a white

figure up ahead – surged forward and tripped on a root. Panic and pain made her blind and she tried to push herself back onto her feet, but her legs wouldn't cooperate. She pictured Love stabbing Greg and Hannah like she'd stabbed her, and dug her nails into the dirt. Stomach flat to the gritty earth, Lily dragged herself after the woman, who slipped away into the trees like a ghost.

A silent scream tore from her throat. *Move*.

Sticks and roots and grit tore at her belly and cut through her T-shirt, but she dragged herself forward, digging her nails into the earth and using her upper body strength to haul herself after Love, whose pace had dramatically slowed.

Gritting her teeth, Lily decided to try standing again. She grabbed a fallen tree and pulled herself to her feet. Her legs held her and she slithered over the trunk and limped towards something large and white that was roughly concealed by branches.

Seconds later, she saw a caravan attached to a green Vauxhall Astra. Rounding the end of the vehicle, Lily limped towards the door. Sirens rang in the distance and she hesitated, turning towards the sound, which grew louder, though not loud enough to signify that help was imminent or definitely heading this way.

A thud came from within the caravan. Chest heaving, Lily approached the door.

Chapter 66

PEARLINE

Now

Dibbs had carried Isabelle and Hannah back to the car, one over each shoulder, and stayed with them there. Backup was yet to arrive at the farm, but Pearline couldn't wait another second, not when Gregory Woods was still out there.

Holding tightly onto Serenity's elbow, she stared into the young woman's blank eyes. The absence of anything in her expression was chilling.

'Where is he?' Pearline said, hauling her up.

Serenity looked at the trees and shrugged.

Pearline whirled her around. 'Who's he with? Is he with Love? Is he alive?'

The woman's cheek twitched at her mother's name, but she said nothing and shrugged again.

Anger surged in Pearline's breast and she clenched her fists as the urge to hit the woman burst forward. 'Is he hurt? Where is he?'

Serenity looked at the ground and closed her eyes.

'Look, if you tell me where he is, I'll put in a good word for you.'

She glanced up. 'What will you say?'

'I'll say that you helped with the investigation. If we find Gregory because of what you tell me, I'll do anything I can to get your sentence reduced. I'll vouch for you in court. Talk about how cooperative you were. How you were coerced into doing this.'

Serenity held her gaze. Her eyes were cold and calculating.

Pearline shivered inside; this woman had not been coerced. Serenity Finch was playing a game and she was good at it.

Again, an impulse to lash out and pummel Serenity into telling her the truth throbbed through her body. Gritting her teeth, she fought back the urge. She wasn't violent. She wasn't her father. But then again, hurting someone to save an innocent child wasn't what he used to do. This was entirely different.

Pearline's pulse picked up. Her body tensed.

The woman sighed as if bored. 'No.'

Pressure lifted off Pearline's chest as the realisation of what she had to do sang in her veins.

'You sure?' she said.

The woman stared at her coldly. 'Yes.'

'You're coming with me then,' Pearline said, dragging her over to the well.

Alarm flashed in Serenity's face. 'What are you doing?'

'This.' She kicked the back of the woman's legs, making them buckle, then held the back of her head and forced her upper body over the well, holding on to the cuffs to stop her falling in.

'Tell me where he is,' Pearline said into the woman's ear.

Serenity thrashed.

'If you don't tell me, I'll push you in.'

The woman stared down into the dark cavity of the well.

Pearline looked down too. A dank, ancient smell rose from the gloom. Vines and moss strangled the stone like entrails.

337

'When backup arrives, I'll say you fought and I defended myself,' Pearline said.

'You wouldn't.' Her voice wavered.

Pearline yanked her up and looked her straight in the eye. She grinned and tried to recreate the mad look that had entered her father's face all those times he'd hurt her. 'I would. I'd do anything to save an innocent child.'

Serenity Finch's expression darkened. She swallowed, licked her bottom lip. 'Are you serious about putting in a good word for me?'

Pearline nodded. She waited, hoping the woman believed her.

Dead-eyed, Serenity said, 'He's in the woods, with my mother.'

Pearline hauled her to her feet. 'Show me.'

Serenity led her out of the clearing into the trees.

Clouds closed in on the final sliver of sun and the sky turned grey. With light ebbing, the gaps between the branches darkened into black slits. Shadows dropped from the canopy onto the woodland floor, and a silent breeze whispered through the leaves like breath.

Fingernails traced her spine. She shivered and told Serenity to hurry up. The woman did so. Pearline tightened her grip on her elbow, worried that her silence and apparent obedience meant she was planning something. There was an inhuman feel about her, an absence of remorse, a terrifying lack of empathy. She couldn't let her guard down with this woman. Not for one second.

The thought that Serenity was leading her into the middle of the woods, further away from Gregory occurred, but she carried on regardless. She had no other lead to follow, and the woman walked like she knew where she was going, which gave Pearline hope.

Then she heard a scream.

Chapter 67

LILY

Now

Love stood in the caravan doorway, pale as milk, clutching a knife in her right hand, a set of keys in her left. Her eyes widened in shock. Lily almost smiled. *Didn't expect to see me here, did you?*

Love hesitated, then glanced at the Astra.

Lily's heart somersaulted. *She's going to drive away to wherever it is she's keeping my babies.*

Their eyes locked.

Lily raised her chin. 'Where are they?'

Love smiled. She looked calm, almost kind.

Lily licked her lips. 'Where are my children?'

Love trailed her eyes down the length of Lily's body and stared at her bleeding leg.

'Where are Hannah and Greg?' Lily said, limping closer.

Love's smile dropped. She lifted her chin and shook her head. 'I'll never understand people like you. So narrow-minded and weak. All we want is to offer a better way to live, but you're all too afraid to explore anything that

339

threatens to move beyond the boundaries of your precious conformism.'

Lily didn't know what to say. Words came and went. Her tongue seemed stapled to the roof of her mouth. She glanced at the knife in the woman's hand.

Love's eyes narrowed. 'You're a terrible mother. Gregory came to us because of you. He's terrified and it's understandable. You've brought him into this world just to die. You can offer your children nothing but short, miserable lives, but I can offer them the chance to live for ever. You choose to die, to let your children die. I choose life. You think I'm crazy, but what's crazier? Bringing children into the world with the promise of death, or bringing them into the world with the promise of eternal life?'

This woman was insane. It was in her eyes; the conviction that *she* was right, that Lily and anyone else who didn't share her beliefs were crazy. Crazy and meaningless and in her way. There was nothing she could say to change Love's mind. The damage had been done a long time ago. By who or what, she didn't know or care. All she cared about was getting the psychotic bitch to talk.

Lily limped forward.

'There's nothing that matters more than living for ever,' Love said, 'as my husband always used to say, the end justifies the means.'

Lily stared up at her. She hadn't driven Greg into the arms of this insane woman; this stranger had wangled her way into their lives and taken him because she was unhinged. This wasn't a case of the God delusion; this was something else. Something deep and dark she'd never understand.

She stared into the woman's crazed eyes. 'I might not be the best mother on earth, but I love my children.'

Love blinked and tilted her head. Her hair slid across her face, but couldn't hide a flicker of confusion.

'What's your point?' she said, tightening her grip on the knife.

Lily hesitated. She supposed she didn't have a point. The intention was to stall for time. If she could keep her talking, maybe the police would get here in time to help.

Begging with her eyes, she limped closer to the caravan, hands up in surrender. Pain slithered around her hips. An invisible needle was plucking her muscles apart fibre by fibre.

Love's eyes narrowed. A vein in her temple throbbed. 'Leave now and I'll let you live.'

'Would you leave if someone had your daughter?'

'Yes, if it meant I got to live. Of course I would. Anyone would. You'd have to be insane not to.'

Lily blinked at the irony. Hot coals scorched her thigh. Her body shook. The police sirens cut off. Was help on its way? Would they find her in time?

'You're wrong. A real parent could never leave their child in danger. Most people would die to protect their children, and I'm the same. Nothing matters more in the world to me than Hannah and Gregory. So I won't leave because I can't. I can't let a monster like you hurt my babies. I won't. I'd rather die than see them suffer.'

Love rolled her tongue around her gums. She held the knife so tightly that her knuckles blanched. A laugh barked out of her and she looked off into the trees. 'You're too late. Serenity's already done it.'

'Done what?' Lily croaked.

Love watched her face. 'Released them.'

'What do you mean? She's let them go? Where? Where are they?'

'Not release in that way,' Love said. 'Release as in she's ended their suffering.'

Lily frowned, unable to catch on – what did she mean by

ended their suffering? That was what people said about pets when they put them to sleep . . .

Realisation hit. Her head roared. The caravan seemed to tilt.

'No. I don't believe you.' But even as she spoke, Lily saw the truth in Love's eyes: her world ended and she dropped to her knees. There was no air in her lungs, no air in the woods, no air at all, none in the world. Her mind went dark. A sheer black chasm opened up before her, endless and terrible.

Love watched her, head askew, eyes glittering. 'I'm sorry, but it's for the best. Because of the life you've chosen for them they'd have died sooner or later anyway.'

Lily's vision misted. 'Kill me.'

'What?'

'Do it. Just kill me.'

Love hesitated. She looked at the knife in her hand and smiled. 'Don't worry, if you don't get to a hospital soon, you'll die. I can't waste any more time here than I already have.'

She turned to go, and Lily looked up, suddenly convinced she'd heard a sound coming from inside the caravan.

Half-twisted away from her, Love froze, back rigid.

'Mummy?'

Lily jumped. Her head snapped towards the little voice.

'Mummy?'

My baby.

'Mummy!'

Love flinched. Lily lunged forward, knocking her backwards into the caravan. Love fought, hissing and snarling and hammering her fists onto Lily's head. A feral scream tore from Lily's lips. Blood was in her throat. Tears blinded her. Blackness pulled at the corners of her mind, but she clung on.

342

Don't . . . stop.

Though every single cell in her body screamed for mercy, she forced her arms to keep rising and falling, her body to keep moving and fighting, her mind to keep working.

After just a few more seconds, Love sagged. She groaned and went limp.

Lily lurched away. 'Greg? Baby?'

'Mummy!'

Trembling, she crawled further into the caravan, raised one hand and pawed at a door. The door opened.

There, sitting on the bed, was Greg. Tied up.

Alive.

He reached out to her. He was saying something, but she couldn't focus, couldn't understand. His words were muffled, as if someone had stuffed rags in her ears.

She reached out to him, then screamed as pain speared her back. A scorching agony pierced her like a red-hot poker. She twisted around as Love yanked the knife out of her shoulder, crawled over her onto the mattress, and raised the blade above Greg's head.

In the space between Love's arm and head, Lily saw the widening of Greg's eyes as he realised what was about to happen. She tried to move, but the injury in her shoulder made movement impossible.

Greg was tied to the bed. He couldn't get away. With a cry, he shuffled back up the mattress until his back pressed into the wall. Love crawled closer to him, hair dripping over her face like oil.

Lily's brain told her to get up, pull Love back, but her body wouldn't work. Tears streamed from her eyes and she stared helplessly as Love lowered the blade to Greg's throat.

'Mummy?' Greg said, eyes wide with panic.

Lily watched, unable to move as Love pushed the tip of the knife against her son's soft skin. A bead of blood appeared.

Love sighed. Her grip on the knife tightened and her knuckles turned yellow as she pushed the blade into Greg's neck. Lily tried to speak, to tell Greg that she was going to save him, but her mouth wouldn't work. Greg began to cry. He reached out to her, 'Mum-me. Mum-me, he-help me, he—'

Love stared into her eyes, delighting in her powerlessness. If the devil was real, this was her; Love was pure evil; a heartless monster that took and took with savage greed and felt no remorse. Nothing Lily said or did would make her stop. She was going to kill her little boy and make her watch, and Lily would watch – she would be here with Greg until the end; until Love turned the knife on her, for she knew Love was going to kill her too. But that didn't matter. All that mattered was Greg. All she needed was to touch her baby boy one more time – but she couldn't. She couldn't move a muscle. Pain had frozen her limbs, manacled her body to the bed.

Tears blinded her as she tried and tried to reach out to Greg.

A smile plucked at Love's lips. She sighed once more then pushed the knife further into Greg's neck.

Lily screeched, her voice a scratched blackboard, body on fire as she strained and reached out, trying to touch him one last time. Her fingertips skimmed Greg's skin and she fought to clutch his hand, to give him the only bit of comfort she could before he died, but it was too much. She was too weak. Her arm went dead and flopped to the mattress.

Greg shook violently. Pain scored lines between his eyebrows – lines she'd never seen before. 'Mum-me. Ple-'

A shadow flew into the room, towards Love. The shadow seized Love's shoulders, ripped her away from Greg and threw her off the mattress.

Love rolled onto the carpet beside the bed. She screeched and clutched her chest and rolled over onto her back, the knife embedded in her breast. A wheeze escaped her lips and she stared up at DI Ottoline and inhaled a rattly breath, eyes bald with terror.

The inspector looked on, but did nothing.

Love's hands twitched against the handle – once, twice – then slipped away and flopped to the floor. Blood dribbled out of her mouth. Tears soaked her eyelashes like dewdrops, and more blood blossomed from the knife like the petals of a poppy. A deep red mist began to spread, soaking into her dress, creeping outwards, dying the cotton crimson, seeping up onto her throat to blend with her bloodied face and down towards her womb to stain her lower half red.

When the blood saturated her groin, Love's chest stilled.

Dead. The wicked witch was dead.

Inspector Ottoline began to untie Greg.

In spite of the pain, Lily fought the need to succumb to unconsciousness, keeping her eyes on her baby boy right up until the moment DI Ottoline lifted him off the bed, looked at her, and said, 'Greg's OK. Hannah's OK. They're both safe now.'

EPILOGUE

PEARLINE

Feet in the corridor. She was coming.

Pearline looked at Isabelle, tucked up in the hospital bed, white as the sheet, eyes blank. Since leaving the woods, she'd not uttered a word. It was as if her experience had stolen her voice. That speaking would be a step too far.

There was an air of hardness about the little girl that tore at Pearline's heart. She'd been through so much. Love and Serenity had robbed Isabelle of four years of innocence, four years where she should have known only love and security, a home with her real family where she felt protected and safe, not an alien domain with two unstable strangers. Love and Serenity had irrevocably harmed her. The damage they had inflicted on the Harts had for ever altered the family's life. Recovery would be long and challenging for everyone involved. Though Isabelle had been found alive, this was not a happy ending.

Looking at Isabelle's little face made Pearline's stomach clench. She'd ended the girl's captivity, but not her suffering. In time, after years of therapy, that suffering would ease, but nothing could restore those lost years, and nothing would bring back the Isabelle she used to be. That person was lost, as dead as Love herself.

Pearline turned as the door opened and a male nurse entered the room. He smiled at Isabelle, who didn't look up from her hands. Another person followed the nurse. Pearline tensed and forced a smile, but Faye Hart only had eyes for the child on the bed.

Mrs Hart stopped a short distance away, eyes roving over her daughter's body, absorbing every detail. After what seemed an eternity, her hands moved to her chest. 'Isabelle? Issy? My baby?'

Isabelle raised her head and stared at Faye Hart. Time hung, suspended by expectation, but the girl continued to stare. There was no hint of recognition, no glimpse of joy or relief, nothing. On her lap, the child's small hands lay limp and lifeless, her chest so still she could have passed for dead.

Faye glanced at Pearline, eyes wide. All colour left the young woman's face, and her lips began to tremble.

A terrifying doubt crept into Pearline's mind. She shook her head, but the thought clung on: they'd made a mistake. She'd made a mistake. The girl on the bed wasn't Isabelle Hart. She'd found the wrong child. The DNA results weren't in yet. What if . . .

Faye Hart released a moan and fell to her knees. Her head shook backwards and forwards in violent jerks, but she was silent; a woman gagged by grief that had returned full force with the realisation that this nightmare wasn't over. She would not be taking her little girl home today. Her little girl was gone.

This child was not Isabelle Hart.

Pearline began to shake. An overwhelming sense of the pointlessness of her life struck with such vitriol she was rendered blind. Her father had been right all along. She wasn't good enough. No matter how hard she tried, her efforts were futile.

350

'Mama?'

Faye stilled.

Pearline blinked, certain she'd imagined the word. She stared at the child, whose eyes were red but sparkling. In a whisper, the little girl said, 'Mama?'

Faye raised her head. 'Baby?'

Isabelle leaped off the bed and threw her arms around her mummy. Both of them burst into tears as their bodies melded into one; mother and child, together again, finally, as they should be.

LILY

Lily raised her head off the pillow and wrapped her arms around John's shoulders. She buried her nose in his neck and inhaled his smell, and he hugged her back. They clung to each other for several minutes. This small act was a big step in the right direction.

He pulled back and stared into her eyes. 'I'm so sorry I didn't tell you. I was—'

'You need to stop apologising. I know why you didn't. You shouldn't have been too embarrassed to tell me, but I get it. Everything makes sense now.' She paused, rolled her eyes at herself. 'I can't believe I actually thought you were cheating on me with Juliet Pickering.'

He smiled. 'Surely some of that fake tan would've rubbed off on one of my T-shirts.'

She laughed. 'When I'm out of this bed, I'll go around with a bottle of wine – or three – and do some serious grovelling.'

'Don't bother. She understands.'

'I don't care. I'm doing it. I need to thank her for everything she's done for you – for us.'

Lily felt as if she could breathe again.

352

The hospital door opened and Hannah and Greg ran into the room and launched themselves on top of her.

'Careful, you two,' John said, ruffling Greg's hair. 'Your mum's still recovering from being a badass.'

'John,' she said, '*language.*'

'Badass! Badass! Mummy is a badass!' Greg sang.

Hannah lay down beside her and stroked her hair. 'I just got a text from Isabelle – her mum's getting her a puppy. A cockapoo. She's so excited. She's going to call it Bumble.'

'That's brilliant news,' Lily said, trying not to think too hard about how much Isabelle Hart and her family had suffered, and would continue to suffer. Four years apart was impossible to imagine. Isabelle might be home, but she would never be the same again. No amount of therapy could rewind the years and give them back that lost time. And nothing would ever make them forget.

Her own children had not escaped unscathed. Greg had started wetting the bed, and Hannah was having trouble sleeping. John said he'd found her reading in bed at three o'clock in the morning. When he'd questioned her about it, she'd burst into tears and told him she couldn't make the worries go away. Lily hoped counselling would help her babies make a good recovery, but she knew they would be for ever changed by what they'd been through.

'Love you, Mummy,' Hannah whispered.

'Love you too, sweetie. So much.'

She stroked Hannah's hair and pulled Greg towards her. They smelt so perfect. The thought that she might never have been able to do this again made her eyes burn. She blinked back tears and felt John watching. He was biting his lip and shaking his head. Tears lined his eyes. She could tell he was thinking the same thing. Nothing mattered more than having her family back. That, at the end of the day, was everything.

PEARLINE

Pearline stood at the top of Glastonbury Tor and inhaled the countryside. The sky was pale grey, but the sun glowed behind the clouds, soon to break free. For the first time in too long, her chest felt light, her shoulders loose. She unclipped her hair from its tight bun and shook it back. Ran her fingers through its soft heaviness, enjoying the sensation, the simple pleasure.

Several people sat cross-legged on the short grass, their faces raised to the sky, backs rake-straight, chests rising and falling slowly. A woman with scraggly blonde hair in bohemian pants and a white vest stood on the mound, lips moving, words silent. Pearline wondered what she was saying and who she was saying those words to. She wondered what happiness and sorrow each and every person on that hill had experienced in their lives so far.

Faye Hart's grief-stricken face appeared in the blacks of her eyes. She exhaled and pushed the memory away. She inhaled and brought forward Faye and Isabelle's reunion. Magical. That's what it was.

She relived the moment she'd told Charlotte Firth's parents that they'd found her body in the well. Their grief had been terrible, but their relief . . . that was what Pearline fixed on; Mr and Mrs Firth had been suspended in horrendous uncertainty for the last twenty-four years. Because her team had tracked down the community's teacher, Hope, and a handful of other ex-members, she'd been able to remove some of the horror Charlotte's parents had imagined. Yes, the little girl had suffered, but while in the community, she had been given food, warm clothes and human contact in the form of weekly educational lessons. Yes, it was awful, but it was not the worst they would have envisaged. Pearline had also been able to inform them that Charlotte's death had been swift and painless; instant from her head hitting the bottom of the dry well – a tiny mercy, but one they'd needed. And, of course, the woman who'd taken their daughter's life was dead.

Tears came. She let them fall.

Dibbs wrapped his arms around her shoulders, moved her hair out of the way and kissed her neck.

Tingles erupted on her skin and when she smiled, the smile didn't hurt.

SERENITY

Serenity sat in the visiting room of Eastwood Park Prison and picked at the grime under her nails. Beneath the table, her legs hopped.

Visitors trickled into the room: fat, thin, young and old. Guards stood next to the walls, watching and waiting for a too-long embrace, sudden sleight of hand, or one-too-many suspicious coughs.

Inmates talked to their loved ones in low voices, longing for privacy they would never get, and their visitors followed suit while trying not to look around and succumb to the morbid curiosity plucking at their eyes.

Serenity watched a mother and daughter embrace. A mixture of loss, shame and disappointment fluttered in her heart. Mother had fought and died. She'd been too weak to triumph in the face of adversity. She had failed.

She sighed. Those blasted migraines had probably played a part, but Mother had always been weaker than she made out.

But Serenity didn't suffer from migraines and she wasn't weak. She was only in for six years, out in three if all went well. And she was good at making sure things went well. She was nothing if not adaptable.

She smiled and stood up, waving at the middle-aged woman who had just entered the room. The woman waved back, a happy smile lighting her lined face.

Serenity had practised what she was going to say to her old foster mother. She knew her words off-by-heart. If she delivered her lines correctly, when she was released from this horrendous place, she would have the perfect home to go to.

'You don't know how much your support means to me, Mrs Harper,' Serenity said.

The woman smiled. A mosquito buzzed around her head. She waved it away. 'Please, call me Martha. Maybe, some day, you'll call me Mum again like you used to before you were – uh – sorry.'

'Don't worry. I can talk about it now. I'm just glad you're here. And I'm so excited about meeting little Poppy. How old did you say she is?'

'She's just turned three. A miracle baby. I thought I couldn't have any – that's why we fostered for a while – but I guess you never know, do you?'

Serenity slammed her hand down on the mosquito and smiled brightly. 'No, you really don't.'

'Poppy can't wait to see you either,' Mrs Harper said. 'I've shown her your picture and she thinks you look like a mermaid princess!'

'How sweet. Does she like fairies?'

'Why yes, she does. She loves them. In fact, I bought her a Tinkerbell costume the other day and she won't take it off.'

Serenity smiled. 'That's great. I must admit, I've always had a thing for fairies. It's such a shame I have to wait so long to meet Poppy. Oh, I've just had an idea! Would it be OK if I start writing to her?'

'Yes, of course! She'd love that.'

'Brilliant. That way, when we meet, she won't feel like I'm a stranger.'

'Yes. Exactly. You know what, dear? I was a little nervous about seeing you again, but I'm so glad I came. Poppy is going to adore you. You'll be her new big sister. I wouldn't be surprised if you soon tire of her following you around like a little lost lamb.'

Serenity laughed. 'No way. Trust me, I'll encourage it. I love children. They're just so delightfully innocent.'

At lunchtime, Serenity tuned out the inane conversation of the other inmates and replayed her meeting with Martha Harper. The woman was so weak and eager to please it was laughable. For some strange reason, she clearly thought she held part of the blame for Serenity's kidnapping and wanted to make up for it, a fact that would make life easier when she moved in with them. Poppy was only the beginning of a bigger plan. Once she'd manoeuvred her way into Mr and Mrs Harper's good graces, she would suck them dry financially, move north and build a community her mother had only ever dreamed of.

Great things were coming. She just had to get through the next three years.

'Hey, Vamp. Hey! I'm talkin' to you.'

She looked up from her plate of straw-dry chicken and stared blankly into the eyes of Hayley Thorn, the meanest bitch in Eastwood. Word was she'd got life for butchering her husband with a hammer, because he'd hit her child. Thorn held queen status around here. A throng of sycophantic women clung to her as if their lives depended on it, half in love with her, half terrified of her.

Serenity couldn't care less about the woman.

'So,' Thorn said, 'I learned somethin' about you the other day. Wanna know what it was?'

Serenity continued to stare, but said nothing.

The other women at the table stopped eating.

Thorn licked her plastic knife. 'Heard you like to suck little kids' blood.'

Serenity looked back down at her plate, thinking how much she'd love to silence Thorn with her father's scythe.

She felt a presence at her back. Someone stood behind her chair.

'That true?' Thorn said.

Serenity speared a piece of chicken and forced it down.

'Cat got your tongue?'

Around them, the canteen buzzed; but the women at the table were still.

Serenity felt the first stirrings of something she'd rarely felt: fear. She broke her rule of ignoring the other prisoners and eyeballed Thorn. 'If you know what's good for you, you'll back off.'

Thorn grinned. 'I don't know much about what's good for me, but I know a bit about what's good for kiddies, and sucking their blood ain't.'

'I'm warning you, fuck off,' Serenity said, clenching her fists beneath the table.

'What do you think, girls? Should I, as Vamp so poetically puts it, *fuck off*?'

No one spoke. Dark glances came her way.

Serenity stood abruptly with the tray gripped in her hands. She turned to leave. A tall, wide woman blocked her way.

'Did I say I was finished with my lesson?' Thorn said in a sing-song voice.

Serenity's heartrate picked up.

Thorn stood up. Chairs screeched as the other women rose from the table and moved to circle her. Serenity looked for a guard, but there wasn't one in sight.

Leaning into her ear, Thorn whispered, 'You might have tricked the law, but I *see* you, bitch.'

Every woman attacked at the same moment. Serenity hit

the ground and an ice-cold fear slithered into her heart and began to squeeze.

Teeth, nails, feet and fists bit, clawed, stamped and pounded. Eyes as dark as death bore into her own. She writhed, fought, spat, and screamed for help until her throat was raw, but Thorn's pack was unstoppable. Only when she was choking on her own blood did the guards stroll forward, and by then it was too late.

Acknowledgements

This is the second time I've had the pleasure of writing the acknowledgements and there is, as with *Mother Loves Me*, a sea of amazing people to thank. Indeed, there's no way this book would be its final, polished self without the contribution of so many selfless loved ones and ultra-clever, dedicated professionals.

My first thanks must go to my incredible editor, Kathryn Cheshire, for reading draft after draft, improving my grasp of story structure and pacing, and for being bloody brilliant at what she does! She's so enthusiastic and astute; a real joy to work with.

Secondly, to my wonderful agent, Euan Thorneycroft, who handles everything with an unflappable cool I will never possess. Without his guidance, I'd sink faster than you can say *Uncle Saviour is a baddie*.

Thirdly, thank you to everyone at HarperCollins who has helped to polish, create, market and sell this book, particularly Katy Blott, Jen Harlow, Isabel Coburn, Alice Gomer, Grace Dent and Caroline Young. Tremendous thanks also to Charlotte Webb for superb copyediting.

I owe immense gratitude to DCI Jerry Waite of Bedfordshire

Police for his invaluable, detailed advice regarding criminal investigation procedures. I am in awe of him and all that he undertakes for his role; his knowledge is astounding. Also, the fact that he gave up his free time to help me is something for which I will be eternally grateful.

Special thanks need to go to my awesome friend, Derryn Wilkie, who read an earlyish draft and offered me a much-needed confidence boost and some brilliant ideas.

Last but definitely not least, thank you to my parents, Steve and Penny, and my husband, Tommy, for pointing out embarrassing 'Abbyisms', re-reading my work time and time again, and bestowing brutally honest feedback! At the end of the day, all I want them to tell me is that it's perfect – no changes needed – but no, they always have to impart some sort of irritatingly useful criticism.

All my love to them and to my little girl, Heidi, who now understands that Mummy's a writer!